Rooftoppers

Katherine Rundell was born in 1987 and grew up in Africa and Europe. In 2008 she was elected a Fellow of All Souls College, Oxford. Her first book, *The Girl Savage*, was born of her love of Zimbabwe and her own childhood there. *Rooftoppers* was inspired by summers working in Paris and by night-time trespassing on the rooftops of Oxford colleges, and has been shortlisted for the Guardian Children's Prize 2013. She is currently working on her doctorate alongside an adult novel.

by the same author
The Girl Savage

Rooftoppers

Katherine Rundell

faber and faber

First published in this edition in 2013
by Faber and Faber Limited
Bloomsbury House,
74–77 Great Russell Street,
London WC1B 3DA

Typeset by Faber and Faber Ltd

Printed and bound by CPI Group (UK) Ltd, Croydon, CR0 4YY

A CIP record for this book
is available from the British Library

ISBN 978-0-571-28059-9

FSC
www.fsc.org
MIX
Paper from
responsible sources
FSC® C101712

To my brother, with love

1

On the morning of its first birthday, a baby was found floating in a cello case in the middle of the English Channel.

It was the only living thing for miles. Just the baby, and some dining-room chairs, and the tip of a ship disappearing into the ocean. There had been music in the dining hall, and it was music so loud and so good that nobody had noticed the water flooding in over the carpet. The violins went on sawing for some time after the screaming had begun. Sometimes the shriek of a passenger would duet with a high C.

The baby was found wrapped for warmth in the musical score of a Beethoven symphony. It had drifted almost a mile from the ship, and was the last to be rescued. The man who lifted it into the rescue boat was a fellow passenger, and a scholar. It is a scholar's job to notice things. He noticed that it was a girl, with hair the colour of lightning, and the smile of a shy person.

Think of night-time with a speaking voice. Or think how moonlight might talk, or think of ink, if ink had vocal chords. Give those things a narrow aristocratic face with hooked eyebrows, and long arms and legs, and that is what the baby saw as she was lifted out of her cello case and up into safety. His name was Charles Maxim, and he determined, as he held her in his large hands – at arm's length, as he would a leaky flowerpot – that he would keep her.

The baby was almost certainly one year old. They knew this because of the red rosette pinned to her front, which read, '1!'

'Or rather,' said Charles Maxim, 'the child is either one year old, or she has come first in a competition. I believe babies are rarely keen participants in competitive sport. Shall we therefore assume it is the former?' The girl held on to his earlobe with a grubby finger and thumb. 'Happy birthday, my child,' he said.

Charles did not only give the baby a birthday. He also gave her a name. He chose Sophie, on that first day, on the grounds that nobody could possibly object to it. 'Your day has been dramatic and extraordinary enough, child,' he said. 'It might be best to have the most ordinary name available. You can be Mary, or Betty, or Sophie. Or, at a stretch, Mildred. Your choice.' Sophie had smiled when he said 'Sophie', so Sophie it was. Then he fetched his coat, and folded her up in it, and took her home in a carriage. It rained a little, but it did not worry either of them. Charles did not generally notice the weather, and Sophie had already survived a lot of water that day.

Charles had never really known a child before. He told Sophie as much on the way home: 'I do, I'm afraid, understand books far more readily than I understand people. Books are so easy to get along with.' The carriage ride took four hours; Charles held Sophie on the very edge of his knee, and told her about himself, as though she were an acquaintance at a tea party. He was thirty-six years old, and six foot three. He spoke English to people and French to cats, and Latin to the birds. He had once nearly killed himself trying to read and ride a horse at the same time. 'But I will be more careful,' he said, 'now that there is you, little cello child.' Charles's home was beautiful, but it was not safe; it was all staircases and slippery floorboards and sharp corners. 'I'll buy some smaller chairs,' he said. 'And we'll have thick red carpets! Although – how does one go about acquiring carpets? I don't suppose you know, Sophie?'

Unsurprisingly, Sophie did not answer. She was too young to talk; and she was asleep.

She woke when they drew up in a street smelling of trees and horse dung. Sophie loved the house at first sight. The bricks were painted the brightest white in London, and shone even in the dark. The basement was used to store the overflow of books and paintings and several brands of spiders; and the roof belonged to the birds. Charles lived in the space in between.

At home, after a hot bath in front of the stove, Sophie looked very white and fragile. Charles had not known that a baby was so terrifyingly tiny a thing. She felt too small in his arms. He was almost relieved when there was a knock at the door; he laid Sophie down carefully on a chair, with a Shakespearean play as a booster seat, and went up the stairs two at a time.

When he returned, he was accompanied by a large grey-haired woman; *Hamlet* was slightly damp, and Sophie was looking embarrassed. Charles scooped her up, and set her down – hesitating first over an umbrella stand in a corner, and then the top of the stove –

inside the sink. He smiled, and his eyebrows and eyes smiled too. 'Please don't worry,' he said. 'We all have accidents, Sophie.' Then he bowed at the woman. 'Let me introduce you. Sophie, this is Miss Eliot, from the National Childcare Agency. Miss Eliot, this is Sophie, from the ocean.'

The woman sighed – an official sort of sigh, it would have sounded, from Sophie's place in the sink – and frowned, and pulled clean clothes from a parcel. 'Give her to me.'

Charles took the clothes from her. 'I took this child from the sea, madam.' Sophie watched, with large eyes. 'She has nobody to keep her safe. Whether I like it or not, she is my responsibility.'

'Not forever.'

'I beg your pardon?'

'The child is your *ward*. She is not your daughter.' This was the sort of woman who spoke in italics. You would be willing to lay bets that her hobby was organising people. 'This is a temporary arrangement.'

'I beg to differ,' said Charles. 'But we can fight about that later. The child is cold.' He handed the vest to Sophie, who sucked on it. He took it back and put it on for her. Then he hefted her in his arms, as though about to guess her weight at a fair, and looked at her closely. 'You see? She seems a very intelligent baby.' Sophie's fingers, he saw, were long and thin, and clever. 'And she has hair the colour of lightning. How could you possibly resist her?'

'I'll have to come round, to check on her, and I really don't have the time to spare. *A man can't do this kind of thing alone.*'

'Certainly, please do come,' said Charles – and he added, as if he couldn't stop himself, 'if you feel that you absolutely can't stay away. I will endeavour to be grateful. But this child is my responsibility. Do you understand?'

'But it's a *child*! You're a *man*!'

'Your powers of observation are formidable,' said Charles. 'You are a credit to your optician.'

'But what are you going to *do* with her?'

Charles looked bewildered. 'I am going to love her. That should be enough, if the poetry I've read is anything to go by.' Charles handed Sophie a red apple; then took it back, and rubbed it on his sleeve until he could see his face in it. He said, 'I am sure the secrets of childcare, dark and mysterious though they no doubt are, are not impenetrable.'

Charles set the baby on his knee, handed her the apple, and began to read out loud to her from *A Midsummer Night's Dream*.

It was not, perhaps, the perfect way to begin a new life, but it showed potential.

2

There was, in the offices of the National Childcare Agency in Westminster, a cabinet; and in the cabinet, a red file marked 'Guardians: Character Assessment'. In the red file, there was a smaller blue file marked 'Maxim, Charles'. It read, 'C.P. Maxim is bookish, as one would expect of a scholar: also apparently generous, awkward, industrious. He is unusually tall but doctor's reports suggest his is otherwise healthy. He is stubbornly certain of his ability to care for a female ward.'

Perhaps such things are contagious, because Sophie grew up tall and generous and bookish and awkward. By the time she turned seven, she had legs as long and thin as golf umbrellas, and a collection of stubborn certainties.

For her seventh birthday, Charles baked a chocolate

cake. It was not an absolute success, because it had sagged in the middle, but Sophie declared loyally that that was her favourite kind of cake. 'Because,' she said, 'the dip leaves room for more icing. I like my icing to be extragavant.'

'I am glad to hear it,' said Charles. 'Although the word is traditionally pronounced *extravagant*, I believe. Happy probably seventh birthday, dear heart. How about a little birthday Shakespeare?'

Sophie had a habit of breaking plates, and so they had been eating their cake off the front cover of *A Midsummer Night's Dream*. Now Charles wiped it on his sleeve, and opened at the middle. 'Will you read me some Titania?'

Sophie made a face. 'I'd rather be Puck.' She tried a few lines, but it was slow going. She waited until Charles was looking away, then dropped the book on the floor and did a handstand on it.

Charles laughed. 'Bravo!' He applauded against the table. 'You look the stuff that elves are made of.'

Sophie fell over into the kitchen table, stood up, and tried again against the door.

'Wonderful! You're getting better; almost perfect.'

'Only almost?' Sophie wobbled, and squinted at

him upside down. Her eyeballs were starting to burn, but she stayed where she was. 'Aren't my legs straight?'

'Almost. Your left knee looks a little uncertain. Anyway, no human is perfect. Nobody since Shakespeare.'

Sophie thought about that later, in bed. 'No human is perfect,' Charles had said, but he was wrong. Charles was perfect. Charles had hair the same colour as the banister, and eyes that had magic in them. He had inherited his house and all his clothes from his father. They had once been beautiful, razzle-dazzle Savile Row one-hundred-per-cent silk, and were now fifty per cent silk, fifty per cent hole. Charles had no musical instruments, but he sang to her; and when Sophie was elsewhere, he sang to the birds, and to the woodlice that occasionally invaded the kitchen. His voice was pitch-perfect. It sounded like flying.

Sometimes the feeling of the sinking ship would come back to Sophie, in the middle of the night, and then she found that she needed desperately to climb things. Climbing was the only thing that made her feel safe. Charles allowed her to sleep on top of the wardrobe. He slept on the floor beneath her, just in case.

Sophie didn't entirely understand him. Charles ate little, and slept rarely, and he did not smile as often as other people. But he had kindness where other people had lungs, and politeness in his fingertips. If, when reading and walking at the same time, he bumped into a lamp post, he would apologise and check that the lamp post was unhurt.

One morning a week, Miss Eliot came to the house, 'to sort out any problems'. (Sophie could have said, 'what problems?' but she soon learnt to stay silent.) Miss Eliot would look around the house, which was peeling at the corners, and at the spiderwebs in the empty larder, and she would shake her head.

'What do you *eat*?'

It was true that food was more interesting in their house than in the homes of Sophie's friends. Sometimes Charles forgot about meat for months at a time. Clean plates seemed to break whenever Sophie came near them, and so he served roast potato chips on atlases of the world, spread open at the map of Hungary. In fact he would have been happy to live on biscuits, and tea, and whisky at bedtime. When Sophie first learnt to read Charles had kept the whisky in a bottle labelled 'cat's urine', so that Sophie would not touch it, but she had uncorked the bottle, and sipped it, and then sniffed at the underside of the cat next door. They were not at all similar, though equally unpleasant.

'We have bread,' said Sophie. 'And fish in tins.'

'You have *what*?' said Miss Eliot.

'I like fish in tins,' said Sophie. 'And we have ham.'

'Do you? I've never seen a single slice of ham in this place.'

'Every day! Or,' she added, because Sophie was more honest than she found convenient, 'definitely sometimes. And cheese. And apples. And I drink a whole pint of milk for breakfast.'

'But how can Charles let you *live* like that? I don't think this can be good for a child. It's not *right*.'

They managed, in fact, very well, but Miss Eliot never quite understood. When Miss Eliot said 'right', Sophie thought, she meant 'neat'. Sophie and Charles did not live neatly, but neatness, Sophie thought, was not necessary for happiness.

'The thing is, Miss Eliot,' said Sophie, 'the thing is, I don't have the sort of face that ever looks neat. Charles says I have untidy eyes. Because of the fleck, you see.' Sophie's skin was too pale, and it showed blotches in the cold, and her hair had never, in her memory, been without knots. Sophie did not mind, though; because in her memory of her mother she saw the same sort of hair and skin: and her mother, she felt sure, was beautiful. Her mother, she was sure, had smelt of cool air and soot, and had worn trousers with patches at the ankle.

The trousers, in fact, were perhaps the beginning of the troubles. When Sophie was nearing eight years old, she asked Charles for a pair of trousers.

'Trousers? Is that not rather unusual for women?'

'No,' said Sophie. 'I don't think so. My mother wears them.'

'*Wore* them, Sophie, my child.'

'*Wears* them. Black ones. But I'd like mine to be red.'

'Um. You wouldn't prefer a skirt?' He looked worried.

Sophie made a face. 'No, I really do want trousers. Please.'

There were no trousers in the shops that would fit her, only the grey shorts that boys wore – and, 'Good heavens!' said Charles, 'you look like a maths lesson.' – so Charles sewed four pairs himself in brightly coloured cotton and gave them to her wrapped in newspaper. One of them had one leg longer than the other. Sophie loved them. Miss Eliot was shocked; and '*Girls,*' she said, 'don't wear trousers.' But Sophie insisted that they did.

'My mother wore trousers. I know she did. She used to dance in them, when she played her cello.'

'She can't have,' said Miss Eliot. It was always the same. 'Women do not play the cello, Sophie. And you were *much* too young to remember. You must try to be more honest, Sophie.'

'But she did. The trousers were black, and greyish at the knee. And she wore black shoes. I remember.'

'You are imagining things, my dear.' Miss Eliot's voice was like a window slamming shut.

'But I promise, I'm *not.*'

'Sophie—'

'I'm not!' Sophie did not add, 'you potato-faced old hag!' but she did very much want to. The problem was that a person could not grow up with Charles without becoming polite to their very bones. To be impolite felt, to Sophie, like wearing dirty underwear, but it was difficult to be polite when people talked about her mother. They were so very certain that she was making it up; and she was so very certain that they were wrong.

'Toe-nail eyes!' whispered Sophie. 'Buzzard! I *do* remember.' She felt a little better.

Sophie did remember her mother, in fact, clear and sharp. She did not remember a father; but she remembered a swirl of hair, and two thin cloth-covered legs kick to the beat of wonderful music, and that wouldn't have been possible if the legs had been covered in skirt.

Sophie was also sure she remembered, very clearly, seeing her mother clinging to a floating door in the middle of the channel.

Everybody said, 'A baby is too young to remember.' They said, 'You are remembering what you wish was true.' She grew sick of hearing it. But Sophie remembered seeing her mother wave for help. She had heard her mother whistle. Whistles are very distinctive. No matter what the police said, then, she knew her mother had not gone down inside the ship. Sophie was stubbornly certain.

Sophie whispered to herself in the dark every night: *My mother is still alive, and she is going to come for me one day.*

'She'll come for me,' said Sophie to Charles.

Charles would shake his head. 'That is almost impossible, dear heart.'

'*Almost* impossible means still possible.' Sophie tried to stand up straight and sound adult; people believed you more easily if you were taller. 'You always say, never ignore a possible.'

'But my child, it is so profoundly improbable, that it's not worth building a life on. It would be like trying to build a house on the back of a dragonfly.'

'She'll come for me,' said Sophie to Miss Eliot.

Miss Eliot was more blunt. 'Your mother is dead. No women survived,' she said. 'You mustn't allow yourself to get carried away.'

Sometimes it seemed difficult for the adults in Sophie's life to tell between 'carried away' and 'absolutely correct but unbelieved'. Sophie felt herself flushing. 'She will come,' she said. 'Or I'll go to her.'

'No, Sophie. That is not how the world works.' Miss Eliot was sure that Sophie was mistaken, but then Miss Eliot was also sure that cross-stitch was *vital*, and Charles was *impossible*, which just showed that adults weren't always right.

One day Sophie found some red paint and wrote the name of the ship, *the Queen Mary*, and the date of the storm, on the white wall of the house; just in case her mother passed by.

Charles's face, when he found her, was too complicated for her to look at. But he helped her reach the high parts, and wash the brushes afterwards.

'A case,' he said to Miss Eliot, 'of the just in cases.'

'But she's—'

'She is only doing as I have told her.'

'You told her to vandalise your own house?'

'No. I have told her not to ignore life's possibles.'

3

Miss Eliot did not approve of Charles, nor of Sophie. She disliked Charles's carelessness with money, and his lateness at dinner.

She disliked Sophie's watching, listening face. 'It's not natural, in a little girl!' She hated their joint habit of writing each other notes on the wallpaper in the hall.

'It's not normal!' she said, scribbling on her note-pad. 'It's not healthy!'

'On the contrary,' said Charles. 'The more words in a house the better, Miss Eliot.'

Miss Eliot also disliked Charles's hands, which were inky, and his hat, which was coming adrift round the brim. She disapproved of Sophie's clothes.

Charles was not good at shopping. He spent a day standing, bewildered, in the middle of Bond Street, and came back with a parcel of boys' shirts. Miss Eliot was livid.

'You cannot let her wear that,' she said. 'People will think she is deranged.'

Sophie looked down at herself. She fingered the material. It felt quite normal to her; still a little stiff from the shop, but otherwise fine. 'How can you tell it's not a girl's shirt?' she asked.

'Boys' shirts button left over right. Blouses – please note, the word is *blouses* – button right over left. I am shocked that you don't know that.'

Charles put down the newspaper behind which he had retreated. 'You are shocked that she doesn't know about *buttons*? Buttons are rarely key players in international affairs.'

'I beg your pardon?'

'I meant, she knows the things which are important. Not all of them, of course; she is still a child. But many.'

Miss Eliot sniffed. 'You'll forgive me; I may be old-fashioned, but I think buttons *do* matter.'

'Sophie,' said Charles, 'knows all the capitals of all the countries of the world.'

Sophie, standing in the doorway, whispered, '*Almost*.'

'She knows how to read, and how to draw. She knows the difference between a tortoise and a turtle. She knows one tree from another, and how to climb them. Only this morning she was telling me what is the collective noun for toads.'

'A knot,' said Sophie. 'It's a knot of toads.'

'And she whistles. You would have to be extraordinarily unintelligent not to see that Sophie's whistling is unusual. Extraordinarily unintelligent, or deaf.'

Charles might just as well not have spoken. Miss Eliot swept him aside with a single flick of her fingers. 'She'll need new shirts, please, Mr Maxim. *Women's* shirts. And, my lord, those trousers!'

Sophie didn't see the problem. Trousers were just skirts with extra sewing. 'I need them,' she said. 'Please let me keep them. You can't climb in a skirt. Or, you can, but then everyone would see your pants, and surely that would be worse?'

Miss Eliot frowned. She was not the sort of person who admitted to wearing pants.

'We'll let it pass for now. You're still a child. But this can't go on forever.'

'What? Why not?' Sophie touched the bookcase with her fingertips for luck. 'Yes, it can. Why wouldn't it?'

'It certainly can't. England is no place for untrained women.'

Above all, Miss Eliot disliked Charles's wish to take Sophie on sudden expeditions. London was dirty, she said, and Sophie would catch germs and bad habits.

On the day of Sophie's probably ninth birthday, Charles stood her on a chair and polished her shoes, while she ate toast with one hand and read a book with the other. She turned the pages with her teeth. Crumbs and spit coated the corners of the paper but it was otherwise a satisfactory arrangement.

They were almost ready to leave the house for the concert hall when Miss Eliot stormed in.

'You can't take her out like that! She's filthy! And don't slouch, Sophie.'

Charles looked with interest at the top of Sophie's head. 'Is she?'

'Mr Maxim!' barked Miss Eliot, 'The girl has jam all down her top!'

'So she does.' Charles looked at Miss Eliot with courteous bewilderment. 'Does it matter?' Then, seeing Miss Eliot's hand reach towards her clipboard, he took a cloth and sponged at Sophie; as gently as if she were a painting.

Miss Eliot sniffed. 'There's some on the sleeve, too.'

'The rain will wash the rest off, surely? It's her birthday.'

'Dirt still applies on birthdays! You're not taking her to a zoo.'

'I see. Would you rather I took her to the zoo?' Charles tipped his head to one side. He looked, Sophie thought, like a particularly well-mannered panther. 'It may not be too late to change the tickets.'

'That isn't what I meant! She'll disgrace you. I would be embarrassed to be seen with her.'

Charles looked at Miss Eliot. Miss Eliot's eyes dropped first.

'She has shining shoes and shining eyes,' said Charles. 'That is smartness enough.' He handed Sophie the tickets to hold on to. 'Happy birthday, my child.' He kissed her forehead – the once-yearly birthday kiss – and helped Sophie from her chair.

There are many ways, Sophie knew, of helping people from their chairs. It is a very revealing thing to do. Miss Eliot, for instance, would prod you off with a wooden spoon. Charles did it carefully, by the fingertips, as though they were dancing – and he whistled the string section from *Così fan tutte* all the way down the street.

'Music, Sophie! Music is mad and wonderful.'

'Yes!' Charles had kept her birthday plans a secret, but his excitement was contagious. She skipped alongside him. 'What kind of music will it be?'

'Classical, Sophie.' His face was alight with happiness and his fingers were twitching at the tip. 'Clever, complicated music.'

'Oh. That's . . . wonderful.' Sophie was an unpractised liar. 'That will be so good.' In fact, Sophie thought, she *would* rather have gone to the zoo. Sophie had heard almost no classical music, and she would have been quite happy to keep it that way. She liked folk songs, and music you could dance to; very few just-turned-nine year olds, she imagined, could have said they liked classical music without lying a little.

The performance did not, as far as Sophie was concerned, start promisingly. The piano piece was long. The pianist had a moustache, and made the sorts of faces that Sophie associated with being very itchy.

'Charles?' Sophie glanced at Charles, and saw his lips were slightly open, and curved upwards in an expression of very listening happiness.

'Charles?'

'Yes, Sophie? And you must try to whisper.'

'Charles, how long does it go on for? I mean, it's not that it's not wonderful.' Sophie crossed her fingers behind her back. 'It's just that I ... wondered.'

'Only an hour, my child, alas. I could live here, in this seat, couldn't you?'

'Oh. An *hour*?' Sophie tried to sit still, but it was difficult. She sucked the end of her plait. She curled and uncurled her toes. She resolved, unsuccessfully, not to bite her thumbnail. She was at last on the borderland of sleep when three violins, a cello and a viola came on stage, accompanied by their musicians.

When they began to play, the music was different. It was sweeter, and wilder. Sophie sat up properly, and shifted forwards until only half an inch of her bottom was on her seat. It was so beautiful that it was difficult to breathe. If music can shine, Sophie thought, this music shone. It was like all the voices in all the choirs in the city rolled into a single melody. Her chest felt oddly swollen.

'It's like eight thousand birds, Charles! Charles! Isn't it like eight thousand birds?'

'Yes! But shhh, Sophie.'

The melody quickened, and Sophie's pulse kept time. It sounded at once familiar and new. It plucked at her fingers and feet.

Sophie's legs wouldn't stay still. She knelt up on her seat. After a moment, she risked a whisper. 'Charles! Listen! The cello sings, Charles!'

When the music closed, she clapped until the rest of the audience had stopped and until her hands were hot and blotched with red. She clapped until everyone was staring at the girl with lightning-coloured hair and a ladder in her stocking, whose eyes and shoes lit up the whole of the second row.

There was a something in the music that felt familiar to Sophie. 'It feels,' she said to Charles, 'like home. Do you see what I mean? Like fresh air.'

'Does it? Then I think,' said Charles, 'we must get you a cello.'

The cello they bought was small, but still too large to play comfortably in her bedroom. Charles unstuck the skylight in the attic, and on the days on which it did not rain, Sophie climbed onto the roof and played her cello, up amongst the leaf-mould and the pigeons.

When the music went right, it drained all the itch and fret from the world and left it glowing. When she did stretch and blink and lay her bow down hours later, Sophie would feel tougher, and braver. It was, she thought, like having eaten a meal of cream and moonshine. When practise went badly, it was just a chore, like brushing her teeth. Sophie had worked out that the good and bad days divided half and half. It was worth it.

Nobody bothered her up on the rooftop. It was flat grey slate, with a stone balustrade running round the edge. The balustrade came up to Sophie's chin; people below, looking up, could see only a shock of bright hair, and a bowing elbow.

'I love the sky.' Sophie said it one night without thinking, at dinner. She bit her tongue; other girls laughed if you said things like that.

But Charles only laid a slice of pork pie on the Bible and nodded. He said, 'I'm glad.' He added a dollop of mustard, and handed Sophie the book. 'Only weak thinkers do not love the sky.'

Almost as soon as she could walk, Sophie could climb. She started with the trees, which are the quickest route to the sky. Charles came with her. He was not a 'no-don't, hold-tighter' sort of man. He stood underneath her and shouted. 'Higher, Sophie! Yes, bravo! Watch out for the birds! Birds look wonderful from underneath!'

The original cello case, Sophie's life raft, was kept at the foot of her bed. For her eleventh birthday, Charles sanded away the mildew and bought some paint.

'What colour?' he asked.

'Red. Red is the opposite of sea-colours.' It was difficult for Sophie to love the sea.

Charles painted the cello case the brightest red he could find, and set a lock on it. She stacked her precious things inside, and midnight snacks. She opened it only as a treat, or if she had one of her dark sea-nightmares.

If Sophie had known how important the cello case would prove to be, she would probably not have stored honey in it, which always manages to leak. But she did not know: it is impossible, Charles always said, to know everything.

Charles warned her not to think too much of the

cello case. 'Be careful not to t   in life,' he said. 'We cannot tell i
Sophie. You may not be able to keep
claim it.'

'Yes, I know!' Sophie grinned. 'Someon
it. My mother will. When she comes.' Sophie   on
her palm and crossed her fingers for luck. It was like a
reflex; she spat and crossed them a hundred times each
night.

'The case may not have belonged to your mother. It
might have been snatched up by her as the ship went
down. Women very rarely play the cello, Sophie. In
fact, I have never heard of a woman who does. A violin
is more usual for a woman.'

'No,' said Sophie. 'It was a cello. I know it was. I remember. I remember her fingers on the bow.'

Charles bowed his head in a courteous nod, as he
always did when he disagreed. 'I remember the ship
well, Sophie. I remember the band. But I do not remember, Sophie, any women with cellos.'

'But I do.'

'Sophie, no. The band was made up of men with
moustaches and greased hair.'

'I *remember*, Charles! I do!'

ow.' Charles's face was too sad to look at. Sophie scowled at her ankles instead. 'But, dear heart, you were a baby.'

'That doesn't mean I don't remember. I saw her, Charles, I really *did*. I remember the cello.' The arguments were always the same. *How did you make people believe you?* Sophie thought. It was too slow, and too unwieldy. It was impossible.

'I saw her floating. I did!' She balled her fists. If she had not loved him so much, she would have spat at him.

'And yet, my child, I did not see her. I was there too.' He sighed so deeply that his breath ruffled the curtains. 'I know it's hard, Sophie. Life is so hard. My God, life is the hardest thing in the world! That is a thing people should mention more often.'

Almost every night, Sophie went mother-watching. She snuffed the candle, and sat on the window sill with her legs swinging, watching the mothers on her street go by. The best ones had faces full of wit. Sometimes they carried sleeping children; fat babies, and toddlers with legs stuck out at peculiar angles. Sometimes they sang as they passed by under Sophie's dangling feet.

That evening, though, Sophie took out her sketch book. It was leather, and soft from being kept under her pillow. She drew in it every birthday.

Sophie's pencil was bluntish, and she chewed at the lead to sharpen it. Then she closed her eyes, and tried to remember. She drew a pair of black trousers, worn thin at the knee ('worn at the knee' is surprisingly difficult to draw, but she did her best) and on top of them the torso and head of a woman. She added hair. She had no coloured pencils, but she bit at a hangnail and used a little blood to paint it red. Then, with her pencil over the face, Sophie hesitated.

'Oh,' she whispered. And then, 'Think.' And then, 'Please.' But she could remember only a blur. At last Sophie drew a tree blowing in the wind, and then drew hair blowing across the face.

Mothers are a thing you need, like air, she thought, and water. Even paper mothers were better than nothing; even imaginary ones. Mothers were a place to put down your heart. They were a resting stop to recover your breath.

Under her picture, Sophie wrote 'my mother'. Her finger was still bleeding, so she drew a flower behind the woman's ear, and coloured it red.

Every night before she went to sleep, Sophie told herself stories in her head, in which her mother returned to find her. They were long and difficult to recall in the morning, but they ended in dancing. When she remembered her mother, she always remembered dancing.

5

By the time Sophie's twelfth birthday came around, she had almost stopped breaking plates, and the books had been moved from the kitchen back to Charles's study. Charles called her in there to give her his present. It stood on the desk, a square tower wrapped in newspaper.

'What is it?' It looked the size of a bathroom cabinet, but even from someone as unusual as Charles that seemed an unlikely gift.

'Open it.'

Sophie tore off the paper. 'Oh!' Her breath got tangled up somewhere on the way out. It was a stack of books, each bound in a different coloured leather. The leather glowed, despite the grey day outside.

'There are twelve. One for each year.'

'They're beautiful. But . . . Charles, weren't they

terribly expensive?' They looked as though they would be warm to touch. Leather like that wasn't cheap.

Charles shrugged. 'Twelve is the right age to start collecting beautiful things. Each of these,' he said, 'was a favourite of mine.'

'Thank you! Thank you.'

'It's the things you read at the age you are now which stick. Books crow-bar the world open for you.'

'They're perfect.' Sophie turned them over. She sniffed the insides. The paper smelt of brambles and tin kettles.

'I'm glad you think so. Although, if you turn down the corners of the pages like that I shall have to bludgeon you to death with *Robinson Crusoe*.'

When she had examined the last one (it was *Grimm's Fairy Tales*, and the illustrated plate in the front looked promising) Charles went to the window sill and came back with a carton of ice cream. It was the size of Sophie's head.

'Happy birthday, my child.' Sophie dipped in a finger; which was not allowed, but could probably be got away with on her birthday. It was rich and sweet. Sophie dug out a chunk with Charles's ruler, and grinned up at him.

'It's perfect. Thank you. It tastes exactly like birthdays should taste.'

Charles believed food was better eaten in beautiful places: in gardens, or in the middle of lakes, or on boats. 'I have a theory,' he said, 'that the best place to eat ice cream is in the rain on the outside box of a four-horse carriage.'

Sophie squinted at him. It was sometimes difficult to tell if Charles was joking. 'Is it?'

'You don't believe me?' said Charles.

'No, I don't.' Sophie struggled to keep a straight face. She could feel a laugh rising. It was like a sneeze; it filled her chest.

'Well, neither do I, to be honest. But it's possible,' said Charles. 'You and I will go out and test it. Never ignore a possible!'

'Fantastic!' Four-horse carriages were, Sophie thought, the best invention in the world. They made you feel like a warrior-queen. 'Can we ask to have the horses gallop?'

'We can. Though I suggest that you change into your trousers first. Those skirts are fascinating creations; it's as though you've mugged a librarian,' said Charles.

'Yes! I'll be quick.' Sophie gathered up her books into her arms. She could only just see over them. 'And then?'

'And then we will locate a cab. Very luckily, it happens to be raining.'

Charles, it turned out, was right. The rain lashed against them as they thundered round corners, and made her ice cream run down over her wrist. It whipped her hair into wet snakes behind her. It made eating a challenge, but Sophie liked a challenge.

When they returned, streaming with water and stuffed with ice cream, there was a letter on the doormat. One look at the envelope made Sophie certain it was not a birthday card. All the happiness went out of her in a whoosh.

Charles read it with a tight-set face.

'What is it?' Sophie tried to read over his shoulder, but he was too tall. 'Who's it from? What do they want?'

'I'm not quite sure.' His face was transformed. He was unrecognisable as the man he had been only a minute before. 'It seems there is to be an inspection.'

'Of what? Of me?'

'Of us. It's from the National Childcare Agency. They say they have doubts about my ability to care for you, now that you are a young woman. They think I will be unable to teach you how to behave like a lady.'

'What? But that's crazy!'

'Governments often are.'

'I'm only just twelve! I'm practically still eleven.'

'Nonetheless, they intend to come.'

'Who is they? Who sent it?'

'Two men; one is called Martin Eliot. The other name I can't read.'

'But why? Why should two strangers get to decide about me? They don't know me! They're just men!'

'Men! I know these sorts of people. They're not men. They're moustaches with idiots attached.'

Sophie snorted with snotty laughter. She wiped her eyes. 'So what do we do?'

'I suppose we should clean.' Together, she and Charles looked around the hall. It was clean enough already, she thought, if you didn't count the poems she had copied onto the wallpaper, or the spiderwebs. Sophie liked spiders, and always dusted around them.

'Do I have to move the spiders?'

'I fear so,' said Charles. 'And I will have to cut the ivy.'

Last year an ivy vine had worked its way in through the window, and spread over one wall in the hall. It had settled like a Sunday hat over the portrait of Charles's grandmother. Sophie loved it.

'Could you leave the part growing on Grandmother Pauline? They wouldn't notice, would they?'

'I can try, certainly.' But Charles was clearly not thinking of grandmothers. 'And then there's you, Sophie.'

'What about me?' Sophie felt herself flushing. 'Is there something wrong with me?'

'To me, of course, you are as close to perfect as a human can be. But I have a suspicion – though please do correct me if I'm wrong – that your hair will not meet with approval. No, not the front – here, at the back.'

Sophie groped around the back of her head. 'What's wrong with it?'

'Nothing is wrong with it, exactly. It's just that it resembles a ball of string. I believe hair is more usually described as a curtain. Or a wave.'

'Oh!' It was true, she supposed. She had never read about a heroine with balls of hair. 'Leave it to me.'

That night, Sophie went to battle with her hair. At first, her hair seemed to be winning. The knot was at the base of her neck, the most awkward place to reach. This was usually the way with knots. Grimly, Sophie tugged, until she had a handful of hair in her lap, but still the knot was enormous. She pulled vengefully, and the comb snapped in two and stayed there, hanging in her hair. She swore, under her breath. '*Damn.*'

Sophie ran down to the kitchen, and found the scissors. She wove them into the middle of the knot, and bit down on her tongue for courage, and cut. It was surprisingly satisfying. When she had cut out the comb and most of the knot, she plaited her hair into a thick rope over her shoulder. Unless you looked closely, she thought, you would barely notice. She felt gingerly at her scalp. Being ladylike was a painful enterprise.

On the day of the inspection, Sophie scrubbed at her hands until her fingernails shone and she had rubbed half the skin off her knuckles. Charles polished her shoes with candle wax and a lump of coal, and, as they had no iron, pressed her clothes with a hot brick. Charles mopped the floor and Sophie soaped the walls until she had taken half the pattern off the wallpaper. She placed jars full of flowers all over the house. Everything smelt of rose petals and soap.

'I think it looks fine,' she said. Sophie had always loved the house, and it seemed especially handsome today. 'I think it looks perfect.'

Then they hovered by the door, unable to sit still. At the last minute, a thought occurred to Sophie.

'How long do I have until they come?' she asked Charles.

'Three minutes, or thereabouts. Why?'

'I'll be right back.' She took the stairs four at a time. In her bedroom, she powdered her nose with talcum powder, and rubbed red paint on her cheeks and lips. There was no mirror. She hoped it looked right.

Charles blinked when she came down. Sophie's suspicions that her cheeks were more 'clown' than 'gracious young lady' deepened, but before either had time to say anything the doorbell rang.

The woman on the doorstep had a clipboard, and an expression like a damp sock. The man next to her had a briefcase and elaborate facial hair. Sophie thought he looked faintly familiar.

Charles whispered, 'Moustache', and Sophie fought not to laugh.

They led the pair into the sitting room. The couple refused all offers of tea, and began their questioning at once. Sophie winced away from them. It was like being under fire.

'Why isn't the child at school?' said the woman.

Sophie waited to see if Charles would answer. When he didn't, she said, 'I don't go to school.'

'Why not?' said the man.

'I learn from Charles.'

'Do you have proper lessons?' The woman looked sceptical.

'Yes!' said Sophie. 'Of course I do.' A useful sentence popped into her head. 'Charles says, without knowledge, you see only half the world.'

'Hmph. And these lessons take place every day?'

'Yes,' lied Sophie. In fact, they did lessons whenever either of them remembered. Sophie found it very easy to forget.

'Can you read?' said the woman.

'Yes, of course!' That was stupid. Sophie couldn't remember not being able to read, any more than she could remember not being able to walk.

'Can you do mathematics?'

'Um. Yes,' said Sophie. That was true. Sort of.

'Although I hate the seven times table. I like the eights and nines, though.'

'Can you recite your catechism?'

'No.' Sophie's insides grew colder. 'I don't know what that is. Is he a poet? I can do most of Shakespeare, if you'd like.'

'No, thank you. That will not be necessary. Can you cook?'

Sophie nodded.

'Plain cooking, pastry, a fine trifle for dinner parties?'

'Um. Yes, I think so.' It wasn't a lie, she told herself firmly. She'd never made a trifle, but anyone who could read could cook, as long as you had the right books.

'You can't be eating well; you slouch, and you're too pale. Why is she so pale?'

For the first time, Charles spoke. 'She is not too pale. She is cut from the stuff of the moon.'

The woman snorted; the man was distracted, looking around the room. 'Is this where you do lessons?' he asked Sophie.

'We mostly do them—' She had been going to say, 'on the roof', but Charles widened his eyes in warning, and his head gave the subtlest of shakes. 'Yes,' she said. 'Mostly in here.'

'Then where do you keep your blackboard?'

Sophie couldn't think of a convincing answer to that one. She told the truth. 'We don't have a blackboard.'

'And how do you expect to learn anything without a blackboard?' asked the woman.

'Well, I have books. And paper. And,' Sophie said, brightening, 'I'm also allowed to write on the walls, and draw, as long as I don't do it in the parlour. Or the hall, unless I do it behind the coat stand.'

For some reason, the woman was not appeased by this. She stood, and turned to the man. 'Shall we begin? I dread to think what we'll find.'

The pair marched through the house as though they were planning to buy it. They inspected the sheets for holes and the curtains for dust, and looked in the larder. They took notes of the rows of cheeses and jars of jam. Finally, they marched up to Sophie's attic room, and looked through her chest of drawers.

The woman drew out the red trousers, and the man shook his head sadly. The green pair – which had accrued some interesting stains around the ankle – made the woman shudder.

'Unacceptable!' she said. 'I find it shocking, Mr Maxim, that you let this go on.'

Sophie said, 'But he doesn't *let it go on*, at all. I mean – they're mine. They're nothing to do with Charles.'

'Please hold your tongue, child.'

Sophie longed to hit her. Charles moved to stand closer to Sophie, but he said nothing. He had barely spoken; and he kept silence all the way downstairs, and only as he shook their hands did he speak a few words to the inspectors. Sophie strained, but could not hear. She closed the door behind them, and sank down on the mat.

'What did they say? Did I do all right?' She chewed on the end of her plait. 'I hated them, didn't you? I wanted to spit. That man! He had a face like a baboon.'

'He did seem excellent proof of the theory of evolution, didn't he? And the woman! I have met wrought-iron railings with more human generosity.'

'What were they saying, when they left?'

'They said they are going to submit a report.'

'That wasn't all, though, was it? You were talking for longer than that.'

'I think we'd better have a talk. Where is the best place for talking? The kitchen?'

Sophie didn't want to be anywhere the inspectors had passed through. The house felt damp and clammy in their wake. 'No, the roof.'

'Of course. I'll fetch some whisky. Why don't you run down to the kitchen, and fetch the cream jug? It helps to have cream, I think, on days like these.'

Sophie ran. The cream jug was cooling in the ice-box. There was jam, and a loaf fresh from the oven; she added that. She found Charles perched on the chimney pot.

'Sit down. Have a little whisky.' He looked about the rooftop for a glass, then handed her the bottle. 'Take a gulp.' The whisky made Sophie cough and spit, but he said, 'Think of it as medicine. Yes, well done. Are you all right?'

'Yes, of course. What's going on? What did they say?'

'Sophie. You must try to believe what I am going to tell you. You must try to understand. Can you do that for me?'

'Of course I can,' said Sophie. She stared at him indignantly. 'Why wouldn't I?'

'Don't be too sure, my love. Believing things is a talent.'

'Fine. I'll believe you. What is it?'

'Have some bread and jam. You can dip it in the cream jug.'

'What *is* it, Charles?'

Charles took some bread and rolled it between his finger and thumb. 'First of all: it will break my heart if they take you away. You have been the great green adventure of my life. Without you my days would be un-lit.' He glanced down at her. 'Do you understand that, Sophie? Do you believe me?'

Sophie nodded. She flushed, in the way she always did when people said nice things about her. 'Yes. I think I do.'

'But there is nothing I can do to stop these people. You are not legally mine. Legally, you are the property of the state. Do you understand that?'

'No, I don't. That's stupid!'

'I could not agree more. It is nonetheless the case, my child.'

'How can I belong to the state? The state isn't a person. The state can't love anyone.'

'I know. But, I believe, they intend to take you. The

pair didn't say anything definite. But they hinted.'

Sophie's whole body suddenly felt cold. 'They can't.'

'They can, my darling. Governments can do both great and stupid things.'

'What if we ran away? To another country? We could go to America.'

'They'd stop us, Sophie. They would tell the police I was kidnapping you.'

'How do you know? I bet they wouldn't!' Sophie jumped to her feet and tugged at his hand, his sleeve, his hair. 'Let's leave. We can just go, Charles. We don't need to tell anyone. Before they send in their report. Please!' He hadn't moved. She took hold of his sleeve. '*Please*.'

'I'm so sorry, dear heart.' He looked twice as old as he had looked this morning, and she almost heard his neck bone creak as he shook his head. 'They would come and fetch you back, my darling. There are people in this world who come out in a rash at the sight of a broken rule. Miss Eliot is one such person. Martin Eliot is another.'

Sophie jumped up. '*Eliot!* I knew he looked familiar! Charles, do you think they're related?'

'Good Lord! Yes, in fact, quite possibly. My God! She once said her brother worked in government.'

'The witch!' Somehow, the idea of Miss Eliot helped. Anger was easier than misery. 'I won't give up, you know.' It made her feel tougher, and meatier, just to say it. 'I won't go.'

It was one thing to vow to be tough. When the letter came, toughness felt very difficult.

It arrived on a grey Monday morning. It was addressed to Charles, but she would have opened it anyway, had he not taken it gently from her. She watched his face, but it was wary and tight: impossible to guess.

'Can I see? Let me see?' she asked, before he could possibly be finished. 'What does it say? Is it good? Can I stay? You have to say I can. Let me see?'

Charles said, 'It's . . . it's not . . .' For once, he seemed to be without words. He handed it to her. Sophie held it up to the light.

Dear Mr Maxim,

We, the undersigned, write to inform you of changes in our policy on the guardianship of

48

female persons aged between twelve and eighteen years.

Sophie scowled. 'Why do they have to talk like that?' She hated official letters. They made her feel nervous. The people who wrote them sounded like they had filing cabinets where their hearts should be.

'Read on, Sophie.' Charles's voice was darker than usual.

The committee has come to the unanimous conclusion that a young woman should not be raised by a single man unrelated to her, except in unusual circumstances. In the case of your ward, Sophia Maxim, it was felt certain elements of her upbringing have been absolutely unsuitable for a female child.

'What do they mean, "certain elements"?' Sophie stabbed at the paper with her finger. 'I don't understand!'

'I don't know. I can guess.'

'They mean my trousers, don't they?' she said. 'That's mad! They're evil!'

'Keep reading,' said Charles.

We must therefore inform you that your ward will be removed from your charge and enrolled in St Catherine's Orphanage in north Leicestershire. Non-compliance will result in a court order and a maximum of fifteen years penal servitude. The committee's decision is final and effective immediately.

'Penal servitude? What does that mean?'
  'Jail,' said Charles.

The Childcare Officer of your borough, Miss Susan Eliot, will collect your ward on Wednesday the fifth of June.

Yours sincerely,

Martin Eliot

Sophie felt suddenly hollow. She fished about for something to say. 'They spelt my name wrong.'
  'They did.'

'If they have to break my heart, they could at least have spelt my name right.' She looked at Charles. He did not seem to be reacting.

'Charles?' A tear was making its way down her face. She licked it angrily away. She said, 'Please. Please say something.'

'So you understood the letter?'

'They're taking me away from you. They're taking you away from me.'

'They intend to try, certainly.'

She didn't want to touch the letter. She dropped it, and stood on it. Then she picked it up and read it again. She couldn't bear that 'absolutely unsuitable'. 'Do you think if I'd worn skirts? And if I didn't slouch? Or if I was prettier? Or, I don't know, sweeter? Would they have let me stay?'

Charles shook his head. She was astonished to see that he was silently weeping.

'What now?' She slipped her hand into his pocket, and drew out his handkerchief and placed it in his hand. 'Here. Charles, please say something. What do we do now?'

'I am so sorry, my child.' She had never seen a man look so white. 'I fear there is nothing.'

Quite suddenly Sophie couldn't bear it. She pelted up to her bedroom, tripping over the stairs. The tears in her eyes were making the world blur. Before she had time to think, Sophie grabbed hold of the poker and swung it at the cello case. It split with a crack. She swung again, at the pitcher of water beside her bed, which shattered over her blanket and pillow. Sophie heard an exclamation below, and footsteps running up the stairs. She stamped and kicked. The case splintered and shards of painted wood flew across the room.

If you have never broken up a wooden box with a poker, it is worth trying. Slowly, Sophie felt her breath become more manageable.

'I won't go,' she whispered with each swing. 'I won't.'

After a while, although the tears and snot still ran down her face, they did not choke her. She found a rhythm – smash, breathe, crash, breathe.

'I won't go,' she whispered. 'No.' Smash. 'No.' Crash. 'No.'

It took her some minutes to realise that Charles was standing in the doorway.

'Still alive, dear heart?'

'Oh! I was just—'

'Quite. Very sensible.' He surveyed the room, then led her by the hand to the bathroom. 'This calls for hot water.'

He would say nothing else, and Sophie could think of nothing to do but to sit curled on a pile of towels, hiccupping and sniffing, while he put every pot they owned on the stove downstairs to boil, and added dried lemon peel and mint to the tub until it steamed. 'Stay in for half an hour. I have some things to attend to.'

Sophie couldn't bear to sit still in the tub. Instead she stamped to the window and back again, and thumped the wall, until Charles's voice floated up the stairs. 'Get in the tub, Sophie, and do some splashing. You will be surprised at what a difference splashing can make.'

Sophie had forgotten that the bathroom floor-boards were directly above the kitchen. She sighed, and undressed, tugging vindictively at her boots. 'All right!' she called. 'I'm in now.'

Having said it, she had to get in or it would be a lie. The hot water came up to her belly button, and the lemon peel lapped against her legs. Once her body was covered in hot water, all the fight seemed to go out of it. Sophie sagged, and lay in the tub. Her heart sagged too. She could think of nothing.

When, at last, she clambered out, she made it only as far as her bedroom rug before her legs collapsed and she dropped down, still wrapped in her towel. She lay there, half awake, and went on with her staring at nothing.

Gradually, the nothing changed into a something. A small dot of light was playing against the wall, and she had been staring at it unseeingly for many minutes.

She turned back to the pile of splintered wood that had once been her cello case to see what was casting the reflection. Then all the blood returned to her, and Sophie leapt up.

Still half-glued to the green baize lining was a long shard of painted wood. Sophie seized it, catching a splinter in her thumb. '*Ach!* Damn.'

Under the green baize, there was a brass plaque nailed to the wood. The light had been glancing off it and reflecting a pinprick of sun on the far side of the room.

On the plaque was an address. It was not in English.

Sophie had to lay the scrap of wood on the table to read it. Her hands were shaking too much to hold it steady.

FABRICANTS
D'INSTRUMENTS À CORDES
16 RUE CHARLEMAGNE
LE MARAIS
PARIS

291054

Sophie found Charles in his study. He was sitting by the window with a newspaper in his hands, but his eyes did not seem to see it. Rain was blowing in and blurring the print on the front page, and he was doing nothing to shield himself.

Sophie ran to him, but he did not turn around. He only blinked, and his dark eyes were blank. Frightened, Sophie clambered onto the arm of his chair, tugged at his sleeve. She later thought she might even have chewed at his eyebrows in a bid to get attention.

'Look! Charles, look!'

Slowly, his eyes woke up. He smiled, just a little. 'What am I looking at?'

'This!'

Charles looked about for his glasses, then, when they did not appear, held it very close to his nose. 'Le Marais, Paris. What is this, Sophie?'

'It was French! The cello was French!'

'Where did you find this?'

'We have to go to France! Right now!' She was choking and breathless. 'Today!'

'Sit down, Sophie, and explain.'

Sophie sat: on Charles's feet, so he would not be able to move. Her mouth was dry, and she had to chew on her tongue until she had enough saliva to talk. Then, as steadily as she could, Sophie explained.

It took Charles less than a second to see her meaning. He leapt to his feet, spilling Sophie into a heap on the hearthrug.

'My God! Sweet singing salamanders, Sophie! You brilliant creature. Why didn't it occur to me that she might be French? I feel I need some whisky. Oh good Lord.'

Sophie turned a backwards roll under the desk. 'What if she's living in Paris?'

'What indeed! It's possible, Sophie. I don't say it's likely, my darling – you know that the cello case still may not be hers - but it's just possible. France, of course, my God!'

'And never ignore a possible!'

'Exactly! Oh my darling creature, what a discovery.' He looked at the letter, still lying on the desk. 'We need to get out of here, at any rate.'

'To Paris?' Sophie crossed every finger and every toe she possessed.

'Of course. Where else? Paris, Sophie! Quick! To packing! Gather up your best pants and your whitest socks!'

It was like a bugle call. Sophie sprang up. Then she said, 'I don't think I've got any that are still white.'

'Then we'll buy new ones when we get there!'

'Paris pants! Yes, please.' Sophie laughed, but the letter from Martin Eliot was lying on the table. It seemed to watch her. She said, 'Will they come after us?'

'Perhaps. Yes. Quite probably. That's why we'll leave tomorrow.'

'What, really?'

'Yes.'

'But truly?'

'I wouldn't joke about such things.' Charles spread the newspaper open at the page with notices of trade, weather, ship departures. 'And if they do choose to follow us – or, which is more likely, alert the Paris police – it won't be for at least two or three days.'

'Days?' Sophie had hoped for weeks. Surely, it would be weeks.

'Days. We need to be wary, Sophie, but we are at an advantage.' He scratched an X next to a column of boat times and high tides, and closed the paper. His eyes were glinting with such excitement that it was like warming herself at the fire. 'Organisations, Sophie, are much less clever than human beings. Especially when that human being is you. Remember that.'

6

The journey was not easy. Very few journeys are, Sophie thought, and they are made even more difficult when you are planning to skip a country illegally in broad daylight.

'Pack light,' said Charles. 'If we are seen leaving, we must look like we're going to the dentist.'

'The dentist? We never go to the dentist.'

'To a concert, then. One bag and nothing else.'

So Sophie took only her cello; she rolled up jerseys and trousers as tightly as she could, and squeezed them into the corners of the cello case. When she was finished there was room for only one thing more; should she take her notebook, or a dress, for just-in-case? 'A dress is camouflage,' she told herself. 'You never know when you'll need a disguise.' Grudgingly, Sophie added it, and snapped shut the case.

Charles carried only his briefcase. Judging by the way he loaded it into the taxi cab, it was heavy. As they pulled away, Sophie thought she saw the curtain next door drop back, and a figure jerk out of sight. She gasped, and looked straight ahead. As they clattered down the street she crossed her fingers and sat on them, for luck.

The train station, when Sophie pulled her case into it, was too full of shouting people and steam. 'Oh,' said Sophie. 'Oh, no.' She said it very softly. Crowds made her ache. They were too much like a sinking ship. 'Oh, help.' She felt a strong urge to scramble up the walls and hide behind the station clock.

Charles, though, was unworried. His eyes were very bright. He said, 'Lord, it's impressive, isn't it? Smell that smell! Engine oil, Sophie!' Then he took in Sophie's taught face and clenched elbows.

'All serene, my child?'

'Of course! Sort of. Almost.' Sophie winced as a horde of boys went roaring by, hitting each other. 'Not really.'

'Do you know, I think the best thing to do in stations is to buy a handful of your favourite food, and then find a corner to sit in and stare at the ceiling.'

'Stare at the ceiling? Why?'

'Railway stations tend to have fantastically beautiful ceilings.' Sophie tilted her head, and her hat fell off. It was true. The ceiling was a maze of glass and bright iron. It looked like a hundred pianos.

Charles felt in his pockets. From a jumble of string and paper and boiled sweets, he extracted some coins. 'Here – there's a sixpence. Or, wait – there's a shilling, and you can buy some tea. Ask for it hot enough to burn your pipes, or it won't be drinkable.'

'Yes – thank you, of course – but *wait*, Charles! Where are you going?'

'To find a porter and secure our tickets.'

'What if I lose you?'

'Then I will find you again.'

'But what if you can't find me?' Sophie laid a hand on his overcoat. 'Charles, wait, don't go!' She hated herself when she was like this, but her nerves were chewing at her insides.

'Sophie, you have hair the colour of a lightning bolt!' He smiled. His smile, today, was a very good one. 'You are not easily missable.'

At the food stall, Sophie hesitated between an enormous Chelsea bun and those round biscuits with red-jam centres that Miss Eliot said were for common children. Sophie had never tried them, but they glinted like rubies.

The woman behind the counter was a reassuring presence. She had a red rash on her cheeks, and nice eyes.

'Chelsea bun, love? Eclair? Strawberry biscuits?'

The thought of what Miss Eliot would say restored Sophie's courage. 'Biscuits, please. Six.'

'There y'are, love. Don't eat them all at once, pet, or you'll be making a closer acquaintance with the station privy.'

Sophie nodded seriously. She bit into one, and found they glued her teeth together in a wonderful way. They did not taste remotely like strawberries, but they did taste like adventure.

'Going anywhere exciting, dear?' said the woman, clanking around in her apron for change.

Sophie tried to say, 'Paris', through her sticky mouthful. She glanced at the station clock. 'Half an hour and counting.'

'Hunting, did you say? That'll be nice.'

Sophie's teeth were now well and truly jammed shut. She only smiled gooily and nodded. It was true, in a way. She was going mother-hunting.

'God and good luck go with you, then,' said the woman. She wrapped a Chelsea bun in newspaper and slipped it across to Sophie. 'For luck. Most luck happens on a full stomach.'

The train was twice the size Sophie had expected, and green. It was the green that emeralds and dragons usually come in; which felt to Sophie like a good omen.

'Look for carriage six, Sophie,' said Charles. 'You are Compartment A. I am told it is usually reserved for the children of the Duke of Kent, but this summer they are shooting things in Scotland. You have it to yourself.'

They edged past porters with straight backs and starched collars, towards the front and the engine. There was a narrow corridor running the whole length of the train, with sliding doors leading to the compartments. Sophie tried not to get in the way; and tried not to look too excited; and tried not to look too much like an illegal runaway. None of the three was easy.

'Here!' Charles manoeuvred her cello case through the door, and turned. His whole face was sparking.

'It was the only one left, Sophie. I hope you don't dislike it.'

Sophie peered round his shoulder. Then she stared. 'Dislike it? It's like an imaginary game!' People were pressing past in the corridor outside; Sophie ignored them. 'It's so ... *gilt*. It's a palace!'

Charles laughed, and pulled her inside, and shut the door on the rest of the train. 'A very small palace. The travel-sized version, perhaps.'

The carriage was beautiful. Everything was child-sized, and made with the delicacy and detail of witch-craft. Sophie tried to look as if she was used to such things – at least while the porter was watching them – but it was impossible, for it was the most polished-clean, gold-edged thing she had ever seen. The pillows were round and fat as a goose's stomach. The mirror was edged in gold; in fact there was almost as much gold edge as mirror. Sophie tapped it. It sounded solid.

'And see your chamber pot,' said Charles. 'It's worth a look.'

She squatted to look under the bed. There, buckled securely to the wall, was a golden chamber pot with red carnations painted round the rim.

'See?' said Charles. 'Even your night-time peeing is accessorised.'

'But where do you sleep? Here, also?' The carriage had two bunks, but they were child-sized. Most of Charles would dangle off the end.

'I will share a bunk with an undertaker from Luxembourg. A lugubrious sort of fate, but I won't die of it; and after all, it could have been worse. He could have been Belgian.' Charles smiled down at her. 'They were the only beds available for three weeks. I thought it would be better than the itch of waiting.'

'Yes!' Waiting would have been impossible, she thought. She would have died. 'Yes, thank you!'

'Now, all serene?' asked Charles. Having no handkerchief, he fished out a clean sock and blew his nose on it. It sounded, to Sophie, like the trumpet of hope. 'You have everything you need?'

'Yes, I think so. Although, actually' – her stomach rumbled – 'have we got anything to eat?'

'Of course! How could I forget? The best part of any journey is the food. There's a restaurant car, but it won't open for a few hours. I smuggled in as much as I could.' Charles crossed to the wooden desk set into the wall and began to empty his pockets. First, six apples; then sausage rolls, shedding their pastry all over his coat, and a thick slab of yellow cheese. From the back of his fob watch Charles extracted a screw of salt. Finally, like a conjuror, he took from under his hat half a roast chicken, wrapped in oiled paper.

'Oh, heaven! Oh, wonderful!' Sophie added her biscuits to the pile; but kept back her Chelsea bun for later. She arranged the rest into a tower. 'There!' It reached up to her nose. 'This is perfect.'

'Now, have we got everything?'

'Um.' Sophie had just taken a mouthful of cheese. The taste was fantastic; salty and creamy, both, together. The train shuddered, and began to steam forwards. She had Charles, and roast chicken, and an adventure. Sophie spoke around her mouthful. 'Everything,' she said.

At Dover, they changed from the train to a boat. The weather was choppy. The sea rumbled in front of them. It was grey, and smelt wild. Sophie tried not to look down at it. She tried not to think of dead women.

'All serene?' said Charles.

Sophie nodded, but she couldn't speak.

To make things worse, amongst the passengers on

the boat was a policeman. It was impossible, she told herself, that he had come for her; he was probably on holiday; but he still made her shiver. To be out of his sight, Sophie inched away down the boat until she was alone on the outside deck. She tried to ignore the sea. Ignoring the sea, though, is like ignoring a man with a gun: it cannot be done. It stretched out as far as the horizon, and though she squinted, Sophie couldn't see France. She gripped the rail, and tried not to panic.

Charles saw her face from halfway down the ship. His footsteps made no sound, and the hand he laid on hers was gentle as a mother's.

'Listen!' he said. 'Can you hear that?'

Sophie could only hear the sea. 'What?' Fear made her more snappish than she had wanted to be. 'What am I listening for, anyway?'

'A murmuration!' said Charles. 'A good omen.'

'A what-eration?'

'A murmuration. When the sea and wind murmur in time with one other; like people laughing in private. There, again! Did you hear that?'

Sophie was not convinced. 'Only people murmur. Sea roars. Wind blows.'

'No. Sometimes the sea and the wind murmur. The

two are old friends.'

'Oh.' Sophie unpeeled her hand from the rail, and gripped Charles's. She breathed in his overcoat smell, and straightened her spine.

'When they sound together,' he said, 'it means luck. A murmuration. A good omen.'

7

The obvious problem did not occur to Sophie until she was standing next to Charles in the Gare du Nord with her cello case clutched to her chest.

The English porter from the train was watching the sky. 'It's due to storm again soon, Sir. I hope you brought umbrellas.'

Charles said, 'I am an Englishman. I always have an umbrella. I would no more go out without my umbrella than I would leave the house without my small intestine.'

'Then I'd get yourself to your hotel before the hour's up, Sir. I don't like the look of the sky.'

It was then that the problem occurred to Sophie. It startled her that she had not thought of it before, but she had not, in the rush, imagined further than the English border control. 'Charles,' she said, 'where are we going to sleep?'

'Very good—'

'And,' she interrupted, 'and also – what are we going to do next?'

'Very good questions, both,' Charles said. 'The first is easy. The undertaker was very helpful. He recommended a very good little hotel, near the river Seine.' He hefted his briefcase. 'We'll take a taxi cab.'

There was a row of carriages waiting by the train station. They varied in smartness; some had interesting bits of carriage-gut hanging down underneath, and others gleamed and smelt of carbolic soap. There was one painted grey and silver that Sophie liked immediately. The horse matched the carriage, and its face was thinner and wittier than the others. It looked like Charles: though Sophie decided not to say so.

'Can we take this one?' Sophie held out her last slither of chocolate to the grey mare. 'The horse looks like he's bored.'

'Of course.' Charles handed the driver some coins, and the man began to load the carriage with their sparse luggage. 'I must say, French horses are very good-looking,' said Charles. 'Paris is making me feel that I should brush my hair.'

Sophie looked about, at the tall trees towering over the buildings, and the cobbled streets curling off in every direction. The women's skirts hung differently to those in London; the women seemed to glide, somehow, as though they were underwater. 'Yes!' she said. 'I know what you mean. Even the pigeons are more chic than in London.' She found her insides were shivering in that way they did before Christmas. She said, 'And when we've got to the hotel? Then what do we do?'

'Then we are going to find a bakery, Sophie, and we're going to make a plan.'

'Why a bakery? I was thinking, more like, a police station? Or, a post office, or a mayor's hall?'

'The most important part of planning is having something to eat. There would be fewer wars if prime ministers ate doughnuts at government meetings.'

'And then?' she said. 'And then what?'

'And then,' said Charles, 'we go hunting.'

High up above the Seine, thirty feet up in the air, a pair of brown eyes was watching the street below. They watched a buggy pull up to the Hotel Bost, and a girl clamber out. The eyes noted the twitch in the girl's fingers, the tense excitement in her shoulder blades. They saw her biting her teeth together in determination and dragging a cello case off the cart; and watched her jump back, flustered, out of the path of a motor car. The eyes saw her anxiously open the case, and pull out the instrument and check it front and back; and then squat on the pavement and pluck out a thrumming tune with her finger and thumb.

The sound was soft, and almost drowned by the traffic below, but the brown eyes flickered, as though impressed.

8

The plan Sophie and Charles made was, of necessity, simple. Sophie wrote it out on a scrap of paper.

1. Find rue Charlemagne.
2.

Sophie's pen hesitated over '2'. Then she drew a large question mark. She underlined it in red ink, and put the list in her pocket, and went to find Charles.

Charles's room was nice, though you could not call it smart. There were two spindly chairs, on which a succession of bottoms had left their mark, and two rugs, on which a good deal of expense had been spared. Even the bedside candles looked second-hand, but the linen smelt of lavender. The wind was blowing from the river, and the air was brackish. Sophie had never felt so much at home in a hotel. Usually they gave her the shivers.

The hotel itself was a tall, gangly building, sandwiched between two more imposing blocks of apartments. It was cheap, because, as Sophie had just discovered, there was no indoor toilet, only a wooden box in the garden, but apart from that it was perfect. From the window, thin streets and pavement cafes wove away from them down towards the river.

Sophie sat on Charles's bed and bounced. Above the bed there was a painting of a man in a beard that curled at the point.

'I like his beard,' she said. 'He could use it as a paintbrush.'

Charles looked up, startled. 'What?' Then he laughed. 'Did you find the bathroom?'

'Yes. We're sharing it with a family of spiders, though. And there's a bird's nest in the ceiling joist. I quite like it.'

'Good. Shall we go and explore your room? Let me carry your case. No? As you wish.'

Sophie's bedroom was in the attic of the hotel. There wasn't much to explore. The doorway was so small that Charles stayed outside, and let her go in alone. Once she had set down her cello case, there was barely room to stand.

'Look!' she said.

The walls were covered in ink sketches, arranged higgledy-piggledy to pick up the most possible light. They were done in quick black strokes; they looked like they were fidgeting in their frames. 'I like these. They look French.'

'They look like music,' said Charles. He tucked his head into his neck and peered further in. Then, 'No window?'

'Skylight,' said Sophie.

A tiny four-poster bed was hung with white cotton at the sides, and open at the top. There was a window set into the slanting roof. Looking up, Sophie realised that the reason Charles hadn't seen it immediately was that it was so thickly encrusted with bird droppings on the outside that it matched the white ceiling.

'Do you think it opens?' she said.

'I can think of only one way to find out.' Charles edged his way into the room, and laid his newspaper on the bed. He set his feet on the newspaper, and prised open the catch. The window did not open when he pushed, nor when he jabbed at the hinge with his umbrella.

'Rusted hinge,' he said. 'Easily solved. It's not painted shut, so it shouldn't be a problem.'

'Do you think the hotel will have some oil?'

'It's unlikely. But we'll find you some oil tomorrow.'

'Thank you.' She stood on the bed and squinted through the gaps in the pigeon mess. She could see red chimney pots, and blue sky. 'My heart feels too large for my body,' she said. 'It all feels so familiar, Charles, and I don't know why. It does, though. Do you believe me?'

'Paris?'

'Yes, sort of. Maybe. But I was actually thinking, the chimney pots. They look familiar; and they're such a good colour.'

Charles was a scholar, and scholars, he always said, are made to notice things. He must have heard in her voice how much she wanted to be alone, because he strode swiftly to the door. 'I'll leave you to explore. Half an hour, Sophie; and then we'll find a map, and get ourselves to rue Charlemagne. If it's near the river it can't be far from here.'

9

Rue Charlemagne was easy to find. It was ten minutes' walk; ten minutes through cobbled streets, and window boxes full of red carnations, and children eating hot buns in the road; ten minutes in which Sophie's heart looped the loop and danced a jitterbug and generally behaved in a way entirely out of her control. '*Hold steady*,' she whispered to herself. And then, 'Stop it. That's enough.'

'Did you say something?' said Charles.

'No. I was singing to the pigeons.'

The shop had a plaque above the window. There was a violin in it, resting on a bed of silky stuff, and some flowers. Everything except the violin was covered in dust.

Inside it was the sort of over-full shop where everything looks ready to fall off the shelves. Sophie pulled in her stomach as they went in, and glanced nervously at Charles. He was so *long*: he did not always take care where he was putting his legs.

'Hello?' said Sophie, and Charles added, 'Good afternoon?'

Nobody answered. They stood stock-still, waiting. Sophie counted five minutes tick past. Every ten seconds, she called, 'Hello? Bonjour? *Hello?*'

'I think it's empty,' said Charles. 'Shall we come back later?'

'No! We'll wait.'

'Hello?' called Charles again. 'I have a cello-child here. She needs your help.'

There was a noise like a horse sneezing, and a man appeared from a door behind the counter, rubbing his eyes. He was stooped, and his paunch sat over his belt like a mixing bowl stuffed up his shirt.

'*Je m'excuse!*' he said. He spoke some quick sentences in French.

Sophie smiled politely but blankly. She said, 'Um.'

'*Pas du tout,*' said Charles.

'What did he say?' Sophie whispered.

'Ah!' the man smiled. 'I said, I was having my nap. You are English.' His accent was thickly French, but he spoke easily. 'Can I *aide* you?'

'Yes, please! At least, I hope so.' Sophie laid the plaque on the desk. She crossed all eight of her fingers. 'It's this.'

'It was screwed to the lid of a cello case,' said Charles. 'Can you tell us anything about it?'

The man did not seem at all surprised. '*Bien sûr*. Of course.' He fingered the plaque. 'This is mine. I engraved it myself. These are tacked to the inside of the cases. Under the green baize.'

'Yes!' Sophie uncrossed her fingers, re-crossed them. 'Yes, that's where it was!'

'It must be old, then,' said the man, 'because we stopped using brass ten years ago. We found it was rusting under the baize.'

'Why are they *under* the baize?' asked Charles. 'Surely that rather defeats the point?'

'But, of course: so they don't scratch the cello, but the address is there, if it is needed.'

'And' – Sophie held her breath: and then had to let it out so she could speak – 'do you remember which cello it went with? Do you remember who bought it?'

'Of course. Cellos are expensive, my child. A man will make only twenty in his whole life, perhaps. You see the serial number – 291054 – that means it was a twenty-nine inch. I have made only three such cellos in the last thirty years. The norm, as I am sure you know, is the thirty-two inch.'

'Who bought *this* one, though?' Sophie inched the plaque closer to him on the desk. 'This is the only one I care about.'

'That particular cello, I think, was bought by a woman.'

'A woman?' Sophie's insides span about. But she held steady. 'What kind of woman?'

'A handsome kind of woman, I think.'

Charles said, 'Could you be more specific? How long ago was this?'

'About . . . fifteen years. Perhaps more, perhaps less. She seemed fairly normal, as beautiful women go. Beautiful women are usually a little odd, I find.'

'What else was she like?' Sophie said, 'Please? What else?'

'She was tall, I think.'

'And what else? What else?' said Sophie. She pulled the neck of her jersey up to her mouth and bit down on it.

'What else? I'm afraid nothing very much.'

'Please?' There was a roaring in Sophie's ears. 'It's important. It's *so* important!'

'Well, I remember she had a musician's fingers. Very pale, like the roots of a tree.'

'Yes? And what else?' said Sophie.

'She had short hair, and a lot of movement around the eyes.'

'What colour hair? What colour eyes?'

'Lightish, I suppose. Yellow hair. Or orange. *Je ne sais pas.*'

'Please! Please, try! It's important.'

'I would like very much to help you,' he said, 'but I must admit that I am not good at faces. I am better at instruments.' He squinted at the two of them, standing side by side in the gloom. 'But she looked, I think, very like you. Not you, Sir. *You.*'

'Are you sure?' asked Sophie. 'Do you swear you're not making it up? Swear that you're sure?'

'*Ma petite belle*: when you are old, you are rarely sure. Being sure is a bad habit.' The man smiled. His skin creaked. 'Don't go.' He lowered himself into a seat. 'I have an assistant. He was there when we sold it. He will have a better memory. These days I only remember music.'

The assistant was hard and angular where the owner was soft and wispy. The two spoke in French; then the younger man turned to Charles.

'Yes,' he said, 'I remember. Her name was Vivienne.'

A name, coming so suddenly, was like being punched. Sophie's breath left her body. She could only stare.

Charles said, 'Vivienne what?'

The man shrugged. 'I don't remember. A colour, I think. Rouge, perhaps. I don't know. Vert, perhaps. *Oui*, I think Vert.'

'Vivienne!' Sophie's insides pirouetted. *Vivienne*. It was a word to conjure with.

Charles said, 'Thank you. Do you remember anything else? Was she married? Did she have a child?'

'She was not, and she did not.' The assistant had tough eyes, and a sneering mouth. 'But she was poor – her clothes were a disgrace – and I would not be surprised to hear of any number of children. She looked the sort of person to end in trouble with the law.'

'What?' said Sophie.

He sniffed. 'She had a lawless-looking mouth.'

Charles saw Sophie's face. He intervened. 'And was

she a professional musician?' he said.

The assistant shrugged. 'Women are not professional musicians in France, Sir, thank God. But she played that cello, in the shop, until I stopped her.'

Sophie said, 'You *stopped* her?'

'Little girl! Please do not take that tone with me. She was disturbing the other customers.'

'Was she good?' This man didn't seem to understand how important it was, and she wasn't sure how to make him see. She drummed on the desk with her fists. 'Was she wonderful?'

He shrugged again. 'She was a woman. Women's talents are limited.' Sophie wanted to hit him, hard, with all the muscle she had. She wanted to bludgeon him with one of the violins on the wall. The man said, 'She was peculiar.'

There was a cough. The old owner had come round from behind the desk and was standing at his assistant's elbow. He held a cello bow like a horse whip. 'Try a little harder, please, Mr Lille.'

Mr Lille flushed. 'I meant, she was peculiar in musical terms. She played funereal marches in double time. She played Fauré's *Requiem* without the necessary dignity.'

'She did?' said Sophie.

'She did!' The owner smiled. 'I remember that! *That* I do remember! She said, she knew nothing but the funeral marches, from living near a church.'

'A church?' asked Sophie. 'Did she say which?'

'Non. But she said, people should be able to dance to music; so she learnt the church tunes and played them double-time.'

Sophie loved the sound of that. It was something she would like to do herself. 'And she was good, wasn't she? I just know she was good.' Her fingers tingled.

'Good has nothing to do with it. It was indecent,' said the assistant. 'She made solemn music frivolous. It wasn't . . . *comme il faut*.'

'Could you demonstrate it for us?' said Charles.

'No,' he said, 'I could not.'

The owner straightened his back. It cracked like a revolver shot, and Sophie winced. 'I could,' he said.

Mr Lille looked staggered. 'Monsieur! Think of what your doctor said.'

'As a favour to the little girl.' He pulled a cello from its case. 'Listen.'

The music started slowly. Sophie shivered. She had never liked the *Requiem*. The old man bit his tongue, and quickened his pace. The music sped up, to a march and then to a run, until it sounded rollicking and sad at once. Sophie wanted to clap in time, but the rhythm was hard to capture. It was music that kicked and spun. 'It's like a rainstorm,' she whispered to Charles. 'That's the music a rainstorm would play.'

'Yes,' said Charles, and the man overheard and called over his playing. 'Yes, exactly, *chérie*! That is it exactly!'

Soon – far too soon for Sophie – the man put down his bow. 'There,' he said. 'Something like that. She was faster than me, I think.'

'But,' the assistant said, 'she did not play as elegantly as Monsieur Esteoule. She rushed with her bow. The young are foolish, and prize speed.'

Charles raised an eyebrow. Eyebrows can be powerful, and Mr Lille looked quelled. 'I admit,' said Mr Lille, 'that I have never heard anyone play as quickly as the girl.'

'Vivienne,' said Sophie. She said it in a whisper. 'She was called Vivienne.'

'Yes, Vivienne,' said Monsieur Esteoule. 'I remember clearly now, I think. She was extraordinary. *Mon Dieu*, the speed! I would not have thought it possible.'

'But it was not a proper way to play,' said the assistant. 'I was *not* impressed.'

'I was,' said Monsieur Esteoule. 'I was. And I am not easily impressed.'

Sophie left Charles to do the thanking and the farewells. She couldn't speak. She needed to keep the music in her head. Sophie had a corner of her brain – it felt near the front, and to the left – in which she kept music; now she stored it away there.

10

Having a name changed everything. Charles made an appointment with the police record office for the next day. He filled in the form with neat capitals.

'*Nom du disparu*,' he said, 'That's "name of missing person": Vivienne Vert.' Then he hesitated. 'It says, "name of supplicant".'

'Is that us? What shall we put?' asked Sophie. 'Are we going to lie? We're not going to give our real names, are we?'

'Certainly not. But even then, it's rather difficult,' he said. 'Technically, my darling, we're on the run. In fact, I think perhaps you had better stay at the hotel.'

'But couldn't we just give fake names?'

'Yes, of course. But London may have sent out a wire by now, to the nearby ports. There will be descriptions.'

'But you said it would be days.'

'I said I *hoped* it would. I would still be far happier if you stayed at home.'

'Why me and not you, though?'

'I am nondescript, my darling. You are memorable. I fear you are, if you'll forgive me, spectacularly describable. The hair, you know.'

Sophie considered. She thought of waiting in her attic bedroom while Charles was gone. It made her feel sick. 'No. I have to come.'

'Are you sure?'

'I won't talk. But I have to come.'

Charles hesitated. 'Do you have a skirt?'

'Yes. At least, I have a dress.'

'Do you have a hat? Something to hide your hair?'

'Yes. Miss Eliot gave it to me. It makes me look like a poodle, though.'

'Excellent. A police description will make no mention of a poodle. Wear it.'

Sophie woke early on the next morning. She got dressed quickly; or rather, she tried to. It wasn't easy to breathe that morning. It seemed there was too much hope in her chest for the air to fit alongside.

The police headquarters was a large building. Too large, Sophie thought, and too cold. But the receptionist was sweet-faced, and Charles offered her his box of mints while they waited. She looked surprised, and then grinned and took three. Sophie refused them; it was hard enough to swallow as it was. Charles and the girl were laughing over something in French, and the sound echoed too loudly around the marble hall. Sophie wished they wouldn't. People were staring. She moved a little further off, and pretended to read the French notices on the walls.

The receptionist was watching her. The girl tugged at Charles's lapel, and, when he politely inclined his head, she whispered in his ear. Then she looked at Sophie, and laughed again. Sophie scowled, embarrassed. The clerk appeared just as the echo of the laugh was dying, and the girl ducked her head and began straightening some papers.

'Come quickly, please,' he said. He spoke English with no trace of accent. 'I can only spare ten minutes. And you, Brigitte, should not be laughing in office hours.'

The clerk had a trick of moistening his teeth before he spoke. Like a toad, Sophie thought, eating flies.

Sophie tried not to look too nervous. Her upper lip was sweating. She dodged behind Charles, and licked the sweat off.

The floor was laid in marble, and rang with the *clack* of Sophie's boots as they followed the clerk down the corridor. She tried to walk on tiptoe, but it slowed her down by half a corridor's length. The clerk turned round and sighed, damply.

Sophie blushed. 'I'm sorry! I'm not doing it on purpose! It's just . . . my shoes are new.'

Charles turned round too, and walked back, and took her hand. 'Don't apologise. Your shoes are excellent; you sound like a tap dancer.'

The clerk turned away. Sophie pulled Charles down so she could whisper. 'What was the secretary saying?'

'Amongst other things, that she thought you very beautiful. I told her a little about you. She said you have the face of a warrior.'

'Oh! Then why was she laughing?'

'She wasn't laughing at you. Anyway, this place could do with a little laughing, couldn't it?'

'Yes! It's like a prison.' She gripped him tightly. 'It's like they've forgotten everything important, isn't it? I mean, forgotten that things like cats and dancing exist.'

'I know. Exactly. Let's rattle the corridors, shall we? Shall we stomp?'

'Yes!' Sophie said, and *Brave*, she told herself. *You have the face of a warrior.*

She straightened her spine, and stomped down the hall. Charles attempted a gangly two-step. He looked like a horse trying to climb a ladder. It made Sophie feel immediately better, and she jumped high, and clacked her ankles together. Charles applauded with his free hand against his thigh. The clerk sighed, pointedly, and his fringe rippled upwards, like seaweed. Sophie put out her tongue behind his back.

The clerk halted outside a room with a large brown desk in it.

'This is our interview room,' he said. 'It's newly refurbished, sir, so please don't let your little girl touch anything.' The pictures on the walls were of men in clothes that looked too tight. One, from his face, appeared to be farting.

'It's very . . . clean,' said Sophie. She pulled her hat more securely over her hair. It was as though, she thought, they had deliberately painted everything grim-coloured. Even the chandelier looked depressed.

'If you'll step inside, Mr Smith,' said the clerk. 'And

the little girl—' the clerk gestured to some chairs lined up in the corridor, 'the little girl will wait outside.'

'What?' said Sophie. 'No! Charles, please? *Please*.'

'Thank you, Sir,' Charles's face was blank and careful, 'but the "little girl" will join us, if she wants to.'

'I do want to stay,' said Sophie. And then, because she had remembered she wasn't supposed to talk, she glared at the clerk with her lips bitten shut.

'Please be seated, then.' The clerk was short, and his nose came up to Charles's collarbone. When he sighed this time it was hard enough to ruffle Charles's tie. 'This will not take long.'

Sophie glanced at Charles. 'Why not?' she whispered. 'That's not good, is it?'

Charles gave a tiny shake of his head. His lips formed the words, 'Be quiet, dear heart.' Sophie fell still again.

The clerk said, 'I'm afraid I must tell you, before we begin, that this is not the sort of request we welcome.'

'Oh?' said Charles. Sophie kept her eyes on him. His face was blank as a brick wall. 'Surely dealing with these requests is your job?'

'It is one small part of my job, yes,' said the clerk, 'but a request for a missing person, if you have not met or even *seen* the missing person in question, seems absurd.'

'Does it?' said Charles. 'How fascinating.'

'You will excuse me if I say that such enquiries lead only to time wasting and disappointment, nine times out of ten.'

'I see,' said Charles. 'And the tenth?'

'Actually I should have said, nine hundred and ninety nine times in a thousand.'

'Quite. And the thousandth?'

'Sir, you will not be the exception. I cannot believe that such a woman exists.'

'There are thousands and thousands of things we have not believed which have turned out to be true,' said Charles. 'One should not ignore the smallest glimmer of possibility.'

'Sir. This is *im*possible. You have asked us about a woman for whom you have no birthplace, no date of birth, and no profession.'

Sophie said, 'She was a musician. You told him that, didn't you, Charles?'

'You will forgive me, Miss Smith, but women are not musicians. We do, in fact, have records of a woman called Vivienne Vert, but—'

'You do?' Sophie sat up straight as an arrow. 'Where is she?' The clerk ignored her. 'What do they say?'

Charles repeated Sophie's question. 'What do these records say?'

'It cannot be the same woman, if what you say is true. She was not a musician. She seemed to be in minor trouble with the law.'

'What kind of trouble?' said Sophie.

'Oh, trespassing, loitering, associating with tramps and vagabonds. Anyway, she vanished thirteen years ago; suddenly no doctor's notes, no bank records. Women of her type often disappear. We have no record of a child. And we certainly have no record of this woman on board the *Queen Mary*.'

'Presumably we may see the records of the *Queen Mary*?' said Charles.

It was a simple question, but the man's face froze. The corner of his mouth twisted downwards. 'Have you any reason to, Sir?'

'Of course we do!' cried Sophie, 'I was—' She stopped.

'Yes?'

Sophie said, 'Nothing.' She was Miss Smith, of course, who had nothing to do with Sophie Maxim.

'Sorry,' she muttered. 'No.'

The clerk went back to ignoring her. Charles said, 'Curiosity is a good reason for most things, I think. Have you any reason *not* to show them?'

'Yes,' he said. Sophie watched his eyes flick to the filing cabinets and back again. 'Or, not precisely; that is to say, I believe the records may have gone down with the ship. That sort of search is not my responsibility.' His voice grew shrill. 'Paperwork, Sir, is a complicated business! I'm afraid I can't help you. No.'

'In that case, could you refer our request—'

'Coffee!' cried the man suddenly. He rang a bell. 'May I offer you some coffee before you go?'

'Thank you,' said Charles, 'but no. I would rather discuss—'

'I must insist!' His eyes were panicked. 'French coffee is the best in the world.' The receptionist wheeled a silver trolley into the room. She winked at Sophie. 'Just put it down and go, Brigitte,' said the clerk. 'Now. What were we saying?'

Sophie took a mouthful, and tried to swallow, but found her throat had stopped working. She spat it, very quietly, back into the cup. A little of it spattered onto her white top and the clerk recoiled.

'Sorry,' she muttered. 'Too hot.'

The clerk turned his back on her, as best he could while sitting down. It looked painful. 'Now, what were we saying, Sir?' he repeated.

'*You* were saying,' said Charles, 'that you are unable to help us find the records of the *Queen Mary*. I am asking you to refer our request to someone who will feel differently.'

Pouring out the coffee had given the man time to gather his thoughts. He moistened his frog-lips. 'I cannot do that, I am afraid. That is absolutely impossible. Protocol.'

Charles nodded. 'I see,' he said. His politeness was deadly. 'Sophie,' he said, 'could you step outside for a moment?'

'Oh! Why? Because I spat? Please, don't—'

'No,' he said gently, 'not because you spat. But please do go.'

Sophie saw his face; without a word, she stood up.

'I'll be just outside the door,' she said, and shut it behind her.

Outside, Sophie dropped to the floor, and gripped her ankles. The corridor felt colder than it had before. It felt darker. Sophie clenched her fists, and stared at the ceiling. She whispered into her knees. 'Please. *Please*. I need her.' Her heart was thumping painfully. 'That's all I want. Just her.'

There were voices coming from inside the room. Sophie shook herself, and then laid her ear against the keyhole. The metal was cold, and made her face squirm, but the keyhole was large and she could hear clearly.

The clerk was speaking. '. . . ridiculous. A child's imagination – a little girl—'

Then Charles's voice. 'You underestimate children. You underestimate girls. Sir, I need an appointment with the chief commissioner.'

'And you, Sir, *over*estimate your own importance. I cannot let you see the chief commissioner.'

'I see.' There was a pause. Sophie held her breath. 'The girl at reception is very charming, isn't she? She was very helpful.'

'I fail to see what that has to do with anything.'

'She mentioned your innovative brand of accounting. Your grasp of numbers really is . . . unique. And your own bank account seems to appear more often than is traditional.'

There was a sputtering noise. Sophie guessed the

clerk's coffee had made a reappearance.

Charles's voice said, 'I have no wish to deal in dirty things; but I feel an appointment with the chief commissioner is in both my interest and yours.'

'This is blackmail.'

'Quite,' said Charles.

'Blackmail is a felony.'

Charles said, 'Exactly.'

The clerk's voice sounded stiff and cold as a corpse. 'Is the girl worth it? Worth committing a felony?'

'She is,' said Charles evenly. 'She is bright enough to start a forest fire.'

'She seemed fairly ordinary,' said the clerk. Crouched outside, Sophie bristled.

'People usually do, until you know them,' said Charles. 'Sophie is uniquely endowed with intelligence, grit; and, at this particular moment, coffee stains. In fact, speaking of which—' A chair scraped, and Sophie just had time to stumble backwards two steps before door opened.

'Come back in, Sophie. This gentleman has good news.'

The clerk was whiter than before. His nostrils were curling. 'I can make an appointment,' he said, 'with the chief commissioner. He may be able to help you.'

'Thank you,' said Charles. 'How kind of you. To-morrow?'

'Tomorrow is impossible. In fact, this week is very busy – I'm not sure if he—'

Charles stood. At his full height, he loomed over the clerk. His eyebrows were at their most alarming. 'The day after tomorrow, then. Thank you. We'll be here at midday. Come, Sophie.'

For the second time that day, Sophie pulled him down to whisper. 'I haven't finished my coffee. Do I have to?'

'No,' said Charles, 'I think I'll leave mine, too. It tastes like liquidated carpet.'

'Good,' said Sophie. 'I thought it tasted like burnt hair, actually.' She spat, for a second time, into the cup.

11

The nights were quieter in Paris than they were in London. Sophie couldn't sleep. Once she was in bed the moonlight shone in brightly enough to read by, but Sophie stared at her book without seeing the words.

She was frightened. She told herself there was no reason to be afraid, but her pulse quickened and quickened until she couldn't breathe. Sophie tried to think of Charles, who was so kind and so amply belegged; and then she tried to think of her mother, who was perhaps only a few streets away. Neither helped. She could think only of being caught, and the horror there would be, and the happy twist there would be on Miss Eliot's face.

Sophie heard the rest of the hotel settle into silence. She tossed in bed until her sheets and blankets were in a pile on the floor, but still she couldn't sleep.

At last, Sophie climbed on to the bed and looked closer at the skylight. They had forgotten to buy oil, and when she tugged at the window-fastening nothing happened. The hinge was rusted and flaking.

An idea came to her. Sophie whispered, 'Yes!'

She ran down the stairs two at a time. Outside the dining room she waited, listening at the door. It sounded empty; she darted in, seized the bottle of olive oil from the nearest table and was out again before a mouse in the corner had time to do more than blink.

Back in her bedroom, Sophie poured the oil over a handful of newspaper and dabbed at the hinge. After a few minutes, nothing had happened to the hinge, but the paper disintegrated stickily in her hands. She needed something tougher.

'Cloth. I need cloth,' Sophie whispered. Perhaps the pillowcase would do? But the hotel might have strong opinions about that. Then she had a flash of inspiration: she pulled off one of her wool stockings, put it on like a glove, and tipped half the bottle of oil over it.

With her tongue sticking out between her teeth, Sophie scrubbed at the hinge. Flakes of rust began to peel off, and beneath them was bright brass. Her heart, inexplicably, began to pound. Once she had got it smooth enough, Sophie clicked back the latch – it was stiff, but the oil on her fingers helped – and pushed, hard, at the window. Nothing happened. She pushed harder. It creaked angrily, and stayed shut.

Sophie swore. She sank down to the floor. There was no reason to be so upset, she told herself. It was just a window. It probably wasn't designed to open. For no reason at all, she found herself fighting that prickling feeling behind the nose that comes before tears.

'Calm down. You're being stupid,' she told herself. 'Think.' She got to her feet, and as she did so, knocked something off her bedside table. It was the station woman's Chelsea bun. 'Oh!' whispered Sophie.

The bun was stale around the edges, but still sweet and sticky in the centre. She finished it in less than a minute.

Sophie licked her fingers (and instantly regretted it: the sugar and oil together tasted disgusting) and pulled herself to her feet. She spat on her hands, and pushed at the corners of the window frame with all her weight. She heaved. Then she leapt back as the skylight opened suddenly with a shriek.

'Yes!' she said. Without waiting to think Sophie scrambled up. She laid one knee against the ledge and one foot on the bedstead; and then she gave a one-footed jump, and both her hands scrabbled for a hold on the roof outside. Then, with a grunt of pain and a tumble, she was onto the rooftop.

Sophie crouched on hands and knees, waiting for her breath to slow. She was bleeding quite vigorously from one knee, and while she waited to stop shaking she licked it, and tied it up with her other stocking.

The roof stretched away, flat and grey and smooth, and decorated here and there with bird droppings. There was a chimney stack, and a weathervane, and black soot layering everything. She thought the rooftop must be one of the highest for miles. A single pigeon watched her. She made a face at it. It looked haughtily at her, and turned its back.

Sophie crawled to the edge and looked out, across the city. Paris lay below her, coloured in shades of night-blue. The city was a cross-hatching of roads and squares. In the moonlight she could see the tops of bright shop awnings – they were surprisingly dirty, seen from above – and the concentric circles of two smart gentlemen's hats as they passed. Top hats look much less stupid, she thought, seen from a rooftop. And from up here, she thought, the streets looked like rivers. The river itself was quicksilver in the moonlight. The wind shifted, and the wet-hay smell of horses hit her.

She leaned further out, and looked straight down. This was a mistake. She softly whispered a swear word, and her stomach dropped down into her pelvis. She found herself retreating rather quickly, and digging her nails into the brickwork of the chimney stacks for reassurance. She had never been this high up, ever. The moon looked close enough to hit with a pebble.

Sophie peeled off her nightgown, and stood up in her knickers and vest. She spun on the spot, and the Paris sky spun in time with her. The wind blew stronger, and a great bubble of happiness was rising up through her chest into her nose. Sophie threw out her arms and danced a war dance round the chimneys, whooping, very quietly, under her breath.

Sophie would have liked to stay out all night, but sometime after the clocks struck two she grew cold and her knee began to bleed again. She wiped off the worst of the blood with leaves, and wrapped it more tightly with her stocking before she lowered herself through the skylight.

Just as her eyeline dropped down inside, she thought she saw something moving across the rooftop opposite. But night shadows, she knew, throw your eyes off-kilter, and it was just a large bird, or a swirl of night air.

12

Sophie did not sleep for long. She was only halfway through a dream when there was a clattering crash and a thump. Sophie jerked awake. She was lying face down, and her scream was muffled by her pillow; even so, a voice spoke very clearly in the darkness.

'Don't *wail* like that. You'll wake the whole hotel.'

Her dressing table was on the floor, next to a broken mug. Mud and soot was scattered across the carpet. And there was a boy standing at the foot of her bed.

The boy said, 'Stop it. *Arrête!* Stop crying! Stop, Sophie!'

Sophie had not been crying, in her own opinion; she had been choking, which seemed reasonable in the circumstances. She pushed the hair out of her eyes.

'Who are you?' She grabbed a book and held it over

her heart. It might help if he tried to stab her. 'I'll scream.'

'No. Don't scream.'

'Why shouldn't I?' It was too dark to see him properly. 'I'm just about to.' *He wasn't much older than she was*, Sophie thought. He was long-legged, and his face was tight and wary, like an animal. He didn't look like a murderer. Her breath came a little more easily.

'Because I don't like screaming.'

'What do you want?'

'I want to talk to you, Sophie.'

'How do you know my name? And what are you doing here?'

'I heard the man saying it in the street. The long one. The one you called Charles. My name is Matteo,' he added, as an afterthought.

'You were watching us?'

The boy picked his nose. 'Yes. You're not special. I watch everybody.'

'And what if I scream for the police? What happens then?'

The boy shrugged. 'You won't. But if you do, I can be gone in . . .' He glanced, calmly measuring, at the skylight. 'Six seconds.'

'Not if I stop you.'

He shrugged again. 'You could try.'

'And what are you doing here?' Sophie sat up. She thought, *Hold steady*. It was lucky that her room was so small. If he tried to attack her, she could get out through the door in three steps.

'I came in from the roof.'

'Yes, I can see that!' The window was open wider than she had left it, and he had brought at least two dozen pigeons' worth of droppings in with him. 'But *why*? Why didn't you come through the door?'

'Don't you lock it? That's dangerous. You should lock your door.'

'Yes, I do, actually – *so that people can't come in*.'

The boy shrugged again. It was difficult to see, in the dark, but he might have been laughing at her. It was not a friendly laugh.

Sophie said, 'And how did you get onto the roof in the first place? I thought the only way onto the roof was my skylight.'

'You thought there was only one way onto the rooftop? *Vraiment*? You really thought that?'

'Why are you laughing?'

'There's hundreds of ways onto any rooftop. I could

have climbed the drainpipe.'

'Did you? I would have heard you, wouldn't I?'

'Probably.'

'Then how *did* you?'

'I jumped. From the roof next door.'

'You jumped?' Sophie tried to look casual. 'Isn't that dangerous?' Her casual face felt stiff.

'No. I don't know. Maybe. Most things are danger-ous. Your eye is twitching.'

'Is it?' Sophie abandoned her casual face. 'Oh.'

'*Oui*. Anyway.' He looked at her, and his eyes were black and hard. 'I came to tell you to keep off my rooftop.'

Sophie was speechless. She had half-expected him to ask for money; or to try to steal her cello. She was so startled that she forgot to be frightened. She said, 'It's not your rooftop! How can it be?'

'All the rooftops between the river and the train sta-tion are mine. I did not give you permission to go up there.'

'But . . . rooftops don't belong to anybody. They're like air, and water. They're no-man's-land.'

'They're not. They're mine.'

'How? How are they yours?'

'They just are. I know them best.'

Sophie's face must have looked as unconvinced as she felt, because the boy scowled.

'I do!' he said. 'I know exactly which chimney pots are going to fall next autumn; and which gutter-mushrooms you can eat. I bet you didn't even know that you can eat those mushrooms that grow in the gutters?' Sophie hadn't known that there were such mushrooms, so she said nothing.

'And,' said the boy, 'I know every single bird's nest my side of the city.'

'That doesn't make the rooftops yours.'

'They belong to me more than to anyone else. I live on them.'

'No, you don't. You can't. Nobody lives on houses. You live *in* them.'

'You don't know what you're talking about.' The boy glared at her. He thumped the wall, and his hand left a sooty mark. The forefinger on his right hand was missing its tip. 'Look, this is stupid: I don't want to hurt you, but you have to stay off the roofs, or I will—'

'Will what?'

'I will hurt you,' he said, as matter-of-fact as a man selling bread.

'But *why*? What are you talking about?'

'You won't be careful enough. You'll give me away. You have the streets. Use them.'

Outside, the clouds moved away from the moonlight, and the room filled briefly with night-glow. The boy's face was darkly tanned (or dirt, perhaps? she thought), and seemed to be made up of sharp angles and eyes.

'I can't stay off the roofs.' said Sophie. 'I need them.'

'Why?'

'I . . .' said Sophie. 'It's too hard to explain. They feel safe.' Sophie blushed as she said it. The boy snorted. 'I mean, they feel important.'

The boy said, 'So? *Et alors?*'

'I feel like I've been here before,' she said. 'I think they might be a clue.' She expected that he would relent. It was what you did: you gave in. Giving in was good manners.

But the boy only stared at her, unsmiling. '*Non*. Rooftops are not a *clue*; they're mine. You'd give me away. You'd be slow. If you're slow, people see you.'

'I'm not slow!'

He looked at her hands, her feet. 'You'd bleed too easily. You look soft.'

'I am *not* soft. Look! No, don't go – *look.*' Sophie held out her left hand, palm up. The fingertips were calloused from her cello strings. 'Do they look soft to you?'

'Yes. They do.'

Sophie could have screamed.

The boy said, 'And you'd be noisy.'

'How do you know? You don't know me.' It seemed too much for this boy to break into her room in the moonlight, and start insulting her volume control.

'All pavement-people are noisy. You'd give me away. Or you'd fall, and people would come searching around and find us all. I mean, find me. No. You're not coming up here again.'

'You can't stop me.'

The boy sighed. He spoke like someone holding onto his temper by a thread. 'Fine! Just, stay on your own rooftop, then. Don't go near the edge. Stay low. Don't stay out after sunrise, or people will see you. Don't make a noise, or I'll hear and I'll come and burn off all your hair while you're sleeping.'

'But I can't!' said Sophie. 'Really, I can't. I need to look around. I need to find out more. Couldn't—' She hesitated. 'Could I come with you?'

The look he gave her was cold as ice. It burned. 'Fine! If you can catch me.'

The boy hadn't been lying when he said he could be gone in six seconds. He gripped hold of the window frame, and had twisted himself up and out before Sophie had counted to five. He seemed made of springs and leather.

Sophie followed, with only a little scrabbling, a little blood. Her legs were long, and she was quick; but the boy, as she clambered onto the slate, was already four rooftops down the road. His run was lilting, and peculiar. At least, she thought it was him; she could see only a black shadow, mixing with the shadows cast by the clouds scudding across the moon.

Sophie set after him. The night had turned damp, and the slate was slippery in unexpected places. Sophie didn't dare follow fast; she jogged, as quickly as she dared, across her own rooftop, and across the next.

Rooftop running was not like other running. Sophie tried to keep her head low, and her back half down. A bottom cropping up over the balustrades and chimney pots would be impossible to explain. Her arms and fingers seemed longer than usual, and got in the way.

Sophie halted, panting. The wind blew harder, and she gripped a chimney pot. Clocks below her began to strike four, and Paris was waking. Its sound was like the hum of a hundred secrets, she thought: it was the mutter of a dozen soothsayers.

But the boy was nowhere. The boy had disappeared.

13

The next night Sophie began training.

She worked harder than she had ever worked in her life. She did sit-ups, and pull-ups on the doorframe. She practised balancing on one leg with her eyes closed, again and again. Her first effort was seven seconds. Her hundredth was one minute and forty-two seconds. She ran barefoot back and forth across the rooftop, and sang under her breath to keep away the pain.

At about one in the morning, she realised quite suddenly what had made Matteo's run look different; it was toe first rather than heel first, which shifted your centre of gravity, she found, to somewhere near the knees. The realisation was like hot water, like a maths problem solved.

At two in the morning, the boy appeared. He was

two rooftops down, crouched behind the chimney pot. She saw him, but she didn't think he realised he had been spotted.

She shouted, 'I can see you! I'm not going to give in!' She turned a cartwheel. It was the most defiant cartwheel ever to have been turned on a Paris rooftop.

Sophie span on the spot. She felt on edge, and tough. It was unlikely, Sophie thought, that her muscles had grown stronger. She had a feeling that took months. It was more that she needed, now, to use them, and they had woken up for her. They felt as a cat's muscles feel: more twitching, and more ready. Muscles, she thought, are a thing worth having. They make the world easier to reach.

The wind up here was strong, and chimneydust blew in her eyes. She looped back her hair with a twig.

The dark was darker up on the roof; it was thick and silent. Down on the street, the dark feels dull and matter-of-fact, like a blackboard. Up here, it felt full of unseen birds and city whispers. The smell, too, was different. From the street, she reckoned she could smell only a few metres' worth of smells. From up here, all the bakers and all the pet shops of Paris mixed their scents. The result was something thick and peculiar and delicious.

From the roof, the moon looks twice as large, three times as beautiful. The moon, seen from the rooftops, is a thing worth spending time on.

Sophie imagined her mother, up here, amongst the stars. Mothers belong on rooftops.

Sophie walked to the next rooftop, and then jumped the three-foot gap to the next, and ran another three rooftops. She shouted, 'Matteo! I know you can hear me. I won't give up! I'm going to keep exploring!' Then, tentatively, feeling foolish, Sophie called into the night, 'Pax? Friends?'

Somewhere below her, a horse whinnied. It sounded as though it were laughing.

On the way back, she ran; ran, properly, not a jog. Her heart was beating so fast that it was nudging against her bones. The wind pulled at her clothes and hair, but she stayed steady. She thought, This is how heaven must feel. She felt confident as a crow. Say what you will against crows, Sophie thought, they do look like they know what they're doing.

14

Sophie prepared for the meeting with the chief commissioner the way other people prepare for war. She washed with cold water, and smoothed her eyebrows with spit. She rubbed lavender against her wrists and neck. She practised an innocent expression in the mirror. She polished her shoes with spit, and washed the oil and bird droppings out of her stockings.

'You look,' said Charles, when they met at the front door, 'as though you're about to sing the solo in the church choir.'

'Do I?' She knotted the bottom of her plait, and tucked it under her hat. 'That's what I was hoping.'

'You do. You look as though you own a minimum of one pony. You look nothing like yourself. Well done.'

As they walked through the streets, Sophie felt she was looking at Paris with newly critical eyes. She kept her head tilted back, and almost without noticing, she judged the rooftops. That one would be too steep; and that one much too low; that one was perfect, except for the flimsy looking drainpipe.

The police headquarters, she thought as they came in view of it, would be wonderful to climb. Its roof was flat, and its drainpipe was thick iron. She tensed as they went in. She would much rather be out on the rooftop than inside.

The meeting was held in a room with high ceilings and large furniture. It seemed designed to make Sophie feel small. A guard stood to attention outside the door.

It became clear immediately that it was less of a meeting, than an ambush.

The commissioner did not stand up to greet them. He waved at two seats. '*Bonjour*. Good day.' His accent was thickly French; it sounded moustachey.

'Please 'ave a seat, Mr Maxim, Miss Maxim.'

Sophie had sat before she realised what he had said. Then it hit her, and she leapt up and jumped towards the door. 'Charles!' she cried. 'Come on! Run!'

Charles hadn't moved. He stood in the centre of the room, holding his umbrella. His face was rigid. He looked like a soldier. Sophie stood with the doorknob in her hand.

The commissioner smiled. 'I could say, welcome to Paris, but I wouldn't mean it.'

'What's going on?' said Charles. 'Are you planning to arrest me?'

'*Non*. I am planning to give you a choice. Sit down.'

'What choice is that?' said Charles. He remained standing.

'Please sit down. You are wasting a good chair.'

Sophie stayed where she was. Charles sat. 'What choice was it you had in mind?'

'A very simple one. If you do not abandon your childish search and leave this country, I will 'ave you thrown in jail.' His nostrils widened as if in pleasure at the thought.

'I see. Well, that is admirably straightforward. May I ask why haven't you done so already?'

'I think we want to avoid fuss, *si possible. Non?*'

'No,' said Sophie. 'No, I'd rather have fuss. I need to find her.'

'Little girl.' He turned on her. All the wealth in the room seemed to mass itself behind him. '*Écoutez-moi*. Listen to me. The *Queen Mary* was a wreck. No women survived. The passenger lists, addresses, staff payrolls, insurance; it was all lost with the ship. I 'ave no wish to start an inquiry. You 'ave no wish to be in an orphanage. We are like twins, are we not?'

'I hate you,' whispered Sophie. 'I hate you.'

'I am giving you a day to book your passage back to England. I recommend the port at Dieppe. It's very fine this time of year.'

Charles bowed. 'You will notice that my young ward has not, as yet, spat on you. I admire her restraint.' For one mad moment Sophie thought Charles was going to spit on the man himself – he had his head thrown back, in spitting position – but he only took her hand, and led her from the room.

They walked down a hundred metres of corridor, until they were out of sight of the guard; then Charles swore, under his breath, and broke into a run. Sophie could only just keep pace with him. Her hat fell off, and she left it where it was. They burst through the grand doors, past the startled doorman, and out into the sunshine.

'I couldn't stand it in there a moment longer,' said Charles. 'He was lying.'

'Yes! His nostrils were flaring.'

'You saw it too. Flaring wide enough to fit a canal boat.'

'But I don't understand.' She stopped, and leant against a lamp post. 'Why does he care? Do you think he had anything to do with it? With the ship?'

'Not with the ship, perhaps. But I think he may be suppressing the records.'

'Why? What do you mean? Why would they do that?'

'Ten years ago there was a scandal in Europe; a series of sunken ships. It was an insurance con: an ancient ship would be certified safe, it would sink, the insurance would be claimed. The survivors were told conflicting stories; the truth got blurred. Smudged. And the records would be burnt or hidden, so that nobody could check who had certified the ship. There were eight cases, in all, before anyone was caught.'

'But . . . did people die?'

'Hundreds of people. It would have looked suspicious had they not.'

'That's disgusting! That's not human!'

'I know, my darling. Money can make people inhuman. It is best to stay away from people who care too much about money, my darling. They are people with shoddy, flimsy brains.'

'And . . . if the *Queen Mary* was one of those ships?'

'Yes?'

'Does that mean they will have burnt the records?' They couldn't have, she thought. They mustn't. She needed them.

'Kept them, more likely. If more than one person was involved, it would be unwise to burn anything.'

'Why? I don't get that; I'd burn them, if it was me.'

'If you are caught, it is better to have proof you were not acting alone. Criminals are only loyal to each other in books.' Charles polished his glasses. Behind them, his eyes were grim. 'I'm not saying that's what happened. But it's possible.'

'And never ignore a possible?'

'Precisely.' He smiled a half smile. 'I couldn't have said it better myself.'

'Where would they keep papers like that?'

'It could be anywhere. In their homes, in their offices, under their floorboards. Or, there's an archive room on the top floor of the building. Four million sheets of paper in one hundred filing cabinets, I am told.'

'Who told you?'

'The young woman at the reception desk. Somebody should promote her. She's wasted on reception.'

They crossed the road, avoiding a gaggle of American tourists.

'Charles?'

'Yes?'

'Nothing, actually.' They walked on. Then, 'Charles?'

'I'm listening.'

'Wouldn't the best place to hide papers be with other papers?'

'Very possibly.'

'So—'

'Yes, I see what you mean.'

'And the archive's on the top floor?'

'Sophie—'

'That's what you said, wasn't it?' The tingle and twitch that come with an idea were prickling at her skin. 'What if—'

'No, Sophie.'

'But—'

'*No*. I am not having you caught. You're not going anywhere near the place. Don't even think of it.'

'But we're not actually going to go back to England, are we.' It was not a question. 'I won't. I *can't*. Not when we might be so close.'

'Of course not. But, Sophie – and I do mean this – you will have to stay inside the hotel.'

'But, you can't do it without me—'

'I can. You will have to trust me to go on without you.'

'But then how will I be able to help? You have to let me help! What are you going to do?'

'I'm going to get a lawyer, Sophie.'

'What kind of lawyer?'

'The best we can afford. Which isn't terribly good, I'm afraid. And I'll lurk in some of these bars, and see if I can pick up any gossip.'

'About my mother? About Vivienne?'

'About cellists of any kind, I think.'

'Oh.' Sophie was sceptical about lawyers in general, but Charles looked so determined and his eyes were so kind that she couldn't bear to tell him so. Instead she said, 'But if I could just get into the archive—'

'No. There's a guard on every floor. You saw the one

outside the commissioner's office?'

'Yes. But, what if the archive—'

'The guard was built like a rhinoceros. There are men like him on every floor.' Charles glared into the sun. 'In fact, Sophie, I need you to keep away from the other hotel guests. Don't even open the door to your room.'

'Fine,' she said. She wasn't lying, she told herself. 'I won't even open the door.'

He looked at her, and she looked back, innocent-eyed.

'I'm sorry,' he said. 'I know it's stuffy in there. I'll bring you some good books.'

Sophie said nothing, but the flickering in her chest did not go away. Never, she thought, ignore a possible.

15

That night, Sophie said goodnight to Charles early, and clambered onto the rooftops the moment the sun had begun to set.

She sat against a chimney pot, and waited for it to become properly dark. While she waited, she tucked her knees under her chin, and tried to muster her options.

She was surprised to find that giving up was not one of them. It was odd. She wasn't, as far as she knew, brave. She was afraid of deep water and large crowds, and cockroaches. And when she thought of being caught and taken back to England she felt physically sick with dread. And yet giving up felt as impossible as flying. Her mother felt so much more real, here. She could almost smell her; she would smell, Sophie felt sure, of roses, and resin. She felt just around the corner.

Sophie got to her feet. Sophie had not thought she had a plan; but she acted purposefully as if she had planned it all along. She pulled off her shoes and held them in her teeth. Then she headed north, in the direction of the boy.

After twenty minutes, she squatted on her heels, and fished the laces from one of her shoes. She tied it round the chimney pot. She wanted him to know that she was not afraid to leave her own rooftop. At each new roof Sophie tied something to the chimney pot: first her other shoe lace, and then her stockings and two hair ribbons, all of which were easy to tie; and then her handkerchief, which was not quite large enough, and kept coming undone at the top. At the eighth rooftop, she wound her dressing gown round the chimney. It was grey with much washing, and she was not sorry to part with it.

At the ninth rooftop, Sophie came to a halt. She stood on one leg. There was a gap, as long as an ironing board, between her rooftop and the next. *It's not far*, she told herself. She would almost certainly make it. But, somehow, she couldn't persuade her feet to agree.

Sophie hesitated. Then she tugged off her nightdress and threw it onto the rooftop. There was one second when she thought it was going to drop straight down the chimney. Instead it landed neatly on the edge and lay there, its arm waving in the breeze, as if it were saluting the dark.

Then Sophie turned and ran, as swift as she dared, dressed only in her pants and with her shoes in her mouth and her arms out for balance, back along the slate, back along the tip-tops of the city, over the heads of a hundred dreaming Frenchmen, and back to bed.

Matteo appeared the next night, carrying her night-dress and stockings. He came at the stroke of midnight, under cover of the chiming clocks. Sophie didn't wake until he was standing three inches from her face.

'My God!' she said. 'You startled me.'

'I know.' He dumped the clothes on her bed. 'I kept the dressing gown,' he said. 'I wanted it.' He sat on the edge of her bed. 'You might as well explain,' he said.

Sophie said, 'Do you swear not to tell anybody?'

'No,' said the boy.

Nobody ever said no. Sophie stared. 'You don't?'

'I never swear anything. Tell me anyway.'

Sophie bit her lip; but the boy looked fearless. Fearless people are not usually telltales.

'If you tell on me,' she said, 'I'll come after you. Remember, I'm not frightened of rooftops.'

She told him everything. She started with the *Queen Mary*, and worked through Miss Eliot and Charles, and her cello, and finished here, in Paris, amongst the chimney pots. 'And the thing is, it feels like I've been here before,' she finished.

'In Paris?'

'In Paris, *and* on the rooftops. But it's so difficult,' she said. 'Charles tries, but he's just one person. And nobody else will help me.'

'Is that a request?'

She looked at the boy. He seemed to be wearing two pairs of shorts, one on top of the other. The red pair on top was missing half the left leg and the blue pair showed through. Together they just about made up one pair of shorts. His jersey was threadbare, but his face, she thought, was not. His face was sharp and clever.

She said, 'Yes. It is.'

'Do you have a plan?'

'Of course. I'm going to make posters. And, there's the lawyers.'

Matteo snorted. 'They won't help you.'

'Yes, they will! Why would you say that?'

'You might find one, I suppose. But I don't think anyone will take on the commissioner of police. All the lawyers in Paris are corrupt, and most of the policemen.'

'How do you know?' Sophie's heart felt suddenly grey. 'You can't know that! Someone's *got* to help! It's wildly important.'

'I listen to people all day. I live on top of the law courts, so I do know.'

'But you can't hear anything from a rooftop!'

'I can. Where I live, I can hear half of the city. It's like a wind tunnel; I can hear all the music in Paris, and all the horses, and all the crime.'

Sophie froze. 'You can hear all the music?'

'Yes. Of course.'

'What music do you hear?'

'All sorts. Women singing, mostly. And men with guitars, and the soldiers' band.'

'Do you hear cello music? Do you hear Fauré's *Requiem*?'

'I wouldn't recognise a requiem,' said Matteo. 'What is it? It sounds like a skin infection.'

'I can play it for you.' Sophie leapt up to fetch her cello. Then she hesitated. 'If I play now, people will hear. They might come up and find you.'

'Come outside, then. I'll go first and you can pass up your . . . cello, is the word, yes?'

Outside, she sat on the chimney pot, and set her cello between her legs. She knew the *Requiem*, but she had never played it double-time.

'It won't be perfect, all right? But I think it was something like this. Listen carefully, all right? And tell me if you've ever heard it.' Sophie stumbled over the fingering, but she thought it sounded at least something like the magic Monsieur Esteoule had played. When she had finished, Matteo shrugged.

'Possibly.'

'Possibly what?'

'*Possibly* I've heard it. What did you say?'

'Nothing.' In fact she had whispered, 'Never ignore a possible.' But she hadn't meant him to hear.

He said, 'I'm not good at music. Unless it's birds. You'd have to come and listen yourself.'

'Can I? Really? When?'

He snorted again. 'Whenever you like. I don't have a busy diary.'

'Tomorrow?'

'D'accord.'

'I don't speak French.' But his face had seemed to say, yes.

'I said, fine. I'll come and fetch you.'

'At midnight?' she asked. It had begun to rain. Matteo ignored it.

'*Non*. It's not dark enough at midnight. Two-thirty. Don't fall asleep. And wear something warm. It can be windy, up high.'

'Yes, of course!' The rain grew heavier. 'Wait a second. Rain isn't good for the wood.' Sophie lowered her cello back into her bedroom. When she turned back, Matteo had vanished.

Back inside, Sophie pulled the window shut, and huddled into the warm patch in her bed, but she did not fall asleep again until dawn. She lay listening to the rain blowing against the glass. Her heart was dancing double-time.

16

If she had obeyed Charles and stayed in her room all day and all night, Sophie would, she thought, have gone straightforwardly crazy. She tried to reassure herself that she was not breaking any rules. She was not opening the door to her bedroom. The thought of the rooftops kept her steady during the day. Sophie counted the hours until sunset.

By nightfall it had grown cold, and Sophie put on her two pairs of stockings under her nightdress. She hadn't packed enough warm clothes, so she pulled the pillowcases off the pillows and knotted them together to make a scarf. It felt limp and not entirely comfortable, but she thought it was preferable to nothing. Then she got into bed, and wedged her hairbrush behind her neck so she wouldn't fall asleep, and waited.

Matteo arrived as the clocks struck the half hour. He knocked on the skylight, and then stood impatiently flicking pebbles down into her room until she climbed out.

'Hello,' said Sophie. '*Bonsoir.*'

'*Oui, bonsoir.*' He wore a pack on his back, and his shorts had been swapped for a pair of trousers. They looked like they had been in a fight, and lost. He said, 'You're learning French?'

'A little.' Sophie flushed. 'It's not easy.'

'Yes it is. I know dogs that speak French. I know *pigeons.*'

'That's different.'

'How? How is it different?'

'Well, I'm not a pigeon.' A thought struck her. 'How long did it take you to learn English? Do all French people speak it like you do?'

'*Je ne sais pas.* I always knew it, a little. There's a bar where the English diplomats go. It has a courtyard. I can hear them speaking from my rooftop. And I learnt to read it while I was in—' He stopped.

'While you were where?'

'In an orphanage.' He shook his head, as if clearing water from his ears, and changed the subject, 'Listen

– I meant to ask – where I live is one of the tallest buildings in Paris. Are you afraid of heights?'

'No, I don't think so. I mean, I'm up here, aren't I?'

'This isn't high! This is practically pavement. I mean, are you good with *real* heights?'

'I'm not bad,' said Sophie. She cast her eyes down at the slate.

'Oh.'

'Quite good, I think.'

'Then you can't come. Quite good isn't good enough. Sorry.' He turned to go.

'Wait! I was being modest!'

'But you just said—'

'I'm very good,' said Sophie. 'I'm brilliant at them.' Matteo was obviously not the sort of boy who understood modesty, and she could not risk being left behind. 'Brilliant,' she said again.

'You shouldn't say what you don't mean, then. Are you ready?'

'Yes.' It seemed wise to change the subject. 'Whereabouts do you live?' said Sophie. 'Near here?'

'Yes. But not on this street. This street is too poor.'

'Is it? Oh.' It looked quite grand, to Sophie, with its tall lamp posts and elegant thin streets. 'Why does that matter, anyway?' She looked at his clothes, and at the mud clinging to the tips of his hair at the front. 'I wouldn't have thought you'd be a snob.'

'Lots of reasons.' Matteo looked haughty.

'Like what, though? Please? I'm curious.'

'Poor buildings are usually pointed; rich buildings are usually flat. Pointed roofs are no good. Poor buildings are . . . unpredictable. You can't be sure if you're going to put your foot through the slate. And they're too low. In the . . . *ach, banlieues* . . . the suburbs, I think you say? Where there are just houses: no offices, no churches? I never go there: the buildings are too low.'

'Really? Always?'

'Almost always. It's like people; rich buildings are tall, poor buildings are stunted.'

'Why does that matter?'

'Why do you think?'

Sophie stared out across the rooftops. 'Because with small buildings they can see you from the street?'

'*Oui.* Otherwise, I can go almost everywhere. At night. Never during the day.'

'Do you go to the parks?' It's what I would do, she thought, if I could.

'*Non*. Of course not.'

'Why not? It would be wonderful to have a park to yourself. And there'd probably be food.'

'I never go on the ground. Not for years. You can't get trapped on a rooftop.'

Sophie blinked. 'Never?' It sounded impossible. 'But what if you need to cross a road? Between rooftops?'

'I go by trees. Or on top of the lamp posts.'

'And you never just . . . cross a road?'

'*Non*.'

'Why not?'

'It's dangerous,' he said.

'Oh . . .' Matteo's voice was sounding increasingly curt. But she couldn't hold it back. 'You know, most people would say it's the other way around.'

'Most people are stupid. It's easy to be caught on the ground. Everyone gets caught.'

'Caught?' Sophie tried to decipher his face in the darkness. He looked serious. 'Is somebody looking for you?'

Matteo ignored that. 'So, you want to see where I live, or no?'

'Yes! Now?'

'Now!' And without looking behind to see if she was following, Matteo took off.

When Matteo was standing still, he was quite an unusual-looking person. When he moved, he was astonishing. He seemed made of India rubber. He ran low, and used his hands as though they were extra feet. She followed as quietly and quickly as she could, tripping over the rough slate. Quite a lot of the skin of her knees got left behind.

Matteo ran for ten minutes, and Sophie followed, balancing along the tips of slanted rooftops, sprinting along the flat ones, and jumping the small gaps between them. Twice, as the buildings grew taller, Matteo showed her how to clamber up a length of drainpipe to reach the next roof.

'The thing about drainpipes,' he said, hanging upside down from one of them, 'is that you mustn't put your foot through a window while you're pulling yourself up. People tend to notice that.'

Sophie tackled the drainpipes without talking. Her nails scraped against the metal horribly, but otherwise they were not so different from trees. When she thumped down onto the slate beside Matteo, he nodded. He almost smiled. 'Not bad,' he said. 'Next time, keep your knees in. It makes it easier to grip. But that was good. At least, good-ish.'

Sophie flushed with pleasure. Matteo ran on. Below their feet, Paris slept.

They were reaching an area full of flags and vast solemn-looking buildings. As the rooftops got wider and larger, Matteo went faster. Once, on the fiddly roof of some kind of chapel, Sophie stumbled, and her stomach inverted. She clutched the cross for balance, and stopped to catch her breath.

The wind was high, and across the road, a shadow was swinging by its knees from the top of the lamp post.

Sophie saw it. She definitely saw it. But by the time she had untangled her hair from her face and could see again, the girl had gone.

It took her a few minutes to catch up with Matteo. 'Matteo! Did you see her? The girl? Who was it?'

'I didn't see it. It will have been just nothing. A paper bag.'

'It was bigger than a paper bag. It was a girl!'

'A broken kite, maybe. A pillowcase. Come on.' He cracked his knuckles, and ran on.

It was ten minutes before Matteo again stopped.

They were a jump across from a tall, curved rooftop. It gleamed greenish in the moonlight.

'Stay there.' Matteo jumped, then bent and rapped lightly on the rooftop. It echoed. 'Copper,' he said. 'Take off your shoes before you come. Jump as softly as you can.'

Sophie pulled off her shoes. 'What shall I do with them?'

'Here; throw your shoes to me. *Ach*, I hate copper.'

Sophie did so. Thank goodness, she thought, that Charles had taught her to throw.

'What's the worst kind of rooftop?' she asked. 'Is it copper?'

'*Non*. Stone tiles; the old ones, from the old days. They're quieter than copper, but too easy to . . . what's the word? Topple?'

'Dislodge?' Sophie held her breath and eyed the gap. It was no wider than her arm, but even so it made her shiver. She jumped, landing messily, but leapt straight to her feet.

'Maybe. Yes, dislodge. And flat rooftops are best.' He handed back her shoes. 'Anything with big slabs is good. Stone, or slate, or metal.'

'Right. Like on the Hotel Bost?'

'Yes. And on most state buildings; you know, hospitals, prisons. Theatres are good. And cathedrals. But anything four floors or under is too low to sleep on. They can see you from the street if you roll too near the edge. Wait, don't put your shoes back on. Tie them round your waist.'

'All right.' Sophie wound her shoe laces round her waist. 'Why, though?' She arranged the shoes carefully, so that one hung over each hip.

Matteo said, 'You need your toes, up here. You shouldn't ever wear shoes.'

'But don't you—'

'People think toes are useless. That's because they're stupid.

'But don't your feet get—'

His face took on an aggravating, headmaster look. 'You thought toes were only good for collecting dirt, *non*?'

'Not exactly, but—'

'But nothing. Toes are life and death. You need toes for balance. I've broken every toe at least twice. Look.' Matteo held up a foot.

It was black. The base of his foot was calloused over. Not one inch of soft skin was visible. He tapped the bottom. 'You hear? It's like tin. You could play music on my feet.'

Sophie said, 'But don't they get cold in winter?'

'Yes.'

'Oh.' Sophie waited for him to say more. He didn't. She said, 'But couldn't you wear shoes, when you're just on your own rooftop? I could give you mine, if you like. I've got two pairs.'

'*Non, merci.*'

'They're not girly.' Sophie held up the shoes hanging round her waist. 'They're like these ones: boys' boots. They were a present from Charles. What size are your feet?'

'You can't wear shoes up here. You never know when you might need to run.'

'But what about when it *snows*?'

'In winter, to stay warm, I wrap my ankles and calves with goose fat and bandages, and feathers between the layers. So it's almost like having shoes, but it leaves your toes free.'

'Oh. Does that work?'

'No. But, almost.'

'Why goose fat?'

He shrugged. 'Fat keeps you warm. Goose fat is best,

but you can use pigeon, if you have to. Sparrows don't have enough fat on them. Squirrel meat's too dry. You need something greasy.' Without her permission Sophie's face formed an *ugh*. He saw, and scowled. 'I never said it was nice, but it helps. Let's go. Are you ready?'

Sophie checked the laces round her waist were tightly knotted. Then, 'Matteo?' she said. 'Where did you learn all this?'

'Accidentally, mostly. Practise.' Matteo lifted his shirt. A purplish scar ran from his belly button to his ribcage. 'Trial and error.'

'My God! How did you do that?'

'Falling. On a weathervane. And this one –' he showed her a bruise, still a fresh green, on his shoulder – 'was when I fell onto a chimney pot.'

'Does it hurt?'

'Of course.' He shrugged. 'We bleed more often than most people. It's not the end of the world.'

'Oh.' Then she said, 'Matteo?'

'*Quoi?*'

'Who is we?'

The look in his face was so different, so suddenly, that Sophie stepped back. 'Me,' he said. 'I said me.'

Matteo took off again. This time, when he reached the gaps between rooftops, he jumped without waiting for her or looking back. Sophie had to stop to gather her courage before each one; they would have been nothing on the ground, but up high they took all the nerve she had. Soon she was a roof's length behind.

'Can we slow down, please? Just a little?'

'*Non*,' said Matteo. He pushed his hair from his eyes in order to glare at her, and sped up.

After half an hour, Matteo did slow. When he turned to face her, he seemed to have regained his temper. He said, 'This is the last gap. It's the next building.'

By now Sophie felt like an old hand. 'Do we jump?' She pushed back her hair and crouched.

'*Non! Arrête!* Sophie! Stop!'

'What? What's wrong?'

'You can't jump onto that roof. It's a . . . I don't know the word – a crumbler?'

'What do you mean?'

'The parapet is too old to jump on to. The tiles snap off.'

'Oh. Goodness.' Sophie stared at the gap. It wasn't very wide, it was true: but it was a long drop to the ground.

'I know! It's so good. It's why I chose to live here: it means nobody can follow, unless they know. If you were to jump without knowing, you'd die, I think.'

'Do you realise that's not very reassuring?'

It was dark, but she thought Matteo smiled. 'I don't bother too much about reassuring.'

Sophie realised she'd been holding her breath. She gulped in air. It was surprising what a difference oxygen made to bravery. 'How do you get across?' she asked.

'It's easy. You step.'

Jumping was one thing. It was a rush and a gasp and it lit up your insides. Slowly stepping across nothingness was quite another. She tried to imagine it. 'I can't. I'll have to jump it,' she said. Terror rose up in Sophie's throat. It tasted green. 'That's too wide to step.'

'*Non*, not for you. Your legs are like drainpipes.'

'They're not.'

'That was a compliment! You were born for roof-tops. And anyway, legs stretch wider than you think.'

'I just don't know if I can.'

'You said you were good at heights.'

'I am!' How *dare* he, Sophie thought. 'We've come miles! And I'm covered in blood and soot and I didn't stop once.'

'So? It doesn't count if you don't get to the end.' He laid a hand on her shoulder.

Sophie leapt away. 'Don't you dare push me!' Matteo was unpredictable. It occurred to her for the first time that rooftops and unpredictable people are a dangerous mix.

'I wasn't going to!' he hissed. 'And keep your voice down.'

'Sorry. I'm sorry.' She peered over the edge again. 'OK. Tell me what we do. I'm not saying I'll do it, though.'

'OK. First, you close your eyes,' said Matteo.

'Matteo. We're on a *rooftop*.'

'Close your eyes. If you keep them open, you'll look down, and if you look down, you'll fall.'

'Oh.' Sophie closed them. 'Ah.'

'I'm going to lead you to the edge. Are your eyes closed?'

'Yes.' In fact, Sophie was peering down under her lashes. She could see her bare feet approaching the edge.

'No, they're not. Close them properly. It will be easier, I promise you. *Et maintenant* – I hold the back of your nightdress, so you can't fall – and you take a step.'

'How big?'

'About the length of a pig.'

The length of a pig, thought Sophie. She was going to die because she had never looked properly at a pig.

'You'll be fine. You're safe.' Matteo sounded unusually serious. 'Keep your eyes shut.'

Sophie extended one leg into the gap. 'They're shut,' she said, and this time it was true. Gripping onto his arm, she stuck her leg out into nothing. It waved around; and still it met nothing. Sophie shot her leg back, and stepped away from the edge.

'That's wider than a pig, Matteo!'

'The *length* of a pig. Pigs are quite long. Shake out your leg. I've got you. Try again. Further! Yes!' Sophie was almost doing the splits when her foot connected with the far edge.

'Now what?' She tried not to sound panicky, but her weight had shifted to somewhere over her knees, too far forward to pull it back, and she felt she might twist backwards into nothing any second. And if anyone was walking in the tiny alley beneath they would be able to see her pants up her nightdress. This is why everybody should wear trousers, she thought. *This.*

'Now you let go of me,' Matteo said, 'And—'

'What? No! Don't you—'

'Just for a second—' Matteo had already detached himself, 'and I step . . .' There was the lightest of thumps. A squirrel would have made more noise.

'And you give me your hand.'

Sophie did so, and blushed. It was slippery with sweat.

'And I pull you over.' His tug was startlingly strong, and she was dragged, shoulders and arms and knees all together, across the gap.

'And now,' said Matteo, 'you stand up. And you wipe your hands.' He grinned. 'You could water plants with your palms. Come on. We're almost there.'

'You said this was the last one! You said this was it!'

'*Oui*. I lied.'

17

Matteo straightened the bag on his back, and beckoned her along the rooftop. 'When the moon comes out, you'll be able to see.' He pointed, and puffed out his chest. 'There – that rooftop there – that's where I live.'

'It's very nice,' Sophie said, politely. Her eyes were shut, but it was what you were supposed to say when people show you their homes.

'Very nice? That's all?'

'Sorry.' Sophie had been gathering together her breath and her courage. She opened her eyes; and then opened them again, wider. 'You live *there*?'

It was beautiful. It was the same dizzying height as the building they were sitting on, but it was built of sandstone, and in the moonlight it glowed yellow. Statues of warriors and women were carved into the walls. It looked like there would be chandeliers inside, and men with power at their fingertips. At the top, a French flag flew from a polished silver pole.

'It's the law court,' said Matteo. 'It's the most important building in Paris.'

'You sound like an estate agent.'

'It's *true*!' He looked furious. 'It's the most beautiful building in Europe. It says so in the guide books.'

'How do we get there?' The gap between their building and Matteo's home was too wide to jump. No tree could possibly reach as high.

'If I was alone, I'd go round the back, up the oak and then the drainpipe.' Matteo took off his backpack. 'But the jump from the tree to the pipe takes practise. See.' He rolled back his sleeve. A scar ran from his wrist to the crook of his elbow. 'The painful kind of practise.' He opened his pack. 'I brought this, instead.'

'Rope?' Sophie looked at the thick coil in Matteo's hand. It was a good length. Rope is heavy; Matteo must have been stronger than he looked. 'What's the hook on the end for?'

'You'll see in a second.'

'Are we going to climb? Is that what the rope's for?'

Sophie tried not to the let the fear in her chest become audible. Matteo, she thought grudgingly, must have been born with a larger than usual portion of courage.

'I said, you'll see.' Matteo walked to the very edge of the building and curled his toes over the edge. Sophie's stomach gave a swoop of protest, but he seemed as cool as if he was standing on the edge of the kerb. 'Stand back,' he said. He whirled the rope above his head, spat over the edge of the roof, and let the rope fly. It hooked onto the bracket holding up the drainpipe on the other side.

Matteo gave it a tug. His face had the same listening expression that Charles had around music.

'That'll be fine,' he said. He pulled it taut, and tied the end in his hand to a hooked nail in the wall. He spat on the knot for luck.

'Now, we walk,' he said.

Sophie stared at him. 'You're joking.'

'You said you wanted to see where I live. This is how you get there. It's easy!'

'It's *string*! A piece of string between the sky and the pavement. *String*, Matteo.'

'Rope.'

From here, Sophie thought, it definitely looked like string. It looked impossible.

Matteo's face, in the dark, was exasperated. 'If you want, you could try to jump from the tree to the pipe, but that would be stupid. This is safer.'

'A tightrope.' It was almost invisible from where Sophie stood; just a slither of grey in the darkness. 'A *tightrope* is your safer option.'

Matteo looked coldly at her over the gap. 'If you don't do it, I won't help you. Cowards don't deserve help.'

'Don't call me a coward. I'm not a coward.'

'*Oui, je sais.*'

'What?'

Matteo shrugged, half apologetic. 'I don't necessarily think you're a coward.'

'Then don't say it, ever again.'

'Look, this is easy. I'll show you.

Matteo spat again, and blew his nose with his thumb. He stepped onto the rope. For one second he hesitated, swaying, and then he paced, foot over foot, until he was right in the middle of the rope. His arms were stretched out. Like wings, Sophie thought. His upper body moved in time with the breeze, and he looked like he was balancing on thin air. The wind ruffled his clothes and flipped his hair on end.

It was the most unexpected thing in the world, she thought. It took the breath out of her.

Very slowly, he turned – Sophie's throat tightened in terror, but the boy gave not a single wobble – and he walked back to her. 'Coming?' he said. He held out one hand.

The thing that amazed Sophie was that she didn't even have to consider. Perhaps because it was so beautiful. Perhaps because sometimes everybody needs to be stupidly and recklessly brave.

'Yes,' Sophie said. 'I'm coming.'

She walked to the edge of the roof. That was easy. She curled her toes on the parapet, and looked down. That was not so easy. Her hands were hot. *Hold steady*, she thought.

'Slowly,' said Matteo. 'You start slowly. Can you put one foot on the rope?'

Sophie felt it sharp and springy beneath her bare foot. 'Oh my *heart*, Matteo!' There was a whirlwind in her chest.

'Give me both your hands. I do the balancing for both of us, *oui*?'

'*Oui,*' said Sophie. 'Yes.'

'Other foot.'

Sophie's right foot left dry land. She stepped out over the air. '*Oh,*' she breathed. 'I think you must be mad. We must both be mad. Oh, God.'

'Good,' said Matteo. She wobbled, and he steadied her. 'Mad is good. Don't look down.'

'But then how do I know where to put my feet?' Sophie's voice came out higher than usual.

'You hold on to me; hold on to my shoulders. I'll go backwards. I'm doing all the balancing, OK? You just don't look down. Can you feel the rope with your feet?'

'Yes,' said Sophie. She dug her thumbs into his skin. 'Yes.'

'Now,' said Matteo. 'Left foot. Right. Grip with your toes. Left. Stop. Do *not* look down. Look up. At the top of my head. Can you feel the balance?'

Sophie's feet tickled against the prickle of the rope. 'I think so. Yes. Maybe.'

'*Bien,*' he said. He felt frighteningly thin and light. She thought his collarbone must be hollow, like a bird's. 'Keep breathing. Step.' Halfway along, he slowed and stopped.

'Why are you stopping?' said Sophie. She tried to keep the rasp of fear out of her voice. 'I think I'd rather we kept moving.'

'So you can look. See, Sophie! Don't look down – look across. There is all of Paris!'

Sophie looked, and gasped. Below her feet, Paris stretched out towards the river. Paris was darker than London: it was a city lit in blinks and flickers. And it was Fabergé-egg beautiful, she thought. It was magic carpet stuff.

'See? Best city in the world,' said Matteo. 'You will never feel as much like a king as up here.'

It was better than being a king. Kings, thought Sophie, would have bruised fingers from a thousand daily handshakes. This was like being a warrior, a sprite, a bird.

Far away, by the river, she thought she could see the Hotel Bost, and her own skylight.

'I wonder if I've left my candle burning,' she said. 'I think I can see it.'

Matteo ignored that. His face was whiter than usual, and his eyes brighter. He seemed to be listening to the rope. He said, 'Shall we feed the birds?'

'Yes.' Then a gust of wind tugged at her nightdress,

and Sophie changed her mind. 'Or, no. No, actually, I think I'd rather keep going,' she said. 'Please!'

'*Ach, non!* To feed the birds while you are in the sky! This is a thing even a king cannot do.'

'But it's past midnight. The birds –' the rope gave a wobble, and a globule of something bitter rose up in Sophie's throat – 'the birds will be asleep.'

'They're just dozing. They'll wake if I call them. Just two minutes more, Sophie! I have hold of you. You can't fall if I have hold.'

'Quickly, then, OK?'

'You have to let go of me with one hand. I have grain, in my pocket; I'll put it in your palm. Yes? I have the balance, Sophie. You just keep your legs straight. *No, don't look down.*'

Sophie tried to take the grain from his hand without looking down at it. She failed. The whole world swooped. She could feel half of the grain slithering through her sweaty fingers. Her knees gave a spasm and the rope shuddered. 'Matteo! Help me.'

Matteo had never looked more calm. He said, 'Steady.' He tightened his grip on her, and shifted their balance. 'Are you panicking?'

'No,' lied Sophie.

'If you start to fall, I'll stop you. You understand, *oui*? Yes? I have never fallen from a tightrope. At least, not far. Not *very* far, anyway. Breathe, please.'

'I am! Stop telling me to breathe!' The rope dug into the soles of her feet. 'I am breathing!'

Matteo said, 'Just one more minute. Unlock your knees. Good. I'm going to call the birds.'

'Matteo, I think I want to get off.' Sophie tried not to think of fifty-foot drops. She was not successful. 'Please, let's just get to the other end.'

'*Non*. Just one minute.' Matteo whistled: a scale of three notes, rising. It was sharp and clean and it rang out through the silent dark for miles. It cut through Sophie's panic. It sounded like rain coming.

He said, 'Can you whistle?'

'Yes.' There was a wind, and the rope swayed under her. Sophie shut her eyes.

'Copy me, then.'

Sophie gripped the rope with her toes. She whistled. It was like playing the cello; it made the rest of the world recede.

'That's good.' He sounded surprised. '*C'est très bien*. You didn't tell me you could do that.'

'Thank you.' She whistled again. It calmed her

breath. She tried to make her throat vibrate, like the nightingales did.

'Open your eyes.' Matteo was grinning. She hadn't ever seen him smile like that. 'Look up!' he said.

Sophie looked up. Three birds were circling above Matteo's head.

'They know me, you see' said Matteo. 'Hold out your seed. Higher than that. It has to be higher than your shoulder, or they'll try to crawl up your arm and onto your head.'

A bird landed on her hand, then a second one.

'*Oh!*' she breathed. They were heavy; their weight on her arms was the oddest delight. Their claws pinched at her skin. 'Hello,' she breathed. '*Bonsoir.*' The rope swayed under her feet as the second bird settled on her wrist.

Matteo shifted their balance. His face was muddy, but the pure white concentration showed through.

'They like you,' said Matteo. 'Look!'

Sophie looked. One of the pigeons was shifting and flapping, up along her forearm towards her shoulder. It was as if it was testing her strength, she thought.

'Please stay,' she whispered to the birds. The birds seemed to approve of her. 'Don't go. Stay.'

The largest one pecked at the seed – which must have tasted rather sweaty by now, she thought – from the grooves in her palm.

Matteo whistled again, and another bird circled down, and landed on her head. Then a red-eyed dove landed on Matteo's shoulder, and pecked at the back of his neck.

'I know this one,' said Matteo. 'He's called Elisabeth.'

'He?'

'He's old. I met him when I was just a baby. I didn't know how to tell the sex, then; I thought he was a girl.'

'He's beautiful.'

'Yes, I know. I didn't think he'd come. He doesn't like strangers.' Elisabeth left Matteo and flapped onto Sophie's collarbone. It looked her in the eye. It bobbed its head. 'He must think he knows you.'

'Maybe he does!'

'He can't, though, can he? Silly Elisabeth.'

Elisabeth flapped his wings against her cheek, but did not take off. To be approved by birds! thought Sophie. To be up in the centre of the sky!

'Matteo! This is too good!' She couldn't think of words. 'This is like music.'

The city, Sophie thought, was different to what she had believed. 'It is kinder than you think,' she whispered. A blue tit landed on her hand. Sophie felt bejewelled. A blue tit is better than a ring. It pecked at her earlobe. 'It is wilder than you think.'

18

It was half an hour before Sophie would let Matteo lead on to the other side. It was only the threat of the rising sun that made her give in. As soon as Matteo had backed onto the roof, and tugged her after him, Sophie's legs started to shake. She staggered three steps towards the centre and collapsed.

'Are you all right?' said Matteo. 'Do you need help?'

'No, I think *I'm* fine; it's just my legs that aren't.' She poked her calf muscle, and it gave a spasm. 'I think they'll be normal again in a second. I'll just sit here, if that's all right.'

'You're an odd colour. Do you want to sleep for a minute? I have a blanket. Or, it's a sack, but—'

'No, I couldn't sleep. I'll just sit.'

'Right. I'll make a fire.'

'Where? Here?'

'Of course not! Don't be stupid. It has to be by the chimney stack, so the smoke looks like it comes from the chimney. You stay there. Don't go anywhere.'

It was a few minutes before her legs would let her stand up and look around. The rooftop was large as a town square, and smooth slate. Sophie stamped, tentatively. Her legs seemed solid again. A plume of smoke rose from the centre of the roof. Sophie walked – or rather, limped – towards it.

Matteo was squatting behind the chimney stack, feeding a fire with wood. From the look of it, it had once been a chair. He wore a sack over his shoulders.

'Matteo!' Sophie's eyes widened. 'Is this all yours?' She hoped he wouldn't be able to see in the dark how impressed she was.

'Of course. Who else's?' At Matteo's feet was a pile of arrows, tied in bundles. Neatly stacked against the chimney there was a pile of apples, a tin saucepan and a kettle, a heap of rough-cut wooden spoons, glass jars filled with nuts. There were two sacks; Sophie peeked inside. One was filled with leaves, and another filled with bones.

'Here. Sit.' He handed her a cushion.

'Did you make this?' It was sacking on the outside, but soft and thick.

'Of course.'

'What's it made of?' Sophie kneaded it. It was softer than anything they had at home. 'What's the stuffing?'

'It's just pigeon . . . *ach*, fluff. I don't know the word.'

'Down?'

'*Non*, not down. Down is like . . . not up. That soft white you get under the pigeon feathers, you know? But,' he said, 'I use the outer feathers too, of course. I use everything. Even the bones.'

'You don't let them go when you've taken their feathers?'

'Let them go? Of course I don't let them go. I mean . . . they're dead. I don't pluck living pigeons. That would be very difficult for me and very confusing for the pigeon.'

'So you eat them?'

'Yes. I cook them and I eat them.' He took out a knife and held it out to her. 'With this. Sometimes, if it's raining and I'm hungry enough, I skip the cooking.'

'Do you eat the bones?'

'I boil them for soup.'

'Is it nice?'

'*Non*. It's disgusting. It's like glue. But it's better than nothing.'

'And the outer feathers? What do you do with them?' He was such a peculiar creature that she would not have been surprised if he had worn them, as a cloak. She would not have been surprised, in fact, if he had sewn them into wings.

'Look. That. There. No, *there*.'

Further along the roof, stretched between the two chimney stacks, there was a sheet. Sophie jogged over to look more closely. It was sewn with layer upon layer of pigeon feathers. It was oddly greasy, but beautiful. Under it was a bed made of sacks. She kneaded the mattress. It was the same soft down as her cushion.

'The feathers are waterproof,' said Matteo. She had not heard him come up behind her. 'It works like a tent. Only it was free.'

It wouldn't be warm, thought Sophie. It would be no real protection from the wind. 'Matteo, what do you do in winter? How do you stay warm?'

'I don't.' He shrugged. 'You get used to it. You don't get to like it.'

'Couldn't you go to the orphanage? Just for the winter?'

'No.'

'But—'

'I did, once. There was a fight, on a rooftop in the north, and I got cut. A bad one. It turned septic.' As he spoke, he tucked his right hand under his left armpit. 'I thought I had no choice.' Matteo poked the fire too hard. It sparked, and Sophie ducked. He said, 'There were iron bars on the windows. I can pick a lock, but nobody can pick an iron bar.'

'But why would there be bars? Did people try to break in?'

'*Non*. Children tried to break *out*. But once they know you exist, they don't let you leave. It's illegal to be homeless in France, did you know that?'

Sophie hadn't known. It sounded the craziest law in the world. 'But you left, didn't you?'

'Yes. Through a chimney. I should never have gone in the first place. They're still looking for me; for me, and for some others. They put notices of runaways in the post offices, did you know *that*?'

'But why? Why did you run away, I mean? What happened?'

'Nothing. Nothing happened. It was like hell: the same thing every day. They shouted if we talked to each other at meals. They shouted if we laughed.'

'Really?' Sophie was stunned. 'I mean, literally?'

'*Oui*. You have no idea, Sophie. It was like being nailed shut. I can't risk going on the ground again. It is better for people not to know I exist.' He turned away, and ran a twig under his toenails.

Sophie wasn't stupid. She turned back to the feather tent. 'Well, I think this is wonderful, up here! I think I'd never leave this rooftop, if I was you.' She stroked the feathers. Water lay in droplets on them, but the slate underneath was dry. 'It's fantastic! I wish I lived here. It's perfect.'

He shrugged. 'It smells in the summer.' But he had that look that Charles got when he was secretly pleased. He said, 'Seagulls have the best feathers – look, there –' he gestured to the sheet, to the white patches – 'because they're naturally greasy, and water runs off them. But you don't get many seagulls, except after storms. Pigeon feathers aren't bad. They're thick, and I add duck grease to them, when I have it.'

'But how do you catch them?'

Matteo looked at her, very hard. 'How do you think?'

'With . . . with a trap?' Sophie had no idea. With a

knife? With his hands? With his teeth? Nothing, she felt, would surprise her.

'I'll show you. I haven't eaten today, anyway.'

Matteo reached inside the chimney and pulled out a bow. He reached under the mattress, and pulled out a bundle of arrows. 'The arrows blow away if you don't tie them,' he said. 'It gets windy up here.' He fitted the arrow on the bow, and his face flicked into that listening expression she had seen on the tightrope. It shut her out as effectively as a door. He turned his back to Sophie. There were three pigeons roosting on the chimney stack on the rooftop they had come from; suddenly Matteo's arm snapped back, and an arrow shrilled across the space and struck the middle pigeon in its neck. The other two pigeons took off, shrieking in fear.

'Always aim for the middle pigeon, if there is one,' he said. He ignored the shock in Sophie's face. 'It gives you more chance of hitting. And aim against the wind.'

Matteo jogged to the edge of the rooftop and crouched to peer over. Then he tipped himself forwards. Sophie watched, certain that he was going to die: but at the last minute he grasped the rope and swung, hand over hand, to the opposite rooftop. He pulled himself up, stuffed the pigeon down the front of his shirt (*So that explained the red patches*, Sophie thought) and swung back over the night sky. The whole there-and-back took less than two minutes.

He dumped the bird at her feet. 'That's how I catch them,' he said, and he wiped his bloody palms in his hair. 'I never said I was nice,' he said.

Sophie tried to look unconcerned, unimpressed. 'Can I help pluck it?' she said.

'*Non.*'

'Why not? Please?'

'You can't help. You can *do* it. This isn't a dinner party.'

Luckily, Sophie had read about plucking birds. You started at the neck and worked backwards. 'I've never had pigeon,' she said. She pulled out a handful of the feathers. The bird's skin was like an old man's, and she tried not to wince. 'What does it taste like?' She tried to pluck briskly.

'Like smoky chicken,' said Matteo. 'Like heaven. But we shouldn't be talking.'

'Oh! Sorry. Will somebody hear?'

'*Non*. Not this high. But aren't you supposed to be listening for music?'

While Matteo gutted and skewered the bird, Sophie listened. What he had said was true. By standing or squatting on different parts of the rooftop, she could hear snatches of conversation and snippets of music from half a mile away.

She circled the roof in a half-crouch, listening to the sounds that came on the wind. She heard an argument, full of what must have been French swearing, and some drunken singing, and a barking dog. Mostly, though, there was just night-silence, and nightingales.

It was a shock when Matteo called, 'Sophie!'

'Yes! What is it? Do you hear something?'

'*Non*. The food's ready.'

Matteo's table manners were not the kind that win prizes. He tore at the pigeon with his back teeth, showing lots of gum, and ate with his mouth open. She tried to follow suit, but the fat on the meat was ferociously hot. The skin on the roof her mouth was flaking off.

She looked around the rooftop, and at Matteo's small piles of possessions. 'Matteo, do you have a fork?'

'No. Why?'

'Don't you need one?'

'I've got fingers, haven't I? And teeth?'

'But don't you burn yourself?'

'Never.' He held out his hands to her. 'You see? Heatproof.' The palms and fingertips were thickly calloused. 'I don't burn.'

'I'd quite like a fork,' said Sophie. 'I'm sorry. It's just, my fingers are blistering.' She needed her fingers to play the cello. 'And do you have any water?'

'For drinking, or for your fingers?'

'For both.'

'Let me see them.' He took her hand in his. 'Your hands are too soft.' Then he spat on his fingers, and rubbed them over hers.

'Keep spitting on them,' he said, 'it helps. Here. This is just for drinking.' He handed her a tin can half filled with water. 'It's rainwater. I can't waste it on burns. And don't drink it all.'

Sophie sipped. It tasted of rust, but not bad at all.

'Right, he said. 'Stay there. I'll make you a fork.'

Matteo tore open the pigeon carcass and tugged out the wishbone and one long leg bone. 'Pass the kettle,' he said. Apparently untroubled by the boiling water, he dipped the bones in the kettle, added a tiny pinch of soot, and scrubbed.

'Soot acts as soap,' he said.

'Does it?' She looked at his face, which was black with dirt. 'Are you sure you're not thinking of . . . um, soap?'

'You'll see.' He kept scrubbing. 'I'm right.' And he *was* right. Soon the two bones shone white. Then he fished some string from his pocket.

'You see. String is the only thing that is never, never boring. String, and birds.'

He tied the wishbone to the top of the leg bone with a figure of eight. 'A fork!' he said. '*Voila.*'

19

Sophie slept most of the next day, and woke in her own bed to find it was raining. It rose to a storm in the night. Sophie counted the seconds between the lightning and thunder, 'One, two' – and then the boom. She did not dare go out on the rooftop. The next day was no better. Charles trudged out in an inadequate borrowed raincoat to look for lawyers.

'I'll keep lookout, if you'll let me use your window,' Sophie told him. 'Come back soon, all right? And don't get spotted.' She rubbed his sleeve, which was too short by an inch.

'I won't. And you, Sophie: make sure you don't leave this room,' said Charles. 'Unless you absolutely have to. If you need to pee, use the chamber pot. I don't want the other guests to see you.'

So all day Sophie sat by Charles's window with a

cup of cocoa in her lap, and kept lookout. She was watching for policemen, and for cello players. Almost nobody went by, and those who did were hidden by umbrellas. She strained her ears for cello music, until her head roared and she heard requiems behind every horse and cart. Every few minutes, she crossed and uncrossed her fingers.

The cup of cocoa grew a skin, and then grew cold. Sophie did not notice. The rain did not stop.

When Sophie went to bed, the rain was torrential. She woke again, though, to hear the clock striking two, and the downpour slowed to a drizzle. The clouds were blowing across the moon, and the moonlight flashed on and off inside her room, like Morse code.

Sophie shoved back her covers, and jumped up. She felt as awake as day. She pulled on her stockings, and over them her trousers, and two jerseys. Then she cut the tips off the stockings, and rolled them back to expose her toes. She clambered out of her window, leaving it open, dripping onto the bed.

Matteo was sitting cross-legged by his fire, leaning against the largest chimney stack. He had a knife in one hand, and something pinkish in the other. It looked suspiciously like a skinned rat. Sophie whistled, and he dropped whatever it was into the embers and ran to fetch her across the tightrope.

When they reached the fire, the animal was smoking. Matteo swore.

'*Ach*. Rat is never delicious; but burnt rat is disgusting.'

'What's rat like?'

Matteo sat, and pulled her down beside him. 'Sit. I didn't think you come, in the rain. It's like . . . hedgehog.'

'I've never had hedgehog, either.'

'Have you eaten rabbit?' He threw a sack over her knees, and pulled one over his shoulders.

'Yes, I've had rabbit.' The sack was wet, but Sophie did not say so. His sack, she could see, was wetter.

'Well, it's not like rabbit, but it's not *not* like rabbit. Here. You can try it.'

Sophie took it, sniffed it. It did not smell inspiring.

Matteo said, 'Leave some for me, though. More than half. I'm bigger.'

'Is this breakfast?' she asked him. 'Or . . . dinner?'

'This is lunch. I had breakfast when I woke up. Sort of.'

'When was that?' Sophie nibbled at the rat's thigh. The rat tasted of charcoal and horse-tails. She swallowed with an effort. 'It's . . . not bad,' she said. 'Here, though. It's yours.'

'I don't know. Sunset. So, about nine o'clock.' Matteo tore at the rat with his teeth. 'I have supper at five o'clock in the morning. If there is any supper.'

'Why wouldn't there be?'

He shrugged. 'It's been a bad week for food.' His face, up close, was tight-pulled and thin, and he said, 'I'm tired. Perhaps you'd better not stay long.'

'I'm so sorry!' Sophie cursed inwardly. 'I should have thought to bring food.' She had forgotten that he might be hungry. 'I didn't realise. But, Matteo, please let me stay. I need to be up here to listen.' Her skin was burning. It always did when she thought of her mother. 'Please.'

'Fine.' Matteo flopped onto his back, and stared up at the stars. 'I'm too hungry to talk, though.'

'Why is it worse than usual?'

'Why?' He half sat, and stared at her incredulously. 'The rain! The rain, obviously.'

Sophie lay down, a little way apart. In the moonlight Matteo's face was the colour of old snow. 'Does the rain make hunting harder?' she said.

'Yes. The birds go and shelter in the station. And rain makes people keep their windows shut at night. There's nothing you can pick up from window sills.'

'What've you had to eat?'

'Seagull, on Tuesday. It got blown in by the storm. It was almost dead anyway. A blue tit for breakfast. I was sorry about that. I quite like them – alive, I mean. I don't particularly like to eat them. And there's not enough meat on them to make it worth plucking them.'

Sophie couldn't help feeling awed. 'Was that all? In three days?'

'*Oui*. Or, *non* – I had a candy cane on Sunday. Anastasia and Safi left it for me in the oak tree by the Opera. I think it was meant for me. If not, it's not my problem.'

Sophie turned onto her stomach. 'Who're they? Anastasia and – what was the second name?'

His face flicked to blank. 'Nobody. Do you have any food in your pockets, maybe?'

'I don't think so.' Sophie fished in her trousers. 'No, wait – I have raisins. I was carrying them for the birds, actually, but you'd better have them.'

'Yes,' said Matteo, 'I had better. I'm hungry. Anyway, I'd just eat the birds once they'd eaten the raisins, so it's just skipping a step. What else?'

Sophie scrabbled deeper. Pockets, she thought, were why trousers were so superior to skirts.

'Yes!' She pulled out a sticky hand. 'Here – there's some chocolate. It might be quite old, though. And it melted and got mixed up with my trousers. But I think it should be all right?'

'Good. Give it to me.'

Matteo did not, as she'd expected, cram it all into his mouth. Instead he took a pan from the fire, and dropped the chocolate into it. He stirred with a whittled stick. 'Chocolate is best cooked. It makes you feel like there's more of it,' he said. He tipped the raisins into the chocolate. 'There. That smells good.'

The scent of melted chocolate was spreading over the rooftop. Matteo's body unwound a few inches. For the first time that evening, he smiled.

'See if you can bring more food, next time you come,' he said. 'It's easier, up here, when you're full.'

Charles had not had luck with the lawyers.

'It's not easy,' he said. 'None of them will take a

case against the commissioner of police. Most lawyers seem to have the decency and courage of lavatory paper. But we'll find someone, my love.' They were at breakfast. Charles spread half a jar's worth of jam on his croissant and dipped it into his coffee. 'Heaven!' he said. 'You're not eating?'

'I thought I might save it for later.' Sophie transferred the croissant to her lap, then to her pocket.

'You're not hungry?'

'No, thank you. I'm stuffed.'

Charles paused. 'Really?' His eyebrow hooked itself upwards. 'You've already hidden your bread roll in your pocket. And, if I'm not mistaken, there's an apple in your sock. What are you stuffed *with*?'

Inevitably, Sophie's thoughts collapsed in a heap. 'With biscuits,' she said.

'For breakfast? Unusual.'

'I thought I'd like to see what it was like, to have biscuits for breakfast.'

'And what was it like?'

'It was good. I had loads of them. I feel a bit sick, now, actually.' She half rose. 'May I go?'

'Not just yet. Sit down, Sophie. Tell me: what sort of biscuits did you have?'

'The chocolate fudge ones.'

'The ones with the soft middle?'

'Yes.'

He smiled. 'And you didn't save me any?'

'I'm sorry. They were too delicious.'

'They certainly sound delicious. And these delicious soft-fudge chocolate biscuits: they came from where?'

'From the baker, of course.' Sophie nodded out of the window, to the baker's bright orange awning. Too late, she saw it was rolled in, and the lights were out in the windows.

'How resourceful of you.' Charles's eyebrows were bristling with irony. 'The baker doesn't open on Sundays, Sophie.'

'I know that. I bought them yesterday.'

'Nor does it open on Saturday.'

Damn, thought Sophie. Her armpits were prickling, and her face was growing sweaty. She hated lying. She wasn't sure if she was good at it; she suspected she was not. 'Oh, yes! I know, I just forgot. I meant, Friday.'

'And you paid for them with . . . what? As far as I know, you have no French money.'

There was nothing to say, so Sophie said nothing.

'Is there something you'd like to tell me?'

Yes! thought Sophie. There were hundreds of things she wanted to tell him. But adults, she thought, were unpredictable, even the best ones. You never knew when they were going to stop you doing what you were doing. She tucked her fingers into her sash, and crossed them tightly.

'No,' she said. 'Nothing at all.' And then, after a pause, 'Can I go?'

'Of course.' Charles hitched his eyebrows into upside-down Vs. 'You're a very poor liar, Sophie. I do not recommend a career as an actress. But, as long as you aren't doing anything too extravagantly illegal, I am happy for you to have secrets.'

'It's nothing illegal.' Or, if it was, she thought, then it shouldn't be.

'Keep your secret, then, my darling. Everybody needs them. Secrets make you tough, and wily.' He waited another moment, but Sophie kept her gaze fixed on the rungs of his chair, and he waved her away. 'Off you go,' he said. 'Go and practise telling lies in front of a mirror.'

In a few minutes, though, he knocked on her door.

'The secret, Sophie,' he said. 'Is it a food-based secret?'

'Oh! Um, yes. Sort of.'

'Is it to do with your mother?'

'Yes. I think so.' *I hope so*, she thought. She crossed every finger and toe.

'Is another adult involved?'

'No,' said Sophie. 'No, not an adult.'

Charles seemed about to say something else. Then he shook his head. 'Good,' he said. 'Keep your secret.'

'Thank you,' said Sophie.

'But, Sophie?' Charles had turned, and she couldn't see his face.

'Yes?'

'Don't dare get hurt, or I'll skin you alive.'

That night, when Sophie went up to her room, her teeth brushed and a French dictionary under her arm, there was a pack on her bed.

The note pinned to it was in Charles's handwriting. It said, 'Everybody needs secrets. Only be sure they are good ones.' On the back there was a P.S. 'I have never in my life had enough sausages in one sitting.'

Sophie hefted the pack. It was heavy, and squelchy in places, and something at the bottom clinked. She went to open it, and then stopped. It would be better if she and Matteo opened it together. It took a great deal of willpower not to open it until she had reached the tightrope.

There was no moon, and Matteo sat with his legs dangling over the edge of the roof, whistling.

'Look what I've got!' he called. He ran across the tightrope, jumped onto the rooftop, and took her hand. 'Come and see! Tomatoes! I've never had so many.'

The pile of tomatoes reached almost to Sophie's knee. They glistened with the dew that had fallen at sunset. She said, 'They're wonderful.' She meant it: they were just ripe, and of the large flattish variety – the sort with a swinging kick to the taste. Sophie took one and sniffed it. 'Where did you get them?' she asked.

'I grew—'

'And don't say you grew them because I won't believe you. You need a greenhouse to grow this sort.'

'Fine.' Matteo sneered, a little defiant. 'I got them from a window sill. An apartment block in the eighth arrondissement. Fifth floor.'

'So you stole them?'

'*Non*. I *took* them.'

'What's the difference?'

'If something's in the open air, that's fair game. That's hunting.'

The thought of what Miss Eliot would say to that made Sophie snort, messily. She grinned. 'What are you going to do with a hundred tomatoes?' she said.

'There's thirty-four,' he said haughtily. 'I counted.' His attention shifted from the tomatoes. 'What's in the pack?'

'I don't know. I thought we should open it together.'

'Why?'

Now that he asked, Sophie found she couldn't explain. She felt herself turning pink, and swore inwardly. 'You know. Like Christmas.'

'I don't understand. What about Christmas?'

'You know, like when you unwrap presents together at Christmas.'

'I don't,' said Matteo. His face was on edge. Perhaps he suspected her of making fun of him. He said, 'I don't know what you're talking about.'

'I think it's food,' said Sophie. 'It's from Charles.'

Food has a power over bad temper that nothing else has. Matteo's mouth elongated into a smile; it reached his ears.

'What kind of food?' He took the pack and squashed it in his hands. 'Meat?' He held it high over her head. 'Maybe I'll keep it for myself.'

'Give that back!' There was no real point in grabbing for it, but she tried anyway. He was taller than her by a head.

'We'll open it together,' he said magnanimously. He jerked it away as she came nearer. 'I'll start.'

The pack was full of parcels wrapped in greaseproof paper. Matteo dipped his face in and sniffed, then lifted out the first parcel. It was bread rolls, four of them, soft in the middle and dusted with flour at the top. They were still warm from the oven, and they smelt of blue skies. The bread had been spread by someone with strong opinions about butter – it was as thick as the first joint of Sophie's thumb.

'I always used to think,' said Sophie, 'that if love had a smell, it would smell like hot bread.'

'What?' Matteo was eating already. 'What are you talking about?' A chunk of butter was hanging from his upper lip.

'Never mind,' said Sophie. Since Matteo looked busy, Sophie unpeeled the next package. It felt sticky in her hand.

'Meat!' said Matteo. He hadn't looked up from his two handfuls of bread roll, but he sounded gleefully certain.

'How do you know?'

'The smell.'

Matteo was right. The package unfolded away from a hunk of brown meat cut in thick slabs. It didn't look familiar. She held it out to him. 'What kind of meat is it? Can you tell?'

Matteo took the largest piece, and nibbled a corner. '*Non*. I've never had it. It's good, though. And it's not pigeon or rat, that I do know.'

Sophie tried some. It tasted of smoke and salt. It was wonderful, up here in the night air. 'It's . . . venison, I think? I've never had it, but this is how I imagine it.'

Matteo's head was inside the pack. His hand came out; his fingers were wrapped around two glass bottles. 'And these? What's in these?'

'Wine, maybe?' The bottles were chilled, and perspiring in the warm air. Sophie held one against her cheek. 'They look like wine, anyway. But Charles knows I don't like wine, except champagne with blackberries.'

Matteo shrugged. 'I've never had that.' He sniffed one. Bubbles flew up his nose and he sneezed, cat-like.

Sophie laughed. 'Lemonade, I think.'

At the bottom there was half a chocolate cake, still wet and sticky in the middle, and a jam jar filled with cream, and a fat parcel wrapped in greaseproof paper and newspaper.

'Sausages!' cried Matteo. They were thick as Sophie's wrist.

Sophie counted them. 'Twenty-two,' she said. 'Eleven each.'

'*Mon Dieu!*' said Matteo. He added something else in French. Sophie didn't know the word, but it sounded unrepeatable. 'Whoever your guardian is, I love him.'

'I know! I do too.' Sophie grinned into the fire. How many other people, she thought, will give you more sausages than you have fingers and toes? 'I think we should cook them all at once,' she said. 'I think he meant us to.'

'*Non,*' said Matteo. 'We should save some for later.'

'But you don't have any ice, do you? If you don't cook them they'll spoil. I'm starving. Go on, Matteo!' A suppressed smile was twitching Matteo's left cheek.

Sophie took that for a yes. 'And I could make tomato soup,' she said.

'Do you know *how* to make tomato soup?' said Matteo.

'Yes,' lied Sophie. 'At least, I'm sure I could work it out.' The sausages had no fat or gristle in them. Sophie prodded them. 'How do we cook them? Do you have a pan?'

'No,' said Matteo, 'but I collect weathervanes.'

Sophie wondered if his English had gone awry. 'You collect . . . weathervanes?'

'Yes. I've got almost a dozen.' Matteo reached into a sack behind him. He pulled out a handful of long metal spikes and dropped them at Sophie's feet. Most of them were fashioned to look like arrows. One, though, was the mast of a ship, and one a chicken. The weathervanes were polished and shone bronze and silver in the moonlight.

'Here.' Matteo took three sausages, and spiked them onto the longest of the arrows. 'You do some.'

'Where do you get them?' Sophie asked.

'From rooftops, of course.'

'Isn't that stealing?' She skewered four sausages on a silver arrow, and laid them on the fire.

'No it's not. They don't use them. They let them rust. *I* use them.'

'They do use them, though. They use them to . . .'

'To what?'

Sophie was stymied. 'Well, to tell which way the wind is blowing, surely?'

'If they are so stupid that they need a weathervane to tell them that, then they do not deserve weather-vanes.'

'But then, nobody would have weathervanes, and there'd be none for you to steal.'

'Find, not steal.' He spat on another metal spike and rubbed it on his shirt. 'Anyway, you want to know about the wind, watch the trees! Lick your finger and feel the wind. Pull out a hair and hold it over your head.'

The sausages were starting to ooze clear juice. Within minutes the smell was quite fantastic.

Sophie rinsed Matteo's largest pot with rainwater. The pot was shaped like a small cauldron, made of brass, and it made an excellent booming sound when she tapped it with the jam jar. 'Do you have something to peel them?' she asked.

'*Non*. But you don't peel tomatoes. You're thinking of oranges.'

'I think you do if it's soup,' she said doubtfully. 'Never mind. It should be all right, shouldn't it?' She tipped in all the tomatoes bar two. She tossed one to Matteo, and they ate them raw. 'I think we leave it to boil,' she said. As an afterthought, she tipped in half a cup of rainwater. Over the next half-hour, the tomatoes boiled down into a pulp. Their skins floated to the surface, and they fished them out – Sophie with a twig, Matteo with his fingers – and shared them with the dozen pigeons that had gathered round at the sight of crumbs.

'Can you pass the cream?' said Sophie.

'Don't use it all!' Matteo took a quick sip from the jar before he handed it to her.

'I won't.' She tipped in most of the jar, but left enough to drink with the chocolate cake. What else would you put in soup? she thought. She said, 'Do you have salt?'

'Of course I have salt! I'm a rooftopper, Sophie, not a savage.' Matteo kept his salt in a scrubbed-out flowerpot, twisted up in a blue square of cloth. There was pepper, too, in a red square. Sophie recognised the cloth of his shorts from the first time they met.

'I don't much like pepper,' said Sophie. 'I'll just put

in the salt, if that's all right. You can put pepper in yours.'

'Yes, you do like pepper. You just eat bad pepper in England,' said Matteo. 'I know. I've had some of the food the English leave behind. Add just a little.' He took the pepper from her, and cracked it between two scraps of slate, and tipped it in. 'Trust me.'

Sophie added the salt to the soup. The smell was so rich it made her nose shiver.

'It's ready, I think,' she said.

They sat side by side, with their backs to the wind, and drank the soup out of tin cans. The taste made her giddy. It made her want to laugh. Matteo ate whole sausages in a single mouthful. Sophie took four and made them into sandwiches with the venison. She added a slop of soup as a relish, and they ate them with both hands. Sophie's hair blew in her mouth, and she tied it back with one of Matteo's bow-strings. She couldn't remember having been so happy before.

They had made their way through fourteen of the sausages and even Matteo was slowing, when Sophie froze.

'Can you hear that?'

''ear wha'?' Matteo spoke with his mouth full. 'It's jusht the wind.'

'That's not the wind.' It was too sharp and too sweet to be the wind. 'It's music. It's a cello. Hear the low notes?' Sophie dropped her food on the slate. She strained her ears. A tune came to her over the rooftops.

She said, 'It's Fauré's *Requiem* played double-time.'

Sophie leapt up, spilling sausages into the fire. 'It's coming from over there!' She tore to the far edge of the rooftop and stood on the tips of her toes on the very edge of the roof, straining to hear. *My mother*, she thought. *I am hearing my mother.* The thought shook her to her bones.

'Can you hear it?' She held her breath to listen. The music had stopped. 'God, Matteo, please! Say you heard it!'

Matteo stood and wiped his mouth. 'I heard it.'

'How far away do you think it was? Can we go now? Come on! We'll go right now! Which way's fastest?'

'I don't know.'

'What? Yes you do! You said you knew the whole of Paris! We need to go, now!'

'No.'

'What are you . . . look, quick, come on! Come *on*!'

'We can't just run.'

'Yes, we *can*!'

'Stop, Sophie! Listen – it's stopped, anyway.' He was white. 'It could be miles away. You can't be sure where it came from. Didn't you know? Sound twists on rooftops. It echoes. It bluffs.'

'But I could tell! It was coming from there!' Sophie pointed across the city. 'There! The Gare du Nord! The train station!'

Matteo didn't look at her. 'I know,' he said.

'Then why did you just say you didn't? Let's *go*.'

'I don't go to the station. You can go, if you like. I can't.'

'Yes, you can! I need you! You have to!'

'I can't. The rooftops there belong to someone else.'

'To who?'

He shook his head. 'I can't explain.'

'Well, in that case can we *go*?' Her heart was booming in her ears. She had heard her mother play.

'We can go. But not tonight. If you want to go to the station, we'll need the others.'

'The others?' This was annoyingly cryptic. Sophie said, 'Who? The other who?'

Matteo sighed. 'The other rooftoppers.'

'But you said there weren't any others.'

'I know. I lied.' Then he turned to her. His gaze was the sort that sees your soul, and makes you wonder where to put your hands. 'You said you could swim, didn't you?' he said.

20

Two days later Sophie sat on a bench in the Tuileries Garden, fidgeting with her clothes. Her heart was hummingbirding. Matteo had sent her to sit there, in the dusk, and wait.

'I sent word,' he had said. 'I signalled. They might come. They might not.'

'Who is "they"?' Sophie had watched him scrubbing the mud off snails in a pan of water. He didn't look up at her as he spoke. She had felt herself growing increasingly tight around the chest. 'And how long do I wait?'

'Maybe four hours, starting at dusk.'

'Four *hours*?'

'Or, five, to make sure.'

'Five!'

'Waiting is a talent. You have to learn it.' Matteo

laid each snail he cleaned upside down in front of the fire. He had a row of them; Sophie counted eleven. Their shells were mottled, and more beautiful than she had realised. Matteo said, 'It's like playing the cello.'

'No, it's not.'

'It will be good for you.'

'What do I tell Charles? I'm not allowed on the streets. I'll get caught.' Just the word, caught, made Sophie turn cold.

'Anything. Nothing. Whatever you want. Lie to him. It doesn't matter. It will be dark.' It did matter, Sophie thought, hugely. But Matteo was a rooftopper, and he had never known what it is like to have to lie to the person who loves you most.

Sophie resolved to say nothing to Charles; it would be better, at any rate, than lying. And she could wear a scarf round her hair. She thought, *It's my hair that they're looking out for*. And she could perhaps pad out her clothes to make herself look fatter; or slouch, to make herself look short. All the same, the thought made her ache with fear.

She said, 'Couldn't you come and keep me company?' From the look Matteo gave her, she might have asked him to eat an unplucked pigeon. 'I don't go on the streets. Ever.'

'Then, couldn't we meet on my rooftop? Or yours? Otherwise I might get lost,' she said. 'Or caught. Please, Matteo. The police here look cruel.'

'*Non*. They don't like roofs much. They like open spaces.'

'What do you mean? You said they were rooftop-pers.'

'They are, sort of.'

'Why won't you just *explain*?'

Matteo shrugged, and threw the snails into a pot of boiling broth. 'You can never know who will tell. Often the ones who look safest are worst.'

'You think I'm going to tell?'

Matteo made a face. 'It will be fine. You'll see.'

She had been sitting there for an hour. It hadn't been easy to get out. She had waited in her room for dusk, climbed out onto the rooftop and shinned down the drainpipe.

She had left a note under Charles's door:

Gone to bed early. Don't wake me. Love, S.

The thought of him finding her gone was gnawing at her insides. And every time a man in uniform passed, she jumped, and bit slithers off the inside of her mouth.

Sophie looked about for something to keep her mind off policemen. The park was emptying as it grew dark, and there wasn't much to see; only flowerbeds, which are boring unless you are allowed to pick the flowers, and sparrows, and beside her on the bench a cheese roll for her dinner. She broke off a corner, and tossed it at the sparrows. Behind her, a voice spoke.

'That won't work. Those sparrows only eat croissant.'

Sophie whipped round.

A girl was sitting on the back of the bench with her feet on the seat. Her blonde hair was inches from Sophie's face, but Sophie hadn't heard a rustle; not a click, not a pigeon's whisper.

'You – how did you do that? That's incredible.'

The girl grinned. 'Good evening to you too. You must be Sophie.' She slid down to sit next to Sophie. 'The birds are very spoilt around here. There's a dove that only eats pain au chocolat.' She took the bread from Sophie, and, instead of throwing it to the pigeons, she bit into it. 'Oh, yum. Oh heaven. I haven't had bread for weeks.'

'It's stale.' Sophie couldn't think of anything better to say.

The girl shrugged. She licked the bread to moisten it. 'Stale means old, doesn't it? Old is wise. Wise bread. This is Safi, my sister. Say *bonsoir*, Safi.'

Sophie jumped half an inch. A dark-haired girl was lolling against the bench. The girl said nothing.

Sophie said, 'But I didn't hear you! How did you do that?'

The first girl shrugged. 'Practise.'

The dark girl came and sat on the bench, tight-rolled, almost in her sister's lap. A clock chimed, and a man began to light the street lamps. For the first time, Sophie could see them clearly.

Both were small, and filthy. The blonde wore a cotton dress; it was greenish-brown but, judging by the stitching, Sophie guessed it had once been white. It looked as if someone had deliberately smeared it with grass stains. A beetle was clinging to the hem. Somehow, the girl made it look like the richest Chinese silk.

'I'm Anastasia,' she said. Her accent was odd, Sophie thought; it was French, but there was an odd twang to the vowels. The girl spread out her arms, as though she owned the place. 'Welcome to Paris.'

'Thank you. I'm Sophie.'

'Yes. We established that,' said Anastasia. She laid her hand on the arm of her sister. 'Safi says welcome, also.' The dark-haired girl had the face of someone who had seen a lot, and wouldn't mind punching most of it. She wore a boy's shirt and a man's pair of trousers, held up at the waist with measuring tape tied in a knot. She had something sticky smeared up one cheek, which might or might not have been blood; but beneath it, she was as beautiful as the blonde. Sophie winced with jealousy.

The blonde girl smiled. 'Matteo said you would be easy to spot. Look out for eyes the colour of candle-light, he said.'

'Matteo told you?'

'Of course. Who else?'

Sophie narrowed her eyes. '*How* did he tell you?'

'We signal. With candles. You know. Morse code, you call it? Shush, just for a second.' She looked Sophie up and down, and then jumped up and circled her to view her from the back, all without any apparent worry of being rude. Sophie tried to keep her face blank.

The girl said, 'You're very like he said. He talked about you quite a lot.'

The other girl raised her eyebrows, and said more nothing.

Unaccountably, Sophie blushed. 'What did he say about me?'

The girl shook her head. 'That's a secret.'

Sophie scowled. She felt stupid, and she looked angrily at the floor.

Anastasia said, 'It was all interesting, and mostly good.' The other girl nodded, and became more emphatically silent. Sophie tried to smile.

Anastasia said, 'Safi wanted you to know that she's very excited about meeting you.'

Safi was hiding it well, Sophie thought. But she only said, 'Why?'

'Matteo doesn't usually like people. So when he does, it matters.'

Sophie burned. She ducked behind her hair, and tried to think of something to say. 'Can I ask you something? You're French, aren't you?'

'Of course,' said Anastasia, and Safi thumped her chest. Anastasia said, '*Vive la France!*'

'Then, who taught you to speak English?'

'The American tourists.'

'Really?' Sophie hadn't expected that. 'Oh. That was nice of them.'

'They don't know they're doing it, but they eat in the cafés in the park and sit on the benches and chat chat chat.'

'And you sit on benches near them?'

'*Non!* Of course not! The park rangers would start to recognise us. We sit in the trees. They never see us. Americans are not good at seeing things.'

'Aren't they?' Sophie had never met an American.

'The adults aren't, anyway. The children are quick-eyed. You've got to be careful of the children. We speak Russian, too, and either Italian or Spanish. We're not sure which it is, but we speak it. Matteo speaks German, but not as well as he pretends he can.'

'And you're sisters?'

'Yes. Safi is younger, I think,' said Anastasia. 'At least, I think I can remember her not being around, but she can't remember the world without me. So.'

This seemed extraordinary to Sophie. She said, 'You *think* Safi is younger? Don't you know how old you are?'

Anastasia shrugged. '*Non*. We don't remember

having a mother. Neither does Matteo. He keeps saying he is fourteen, but he forgets it has to go up every year.' Anastasia looked Sophie up and down again. There was a straightforwardness in her look Sophie had never seen in the girls at home. She seemed fearless. 'How old are you? We're about the same height, aren't we?'

Sophie shook her head. 'You can't tell that way. I'm tall for my age. You look about thirteen, to me.'

'Good. I will be thirteen. Safi can be . . . what do you think?'

'Eleven? Ten, maybe?'

'Let's say ten,' said Anastasia. 'I like to be older.' She smoothed down her dress, like a princess at a birthday party, rather than someone with algae caked in her nails. 'Please excuse my dress. It was white brocade, once. It was so good, I found it in a dustbin. People throw away so much in Paris. But, you can't wear white, if you want to stay safe. So we stain everything, with . . . *ach*, what's the word?'

'With paint? With grass?'

'There's a green dust you get coating the trees. Like tree powder, you know?'

'Yes! I know what you mean! You can find it in

white, too, actually, on willow trees. Charles – my guardian – calls it wild paint. I don't know what it's really called.' Sophie looked down at her own, cream-coloured jersey. 'Will this be all right?'

'The trousers, yes. The top . . .' The girl shrugged. 'No, not really. White, and yellow – those are the most visible colours at night. And cream, and pink. They are like wearing a sign, "look at me". They're for people who want to be at the centre of attention.'

Sophie did not agree. Her cream jersey was very plain, and she had knitted it herself, in thick and uneven stitches. It had never occurred to her that it might be attention-seeking. She crossed her arms defensively across her chest.

Anastasia laughed. 'It's a very good jumper. You mustn't be offended. But if you don't want to be caught, you can't ever allow people to look too much at you – you see?' Her English seemed to be faltering. 'In exchange, we have the sky. *Tu comprends, oui?* You understand?'

Sophie nodded doubtfully. 'Yes. Or, sort of.' Anastasia watched her with steady eyes. 'Not really.' Sophie grinned. 'I don't see how you can *have* the sky.'

'More than anyone else, the sky belongs to us.' It was what Matteo had said about the rooftops.

Sophie said, 'How? In what way?'

Safi tapped Sophie on the elbow. She rubbed her arms, and pointed at the clouds.

Anastasia smiled. 'She says, because we live nearer the sky than anyone else. She says, look up.'

Sophie's eyes followed the girl's pointing finger. Amongst the uppermost leaves of the tallest tree in the park, which towered above all surrounding buildings, there were strung two hammocks. They were greyish-brown, and – Sophie shaded her eyes against the setting sun – it looked as though they might be made out of sacking. She would never have spotted them, if she hadn't been shown where to look.

'They are made from the sails of a ship which washed up down the river,' said Anastasia. 'Before that we used curtains from a theatre that burnt down, but the sails are better. The canvas is very strong, especially if you sew it double-thick. We dyed them with squid ink.' Anastasia's face was lit with pride. She might have been showing Sophie a country estate. 'We use sacks for blankets. You only need six or seven to keep properly warm. In the summer, we don't use them, and we hide them on the rooftop of the opera house so they don't get stolen.'

'Who would steal a sack?'

Anastasia looked shocked. 'Hundreds of people. I would. Sacks are valuable.'

The hammocks rocked very slightly in the breeze. They looked wonderfully comfortable. Sophie's heart screwed tight with envy.

Anastasia said, 'You see, Matteo, he is a rooftop boy. But, we are better with trees than buildings. We're called *arbroisiers* – tree-dwellers. And there are some boys who live in railway-station roofs: railway is *gare* in French, so we say, *gariers*.' She screwed up her face. 'The *gariers* are . . . *pas bien*, you know? Bad. They steal, they cheat, they cut.'

'Cut what?'

'People. Each other, sometimes. Matteo, once. But they are still sky-treaders.'

'Still what?'

'Is that not English? Um . . . *danseurs du ciel*. Sky-steppers. It's what we call the children who live outside, but not homeless. Not on the streets; those are just street children. They're no good. Streets can never be a home, because other people use them, all the time, and your home must be private. The trees are our home, Safi and me. Sky-treaders, you see?'

'Why do you do it, though? I mean, your hammocks look lovely – but don't you get wet? And hungry? And how do you wash? And . . . the toilet? It must be difficult.'

Anastasia's gaze shifted from Sophie's eyes to the space above her head. The shutters of her face came down. 'We prefer it. Nobody can lock you in a tree.'

Sophie was not stupid. She changed the subject. 'So – should I stain my jersey, before we go?'

Safi glanced up at the sun, and then shook her head. She motioned to her chest, and Anastasia nodded.

'Safi says no. She says, there isn't really time. If you want to come with us, you can wear her spare jumper. She stores it in the oak next to the statue of Napoleon.'

'That oak?' It was a great pillar of a tree, the first six feet wide as a giant. 'She can climb that one?'

'Yes. We both can. I have a scarf and gloves in a hole in the cedar tree. We spread our things out; all the sky-steppers do. That way, if one thing gets taken, you've got more.' She looked again at Sophie's jersey. 'Safi's jumper is grey. Grey will be better. Where we're going is very grey.'

'Thank you,' said Sophie. She looked doubtfully at the smear on Safi's cheek. 'Are you sure? I mean – it's very kind of you.'

'Safi will go and get it now.' The girls seemed to be waiting. Anastasia said, 'You have to give her your jersey, in exchange.'

'Oh!' Sophie flushed, deeply, and began to pull it off. 'Of course, yes,' she said, her voice muffled by the wool. 'Sorry.'

As Safi ran off with the jumper bundled in her arms, Sophie gathered the courage to ask a question. 'Doesn't she talk?'

'Of course, sometimes. But not when other people are around.'

Sophie tried to look like she understood. 'Was she always like that?'

Anastasia looked as though she were deciding whether or not to be insulted. Then she said, 'We – sky-treaders – we're different. I guess you become strange, even if you didn't start out strange.'

That made sense to Sophie. It was something she'd thought about before. 'I think, actually, everyone starts out with some strange in them. It's just, whether or not you decide to keep it.'

'Maybe. Yes. I could believe that.'

They watched Safi glance around, then launch herself at the oak. There were no low branches, but she gripped with her knees and dug with her nails. In ten seconds she had disappeared amongst the foliage.

Sophie's head was swirling with these new revelations. 'How did she do that?'

'Practise,' said Anastasia.

The sun had almost set. Sophie wrapped her arms around her knees and shivered. Sunset seemed a good moment to ask questions. Sophie said, 'Anastasia? Why do I need a grey jersey? Where are we going?'

'Matteo didn't tell you?'

'No. He doesn't tell me much. And he's hard to guess.'

'Ah, I know! Safi is too. Likes cats, *non*? We're going to visit someone. A fighter. To go to the station, we need numbers, you see?'

'And do they . . . does this person live in the river?'

'Why?'

'Matteo asked if I could swim.'

'Ah! The person we're going to see can't swim, and he always wants money.'

'Where will we get the money? Why does it matter he can't swim?'

'You'll see. I think Matteo didn't want me to tell.'

'Doesn't he beg, this person who wants money? I've seen street children doing it.'

'Of course not!' Anastasia glared and moved a few inches down the bench. 'I told you, we're not street children. Begging would be boring and stupid and dangerous. We buy food, like normal people. Only, mostly from stalls, at night, because—' She held up her hands. They were layered thick with calluses. 'My hands make me memorable, you see? It's dangerous to be memorable. But I need them like that for climbing; it's like having gloves. And Safi won't go near stall owners.'

'Why not? What's wrong with stall owners?'

'*Rien*. I mean, nothing.' Anastasia shrugged. 'Safi's like Matteo. She does not want too much human in her life. She'd like it better if it was just her and me.'

Sophie knew that feeling. But before she had time to reply, someone tapped her on the shoulder. Safi stood behind her, clasping a grey rag to her chest.

'Don't *do* that!' cried Sophie. 'I swallowed my tongue.'

Anastasia laughed. Even Safi twitched around the lips.

'Let's go,' said Anastasia. 'Matteo will meet us there, half an hour after dark. It should be dark by the time we get there.'

'Where are we going?'

'It's not far. The Pont de Sainte Barbara. It's a bridge.' She took Sophie's hand. 'You'll like it. It's beautiful; it's like you, actually.'

21

The bridge was indeed beautiful, though it wasn't much like Sophie; at least, Sophie couldn't see it. It was fine wrought, with gold-painted railings and pigeons roosting on each end.

They ran, the three of them, down stone steps and came to rest under the bridge. Matteo wasn't anywhere.

'Did he say he'd be waiting?' said Sophie. 'Can you see him?'

'He'll be here somewhere,' said Anastasia. She whistled, not very well, the same whistle Matteo had used on the tightrope. They waited. Matteo was still nowhere.

'You try,' said Anastasia. 'He said you had a good whistle.'

Sophie tried to remember the shape her lips had

made. She whistled; and then again, louder, and sharper.

'Again,' said Anastasia.

Sophie whistled until her lips buzzed and her ears hurt. She was just about to give up when there was a thump, and Matteo appeared, walking swiftly along the railing of the bridge.

'*Bonsoir!*' He sat on the rail, and called down to them. 'Are you ready?'

'Ready for what? Why won't you tell me?' Sophie hissed. 'And keep your voice down. I can't be seen.'

'I thought you might not come if I told you. Take off your shoes.'

'Why wouldn't I come?' Sophie bent to untie her laces.

'Because the water's so cold,' he said, matter-of-factly. 'It's like swimming in frostbite. We're going river-sieving.'

'River-sieving?' Sophie halted, one shoe in her hand.

'Diving for coins. If I really need money, I collect coins, from under the bridges. And sometimes there's wedding rings. People throw them in. I don't know why—' He shrugged. 'But you can sell them, sometimes.'

'But those coins are wishes! You're stealing other people's wishes!'

The look Matteo gave her was so flinty she could have chipped a tooth on it. 'If you have money to waste on wishes, you don't need the wishes as badly as I need the money.' He stood on the rail, rose onto his toes, and disappeared in a flawless dive.

Sophie stood at the edge, waiting. It was almost two minutes before his head came up. He swam to the edge and dropped a handful of coppers at her feet.

'You said you could swim?' he said. 'Safi and Stasia can't, much.'

'I can, yes. I might not have told you if I'd known why you were asking.' Sophie crouched at the water's edge. It was midnight blue, and the stars shone on its surface. It looked secretive. Sophie bent until she could see her reflection. She looked secretive, too, and more beautiful than she had expected. She dipped a finger in the water. 'My God, Matteo!' It was icy. Her toes contracted in protest.

'Then come on,' said Matteo. 'There's a lot. If we leave it there, the *gariers* will take it.' And, as Sophie ran to the edge, he hissed, 'Take your other shoe off, first! And quietly.'

'I was going to!' She pulled off her shoe and trousers and jersey and bundled them into a corner under the bridge, but left her pants and vest. She glared at him, and dived – with some splash, but still quite well, she thought – into the water.

'Ugh. It's freezing!' Sophie gasped and retched as the water clutched at her. She spat out a mouthful.

'You sound like a water buffalo,' said Matteo, treading water. 'Come this way. The tides shift most of the coins to the left – over here. Keep moving, or your heart stops.'

He dived under and she waited, kicking her frozen feet, until he came up.

'Matteo!' she said. 'Listen to me. I won't help until you tell me something.'

'What? I'm icing over inside, Sophie. This isn't a good moment.'

'Those boys who live on the station. What's wrong with them?'

Matteo shrugged, which is not easy to do whilst treading water. He said, 'They're dirty.'

Sophie said nothing. She tried not to let her gaze flick to the girls standing on the bank, dressed in mud and rags.

Matteo saw. Matteo, Sophie thought, saw everything. It was very annoying. 'There's good dirt and bad dirt,' he said to her. 'The *gariers* are bad dirt.'

'Which is which, though?' said Sophie. 'What counts as good dirt?'

'*Je ne sais pas.*' Matteo scowled at her, as he always did when she asked questions. 'I don't know. *Ach, je m'en fous.*'

'He says, he doesn't know, he doesn't care,' called Anastasia. She must have been listening from the bank of the river. 'I suppose, good dirt is soil. And roofdust.' Safi made a sign. Anastasia added, 'And treedust, also.'

Matteo said, 'And the grit you get if you run your hand along the top of a stone bridge. Bad dirt is dried blood.'

'And sewerage. And the chimneydust on bad days.'

Sophie knew that by now. The chimney smoke could be corrosive in the nostrils.

'Usually it's not too bad,' said Anastasia, 'but when there's no wind and the air is damp, it sucks up the smoke and wipes it over your face.' Sophie had noticed. She had also noticed that Matteo picked his nose a lot more than most people; and that on smoggy days the snot was black.

'And pigeon fat,' said Anastasia. 'Pigeon fat's bad dirt.'

'*Non!*' said Matteo. He turned and swam away from them. 'No, pigeon fat's good dirt.'

Anastasia exchanged a meaningful look with Sophie. 'A tiny bit is OK, maybe. More than a tiny bit and you start smelling like an open wound. Anyway, it's not just dirt. They're vicious, the *gariers*. They're like animals.'

Sophie thought about that. Matteo had always struck her as being like an animal: a cat, or a fox. Anastasia and Safi moved with the same shifts and swing as monkeys. 'Is that bad? To be like animals?'

Anastasia said, 'They're like dogs. Have you ever seen a mad dog? They're cruel in the eyes.'

'Do they . . . bite?' She had expected the two girls to laugh, but they just stared back at her. Nobody moved, or smiled.

At last, Safi nodded. Matteo popped up next to her, panting. He said, 'Yes. They bite. Come on. Before my teeth freeze together.'

There was very little current, so the swimming was easy, but the water was murky and in the dark it was almost impossible to see the glint of copper. Sophie found what she could by groping about the riverbed. She and Matteo dived six, then seven times, swimming to the side whenever they had a handful. She was gratified to find that her pile on the bank was double the size of his.

'*Ach!* It's my fingers,' he said. Sophie and Anastasia exchanged another glance. 'I can't feel what's a coin and what's a stone.'

'Of course,' said Sophie. 'Of course it is.'

When Anastasia called out that they had more than three francs, Matteo said that was enough. They swam, half racing, to the bank. Sophie was faster, but Matteo reached out and ducked her under just as she was reaching out for the edge.

'Cheat!' She came up spitting. 'You're a filthy cheater.'

'Cheating doesn't exist for rooftoppers,' said Matteo. 'There's just alive, or dead.'

'Anyway, that's not cheating,' said Anastasia. 'That's fighting. Fighting's better than cheating.' She hauled Sophie out of the water, and handed her a square of chocolate.

Matteo stayed in the water. Anastasia passed him

another square, and he ate it treading water.

'Thank you,' said Sophie. Her voice came out in a croak. 'Swimming always makes me thirsty. Can I drink the river water?'

'No! Sorry. Rat disease. Even Matteo doesn't, and he's immune to most things. There'll be water when we get to the cathedral, though,' said Anastasia.

'The cathedral?' Sophie pulled on her borrowed jersey, and stuffed wet feet into her shoes. 'What cathedral?'

'*The* cathedral, of course. Matteo'll meet us there.'

'Meet us there? But he's here—' Sophie's head whipped round. Matteo had gone.

'He's like that,' said Anastasia. 'He'll be going by the river, and then the trees.'

Safi approached her silently, and stroked down the parts of Sophie's hair that were scarecrowing, and picked out the pondweed. She took Sophie's scarf from the ground, and wound it round Sophie's head.

'Oh!' said Sophie. 'I almost forgot about my hair!' Her whole body swept with terror, and she tugged at the cloth, far down over her ears. 'That was so stupid of me. Thank you.' Safi smiled; and then she suddenly blushed purple. She darted up the stairs and into the leaves of one of the trees lining the pavement.

'Will she be all right?' said Sophie.

Anastasia gathered up the coins and stowed them in her pockets. 'Of course. She'll go by treetop too,' she said. '*Allez*. If we walk quickly you'll be dry by the time we reach Notre Dame. Race you up the stairs.'

22

Dark pavements are one of the best places in the world to talk. They walked quickly, so Sophie wouldn't get cold. Anastasia hummed under her breath. Sophie waited until she was sure Matteo was nowhere close before she spoke.

'Anastasia? If I ask you something, could you not tell Matteo I asked?'

'Maybe. Probably. I'll try, anyway. What is it?'

'It's the . . . is it, *gariers*? The train station boys. Why does Matteo hate them? He goes blank when he talks about them.'

'Oh. If you don't know, I don't know if I should tell you.'

'Please. It frightens me. His face goes dark.'

Anastasia ran her nails over iron railings as they passed. Under her touch, they played music. 'There was a fight. A few years ago. The *gariers*, they didn't want anyone else on the rooftops. Safi and I, we didn't care much. We moved to the trees. Trees are better. But Matteo, he loves being a rooftopper. Rooftops are . . .' She stopped, and made a face. '*Ach*, this will sound too poetic.'

'Say it anyway.'

'They are all he has,' said Anastasia. She flushed. 'Sorry. *Alors*, he couldn't give them up.'

'What happened?'

'Nobody won. They bit . . .'

'Bit what?' Sophie stared at the girl, who looked away. 'Bit *what*?'

'Nothing. Matteo lost the tip of his finger. A *garier* lost his hand. And, have you seen Matteo's stomach? The scar?'

'He said he fell on a weathervane!'

'Did he? Well, he lied. He almost died. He had to go to an orphanage for medicine. You know about that, *oui*? And now he never goes near the station, and never goes on the ground.' Anastasia halted, and grasped Sophie's arm.

'Stop. We're nearly there. Matteo will be some-where around.' Her face was restless in the starlight.

She bit her lip. 'Promise you won't tell him I told you?'

'Of course,' said Sophie, but the buildings around them were distracting. They stood at the foot of a great white building. It rose up into the night sky, majestic as a god. 'What is this? Where are we?'

'Notre Dame, of course! And Matteo's in that tree, you see? By the door.' Sophie couldn't see; but Safi was standing underneath it, looking up at the leaves. The courtyard was empty. Anastasia said, 'Let's go.'

Notre Dame was as painful to climb as it was beautiful to look at. The scramble to the top took twice as long as Sophie had expected.

Matteo went first, followed by Safi. They seemed to know it as well as Sophie knew her home in London; their hands found grips and holds in the stone without a second's hesitation. Sophie followed more slowly. Anastasia came last, giving advice on handholds and guiding Sophie's feet when she got stuck.

Balancing came more easily to Sophie now. Her feet were still tender against the stone, and her toes bled a little, but she was determined not to wince in front of the rooftoppers. They were not, she thought, the wincing sort. She rubbed her foot with spit, bit the inside of her cheek. By the time she was halfway up it was pulpy with chewing. Twice she lost her footing, but she did not think anyone noticed.

To most things in life, there is no trick; but to balance, Sophie thought, there was a trick of sorts. The trick was knowing where to find your centre; balance lay somewhere between her stomach and her kidneys. It felt like a lump of gold in amongst brown organs. It was difficult to find, but once found, it was like a place marked in a book; easy to recover. Balance is also to do with thinking. Sophie tried to think of mothers, and music; and not of dropping backwards onto the pavement below.

Paris lay still below them. From where Sophie stood, with both her hands wrapped round the neck of a carved saint, it was a mass of silver, except where the river shone a rusty-gold colour in the lamplight. 'It's beautiful,' Sophie said. 'I didn't realise the river was so beautiful!'

'Yes.' Anastasia looked taken aback. 'It's . . . brown, mostly.'

When they reached the base of the tower, Matteo and Safi were perched close together, scratching noughts and crosses into the slate with a nail. From their faces, they might have just sauntered up a flight of stairs.

'A tie,' said Matteo. He scratched out the game. 'Sophie, can you whistle? We need to call Gérard.'

'Yes, of course.' The three waited. She felt suddenly self-conscious. 'Um. The tune you use on the birds?'

'Yes. Make it loud; as loud as you can. He might be asleep.'

Sophie whistled the three notes she had heard on the tightrope. There was a pause; then the three notes came back, deeper and richer than she'd sent them.

'Was that an echo?'

'*Non.*' Matteo cupped his hands, and gave two owl hoots. 'That was Gérard.'

Up above them, from the bell tower, there was a small avalanche of dust, and a boy appeared. He swung down hand over hand, finding footholds on the open jaws of the gargoyles. He somersaulted down the last four feet, and landed facing Sophie.

'*Bonsoir,*' he said.

His face was younger than Matteo's, but his legs were so long that he towered above them both. He was so thin that Sophie could have snapped him, she thought, with one hand. He did not look like a fighter.

'*Salut*, Gérard,' said Matteo. 'We want to borrow you.'

The boy grinned. '*Bon*. I know. Anastasia signalled.' He wore a musty, weevil-eaten jacket, which looked as though he had made it himself from a selection of doormats. Sophie coveted it immediately.

'Hello,' she said. 'I'm Sophie.'

'*Oui,*' he said. 'I know.' His English was a little halting, but he had a good face. His eyebrows were thick enough to shine shoes with, and his eyes were gentle. 'You need to go to the station, yes?' He hesitated. He was obviously too polite, Sophie thought, to be good at life. He said, 'Did you . . . bring me anything?'

'Yes,' said Anastasia. 'Of course.' She tipped the still-wet coins into his cupped hands.

'*Merci!* Did you know, the candles in the cathedral, they have gone up to twenty centimes? *C'est fou!*'

Sophie said, 'Couldn't you just . . . take some? If you needed them? I'm sure they wouldn't mind.'

'*Non!* You can't steal from the church! That's a sin.'

'What do you do for light, then? When you can't get candles?'

'Mostly, nothing. Your eyes get better at dark. Dark is a talent. Or, you can put oil-soaked cloths in tin cans and light them.'

'If you have cloths,' said Anastasia.

'If you have oil,' said Matteo.

Gérard laughed, an inward, guilty laugh. 'So. We go to the station, yes? To fight, *oui*?'

'Perhaps to fight,' said Anastasia. 'Hopefully just to listen.' She turned to Sophie. 'Gérard is good at listening.'

Matteo did not seem jealous. He nodded. 'It's true. Listening is unusual. Animals have it. Most people only think they do.'

Gérard said, 'I can hear a harmonica played in a classroom halfway down the river.'

'That's impossible!' said Sophie. 'Isn't it?'

'Not impossible,' said Gérard. 'Just unusual.'

It wasn't polite to whisper, but she had to. She pulled Anastasia to one side, and cupped her hands round the girl's ear. 'Is he telling the truth?' she breathed. 'Is he just boasting? It's *so* important. Does he realise how important it is?'

Gérard laughed. It was hard to tell in the dark, but he seemed to be blushing. 'Yes, he is,' he said, 'and yes, he does. Whispering doesn't work around me. I didn't ask to be born like this – it makes sleeping difficult. I have to wear acorns in my ears. But it is true. I think it comes from living on a church.'

Anastasia said, 'He sings, too. He practises the choir's songs every night, when they've left.'

Matteo scowled. 'I *said* he sings. Didn't I, Sophie?'

Anastasia rolled her eyes. '*Boys.* He doesn't just sing. With him, it's like the first snow. Sing something, Gérard.'

Gérard wrinkled his nose. '*Non.*'

Safi tapped her chest, and held out her hand towards him. She tilted her head.

'Please, Gérard?' said Sophie. 'One song. For luck.'

'*Ach, d'accord,*' said Gérard. 'Fine. *Half* a song.' He glanced around, and licked a finger to check which way the wind was blowing. He cleared his throat.

The first notes from Gérard's mouth were so clear and sweet that they sent tingles from Sophie's scalp all the way down to her toes. The words were in French, but it certainly wasn't a hymn. It made you want to bunch up your skirts and dance with the people you love. It made Sophie want to twirl. It made her want her mother so much it hurt.

There was silence when Gérard stopped. Even the river was hushed.

Then Sophie and Anastasia burst into cheers. They

clapped, and stamped against the cathedral roof. Safi made a shrill whooping in the back of her throat. It was the first noise Sophie had heard her make.

A throat was cleared. 'If you hadn't been making enough noise to wake the saints,' said Matteo, 'you would have heard the clock strike midnight. We should get a move on, if we want to be at the station at two.'

'Why two?' said Gérard. 'Two is a bad hour for *gariers*. We should go later.'

'Two was when Sophie heard the music last.' Matteo gave a grunt. 'I know it's not much to go on,' he said, 'but I thought it would be better than nothing.'

'It's a possible,' said Sophie. She said it quietly, so the others wouldn't hear. 'You should never ignore a possible.'

23

They reached the neighbourhood of the station just before two o'clock in the morning. The rooftops had grown steadily lower as they had moved away from Notre Dame, and the others were on edge and anxious.

Twice, they had to cross a road between buildings. Matteo, Gérard and Safi jumped from a cedar tree to a lamp post and swung effortlessly to the drainpipe on the far side. Anastasia and Sophie slid down one drainpipe, ran across the road, and grasped the next pipe. It had handholds at regular intervals, but there is nothing like climbing a drainpipe at night to remind you just how dark dark can be.

The five came to rest on the roof of a school. The four rooftoppers sat, alert, in a square, facing outwards. Sophie sat a little to one side. She held her breath, and prayed. She whispered to herself, 'Please.

Please let me find her.' Her heart was thumping hard enough to break, but the words sounded too small and thin in the night air. Sophie clenched her fists, and sat on them.

An hour passed. Sophie grew restless. None of the rooftoppers had spoken. They had not moved a muscle.

At last she whispered, 'Can I ask you all a question?'

Matteo grunted. Gérard said, 'Of course you can. What?'

'What happens when rooftoppers grow up?'

'Oh!' said Matteo. 'I thought you were going to ask about toilets.'

Gérard said, 'Mostly, they go down to the ground, but they still lead wildish sort of lives. It is easier to be a wildish sort of adult than a child.'

Anastasia sniffed, haughty as a Cleopatra. 'Especially,' she said, 'if you happen to be a boy.'

'And have there been others?' said Sophie. 'In the past?'

Anastasia said, 'No', just as Matteo said, 'Yes.'

'Yes,' he said again. 'I think so. Look. I found this on my roof, when I first moved there.' Matteo took from his pocket a small knife. It was ornate and heavy.

'See the handle?' It looked at least a hundred years old. On the handle, finger grooves were clearly visible. The hand that had made them was smaller than Sophie's.

'Whose was it?' she asked.

'Some kid.' He shrugged. 'A clever kid. I found it wrapped in rope. Rope is the best way to store a knife. Not everyone knows that.'

'Did you ever go looking for them?' Sophie thought she would have, if it had been her. 'Why didn't they come back for it?'

'*Non*. It was rusted a centimetre thick. It must have been years ago.'

'What do you think happened to them?'

He shrugged into the night. 'Maybe they got caught. Maybe they went south. The sun is hotter in the south, and there's less people.'

Sophie said, 'How many do you think there are? How many rooftoppers?'

Gérard said, 'I would guess more than ten. Less than a hundred.' The girls nodded. Safi held out ten fingers and thumbs, closed her fists, opened them again. Anastasia said, 'I think that's right. About twenty or thirty. I see shadows, sometimes. I think there's probably someone living on the Louvre.'

They fell silent again. Two hours passed by. Sophie sat with her ears stretched wide.

No *gariers* appeared. There was no music. By five in the morning, Sophie was cold and tired enough to weep.

'We should go,' said Matteo. He knelt, and dusted off his backside. 'The sun's coming up.' He stood.

'Wait!' Gérard pulled him down. 'One second! Listen!'

'Cello?' Sophie snapped alert, and she balled her fists. '*Gariers?* Or music? Can you hear her?'

'No, neither. But listen.'

The rooftop was very still. Far away and down the road, there was a sound that might have been a horse, or someone coughing, or nothing at all. Then a cloud appeared; a grey cloud, which span and zagged across the sky.

Anastasia breathed, 'Birds.'

Sophie said, 'Starlings.'

The air was suddenly thick with them. There were five hundred, a thousand. Their wings hummed, and they swooped down over the rooftoppers' heads as fearlessly as if the children were a cluster of chimney pots.

'They're like a ballet!' said Sophie.

'Maybe,' said Matteo. 'I don't know ballet. They're like starlings.'

'What do you call a group of starlings?' whispered Sophie.

'You call them starlings, don't you?' said Anastasia. 'I don't know what you mean?'

'Like, a flock of crows is called a murder. A group of owls is a parliament.'

'Oh. *Je comprends*. I don't know, though.'

'A ballet of starlings,' said Sophie

They spoke without moving anything, not even their lips. The birds circled and dived. Each time they came near Sophie gasped: the others did not, but Sophie couldn't help it. It felt high-day-holiday miraculous. It felt like an omen. Her heart was hot, and enormous.

'An army of starlings,' said Matteo.

'A tornado of starlings,' said Gérard.

'An avalanche of starlings,' said Sophie.

'A fountain of starlings,' said Anastasia. 'A sunray of starlings.'

The boys snorted, but Sophie said, 'Yes! I like that. Or, an orchestra of starlings.'

'A rooftop of starlings,' said Matteo.

24

They went home slowly. The roar of adrenaline had died away, and Sophie felt only exhausted. They went an unfamiliar route, single file, Matteo first and Safi last. Nobody wanted to talk.

Matteo and Sophie left the two sky-treaders and Gérard at the cathedral, and went north alone.

Once they were alone, Sophie said, 'Matteo? Just out of interest? What *do* you do about toilets?'

'Drainpipes,' he said. He did not elaborate.

Sophie laughed, and looked away. The surrounding buildings were becoming familiar. But— 'This isn't my street, is it?' Sophie hesitated. 'Matteo? Where are we?'

He looked half asleep. 'Near the river.' He shook himself. 'It's a shortcut. Quite close to you, now. Ten more minutes.'

'But what building are we on?

'The police headquarters. You should know that. You said you've been here twice.'

'And we're . . . on the roof?'

'Yes.' He looked confused. 'We're on the roof.'

'How long until sunrise?'

Matteo's mouth moved as he counted the remaining stars. 'Half an hour. Maybe forty minutes.'

'And the city archives are on the top floor of the police headquarters, aren't they?'

'I don't know.'

'Well, they are. I know they are. Could we . . . have a look? Just in through the window?'

'If you want.'

She laid a hand on his wrist to make him concentrate. 'How, though, do you think? How would you do it?'

'If you lie on your stomach and hang over the edge, I'll hold your legs.'

'And you won't . . . drop me?'

'You'll be fine.' Which was not, Sophie thought, exactly an answer. 'You just have to hope they don't have curtains.'

If he said she would be fine, she believed him.

Sophie lay down near the edge and shuffled forwards on her stomach. 'Have you got me? Hold tight, won't you?'

Sophie shimmied forwards until her ribs were hanging over the edge of the rooftops. She gripped the brickwork and bent herself slowly forward, but she couldn't see in. The top window was some way below her. Sophie forced herself not to look down.

'A bit further,' she said. The blood was going to her head. 'A bit further!' It was no good. The window was too far down.

'Pull me up again,' she said. 'Quickly, please.'

Matteo gave a grunt, and tugged. Sophie's chin scraped against the brickwork as she rose. She sat up and rubbed it. Blood wetted her fingers. 'Damn,' she said.

Matteo pulled a scrap of cloth from his pocket. 'Spit on it,' he said. 'There'll be brick-grit in the scab if you don't.'

'Thank you,' said Sophie. She said it to Matteo's bottom, because he was peering over the edge. There was a pause, and then his feet started drumming on the rooftop. If feet can sound excited, Matteo's did.

He straightened up. 'You're right,' he said, 'it's too

far to bend over. But what if I dangled you by your ankles?'

'What? No!'

'Why not? I'll hold tight, I swear. I'm strong.'

'By my ankles, though?' she said.

'How else? You said you wanted to see, didn't you?'

'I do.' Sophie's skin was suddenly itchy with terror. It was like wearing a sandpaper suit. But it would be too terrible to give up now. 'All right,' she said. 'But make sure your hands don't get sweaty. I don't want to die upside down, thank you very much.'

She scooted forwards again, and Matteo took hold of her feet. His grip on her ankles was cutting off the blood supply. 'I'm going to lower you,' he said.

He pushed her forwards until only her knees could still feel the roof; then only her toes were touching the parapet. She could feel the muscles in his arms shaking, and she grasped the bricks for support. 'Don't look down,' she whispered. Her hair hung down over Paris. She shook it out of her eyes, and peered in the window.

The room stretched the length of the building. It was lined with filing cabinets. There must have been hundreds, for there wasn't a single gap. In the centre of the room there was a large table. She blew on the window, *hah*, upside down, and wiped the window clean with her fingertips. There were no pictures in the room, and no lights. Sophie's vision started to swim with red spots.

'I'm going to have to pull you up,' called Matteo's voice. 'Unless you want to take the fast way down.'

When all the blood in Sophie's body had returned to its proper place, the two went on, quicker now, for fear of the rising sun.

'The filing cabinets had locks on them,' she said. 'Do you think I could hammer them open?'

'*Non,*' said Matteo. 'The whole of Paris would hear you.'

'Damn. How else, though?' she said. 'Could I crow-bar them?'

'But you pick the lock, of course.'

'How? Ouch!'

Sophie's nose met Matteo's foot. They were crawling over the peaked roof of a butcher's shop, and Matteo had stopped to stare at her.

'You've never picked a lock?' He sounded genuinely incredulous. 'I thought it was . . . I don't know, like breathing. I thought everybody could.'

'Why would I know how to pick a lock?'

'Really? You really don't know? I can do it with my *teeth*.'

'For goodness sake, no, I don't!' They were in sight of Hotel Bost now.

Matteo stared at her. She felt herself turning red, and brushed her hair over her face to hide it. At last he said, 'I guess I'll teach you, then. It's easy. And it's useful. More useful than the cello.'

'When? Now?'

'*Non*. Your hands will be too stiff. You need to sleep first. Tomorrow.' He nodded towards the hotel. 'Can you do the last part on your own? I need to get home. The sun'll be up in ten minutes.'

'I'll see you tomorrow,' she said. 'And, Matteo—' She scrubbed at her eyes, to give herself time. It was difficult to think of the right words to thank him. But, when she opened her eyes, he had already vanished.

When Sophie dropped back into her room, the first strong sunbeams were warming her bed. The palms of her hands were black. There was soot and leaf mould all across the soles of her feet and up over her ankles. The bed looked wonderfully inviting, but before she climbed into it she fetched the English dictionary from the bookshelf on the landing. She wiped her hands clean on the backs of her knees, and flicked through the pages.

A flock of starlings was called a murmuration.

25

Sophie opened her eyes and saw Charles bending over her with a mug of something hot. Mid-afternoon sunlight streamed in through the skylight.

'You're back,' he said.

Sophie took the mug. She tried to look innocent. 'Back from where?' It was hot chocolate. It was rich and sticky, the way Charles made it at home. As a baby she had called it 'cocoa-extragavant'. It took half an hour to make it that particular, chewy thickness. Sophie's guilty feeling deepened.

'I don't know,' said Charles. 'You tell me.' He sat on the bed. 'I came in at eleven last night and you were gone.'

'Was I?'

'I don't want to be a boring old fart, my darling, but I thought you'd been taken. I thought you had been ... I don't know.' He wasn't smiling, and there was no light in his eyes. 'Where were you?'

'I can't tell you.' She wrapped her fingers round his wrist. 'I'm so sorry. I would, honestly, but it involves people who aren't me.'

'Sophie, are you telling me—'

'But I promise, nobody could have seen me. I *swear*. I didn't go on the streets until it was dark. And I covered up my hair.'

'Why didn't you at least tell me you were going out?'

'I couldn't. I thought you might stop me.'

Charles took her mug from her, sipped, handed it back: all in silence. His eyebrows were raised so high they were almost on top of his head.

Sophie asked, '*Would* you have stopped me?'

'I wouldn't, no.'

'Oh!' Guilt caught at Sophie's chest.

'At least, I hope I wouldn't.' He took another draught from her mug. 'I might have. I don't know, actually. Love is unpredictable.'

Love is unpredictable, thought Sophie. She hesitated. Then, 'Charles? Can I ask you something?' she said.

'Of course. Always.'

Sophie tried to find the right words. To give herself time she gulped the rest of the chocolate, and ran her finger round the inside of the cup.

'It's only that I've been thinking – if she *is* alive – and I'm sure she is – why didn't she come for me?'

'But she would have been told you were dead, Sophie. If we couldn't get a list of survivors, neither could she. You wouldn't have been in the hospitals. Nobody in France would have known about you.'

'I know. I do know that. But . . . they told *me* that *she* was dead, and I didn't believe them. Why did she believe it? Why didn't she keep looking?'

'My darling, because she is an adult.'

Sophie ducked behind her hair. Her face was hot and tight and angry. 'That's not a reason.'

'It is, my love. Adults are taught not to believe anything unless it is boring or ugly.'

'That's stupid of them,' she said.

'Sad, child, but not stupid. It is difficult to believe extraordinary things. It's a talent you have, Sophie. Don't lose it.'

26

That night, before Sophie climbed out of the skylight, she left a note for Charles on her pillow. It said that she was going to the police headquarters – though not that she was going via the sky – and it promised she would be back before dawn. Then she pulled on trousers, and Safi's grey rag of a jersey. She put a candle stump in her pocket, and flexed her fingers, and headed out into the dark.

Matteo was waiting for her on the roof, hopping from foot to foot. Sophie had expected that; but under the chimney stack sat Anastasia, Safi and Gérard, passing round a bag of raisins. Both Safi and Anastasia were dressed in black jerseys and grey trousers, and their faces looked silvery-white in contrast. She had forgotten how beautiful they were. It gave her a shock.

Gérard saw her face and laughed. 'I know! *Mon*

Dieu, non? But you get used to it, eventually.'

'We're here to keep watch,' said Anastasia. 'Gérard has hearing like a rabbit. He'll know if anyone's coming. And we brought food.' She tipped a dozen raisins onto Sophie's palm. As she ate them the sugar warmed her, and she turned to Matteo.

'Shall I go first?'

'*Non,*' said Matteo.

'No, but please. I'd like to.' It felt so important to do it right, but Sophie couldn't properly explain. She felt she was so close. Every thought of her mother made her quiver.

Matteo said, 'Do you know how to break open a window latch?'

'Oh. I don't, no.'

'Then I go first.'

Matteo slid down a metre of drainpipe until he was level with the window sill. Sophie lay on her stomach and watched. She didn't want to say, 'Be careful!' She didn't want to be a 'be careful' sort of person. So she called, 'Good luck!' and after a second, unnecessarily, 'We'll keep watch!'

Matteo was facing the wall. Embracing the drainpipe with both arms, he swung one leg, then the other, to rest on the window sill, pressing his body flat against the brick. One hand let go of the drainpipe, and latched onto the brick. It made Sophie giddy to watch. Then the second hand swung across, and Matteo stood upright on the window sill, balanced on his toes. Slowly he bent his knees, gripping the window pane with his fingertips, until he was crouching. The window sill was thick, but even so, his back half was sticking out over nothing. His face, though, was as calm as a Sunday afternoon.

He attacked the window latch with his penknife. 'It's open!'

'Good! Oh, please be—' Sophie caught herself just in time. 'Wonderful!' she called.

He hitched his nails under the sill and heaved. There was a ripping noise, and Matteo said, '*Ach*.'

'What? Are you all right?'

'Nothing. Just a little blood.' The window opened. 'We'll wipe it before we go.' He rearranged himself so that he was sitting on the sill with his legs dangling inside the room. 'OK!' He patted the sill. 'You can come down now.'

Sophie copied his movements as exactly as she could. Matteo guided her feet with both his hands.

She forced herself to think of cellos, and mothers, and not of the noise her skull would make on the pavement if she fell. 'Mothers,' she whispered to herself. 'Mothers are worth hunting for.'

Sophie ducked in through the window. The archive room was chill and dark. It felt secretive, and wary. She said, 'Are you coming in?'

'*Non*. I never go inside.' Matteo kicked his heels against the wainscoting. 'I'll be fine like this.'

Sophie pulled the candle from her pocket and struck a match. 'Right.' She wrapped her hand in her jersey so that the wax wouldn't drip on her fingers. 'Where do I start?' She peered at the labels on the cabinets. 'Matteo, they're in French!'

'Of course they're in French. Read them out to me.'

'This one says, *meurtre*.'

'That's murders.'

'*Incendiaire?*'

'Firebombs. Probably not.'

She crossed to the far end of the room. '*Assurance?*'

'That's insurance. Try that one.'

Sophie tugged at the cabinet door. 'It's locked.'

She couldn't believe she had forgotten. But Matteo's face, framed in the window, was excited.

'Of course it's locked. Do you have a hairpin?'

'Yes.'

'Good. Now—'

'Wait a second.' Sophie fumbled at the pin holding back her coil of hair. Her fingers were shaking, and somehow fatter than usual.

'OK,' he said. '*Bon*. Now, you have to concentrate. A lock has *cinq* pins inside.'

'Sank?' It was the one word she was trying not to think. That, and 'drowned'.

'*Oui, cinq*. Oh! *Ach* . . . five. Numbers are ugly in English. A lock has five pins, *oui*? And the key moves the pins and opens the cross-bar. Where's that match you used? Did you drop it on the floor?'

'No. It's here.'

'So, you put the match in at the base of the lock – like that, yes – and you push a little, left or right.'

Sophie licked her fingers to calm them, and inserted the match into the fat part of the keyhole. 'Which one?' she whispered. 'Left or right?'

'You can feel it. It's like water. It has a flow. One way is upstream.' Sophie wriggled the match. She couldn't feel anything.

Matteo said, 'Stop! You're trying too hard.'

This is one of the most annoying things anybody can say. Sophie glared at him, her tongue still sticking out between her teeth. 'That's not terribly helpful, Matteo.'

'I mean, you're forcing it. You're poking it like it's a sausage. Imagine it's alive.'

'It's not.'

'How do you know? *Imagine* it is.'

And it was true. To the right, it stayed stiff; inched to the left, the lock gave a shift. It was soft as a whisper, and she repeated it a few times until she was sure.

'Now what?' she said.

'Hold it there. You mustn't move it a millimetre.'

'Right.' Sophie rearranged her grip so she could hold the match in place with her left hand. 'And now?'

'So, you push in the hairpin at the top of the lock.' He was watching her carefully, squinting through the dark. 'And you start at the back with the fifth pin. You slide the hairpin under it and you push upwards until it sticks.'

'How you do you mean, sticks?' Sophie's hands were wet with sweat. She licked her palms, and dried them on her front.

'I don't know how to explain. It's easy. You just—'

'Couldn't you just come in and do it?'

'*Non*. But, you wriggle the pin until it feels . . . more solid. You just feel it. You hear a click, sometimes. But so quietly, if the lock is oiled. Like an ant coughing.' His mouth was slightly open, as though he were listening to music. 'That lock is oiled, I think.'

'And then?'

'Then you do the fourth pin, and the third. And then the—'

'Second, yes, I understand.'

'Can you feel the stick?'

At first, Sophie couldn't. She wriggled the hairpin up and down, feeling increasingly furious. And then, quite suddenly, she could feel it. It was the smallest possible shift, but suddenly the pin felt stiffer. It no longer wobbled.

'I think that's it! Now what?'

'Good. The first is the hardest. Now you pull the hairpin towards you – less than a millimetre – and wriggle the next pin.'

Sophie held her breath, and pulled the hairpin back a hair's breadth. She made tiny digging movements with the hairpin to hitch it under the pin. It was easier, once she had got into a rhythm. 'That's the third,' she called. 'Second.' The final pin was the hardest. 'Done, I think!'

If she had expected congratulations, she would have been disappointed. Matteo gave a curt nod.

He said, 'Right. Now you keep hold of the hairpin – your hands are shaking, you must stop that – and you jerk the match to the left.'

The lock clicked open. Sophie hefted the file to the window and the two of them sifted through the papers. Sophie's fingers were quivering. It was hard to tell in the dim light, but she thought that Matteo's were too.

'There's nothing here on the *Queen Mary*,' she said. 'It's all from the last two years.'

'Don't worry,' said Matteo. 'We have time.'

'But there's thousands of files in this room!'

'We have time,' he said again. 'Don't panic.' His voice was more gentle than it usually was.

'Maybe I should try the older filing cabinets?' said Sophie. 'The green ones. They look rusty. They look less honest.'

He nodded. 'Put this back first, though. They mustn't know you were here.'

Sophie read the labels out to him. Pickpockets, theatre fires, beggars. But nothing that sounded promising.

'*Divers*,' she said. 'What's that?'

'It means "a jumble". Misc . . . miscellaneous, you know? Try it.'

This lock was bigger, and the pins were easier to feel. It took Sophie and her hairpin less than five minutes to open it.

The files inside were fat, and the dates on the outside went back twenty years. Feverishly, Sophie found the right year. Then her whole body quivered and burned.

'"*Queen Mary*", paquebot *Anglais*.'

'What is *paquebot*?' she asked.

'I think – a large ship?'

The file was marbled cardboard; Sophie ran with it to Matteo's window sill, and handed him her candle. There were about two dozen sheets of paper, in all. She split them into two piles, and handed half to Matteo. 'Don't let them blow away,' she said.

Sophie flipped through the papers as fast as she could. There were printed lists of names, and handwritten letters. There were photographs of the waiters, staring unsmiling at the camera with napkins over their arms, and their names and addresses inked on the back.

'Ha!' cried Matteo. 'This is the passenger list, I think.'

Sophie took it from him. Under M, there was 'Maxim, Charles'. But there was nothing under V; no Vivienne Vert. She ran one shaking finger down the staff list with the same result. No Viviennes.

'Look!' said Matteo. He held up a photograph. 'Sophie! The band! Is she there?'

'Let me see!' Sophie almost tore it from his fingers. 'But . . .' she said. 'They're . . . they're all men.' The darkness in the room was suddenly terrible. 'The cellist is a man.'

'Oh,' said Matteo. His smile dropped downwards. 'Oh, *Dieu*.'

Sophie turned over the photo. 'It says the cellist is "George Greene, 12, Appartement G, rue de l'Espoir".'

He was young and handsome, staring out at the world on the brink of laughter. He might just as well have been one-eyed and pot-bellied for all she cared. Sophie licked a tear off her nose. She hadn't realised she was crying. 'It's a man,' she said again.

'It's odd, though. Because George Greene looks very much like you,' said a voice.

Sophie nearly fell off the window ledge. A shadow was hanging from the drainpipe, watching.

'Move over, please,' said Safi. 'I want to sit down.'

Sophie ducked back into the archive room to make space on the sill for Safi. She gripped the girl's wrist. 'I don't see it. He doesn't! Does he?'

'He has your eyes,' said Safi. Her voice was deeper than Anastasia's, and more French. 'People never really see their own eyes, so you wouldn't notice.' She turned to Matteo. 'I'm surprised *you* didn't see it, though. You talk about her eyes enough. Do you think it could be her father?'

Matteo flushed, but Sophie was busy looking at the picture. She held it up to the moon.

'My God,' she whispered.

A prickling started in Sophie's neck and ran down her back. She said, 'He's wearing a woman's shirt.'

'What?' said Matteo.

Sophie said, 'Women's shirts button right over left.'

'What?' said Matteo. 'How do you know that?'

'Of course I know. Buttons,' said Sophie, 'are important. Matteo, that's a woman's shirt. Why would a man wear a woman's shirt?'

'And,' said Safi, 'look at the shoes. Only women lace their shoes crossways, like that. See!'

Sophie did see. And she saw too that the trousers were black, and worn greyish at the knee.

'And,' said Sophie, 'look at his moustache!'

Matteo and Safi looked. 'What about it?'

'It's too short. It should come over the lip, surely? Look at all the other moustaches. They're huge! But this is just the hairs that women have, painted darker.'

Safi took the photograph. 'I don't think that's a man,' she said. 'It's just a very clever woman.' She studied the picture, and then she reached out to Sophie, and pushed the hair away from her face. 'She looks like you.'

27

Sophie was still staring – at Matteo, at Safi, at the photograph – when there was a scuffle, and a thump, and a voice called from above their heads.

'Sophie? Are you down there?'

'Who's that?' said Safi.

Matteo said, 'The police! Run!'

Sophie gripped them both round the wrist. 'Wait! I think it's—'

'Would you mind coming back up?' said the voice. 'I have no doubt it's unintentional, but you are, metaphorically, scaring the hell out of me. Come back, please.'

It was Charles.

The three of them scrambled up the drainpipe. Matteo wiped a patch of blood off the sill with his elbow as he went, and slammed the window behind him.

Sophie carried the photograph in her teeth.

Charles was leaning against the chimney pot, watched warily by Gérard and Anastasia. He held Sophie's cello in one hand, and his umbrella tucked under his arm.

'This young lady,' he said, pointing at Anastasia, 'very properly tried to kill me, until I explained I was your guardian. This young gentleman has convinced her I was harmless. I believe your cello convinced him.'

'You brought my cello?' Sophie stared blankly at him. 'Across the rooftops? How? Why?'

'I tied it to my back.' He looked ruminatively at the cello. 'I rather thought you might need it, if you discovered something . . . something grey.' He crouched down, and studied Sophie's eyes. 'From the look on your face, that is not the case.'

'I've got an address,' said Sophie. She was still shivering from head to foot. 'It might be her. I don't know.'

Matteo took the address from her. 'Rue de l'Espoir. That's *garier* country, near the church of Saint-Vincent-de-Paul. It's east of where we were last night.' The other three nodded.

'How do you know?' said Sophie.

Gérard shrugged. 'Rooftoppers have maps in their heads.'

Anastasia said, 'They'll be angry, Sophie. The *gariers*. Rue de l'Espoir . . . that's like going into their front hall and singing Christmas carols.'

'I don't care,' said Sophie.

'You don't understand,' said Anastasia. 'Rue de l'Espoir is their headquarters. They carry knives.'

'You can stay here if you like. I'm going.'

Matteo said, 'Sophie, we never go there—'

'I don't care,' Sophie said again. She meant it. She had never felt less afraid. Perhaps, she thought, that's what love does. It's not there to make you feel special. It's to make you brave. It was like a ration pack in the desert, she thought, like a box of matches in a dark wood. Love and courage, thought Sophie: two words for the same thing. You didn't need the person to be there with you, even, perhaps. Just alive, somewhere. It was what her mother had always been. A place to put down her heart. A resting stop to recover her breath. A set of stars and maps.

Charles had been politely silent while the others were talking. Now he said, 'If we're going anywhere, Sophie, you and I should go at street level. I don't want to accidentally smash your cello on a chimney pot.'

'No,' said Sophie. 'I'm staying up here.'

'Why?' said Matteo. He was kicking at splinters of slate. His face was clenched tight.

'The police. If they caught me now . . .' She didn't finish her sentence. Instead she said, 'Charles, I'll meet you there, all right?'

'No,' said Charles. 'That is very far from all right.'

She looked up at Charles. 'Please,' she said. Her gaze took in his long legs, and sharp bones, and the kindness of his eyes. 'I promise not to get hurt. You said to do extraordinary things. This counts as an extraordinary thing.'

Charles sighed. 'That is not untrue, perhaps.' He tried to raise his eyebrows, but they only flickered, and sank down. 'I can't think what Miss Eliot would say, but yes, that is certainly true.' His smile was strained. 'I suppose I will see you at rue de l'Espoir, then. If you're not there in an hour, I will . . . I don't know what I'll do. Just be careful.' He hitched the cello onto his back, and turned to the drainpipe.

'If you're going,' said Matteo, 'you'll need us. You don't know the way.'

'I know,' said Sophie. 'Yes. Thank you.'

Anastasia said, '*Mais, non*! Rue de l'Espoir—' She launched an angry stream of French at Matteo.

Sophie uncurled her spine. She had not realised how often she slouched. At full height, she was taller than Anastasia, and almost as tall as Matteo. Sophie raised her eyebrows, and Anastasia and Matteo fell silent. 'You don't have to come,' she said. 'But if you're coming, let's go.'

28

They were twenty minutes past the river when Matteo's back began to tense. They were walking single file along the wide roof of a hospital, with Gérard bringing up the rear and humming to himself. They were going more slowly, more carefully than usual. Sophie and Matteo were in the lead, and she could see the hairs rising on the back of his neck.

'They've been here,' he said. 'Smell that? Tobacco.'

'Lots of people smoke tobacco,' said Sophie reasonably.

'But they smoke the butts of other people's. It has a twice-burnt smell.'

'I can't smell anything. It just smells like chimneys to me. Can you, Anast—' Sophie turned. Anastasia was on the far side of the rooftop. Her face was yellow with terror. She was surrounded.

The boys had come noiselessly up the walls and across the neighbouring roof. They were tall, and pale. Their faces were arrogant, and sharp as acid. There were six; four of them had encircled Gérard. Nobody was moving.

Matteo backed towards Sophie. Sweat had flattened his hair against his face. He bent, snapped a piece of slate from the roof.

'They're angry,' he said. 'This was a bad idea.'

Nobody was laughing, nobody was jeering. The *gariers* held piping, broken shards of iron. *A wolf pack*, thought Sophie.

'Where's Safi?' she whispered.

Matteo shook his head. *'Je ne sais pas,'* he said. He pushed Sophie behind a chimney stack. 'Sophie, stay here. Don't move, or I'll kill you later, *d'accord*? And if Safi comes, hold her down, if you have to. You understand? Don't let her fight.'

Matteo pulled a pigeon bone from his pocket, and snapped it in half. The broken end formed a jagged edge, like glass. He handed half to Sophie. 'If they come for you, go for their eyes.' Matteo switched to French: he shouted something raw and bitter into the night, and then he hurled himself at the *gariers*.

The moon was covered and it was dark, but Sophie's eyes had grown accustomed to it. Sophie saw Anastasia catch sight of Matteo, and shout. She seemed to grow taller. One of the *gariers* had turned to meet Matteo, and Anastasia threw herself at the other. Anastasia didn't fight nicely. She hacked at his neck and chest with her nails, with her teeth. What terrified Sophie was how little noise was made. They fought in grunts and spits. Matteo saw Anastasia struggling, and he pulled a chimney pot from the roof and threw it, straight at the back of the boy's head.

'It pays to know,' he panted, 'which ones are coming loose. Gérard, help me!'

Sophie understood, then, why they had called Gérard a fighter. His legs, which had looked so awkward on Notre Dame, were strong, and dangerous. He kicked two boys in the eye, raking at their faces with a flint held between his toes. But four to one are bad odds, and he was panting, and clutching at his left arm.

He called, 'Matteo!'

Matteo fought the way a cat fights. He darted in and out, aiming his shard of bone and his fists at the boys' eyes, their ears, their lips. In any playground, against any child, Matteo and Gérard would have won, but the *gariers* were not children. They were rooftoppers, and vicious. Gérard slipped, and hit the back of his head against the roof. One of the boys made as if to kick him the face.

Sophie scrambled on the rooftop for a weapon. She had no idea if fighting was difficult, but sitting crouched here was impossible. She jumped up and ran, head first, at the boy. He shouted and staggered, but he was up before she had wiped the dust and hair from her eyes. He stood over her, and she raised her knee and kicked him in the crotch. He groaned and collapsed.

Sophie retreated, and ducked behind the chimney pot again. As she watched, the tallest boy pulled a knife from his belt, a plain kitchen knife with a wooden handle. She used one like it at home to peel potatoes. He moved towards Anastasia. Sophie let out a noise that was half shriek and half roar. She jerked a slate from the roof, and threw it at the boy. It cut at his knuckles, and he swore and dropped the knife. Anastasia grabbed it, and dropped it down a chimney. The boy ran at Sophie. She gasped and tried to punch him, but swung at nothing. He spat something in French. She ducked his fist.

'He says, punch like you mean it,' said a voice.

Sophie turned, but she already knew it wasn't Matteo. A flat palm on her shoulder pushed her out of the way, and Safi's fist connected with the bridge of the boy's nose. Blood spattered the rooftop.

'Kick him, if you can't punch him,' said Safi. Her voice was soft, but the expression on her face was not soft at all. 'Kicking is less personal.' Safi brought up a sharp knee, and slammed the heel of her hand into the boy's eye. 'You have to *mean* it.' He rolled to the ground, choking, and she vaulted over him.

'Where's Stasia?' said Safi.

'I'm here.' Anastasia scrambled towards them on hands and knees. 'Sophie! On your left!'

Sophie had always found it difficult under pressure to remember which was left and which right. Luckily, so did Anastasia. Sophie's hair was in her face and mouth and she kicked out blindly to the right, and felt her foot connect with a shin. Safi jerked an elbow at the boy's face as he went down.

There was only one *garier* standing now. Gérard was hunched over on the slate, coughing, and Matteo was leading the *garier* away from him. Matteo was white. He had a scrap of bone in each hand, but the boy had a piece of pipe, and was backing Matteo towards the edge of the roof.

Safi took a stone from her pocket, squinted into the dark, and flung it. It hit the boy on the temple. He screamed and whipped round.

He saw the three girls standing, unblinking, in the night air. Two unconscious boys lay at their feet. Sophie whispered, 'Do not mess with a mother-hunter. Do not mess with rooftoppers.' She whispered, 'Do not underestimate children. Do not underestimate girls.'

The *garier* vaulted onto the next rooftop, turned, spat, and disappeared into the dark.

'Let's go,' said Matteo to Sophie. He was standing behind her. 'Quick. I don't want to be here when they wake up.'

'Are you sure? You can go back if you need to. I can go on alone.' The girls looked so fragile, now, in the moonlight. They looked like china dolls. 'Will you be safe?'

China dolls do not wipe their noses on their hair. Anastasia did so, and grinned. 'Come on, before it gets light. We'll be fine, Sophie. We're rooftoppers.'

29

Rue de l'Espoir was deserted. Charles was waiting, stamping his feet, in front of the apartment block. Sophie leaned over the edge of the building and whistled down to him.

'You were longer than I expected,' he said. Then he saw Gérard's bleeding temple, and Matteo's hands. He said nothing; only strapped the cello more securely to his back, and climbed up the drainpipe to join them.

They sat, the six of them, under the stars. It was a beautiful night, but it was too silent. There was not a single cat, drunkard, or piece of litter. Sophie peered down at the street.

'Where is everybody?'

'There was cholera here; three times in four years,' said Gérard.

Anastasia added, 'That's why the *gariers* like it.

Nobody will live here. People think it's cursed.'

Matteo snorted. 'People are stupid. Shall we break in to the apartment block?'

'No,' said Sophie. 'We'll call her.' Sophie cupped her hands to her mouth and then hesitated. What did she shout? '*Maman?*' she called. 'Mother?'

Matteo shook his head. 'Half the women in Paris are called Maman.'

'Vivienne?' called Sophie. 'Everybody, try together. On three. One, two, three—' All six of them bellowed, '*Vivienne!*'

There was no answer, and no sound except the tin drum of Sophie's heart.

Charles handed her the cello. 'Here. Play the *Requiem.*'

'Why? Charles, I can't.' She felt awkward. To her surprise, the other rooftoppers were nodding.

'Play,' said Safi.

'Why, though?'

Anastasia said, 'Music will work the same way as magic does, sometimes.'

Matteo nodded. 'Only an idiot doesn't know that. Play, Sophie.'

Sophie had never been so nervous. Her heart had

269

migrated down into her stomach, and her fingers felt thick on the strings. They were shaking. *Play*, she told herself. *Remember how it sounds when you dream.* The first notes were flat, and Gérard winced. Charles did not seem to notice.

'Yes!' he said. 'Quicker, Sophie!'

Sophie spat on the ground, and straightened her back. She played quicker.

'Louder!' said Matteo.

Anastasia kicked and span on the spot. 'Quicker!' she called.

Sophie did not hear them. She played on, willing her fingers to go faster. *Come on*, she thought. *Please.*

When her arm ached too much to keep bowing, she stopped. Matteo clapped. Charles whistled. Safi and Anastasia whooped. The stars stopped spinning.

The music, though, kept going.

30

'Is that ... an echo?' Sophie looked round for Charles. 'Is it?' Her voice hurt her own ears. 'I can't hear it!' she cried. 'Has it stopped?'

It hadn't stopped. It had only grown fainter.

'It sounds like no echo I have heard,' said Charles. 'Echoes do not change key.'

It was Matteo who jerked them out of their shock. He shoved Sophie in the small of the back. She almost dropped her cello. 'Go! Now! *Vite! Mon Dieu*, are you deaf? Go!'

'Where's it coming from?' she said. '*Where? Quick?*'

'It's coming from the north-west,' said Anastasia. She started to run, pulling Sophie along. 'Go west first.'

'Which way is west?' cried Sophie. 'Left or right?'

'Left!' said Safi. 'There, the roof with the black weathervane. Then the public baths; and then you have to jump.' Sophie turned and ran; Charles thundered after her. The slates under her feet cracked. The steps of the others faded.

'Sophie!' called Matteo. 'You're going too fast!'

Sophie was not, in her own opinion, going too fast. She was going not-fast-enough, and the music was swooping, as though to an end. She jumped two feet to the bathhouse; then there was a solid street's worth of pointed rooftops, and she ran, not bothering to keep low, along them. Anyone looking up would have seen a dark, soft-shoed blur.

'Sophie! Stop!'

Sophie came to a sudden halt. There was a side street between her rooftop and the next. The next rooftop was flat, but the gap was twice as long as her own body. It would be so great an anti-climax, to die now.

She stopped, choking on her own breath. She tried to prepare to jump, but her legs would not bend. 'I can't,' she whispered.

'You can.' Suddenly, Charles was behind her. 'I'll throw you across. Curl into a ball.'

She couldn't understand him. 'What?'

'Crouch!' He sounded like a sergeant major. Sophie crouched.

He said, 'Make sure to land on your feet and hands, not your knees. Knees are brittle. Not your knees, you understand, Sophie?'

Sophie nodded. 'Quick!' The music was fading.

'On three, Sophie. One. Two—' Charles hefted her in his arms, and swung her backwards. '*Three.*'

Sophie had not known that Charles was so strong. He had always looked spindly; but he lifted her with ease, and now the wind bit at her face, and then she hit the opposite rooftop with a thud and felt the skin scrape off her palms.

There was another shout of 'Three!' and a thump. Matteo landed next to her.

'You! How did you get here?'

'I thought I'd catch you up,' he said. 'I didn't want to miss it.'

Then Charles jumped, with his legs outstretched, silhouetted against the streetlamp. He landed on one knee, awkwardly, and brushed some dust out of his eyebrows. He spoke gruffly. 'I suggest, Sophie, that you don't mention this to the educational authorities. Throwing children across rooftops is frowned upon, I believe.'

Sophie stared at him.

'Go!' he cried.

Sophie ran on. Sometimes her panting covered the music and she thought it had stopped; but it kept playing, and always quicker, even when quicker should have been impossible.

Matteo was limping on his left foot, and she could hear him grunting in pain, but his face was steady.

Then Sophie heard Matteo gasp and turned back just in time to see his legs slip from under him. Charles was closer – he thrust his umbrella at Matteo as he slid, and Matteo grasped the hooked end. 'Hold tight,' said Charles. He tugged Matteo back up the slope, hauling hand over hand.

'You – are – more – substantial – than – you – look,' Charles grunted.

Using Charles like a stepladder, Matteo clambered to his feet. Charles must have seen how white the boy's face was, because he smiled through the strain. 'An Englishman without an umbrella is less than half a man,' he said.

Matteo stood, and as he did so a tile slipped down from under him and smashed in the street. Someone below shouted and pointed. Charles said, 'Speed would be ideal, here, I think.'

Sophie ran.

Music was not as easy to follow as she had imagined it would be; but surely, now, it was sharpening? It was coming from somewhere nearby. It was beautiful.

Then a voice, singing in French, was added to the music. Stars, Sophie told herself, do not sing, except in bad poetry; but, otherwise, she would have said the stars themselves were singing.

Sophie scrambled over the tip of a sloping roof, and stopped.

On the rooftop opposite, a single leap away, there was a woman. She sat with her back to Sophie. She sat on an upturned box, and she held the dark curve of a cello against her body.

Even in the dark, Sophie could see that the woman had hair the colour of lightning.

31

Sophie felt her heart physically shiver. 'Charles!' she cried. Her voice came out cracked and unfamiliar. She sounded starved. 'Charles! Is it her? Is that her?'

What if it wasn't her, she thought. She felt sick. What if it was?

'Go on, Sophie.' Charles pushed her forward, very gently. 'Carefully. Mind how you jump. We'll wait here.'

Sophie jumped. Her left knee cracked against the tiles as she landed, and a rivulet of blood ran ankle-wards. She ignored it.

She realised she hadn't thought about what she would say. She had never got further than this in her imagination; but she would have to say something. What did you say? 'Good evening'? 'I love you'? 'What excellent weather'?

She need not have worried. The years of living with Charles meant Sophie stood upright as a weathervane and courteous as a cat as she walked towards the back of the cello player.

Sophie said, 'Excuse me?'

The playing continued. Sophie stepped a pace closer, and laid on trembling finger on the woman's arm. 'Excuse me,' said Sophie. 'Excuse me? *Bonsoir?* Excuse me.'

The playing stopped. The woman turned round.

Sophie said, 'Hello.' She swallowed. 'I'm . . . I'm hunting. I'm mother-hunting. I think you might be the thing I've been looking for.'

The moon shone down on them. The woman's eyes and nose and lips were Sophie's eyes and nose and lips. She smelt of resin, and roses. She had the sort of face, Sophie thought, that looked as if it had been around the world two dozen times. Her eyes were a colour that you do not expect to see outside of dreams.

Charles watched from the opposite rooftop. He saw the woman cry out; and then bend, and stare. He saw her kiss Sophie's ears and eyes and forehead; and then he saw the woman swing Sophie into her arms, and spin round and round until they looked less like two strangers and more like one single laughing body.

Charles squatted down against the chimney pots. 'Sit, Matteo.' He patted the rooftop beside him, and fished in his pocket for his pipe. It took two attempts to light – the first match was extinguished by the tears inexplicably running down his nose.

'Sit, come. Here, next to me. Have a puff of pipe. No? Let's leave them, for a little while.'

The music must have stopped, Charles knew, because the cello was lying on the rooftop, forgotten; but there seemed to be music still playing, somewhere, faster and faster, double-time.

Daughters *of* Jerusalem

CHARLOTTE MENDELSON was born in 1972 and grew up in Oxford. Her first short story was published in *New Writing 7* and broadcast on Radio 4. *Daughters of Jerusalem* is her second novel, following *Love in Idleness*. She lives in London with her family.

Also by Charlotte Mendelson

Love in Idleness

Charlotte Mendelson

Daughters *of* Jerusalem

PICADOR

First published 2003 by Picador

This paperback edition published 2004 by Picador
an imprint of Pan Macmillan Ltd
Pan Macmillan, 20 New Wharf Road, London NI 9RR
Basingstoke and Oxford
Associated companies throughout the world
www.panmacmillan.com

ISBN 0 330 48278 5

5 7 9 8 6

A CIP catalogue record for this book is available from
the British Library.

Typeset by Intype London Ltd
Printed and bound in Great Britain by
Mackays of Chatham plc, Chatham, Kent

For Joanna

and for Max, Kati and Rachel

with love

Acknowledgements

I am extremely grateful to both
the New London Arts London Writers' Award scheme
and the Kathleen Blundell Trustees,
whose generosity helped me to complete this novel.

Thanks also to:

Carol Ann Duffy and Anvil Press Poetry for kind permission
to use an extract from 'Oppenheim's Cup and Saucer'
(*Standing Female Nude*, 1985)

Maria Rejt, Stephanie Cabot, Candice Voysey, Kate Saunders,
Sarah Turner, Lucy Hale and the sales team

Theodore Mendelson

and Joanna Briscoe, whose book this is.

King Solomon made himself a chariot of the wood of Lebanon. He made the pillars thereof of silver, the bottom thereof of gold, the covering of it of purple, the midst thereof being paved with love, for the daughters of Jerusalem.

The Song of Songs, 3:10

Prologue
October 1979

NOUGHTH WEEK

A children's tea party in the land that style forgot. One small pink-cheeked boy, white old-man's braces over the top of his padded navy jacket, is laboriously spreading cream cheese on wholemeal bread. Another, in a mis-toggled duffel coat and, unmistakably, pyjamas, is building a scale model of a Roman catapult on a pile of monochrome periodicals, with matchsticks for timbers and a half-sucked Polish liqueur chocolate for the stone. In the corner a tiny child of indeterminate sex is reading *Asterix*, in French, back-to-front. It has mistaken it for Hebrew, a scholarly language which every child should know. Underneath the table, eight little girls in party-corduroy and smocking are giggling under a purple towel, entirely invisible, if only to each other. And in the doorway, the sister of the most giggly and sugar-glutted girl, her private counting games forgotten, is watching them silently though a bright cold tunnel of envy, her body as still as a sentry's, her mind a frosted bowl.

Where are the adults? Behind the standing girl, in the kitchen. Five women are drinking coffee and looking for a place to hide their own inedible chocolates. Four men are on their knees on the cold flagstones, playing an ancient word-game in the dead languages of their choice.

'Victor,' says the Bannett Professor of Morbid Anatomy, who has something sticky, like honey, all up his sleeve, 'I can't believe you thought we wouldn't notice. It's only a diphthong in Hittite, as well you know.'

'Hrm,' growls Victor, a black-haired stooping wolfhound of a man. He lowers his white-seeded eyebrows and frowns at his young wife, less unkempt than the other women, who is washing chocolate off their hostess's milk-jug. Jean knows no Hittite; that is not her place. Although she can feel his glower against the back of her blouse, she keeps her eyes on the stained sink, and the apple-cake beside it.

Too irritated to persist with this manly gamesmanship, Victor mumbles an excuse and, wiping his hands on his old grey jacket, rises to his feet. It takes some time. Eventually, scratching the skin between his fingers, he turns and sees his elder daughter in the doorway, staring into the other room. She is dark-haired, pale-eyed, fierce-looking: an unfortunate combination of her parents' genes.

His head is uncomfortably inclined beneath a beam. 'Eve,' he says irritably, 'come here. You can learn from this.'

Reluctantly, still luxuriating in hatred, she turns. Her pinafore dress is too tight across her shoulders, her nine-year-old thighs hot and prickly in her eight-year-old's tights. 'Mum?' she says. 'Are we . . . can we . . .'

Her mother, preparing her expression – tolerant, calm – finishes drying the jug, wipes her hands, glances at her new chestnut-coloured knee-boots, breathes in, looks up, and at Eve's sullen, plucking face she feels her smile fade.

'Mum?' she says. There is chocolate on her chin.

'Later, love. Soon. Ask your . . . Victor, didn't you want her for something?'

Victor, with an air of hermit-like patience, has been watching the men's game from above. 'Gerundive, surely,' he says, and then remembers his daughter. 'Come on then. Stand here, where you can watch them.'

There is a thin black shelf running along the wall of this semi-country kitchen, above the fireplace. It matches the beams exactly and, like her father, Eve must bend her head slightly to fit beneath it. She is not particularly tall for her age but, with this baby beam, and the babies playing under the table, she feels like a giant.

'*Dimitos*,' says the Junior Dean, Potson, whose hair is too long and trousers too short and who wears, whenever possible, a monk's habit instead of normal clothes.

'*Mugga*,' says a thin man from America, almost as tall as Eve's father.

'Query?' says Eve's father. He stares at the thin man for a long time; he doesn't seem to realize he's being rude.

The thin man's sharp smile does not wobble. 'Old Norse. Muggy,' he says eventually, sitting back on his heels.

Eve's father narrows his eyes. She must distract him, or he will grow crosser, like water boiling, and when eventually they force her giggling sister from under the table and into the car, their journey home, which could be full of night and adult conversation and the strangeness of the fields, will be a long angry rant, and her sister will insist on resting her tickly Rapunzel hair against Eve's knees, and Eve will be unable not to pinch her, and it will all be black.

The other mothers are talking as if they're friends, which they aren't. Her mother is fatter and prettier than any of them, particularly the one she is with now, who is tall and unfamiliar in awful clothes: the mother of the Roman-catapult boy. She looks like a Roman herself, thinks Eve, but she has, at least, made Eve's mother laugh by hiding her chocolate in a boot by the door, and has smiled at Eve and shown her a woodlouse which Eve, unfortunately, squashed. Eve is not in the mood to be charmed. Her mother is laughing again, although she said all week she was dreading this party. Are they talking about her? Eve concentrates on the game and tries to feel her brain work. Her brown fingers pull at the stitching on her collar.

'*Sula.*'

Her father's eyebrows are a question-mark.

'Gannet.'

'For God's sake.'

'Daddy—' she begins, ducking her head out from below the shelf and, with a terrible crash, like the end of the world with her in it, something smashes all over the tiles at her feet.

The air goes thick. The room is still. She has the attention of every adult. Confused, she smiles, and sees they are waiting for her to speak.

'I – what?' Her lips feel like wood. 'I didn't—' she begins, because it seems expected, although she knows, for certain, that it was nothing to do with her.

There is a horrible pause before everyone leaps into life, like statues animated: green and brown and hands and trousers speeded up, as if seen from a roundabout, and the china that broke, splinters of icing and dark red glaze, is piled carefully on the kitchen table. It had been a plate, someone says, and Eve's mother is repeating, 'I'm so sorry, I'm so, so sorry,' and all Eve can think is: how strange. She is sure she'd have seen the plate if it had been on the shelf above her; besides, how could she have smashed it with just a turn of the head? It cannot have been her; they are all terribly mistaken.

However, there is now a frenzy of clearing-up and comfort, and she realizes, from the way that no one looks at her, that the plate was precious and everyone thinks she broke it: the most precious thing in the house.

'It wasn't my fault!' she says again, more urgently, but fat tears are running down the birthday girl's mother's cheeks, and although she smiles bravely at Eve it is obvious she blames her. 'It really wasn't. It wasn't *there*—'

'Never mind,' she says, and now Eve is forgiven it is too late to explain, although she will keep on explaining it in her head, for days and decades later, the frozen horror undiminished, forever hoping her certainty was not misplaced. In the meantime, however, until her mother decides they can leave, she wedges herself into the small chair by the doorway, picking red-facedly at a stick for the fire and listening, over the sound of sweeping and small-talk, to Phoebe, her sister, under the table, who will have heard what happened, who will glow beside it, who is laughing, blameless and free from it all.

Later, driving back into Oxford in the world's oldest Volvo, Eve listens. Her parents have not mentioned the plate, to her or to each other, which makes it worse. She still cannot see how she could have done it. However, as they all said goodbye in the cramped dark hallway, sidestepping newspaper bales and child-high towers of books, there was a rustle of frost in the air, and she knows that her mother and father hold her responsible.

The car slides, smooth as a boat, down the road into town. Phoebe has claimed exhaustion, as she always does, and is now lying across Eve's lap, chattering herself to sleep. Although her soft fair hair cannot penetrate the diamond holes of Eve's tights, even the idea of its tickliness is an outrage. Her hot head rolls heavily against Eve's thighs, pinning her to the seat. To calm herself, Eve draws magical patterns in the steam inside the glass and waits for a natural pause in the conversation. She has a plan.

'I don't think she saw him,' her mother is saying. In the multicoloured darkness her bob shines silver as armour, or a beacon blazing for Phoebe. The back of her father's neck, a good head taller than her mother's, shows where he needs a haircut; wispy fluff-prongs are heading into his collar. From behind they look older. When Eve has lived her life only two more times, he may be dead. She begins to stretch out a finger towards his secret grey hair.

'That is ridiculous,' he tells her mother. 'Of course she did. A, she is not an idiot and, B, she knows about it. However, were you to have said—'

'But his hand . . .'

There is a pause. Eve's eardrums shimmer with the effort of waiting. '*Cave puellam*,' her father says.

Latin is a flag, and a screen. She will have to master it in private, better than her mother, better even than her father, and find out all their secrets for herself. Which reminds her of her other, much more exciting, plan.

Her sister has recently learned to swim. Her splashy flurries across the pool amaze and delight their mother and, when captured and brought there, their father too. Eve can swim, just about, and recently passed some exams for a school, Oxford Girls' ('And so she should,' her father said gruffly, as she stood on the step and received his embrace), and has done Grade 1 piano and has a chemistry set. But now she has run out of things to do. The pool's chlorine fug, the tough children with cold sores and shiny tracksuits, alarm her. She waits by the glass while her mother, at the baby pool's hot and stinking edge, encourages her sister with smiles and waves and looks of love. Eve stares at the deepest point of the deep end and thinks of ways to win her mother's heart.

She has thought of one, but it may not work. Her father, who should approve, isn't exactly easy to please, although somehow Phoebe always manages. Their mother is softer, but somehow Eve fears she won't be pleased either, for reasons which elude her. She needs something guaranteed to charm them both, at the entertaining, athletic level Phoebe has claimed as her own, but she cannot imagine what it might be (Eve, an eyesore in a leotard, falls off the horse in a gym display; Eve, stained, presents her parents with a dollop of khaki papier mâché)—

'Did you see Phoeb's onslaught on the chocolate cake?' her father murmurs. He seems to be growing happier with every minute they put between them and that cold house. 'Went right past all those bloody flapjacks and stuck her hand in. Under everyone's nose. Hilarious.'

'I did,' says Phoebe, conveniently awake. 'And scoffed it all.'

'Not all,' their mother reprimands, gently. 'I saw you leave a little tiny bit . . .'

'Well, I wasn't going to eat those pesky nut things. Or the cucumber. I had to zoom.'

'Zoom!' says their father delightedly. 'Zoom! Precisely.'

'Dad,' says Eve. The time has come. 'Dad. Um. Listen. Will you, will you teach me Greek?'

The car is silent. Eve holds her breath as, simultaneously, her mother turns in her seat and Phoebe rotates her silky head to look at her: Phoebe amused; her mother not.

'Well,' says her father. He changes gear with a grinding scrape. Eve wishes she could wind the moment back on a great spool. She doesn't care about Greek, barely knows what Greek is. It had just seemed the sort of thing she ought to do.

'Or . . . maybe – I—' she begins, with a mouth full of sand.

Her mother turns back and, it seems, although the car is dark, minutely shakes her head. Phoebe sits up, pretends to stick her finger down her throat, and starts picking again at the rubbery ribbon between the window and the door.

'Well,' her father says, and something unexpected but longed-for is curling at the edges of his voice, 'that is not an entirely bad idea. Perhaps we might try it. I shall pay a visit to Blackwell's tomorrow. No, Jean?'

Eve smiles, feeling at this moment that, at the end of the journey, she might be sweet and sleepy and light enough for her father to carry her in under the stars, her mother dazed with love, Phoebe locked safely in the car. Then she hears a sigh, and her mother's voice.

'Well, I wouldn't have thought . . .' she says, doubtfully. 'It's really not something I know about.' She looks out of the window. 'If she thinks she'll have time with the music and the extra drama, I suppose . . . will they have books for young ones, even?'

'Probably. This is Oxford, after all,' says Eve's father.

'Well, try if you want,' says her mother, with that same crushingly doubtful tone, and then her voice goes bright and strengthening, for Phoebe. 'Why not? And while they're at it, sweetheart, let's go to the pool again, shall we? I *know* you could do ten metres; you'd get that lovely badge with the dolphin. It might even be worth a new swimming costume. Let's give it a try.'

The light goes out. Eve can feel Phoebe staring and staring, until she is forced to turn. Her sister's smile catches a flash of streetlight; shining eyes and sharp white teeth. Triumph – they both know it. Eve looks away.

Part One
Michaelmas Term
October 1986

First Week

All grown up. It is autumn, a bright blue day, filled with the rustle of turning leaves and bells everywhere, like beautiful moans. Jean Lux pedals slowly, as if in pain, cool air snapping at the open neck of her shirt. She is wearing rather a flattering knitted garment, like a stylish tank-top, if such a thing exists, and as she cycles she wonders whether the women she passes take her for someone quite different: more angular, more upright, a wife like other wives.

This afternoon, instead of going straight back, she cycled to the Iranian shop on Aristotle Lane for bread, and then took the longest possible route home. However, the cobwebs in her mind will not be shifted. It has been a long slow Archive afternoon. Jean's current purpose is to transcribe, with infinite care and boredom, the details of every book and object in St Thomas's collection into an enormous leather-bound book whose predecessor, since a recent and barely-wanted benefaction, is now too small. Jean suspects that there are mechanical alternatives: computers, or perhaps a device to photograph the existing pages. However, Hedley, her chief curator, is too full of self-advancement to care. Besides, suggesting it might deprive Jean of her job.

She has, therefore, spent her day on a translation, with difficulty, of several entries in Italian; a small disagreement with Hedley over his use of her Anglepoise; and a description of thirty-one grainy photographs of the excavations at Aleppi which the recent benefactor, a Rhodes Scholar with secrets, had felt should be preserved.

Now, as she cycles, she tries to feel the potential in her soft muscles; just as, at the end of every Archive day, she gently stretches at the edges of her mind, pretending she is merely waiting for something a little more taxing, a little – well, worthier.

This last, however, is not a thought she usually allows herself. She puts the fingers of her right hand on the hot skin below her throat – while still steering, inexpertly, with her left – as if to remind herself who she is. Think of small things, she tells herself.

– Tomorrow she will have lunch in college with her dearest friend.

– Her father is still taking his pills; her bicycle mudguard appears to have self-mended.

– Against this bright blue sky, the pale precision of the spires and domes and turrets does still sharpen her mind, even after all these years.

– From the window of the Cupboard, the archivists' office, this afternoon, she watched a college mason carving a replacement section of scrolling across the quadrangle. She has seen the back of this mason before, to whom she is as nameless as cobblestones or trees, and something about the swing of that fat-headed mallet, the soothing tap-tapping and the hot live smell of stone-dust moved her. She watched the jump and stretch of cottoned muscle as

16

if in a trance. It was some time before she noticed that this mason was a woman.

- Victor, provided none of the new undergraduate intake proves deranged, and he manages to stay off the Accommodation Committee subgroup (B: curtains), which will be decided in this, the first week of the term and academic year – the date every don's wife dreads – is moderately cheerful, for Victor.
- And best of all, most alarmingly of all, tonight is the night that her small plans begin.

She has realized that she does, quite simply, nothing for herself and, beginning this evening, she has decided that this must change. Money and time permitting, she will, occasionally, indulge herself. She is going to live. She tightens her soft fists around the handlebars. Whatever they say, she will be ready.

For Jean has had enough. Not of her marriage, although she knows other women would baulk at the challenge that is Victor: keeping him presentable, excusing his social idiosyncrasies, hardest of all, protecting his huge but fragile ego from enemies, without and within. Nor of her job, despite the hot afternoons in the Cupboard, surrounded by learned papers and the slow death of flies, which fill her with schoolgirl torpor. Nor of her body, slow-moving and suddenly-ageing as it is, nor her shabby house, nor, for the sake of argument, her daughters.

No, she thinks, decelerating still further while a stooping old man, flat-shouldered as a cow, mumblingly crosses the road, she is sick of *this* – the sooty castles of the Banbury Road, filled with departments of Old German, Philology and Chinese Art, the stringy-haired pedalling mothers like moulting hens on wheels, the damp, the incessant sound of violin practice, the querulous old men and twitching young men, the tourist crush . . . all of this. She is sick of the fact that every dowdy woman or soiled geriatric she passes is *not* her equal, but is likely to be one of the world's cleverest people: a Nobel Laureate, a pioneering biochemist, the head of a college whose furniture is five centuries old. She is sick of navy-blue corduroy, Gothic arches, famous fig-trees, shabby dons' wives, cellars, rivers, genius children, stuttering and gold leaf. It is *your* fault, she thinks, approaching her husband's college, as she glimpses her neighbour, an entirely silent botanist, attempting to untangle his own beard from a hawthorn tree. None of you are normal. *Is* normal. And I am.

She streams angrily across several lanes of traffic and freewheels into the cobbled cyclists' entrance of St James's College, smiling politely at Arthur, the retired University Marshal (MA status) and now gate-porter, as he clicks open the turnstile to let her pass. Arthur, who is scowling at the unseemly rattling made by her mudguard, barely acknowledges her. Then, because cycling within the bounds is forbidden by the college statutes, even to her, a thirty-nine-year-old, she wheels her bicycle dutifully towards a little row of Victorian dons' families' houses which lie under the cold concrete shadow of the Sir David Milthrop Building, and up the path to the last, or first.

Behind the side gate, her elder daughter's bicycle is waiting. She has, Jean notices, helped herself to two of her sister's star-stickers and put them, slightly askew, on her handlebars. Phoebe will be upset: she may not have enough to cover her frame, as discussed at breakfast this morning.

Jean will give her money to buy some more – later, after her announcement.

The house smells of caraway. One of Victor's occasional angry bouts of cooking elapsed last night. She takes a package of frankfurters from her bag: Phoebe is eating little else this week.

'I'm home,' she shouts. 'Is anyone here?'

There is a tiny knowing resentful pause. Then Eve's voice: 'I am,' from the kitchen.

'No sign of your sister?' calls Jean. She is becoming nervous; her breathing is quick and tight. She must not stumble. She will be resolute.

Another pause. Mute accusation is filling the hallway like poisoned gas. Jean Lux, of all people, who tried so hard, has produced a difficult, grudge-bearing daughter. She tries to think of an excuse not to go downstairs.

'Not as far as I know,' Eve answers.

Jean sighs, practises a smile, takes off her bicycle clips, smoothes her hair. She is already so unnecessarily excited, so tense, that she may blurt out her plans prematurely, and endanger them. I am capable of handling this well, she tells herself. I am a youngish woman, although my name and body and daughters and husband all make me feel old, and I do have my own mind, of sorts. No one, least of all a sixteen-year-old, should make me doubt that. She hangs her bag over the newel post, on top of Eve's. Then, her smile already fallen, she descends.

It happens later that evening. Phoebe, inevitably late for dinner, is entertaining her parents with tales from school.

Thanks to her father's college, which owns much of that part of North Oxford, she attends the Gate, where children learn grammar in second-hand corduroy bomber jackets, where independence and knitting are prized, where sports day takes place largely in and on the River Cherwell. Phoebe is describing today's swimming lesson, in which a student teacher was led to believe that the whole of Phoebe's class had drowned. Eve keeps her face closed.

'So I stood on the bank,' Phoebe says, 'and pointed down the river, and because I couldn't remember the *name* of the bit they were hiding in, I sounded even more hysterical, and by then he had *hitched* up his dress—'

'His dress?' asks their mother, plainly loving it. They can't get enough of this, the frisson provided by their thirteen-year-old ringmaster. Phoebe is all schoolgirlish semi-innocence: a few peppery freckles, big narrow eyes, thick dirty-gold plait. Her family's gene-pool has taken sides: their mother's pink-and-white lost prettiness, their father's dark scowl, have produced one honey-skinned greenish-eyed beauty, and one who is beige, the colour of undrinkably milky coffee, with biblically black ungovernable hair and brows and an expression people look away from.

'Oh,' smirks Phoebe. Even the kitchen conspires in her favour: all that pine makes Eve look jaundiced, but it suits her sister. 'Didn't I say? He's a vicar, or something. And there's pondweed all over his skirty bits, and he's crying, or maybe that's water . . .'

The parents lean forward. It's in her eyes, thinks Eve: the way they look as if she's only just woken, which makes them narrower, but probably sexier, which is worse. And, of course, Phoebe doesn't have to wear glasses whenever she reads, or writes – which, if you're Eve, is most of the time.

She looks at their mother, who smiles at her; but by now Eve is too irritated to join in. 'Get on with it,' she says impatiently, although she hadn't meant to speak at all.

'I *am*,' Phoebe says, hands in pockets, leaning back in her chair. No one will dare to tell her to stop.

'Do you want some more orange juice?' asks their mother. 'You should, for your cold. Eve, not all of it. Save some for your sister.'

'Anyway,' says Phoebe, downing her third glass. 'And I realize a bit more is needed, so I sort of do a little sob, and stumble back against this tree trunk, sort of weakly pointing where I think the others have gone, and he looks at me, and—'

The parents are by now virtually on her lap.

'He turns—'

Saps.

'And wades right into the river!'

Eve watches as Phoebe triumphantly surveys her audience. Her father is giggling helplessly; her mother, the representative of sense, is trying to look horrified, but she's half laughing as she clears their plates, helped by Eve. Phoebe crashes her chair forward against the table to pour more orange juice, and a purple cigarette-lighter drops out of her cuff on to the butter dish. Her mouth forms a tight O, as in O Fuck, but neither parent has noticed. There is now a sloping crater in the butter.

For Phoebe, Eve knows, fear is exciting, not the miserable paralysis it is for her. She only understood this a couple of months ago. She had accompanied her father into the soft summer darkness at the end of the garden; although it was after ten he had wanted to repot the mint and explain historical determinism, and she could not refuse him. As they approached the shed, Eve saw Phoebe, wide-eyed and grinning, standing by the compost heap with something held between her teeth. Eve, moved to solidarity, smiled back before realizing that her sister's mouth contained a lit fag-end, pointing inwards. Their father, to Eve's many-layered shame, began reciting something in Latin, a metre from where Phoebe stood, and got up to leave: the mint was dead. Eve, although seized by the desire to expose her – didn't she know smoking was *dangerous*? – merely nodded and followed him back in, leaving her sister, still grinning, in her own starry universe.

Now Phoebe grabs the greasy lighter and hides it under the table. She takes a knife, sweeps it across the butter, and spreads it on to her potato. Then, her face relaxing, she looks up and finds that her sister is staring at her.

'What?'

'Nothing,' says Eve. Like cats restaking their territory, the girls turn away, then back. Phoebe lifts her chin and fixes her with her gooseberry eyes. Eve meets her stare, and quickly begins to buckle. Phoebe holds it, holds it, until Eve looks away.

'And then what happened?' asks their mother.

Phoebe begins to describes the student teacher's pale panic and gradual realization of the truth, but Eve is no longer listening. She is feeling sick, again. For weeks, ever since the sixth form began, she has felt like a squirming girl-shaped sack of nerves, and the more she tries to calm herself down the worse it becomes. Her father is no use; to him, once a child refugee, A levels are nothing. He won a scholarship to Oxford just after the war, practically an orphan and the family's sole provider, and English hadn't even been his first language – not even his third. Her mother, whenever Eve dares to mention her exams – much less often than she would like – simply repeats: 'Well, I'm sure you'll get by.'

This infuriates Eve, because getting by is not the point. It's what happened with her O levels, as she keeps trying to explain: only A-grades count, and some girls, including most of her friends, got ten or eleven, not to mention the odd one from the year before. This year she will be constantly assessed; next year is Oxbridge and the A levels themselves, and in all of these she will be tested and found lacking. The thought makes her shivery with fear, as if acid is shifting in her stomach, as if ice scrabbles at the roots of her hair. For Eve is going to fail her A levels: Cs and Ds if she is lucky. She is not her sister or her father: she is plain, and doomed.

Besides, her mother is making her nervous. She keeps offering things: more soup, more chicken, like a penitent. What is she trying to hide? Eve, unlike half her sister's friends, does not suspect herself of having psychic powers. However, she is sure that something is going on.

She looks at her father, but he will not meet her eye. This is normal; his mind is usually among the warring Picts, or guest rotas for his college's High Table, where the dons sit. Like him, she should be improving herself: practising on their borrowed piano, whose crazed keys she is afraid to touch, or working on her music theory, or trying to improve her back-hand in the lane, or teaching herself German. There is no end to the things she should be doing, but she feels too hot and heavy to move. She presses down on her forearm under the table and tries not to wince.

'Does anyone want an apple?' asks her mother, who seems to be trying through sheer nervousness to make her father look up. He is writing in his notebook, oblivious. What is wrong with her? Has there been, unprecedentedly, an exciting event at her work? Is she ill? 'Phoebe, have an apple,' she says, biting her thumbnail. 'Victor?'

She doesn't look ill, Eve decides. She's too plump; not quite officially fat, but her cheeks are, and her soft hands. She is still, Eve supposes, young for a mother, but her neck is beginning to crease in bands, like a tribal necklace, and her thick once-fair hair is greyish-mouse now, miles from Phoebe's. Yet her bright blue eyes and neat features save her. They make her prettier than Eve will ever be.

What would it be like, wonders Eve experimentally, if she *was* ill?

Her mother dries her hands, as if preparing for a fight.

'Victor,' she says, anxiously.

Eve sits up. Phoebe, who has begun surreptitiously drawing yin and yang signs in the margins of their father's untouched marking, puts down her turquoise rollerball and cocks her head. Only their father, in his smelliest jacket, is undisturbed. The cover of his notebook is grey and seamed, as if bound with elephant skin; he is humming as he writes. Does he usually hum?

'Victor,' says their mother. 'Victor!'

He looks up, frowning, as if twisting an eyepiece to reinclude the world.

'Mmhmm?'

'I . . .'

Each stare has a different texture: Phoebe's solid, like a frozen wave; their father's seething, too full of dark thoughts to focus; Eve's own a yellow sponge, waiting.

'I've decided . . .' their mother begins. She does up and undoes a shirt button, over and over again. 'I've decided—'

'Something, clearly,' says their father. 'Now what might it be?'

Eve watches her mother's resolve set, like blancmange. 'Well,' she says, abandoning the button. She puts the salad bowl back on the table. 'I've been thinking. You know I've been worrying about my aunt, aunt Rose, in France, and feeling I should visit before — Victor? I did say.'

'That may be,' says Eve's father. He has, however, put his notebook down.

'Well, now term's begun, and you and, um, Eve are settled in, I thought . . . it was so wonderful how well Phoebe did with the magazine—'

Eve prepares to snort scornfully – her sister took two blurry photographs, and her parents are still stupid with pride – but their mother silences her with a look. Her arms are crossed. She waits, growing hotter. In a small part of her brain she has known, from the moment she noticed their mother's nervousness, that this is about Phoebe.

Phoebe's lids are low, like a sleepy lizard's.

'—and so I thought perhaps, as a reward, and to, well, you know, inspire her, I could . . . Eve went there on her French exchange, but Phoebe hasn't . . . so . . . oh, and of course Phoebe's still doing French, aren't you Phe, unlike Eve, so, so—'

She gives Eve a quick guilty look, biting her lip. Eve lifts her face, but their mother has glanced at Phoebe, whose hands are clasped in expectation. It strengthens her – Eve can see it. 'So,' she says in a rush, 'I thought I could take her with me.'

Eve's mouth opens. Her body seems to have congealed. Slowly, the table swims into life: Victor, tapping his ear with his pencil; Phoebe, eyes wide in an exaggeration of happiness, lifting her arms and clattering towards their mother; their mother herself, looking pleased and astonished, trying to answer her husband and receive embraces and avoid Eve's eye and bask in her courage all at once.

'Just a few days,' her mother is saying. 'For my birthday – or you could call it a very early fortieth. We'll go by ferry, and I'll use all the rest of my money and, maybe—' she says, looking at Eve, who ignores her, 'maybe we could all go together another time? Victor, please?'

Victor is scowling, but it is the kind of scowl that is longing to yield. His primary emotion, the one he is allowing himself to feel, is relief that he will be staying at home with his books, aunt-free, not shopping. He is, moreover, secretly charmed by the thought of his wife and younger daughter, girlishly among the boulevards together.

Then he looks at the other one. She is picking at something invisible on the table. A dark eye of tears has already splashed the pale wood.

'Hmm,' he says, as loudly as possible. She looks up, flushed with self-pity: never Eve at her best.

'Hmm,' he says again. The other two, the ones going to Paris, are locked in a cooing knot of exclamation and self-delight. He thinks of Jean's mother's money: a poor woman, she died with nearly a thousand pounds wrapped in a kitchen towel underneath her bed. In wobbly ink on the kitchen towel was: 'Jean's, for when she needs it.' Victor knows what this means; it means: 'for when she needs to escape'.

They cannot spare what remains of this money, but to say so, to prevent the trip, would be precisely what his mother-in-law would have expected of him, the man who stole her fair pale daughter. He will say nothing to Jean. They will manage somehow.

'Well, Evie,' he says shortly. 'Not much call for us, it seems.'

She shakes her head, wipes her nose with a knuckle. It leaves an unattractive sheen on the back of her hand.

'You'll have to keep an eye on me,' he says. She gives a little smile, at last. The rejects of the family Lux have decided to stick together.

Twenty past twelve at St Thomas's. A little early, Jean Lux locks the inner door of the Cupboard and pulls out the name-plate to show she is absent. There is always the possibility that, for the first time in a decade, someone might come looking for her with an urgent enquiry. Then, rather more rapidly than usual, she winds her way down the steep wooden staircase into the quadrangle.

She fails, as usual, not to be flustered by the time she reaches the bottom; she smiles, as usual, at the unsmiling Crushard, who despite his bowler, girth and hypertension is as far from the ideal Head Porter – respectful, facilitating – as it is possible to be; and she is trapped, as usual, in the raging herd of youth charging up the steps into the college Hall for lunch, despite her efforts to thread obliquely through them. Then, a little breathless, she enters the Senior Common Room Pantry, where she, neither a don nor a student, is permitted to eat.

Not, she reminds herself, that there is anything wrong with the Panty, as her lunch-date has renamed it. It is round and barrel-vaulted and, because so much less grand than the Fellows' Luncheon Room, better suited to the odour of mashed potato that pervades them both. What's more, it attracts an interesting selection of fellow diners.

Here is Giuseppe Bowker, pale-eyed son of the famous Bowker and his unsuitable Neapolitan wife. Giuseppe's life is Imperial Latin – he was conceived, it is believed, solely to inherit his father's extraordinary library – but his heart is in the South. Perpetually haggard and haunted, his great brain is oppressed: not by the mysteries of Pliny's sources, but by whichever purring female scholar has currently enraptured him at one of the many conferences he attends in Italy, his mother land.

Here is Godric Nestor-Stears, as ever in his mackintosh, his leather satchel tight across his paunch like an ageing schoolboy, or a fisherman one might try to avoid. Nestor-Stears, like Jean, is attached to the college only by a fine thread of sinecure and patronage; his work is for the Oxford English Dictionary, but he does it here, in a courtesy room rumoured to contain a stuffed bear, live birds in cages, and every dictionary published since Dr Johnson's, or beyond.

'He could lend them to the Bodleian,' Jean once joked to a college acquaintance, knowing full well that the Bodleian neither lends or borrows.

'Return them, surely,' he replied.

Godric, however, can read thirty-four languages, so no one particularly minds. His file-stuffed bookshop carrier-bags – the Oxford briefcase – form a puddle around his chair. He takes a bite of kipper, puts down his fork, and twitches and nods for several fascinating seconds, until that particular tic has passed. Then he retrieves his fork and begins the process again. He also talks incessantly to himself, with disdainful shakes of the head and an air of smiling impatience, looks no one in the eye, and frequently consults a compass. Jean enjoys watching him most when a new servant faces him for the first time.

Beside him is Clive, almost too translucent with age to focus upon. Clive was once a Middle English Fellow, but his function now is to oversee the college gardens, where he is said to know the age and health of every plant. He is, it is believed, also the Head of something; a think-tank, perhaps, or a global charitable foundation, but he is considered too boring to ask.

Clive, Godric, Giuseppe; these are the Panty regulars. Like Giuseppe, she always chooses from the short menu, although without his air of strained enthusiasm. The other two invariably have the same: Godric, a kipper and white toast; Clive, vegetable soup. Jean does not know where these provisions come from and suspects that, were she too to request a kipper, or to demand an alternative of her own, Hever, the embarrassingly elderly Panty butler, would demand her removal.

As she waits, Jean decides that one day, perhaps, she will buy Phoebe a kipper. It contains oily somethings which might, she hopes, prove beneficial: restore the gleam to her daughter's hair, give her new energy. She does seem, these days, a little tired.

Still no sign. She looks pleasantly at Giuseppe, in whom disdain for greying Anglo-Saxon women, and awareness that even here he is out of his depth, merge in a daily nod of proud self-loathing. Discomfited, as ever, she looks away. Godric is patting his pancake fringe and searching for something anxiously in his satchel. Clive, who looks ever nearer death yet walks, it is said, ten miles a day around the Botanical Gardens, wavers a watery smile.

'I am dying, Oxford, dying,' runs unsummoned through her mind.

And then there is a rattle of footsteps over the floorboards, reverberating off the blackened panelling of the passage. Relief: Helena has arrived.

Jean's news is too exciting to contain; she can feel it bulging like a cartoon dog in a sack. She announces: 'I told them about France.' Far above her, Helena's eyes – or do they? it is all too quick to be sure – grow strangely bright.

Perhaps it is the angle. For, as soon as Helena has found a chair and arranged her Paraguayan bookbag and sea-green poncho and carrier-bags of papers and vegetables, and herself, upon it, and turned back to her friend, she looks perfectly normal, for Helena.

'Good Lord,' she says, and now she looks delighted (perhaps, after all, Jean imagined it). 'You brave thing. What was it like?'

Her tufty hair seems more grizzled with every meeting, the bridge of her Roman nose bonier, her height, if anything, a little more extreme, yet, thinks Jean, she is a marvel. Godric, Giuseppe, ignore her at your peril. She is more than you will ever be.

For Helena is famous. Her fine-lined pink-scrubbed pallor, her Woolfian shabbiness, her dreadful hair and unfortunate clothes make her indistinguishable from half of North Oxford's mothers, yet she knows so much about insects, about pupae and egg-sacs and the tiny chromosomal chances to which our futures are hostage, that foreign professors leave presents at her door, and undergraduates come from Boston and Dar es Salaam to be near her. Her second monograph, a masterpiece of apocalyptic Darwinism, still outsells most of her peers in twenty-three countries; her recent acclaimed lecture series is at the printers. She has toast-crumbs in the smocking of her Breton blouse.

She rubs her ear energetically with a dry bare hand. Since the death of Simon, her unexpectedly handsome husband, she wears her wedding-ring on the other side.

'Irish stew, please, Hever,' she tells him.

'And I think for me too, please, if you don't mind, Hever,' says Jean, smiling cravenly. She is afraid of Hever, and he knows it.

'So tell me,' Helena says, '*all* about it.'

Jean sighs, smiles, revelling briefly in the possession of her tale of heroism.

'Well . . .'

Her sole audience member looks alert and welcoming; the men at the far edge of the table twitch and mumble, oblivious. Suddenly she is afraid of telling her, as if by removing the coverings she will fatally aerate it, expose its many flaws, and leave a soft crust of dust in the place of her excitement. Be bold, she tells herself: remember, I can be bold.

The first time she met Helena she was bold, seven years ago. It had been Jean who had approached her, desperate for a diversion, and within ten minutes Helena had proved herself superior to everyone Jean knew. She saved her – not just from that party, but from a more frightening, slowly-creeping boredom. To whom else can she tell her achievements, however minor? Only Helena. So she begins.

Helena, under the table, is rolling and unrolling the hem of her long navy-blue blouse.

'Well, dear,' says Jean. 'Obviously, I was longing to say something and dreading it all evening. I mean, I know it's hardly a huge announcement, by normal standards.'

'No,' says Helena.

'But for me it is. It's so long since I made a plan for *myself*. It feels . . . like liberation, in a small way. Or the beginning of it. You know?'

'Well . . . yes. In theory.'

'So, I was trying to make dinner, do things to the chicken, find the peas, make Phoebe's frankfurters, and all the time my mind was completely elsewhere – there was nothing but *it*. You know.'

Helena nods; she knows.

'And then Phoebe was telling this very silly story—'

Helena lowers her eyes; she has her own view of Phoebe's stories, her dietary whims.

'—and Eve was baiting her, as she does – and you know everyone says it's water off a duck's back to her, at least Victor does, but I'm *sure* it hurts her, only she won't let it show. But I—'

Helena, as if for the first time, is noticing how a green pattern of tendrils overlays the blue of Jean's irises, like a snowflake. Nature's repetitions are a private thrill; she keeps them close, for moments of need. These moments, unfortunately, have become increasingly frequent.

'Helena, are you all right?'

She looks away. While hardly a believer in iridology, she fears that one day, one day soon, with a single attentive glance at her eyes, Jean will see the truth. For Helena has a secret, like a parasite, and her life is consumed by the effort of keeping it hidden. It must remain hidden.

'No, I'm jolly well actually,' she says cheerily, and to her surprise she does feel well, though her muscles are stretched tight. 'Go on.'

'So.' Jean begins uncertainly, but her story has wings. 'Victor was writing away in his notebook, leaving them to me – he's got stuck with this class on Pictish law, and you know he hates the Picts—'

Helena makes a noncommittal noise. She was brought up in drawing-rooms and, though now far from that world, she still excels at meaningless social lubricants.

'—so it was just me and the warring girls, beside whom the Picts were a peaceable nation, and of course all that's *why* I need to escape. So I just . . . well, burst forth.'

'Well *done*,' says Helena.

'As we planned, practically verbatim.'

'What did everyone say?'

'Well, Phe of course was wild, it was so sweet. She's the most rewarding creature to do things for. And Victor . . .'

'How *was* Victor? Do you think he minded, at all?'

'No – well, if he notices we've even gone, which is doubtful – no, he won't miss me. Why would he?'

Their food has arrived. 'Of course,' says Helena, with effort, filling their water-glasses so clumsily that a thin pool of water spreads over the tarry wood, seething into the knots and crevices. 'Of course he will.'

As a girl, on holiday in Scotland, she had once climbed to the top of a grey slide of choppy rocks, high above black water. Her many sisters had spent the day hiding her books and laughing, but now they were ignoring her, tanning themselves like seals in the weak northern sun. Helena, teeth gritted, thin arms goose-pimpled in her sagging bathing costume, had looked down on them over her shoulder and back at the waves. Then, without quite intending to, unexpectedly seized by a moment of grace, she had arched her back, lifted her arms and leapt into the sea.

Now, she tells herself. Do it. The water shivers over the table-top, trapped by its own invisible skin. Jean lifts her eyes and beams at her. No, not now.

'And Eve – Eve was Evelike. I mean, yes, it's disappointing for her, I suppose, but . . . actually, I . . . I've a confession to make.'

'Confession?' asks Helena dazedly, stepping back from the brink.

'It's, it's . . . I don't know. We seem to *anticipate* each other.'

'Who do?'

'Me and Eve,' says Jean, looking confused. 'Who did you think?'

'Sorry. Sorry. Go on.'

'It . . . I don't like myself, feeling this, let alone saying it, but . . . everything she says makes me . . . it makes me want to get in there first.'

'Oh,' says Helena. 'I see. I see what you mean. Do you find her . . . irritating?'

'To be honest . . .'

'Ah.'

'I . . . there's this defensive tone to her voice, but she makes *me* feel defensive, and protective, too, I suppose – well, of Phoebe . . . I feel watched by her, all the time. She's so . . . beady, somehow.'

'She's only sixteen.'

'I know. But you should see it. And the thing is, because they're so different I don't want Phoebe to feel . . . well, deflated . . .'

'No, you're right.'

'But Eve's relentless over-achievement . . . I mean, poor Phoebe, what with Eve's O levels being so, well, predictable, and this year of course the bloody A levels begin—'

'How many Os was it, in the end?'

'About a thousand.'

'And all As?'

'Mostly. Near enough. Same thing. So she's fine, she's got those to think about, but poor Phoebe – it's no fun for her being under that shadow. She needs something of her own. Besides, Eve has been to France already. And probably she wouldn't *want* to come with me. Not in the middle of term.'

'But you will take Phoebe?'

'Of course. It's only a few days.'

'When will you go?'

'By the end of the month; the weekend after next, if we can get a crossing. It'll mean the end of my mother's savings, but that way it really can be, you know, a proper little holiday, not a spread-out family thing. I don't know why Eve always feels so hard done by – I did explain it . . . Well, never mind. I can't not live because of her. We'll have a lovely time.'

'You will,' says Helena, trying to sound glad, and failing.

Second Week

Victor is writing letters. His hair, which ordinarily lies flattish, is almost vertical with worried sweeps of his hand, and traces of the lemon pudding he had for lunch. He scratches at his knee and growls to himself. This is not going well.

Four weeks ago Henry Glover, his close colleague and, relatively, friend, suffered a stroke during Evensong. He is not going to teach again. Victor has visited him at home in St Bartlemas, awkwardly holding a bunch of marigolds and unable to tear his eyes from the missed patches of silver stubble, the soft feminine wattles, of his once invulnerable-seeming fellow tutor's neck.

Self-interest, however, wonderfully concentrates the mind. Even as he mumbled goodbye to Ursula Glover at the door, he was deciding to whom to write. He will suggest Lewis Depuise, a former student, for the vacant fellowship: a fair scholar, and someone Victor could bear to see around the place, if pushed.

When he, Victor, was relatively young, an older tutor gave him a similar opportunity – to write an essay for a book on slavery. Victor had seized the chance. He laboured for one extraordinary, exhausting night, and at the end of it had produced a jewel: On the Usefulness of Slaves to Democracies. It spanned Ancient Greece to 1930s Germany and was dedicated to his mother – who as a slave had survived the death camps where her parents and brothers and sisters and husband and elder son were murdered, democratically. The essay was both lauded and vilified. It won him a post coveted by his rival, a little gratifying notoriety, some gloriously well-attended lectures and, ultimately, a wife. While his subsequent career has been rather less fêted, gratitude, superstition and, chiefly, guilt, make him feel the kindness must be repaid.

However, Lewis has never covered the period 300–1200, leaving Victor solely responsible for the first section of the Modern era, and a great deal happened in those 900 years. The very thought of teaching elementary Byzantine schisms to spotty and ungracious youths, and girls, leaves Victor exhausted. What is more, it means his interesting work on Ostrogothic law will remain incomplete for years to come.

He has, however, no choice. The alternatives to Lewis Depuise are too dreadful to consider: one, in particular. Last week, processing towards High Table a little behind the Junior Dean, who is not known for tact (or, indeed, much else), he thought he heard that one person's name mentioned. He stumbled – the passage seemed to go black – and found himself standing stock still in the middle of the stairs, skin chilled, as if a ghost had reared out of the rib-vaulting at him alone. He forced himself to continue into Hall, his mind shut in on itself like an empty box but, despite discreet enquiries, he could discover nothing further. He has not heard that name again. There is no reason for concern, he tells himself. He will concentrate instead on the election of Lewis Depuise. So.

Victor has written to everyone he can think of, but

something, he senses, is still lacking. He is not a great recommender; he knows that his references may sound a little dry, particularly to those who favour rowing and leadership skills. What is more, which makes his task even more difficult, whoever wins the post will become his rival in one critical respect. The Sir Henry Spenser Memorial Lecture, which has been given every ten years since 1627, will take place this Trinity term, on or around the sixteenth of May. To be asked to give the Spenser Lecture is an honour most historians would kill for – and, in the eighteenth century, reputedly did. It has gone to scholars as far afield as Bombay, St Petersburg and Cambridge, but never in living memory to someone from Victor's college, where it is endowed. Now, however, as every half-century, it is the turn of a historian from one of four named Oxford colleges, including Victor's own. Victor has published virtually nothing, does not attend avoidable dinners, has never complimented professors on their work, or ties, or wives. He is, however, at the age where honours are to be expected. Moreover, the endowment specifies 'a goode man', in the sense of well-reputed, morally upstanding, scandal-free. He is, at least, the latter. It is not unreasonable to suppose that his time may have come.

He looks out of the window, at the great horse-chestnut tree at the edge of the quad. Tendrils of ivy like tiny tongues are beginning once more to ease between the stone windowsill and the leading. He has a scout, Kenneth, who does not clean his rooms like other scouts but merely hides essential items and empties the waste-paper baskets. He will ask Kenneth to see to it.

Today the percussion in his left ear is infernal, as if an undergraduate has left a radio under a chair. He even looked for it, half-heartedly, and now he feels foolish. You are, he tells himself, a fearful old man.

In the red and gold reflection of his room in the glass, he imagines a sleek dark cow-lick, a thin self-satisfied hateful face. Behind his shoulder, where nothing should be, he seems to see Raymond Snow, currently Lecturer in Medieval Studies at Liverpool, his erstwhile contemporary and greatest foe, bare his small white teeth and smile at him.

The house is empty. Eve hates coming home to nothing; she worries in the gaps.

'Hello?' she calls, in case her father has forgotten his gown, or her mother is working, guilty and greedily, at home, or her sister is here with her alarming friends, boasting about Paris. Eve has had wonderful dreams of knives and soft revenge. She hitches up her enormous book-bag and puts down her clarinet. The house holds itself open at her voice: silence. She descends through cold October light to the kitchen.

Down here, as below deck – the garden a strip of brown leaves, the shadow of St James's invisible – the outside world ceases to exist. Their kitchen smells of water: cold plaster and a tap which Phoebe insists on leaving dripping – she pretends it's too stiff for her hands. Eve goes to turn it off, hesitates, turns it off anyway. She slides a knife through a waxy shank of cheese, makes tea, drops a dried apricot, kicks it under the oven, fishes it out, reads a letter from Jericho Cycles ('Were we to order the part in question, it would take over a month; this bell was made in Sweden and is no longer in stock. May we suggest the Dupree? A reasonable bell, audible but not intrusive, price £1.29 (less college discount @ 20% = £1.03)'), thinks of the rumoured arms factory behind the cycle shop, thinks of guard-dogs, sits down.

She feels pent-up and irritable. Everything reminds her of Paris. She should begin her homework, but it stretches far above her, a looming tangle of verbs and homonyms and syntax she will never, ever, be able to climb. Her stupidity disgusts her. She stands up straight against the wall, navy blue against the whitewash, and gently beats her head against the brick.

Where *is* everybody?

She could go for a walk, but the University Parks will be full of rebels smoking under the trees, making her feel self-conscious and alarmed. She could read, but she is hating *The Brothers Karamazov* and hasn't the heart for anything new. She could have a friend round to discuss teachers' husbands, and who, if they ever get round to it, they might eventually kiss. However, there is so much she can't talk about, all the shameful details of Lux-hood and Eve-hood, that she is beginning to find that being with friends makes it worse. Besides, she is heartsick.

I AM HEARTSICK

she announces.

The kitchen's acoustics are good for declarations.

She leafs idly through her father's bills, finding only a used St Thomas's library slip in her mother's thin fast writing:

Confirm ferry 12.15 am Thurs. CASH

Despairing of finding a distraction, she is about to read a recipe for mackerel pâté in the newspaper when she notices a package. Books, she thinks hopefully, and then notices the strange animal on the stamp. Per, her father's depressed Finnish ex-student, has sent his annual box of peculiar artefacts.

Per, like her father, is Early Medieval; an archaeologist, despite the snow and endless night. The paper wrapping is open, but the box inside looks undisturbed. Eve takes off the lid and sniffs the cardboard: rich and sour, like foreign wood. Inside the box, under yellow-pink fragrant shavings, are a tiny curved horn with a dark stopper, tightly jammed; a thin disc, also the curdled colour of horn but dappled under its surface gloss; a heavy ball, grey-brown suede, with a rim of soft grey fur along the seam. She thinks of poison, of grave-goods; imagines shaking their spores on her sister's plate.

In the corner of the box something else lies hidden. She should not be going through her father's post like this but she is, she tells herself, interested in archaeology. What's more, however much Phoebe is bought in Paris, however sleek and secretive she is when she returns, she will not know about this, she thinks, sliding her hand through the shavings, half prepared to scream. Then her fingers touch metal. She lifts it into the open: a flat silver rectangle, the size of a small mouth-organ, with a big golden bean or pebble at one end.

She should put it back in the box, she thinks, running her fingertip along the silver casing. It is engraved with a pattern like petals overlapping, or water-pitted water – rain on a river, perhaps, or a distant sea. They notice these things in Finland too. Perhaps there the rivers are frozen, so this is instead a pattern of seals packed together, or of sperm . . .

She smiles in what is, she hopes, a sophisticated manner, but she has managed to make herself blush, even here, alone. The metal is cool and mineral-smelling; she holds it to her cheek, up to her eye, and notices a little catch against the pebble-handle, like a tongue in a frame. She flicks it with her nail, and it is not tight, as she supposes, but easily moves away.

Suddenly the kitchen contains nothing but Eve and this little box. There is a feeling in her stomach like a spreading grain of ice, a tiny flame. She knows what this is. Her mind floats free. Her body acts. Or is it the other way around? The catch is up. She holds the yellow pebble in her hot right hand and pulls: Excalibur. Her left hand holds the empty metal casing. Her other holds a silver blade.

Upstairs, Phoebe arrives, like a rocket.

Eve has no private places; her sister has invaded them all. Slowly, slowly, she slides the knife back in its filigree casing.

Phoebe is throwing her bag on to the stairs.

She holds it tightly; how can she let it go? Its blade may be covered with ancient poisons. It is the most beautiful thing she has ever seen.

Phoebe is running along the hallway.

Eve puts the case in her pocket.

Phoebe's feet are drumming towards her down the stairs.

Eve's mouth is dry as bone; she had not meant to do this. The cold metal burns through the fabric of her skirt, heavy against her thigh. They are going to Paris, but she has consolation.

The kitchen door bangs open. Phoebe has arrived.

On Thursday Eve wakes very early, full of fire. She could spring from her bed and walk across the ceiling, if she chose: a girl high-flyer, her shapely leotard a mesh of stars. For a few leisurely moments she flexes her fingers pinkly in the sunlight and plans the equipment she would need for public performances, if it came to that. Her mother's footsteps creak towards the bathroom. It is only then, idly noticing her hurried pace, itself rare and exciting, that Eve remembers: it is today.

Her stupid mind has deceived her. She trips over the tightrope and falls – fool, thought she was too good for a safety-net – like a lost angel through the spotlit air. By home-time today her sister and mother will be in another land, a foreign city, without her. Unprecedented. They have pulled apart so cleanly that she wonders if they were ever a four at all.

'Phoebe,' calls their mother up the stairs, over the dragging of the stuck bathroom door, 'it's time. Hurry, love. Remember that purse I gave you.'

What purse? Eve has returned to her own body; her nightdress is twisted around her back like a damp shroud. A million sequin-fragments fall on her face through the green curtains. Purse?

'I can't find it,' Phoebe shouts, croaky with sleep.

'Never mind. You can use one of mine.'

Oxford is full of houses like these, so tall and thin and paper-muffled that only shouting, floor to floor, keeps its inhabitants in touch. Eve has heard that a schoolfriend's father, obsessed with the microbes on library books, apparently insists that his children address him at a distance on home-made intercoms. Eve sympathizes: certain objects do seem contaminated by the dirty silver-ringed nicotined hands of some of her sister's friends. She has taken to opening doors with her sleeve; of course, no one has noticed.

The alarm clock ticks closer, closer. Phoebe, alone in her bedroom, is singing her school hymn, rousingly. It is barely seven o'clock. The bath tap roars shut.

'Found it,' bellows Phoebe. 'But Mum, it's practically bust already.'

'Just pack it. We can always buy another there.'

In a minute Eve will go resentfully to her sister's bedroom

to view, under mounds of clothes and trashy paperbacks, whatever else their mother has dug up: a cracked red leather travelling case, an umbrella, a hat. It will be a mistake, but she knows she will be unable to keep away. Until then, however, she will lie here, flat with longing.

And then it is over. She sits in double Greek, the room a green soup of sunlit leaves, and waits for her neighbour, Olive Joll, to notice the pencil that someone has stuck through the bottom of her cardigan. *They* are on the train; Kent, the garden of England, is roaring towards them, and the ferry waits. Her teeth taste salty; her lip is bitten sore. Other girls in this class have had strange losses: Nancy, the new girl from Scotland, claims her mother has gone to Las Vegas; Janey Sebastopol, Latin star, has an older brother at the Warneford Hospital, his wrists bound to his body, four big blue pills a day. Eve knows perfectly well that her own loss is temporary, minuscule – a brief exclusive holiday, with her father at home every evening until their return. However, her throat is hard and tight, and she cannot concentrate on anything, even Mrs Dicken, their fascinatingly pale Greek teacher, whose hair has turned prematurely white in mysterious circumstances.

In five days—

'Eve Lux,' says Mrs Dicken, white head still bent over her marking, 'kindly attend. You have a great deal of work to do.' It is true; Eve bows her neck. Three desks away Apricot Hause, sister of Dido and Lavender, tightens her plait and aims for 100%. Three hundred miles away the left-handed female Luxes, the winter-born ones, sleek-haired, blue-eyed, will soon be shopping, arm in arm. This holiday will make them impermeable. They will become, with every hour, every purchase, more lovable than before.

In five slow days they will return. Until then, however, she is her father's.

They have agreed how the first evening will be. Eve and her grateful father will eat a simple stew of beef and carrots, followed by oranges. The oranges are no problem. The stew, however . . .

'But,' she said that morning, as her mother addressed Phoebe's luggage tags. 'I don't see how—'

Her mother, looping the tag expertly against itself, pointed her chin in the direction of the cookery books. 'Oh, come on,' she said, her voice gentle.

Eve, like an idiot, imagined a reprieve: darling, come with us – the trip will be nothing without you. Their eyes met.

Should I say something? thought Jean. She busied herself with another label, considering how to introduce the subject. Is there, she wondered, glancing anxiously at the clock, any way to suggest regret without encouraging a fuss? It isn't fair to mention money – it will only worry her. Surely Eve is old enough to understand? She will say something, once these tags—

'Shit,' she said, as the elastic snapped, and the thought was lost.

Oxford mothers do not swear. While Jean Lux, superficially, is one of them, here and there are signs. Her clothes are better; her hair is not self-cut. She does not make her own yoghurt. And other mothers, Eve suspects, would *prefer* a more book-loving, worried daughter: someone a little less like Phoebe.

'Mum?'

'I'll have to start again. Can you . . .' She held out the pen.

Eve lowered her dark eyebrows and looked at the floor.

'All right,' said her mother, beginning to fill in another label. 'But really—'

'There's hardly any time. You've got to tell me what to *do*.'

'We'll go through it again. Chop the onions, sweat the carrots, add the bay – those leaves. I'll leave them out. Chuck in the meat, the wine, the water, and simmer, simmer, until he comes home.'

'What if he doesn't come home?' said Eve.

Her mother frowned. 'Why wouldn't he? He always does.'

'There might be a dinner, or a guest that he's forgotten, or . . .'

'Eve. You know perfectly well that he will. Besides, you *are* sixteen. You'll be fine.'

Her mother, as so often, was refusing to see the point. However, she has been left her father, and she will make the most of it. They have five days together, and Eve, by whatever means necessary, is going to cement their own particular bond.

Today, although it is Thursday, Helena will lunch alone. Jean is on her way to Paris. She is too preoccupied to work. Instead she sits on the window-seat, looking through bubbled glass into the quad below.

A strange phenomenon has taken place. Ordinarily, when Jean is in Oxford, telling her anything seems out of the question. She is, after all, Helena's closest friend, and when temptation strikes, as of course it does, Helena merely has to imagine her friend's face for her secret to sink back down, vanquished. However, it is as if one end of the secret has stowed away in the guard's van, or wrapped itself around Jean's heel and, the further she goes from Oxford, the more tight-stretched and agonized it becomes. Now it seems imperative that Helena tell her without delay, and nothing, not even the thought of Jean's expression as the truth is unfolded, can distract her.

She has had secrets before, of course. In motherhood, in marriage, in girlhood, primarily, trying to conceal her reading and her centipedes from the five long-legged sisters who gambolled around her, impatient for husbands, avid for amusement.

Helena wedges a finger into the corner of the window-leading and examines the darkened tip. Perhaps she could arrange an emergency research weekend at the Sorbonne and track Jean down. She sticks out her tongue to taste the poison and sees herself, striding across the Place de la Concorde, a black-skirted torturer.

Yet Jean's absence is also a relief, and relief is difficult. She has spent the morning knowing that at lunch she will be free, with no role to play. The knowledge has been like too much oxygen, or flesh freshly unbound. She feels loose, and dangerous.

I am Helena, she repeats: being myself. No need for concealment.

This is, of course, a lie.

In the quad below her, two dons are feebly rushing, gowns

billowing, to the Palfrey Room. A minor royal person is visiting today, and Dr Ruske and Professor Something – a former Soviet sleeper, which explains the decline of communism – are obviously feeling thoroughly Cavalier. Since she moved here a term ago from St Anne's, exchanging a lowly yellow-brick-and-varnish room for this chill pale professorial hangar, a mere five of her fellow fellows have addressed her, only four directly. She is beginning to accept that this will not change.

Jean is in Paris. She does not have to pretend. Heat pours from her skin like a furnace; her secret is the only source of warmth in this room. Her hands and feet are cold, but her heart is ablaze, enormous.

Victor is in trouble. His wife, were she here, would have remembered that today is Matriculation day, for complex reasons to do with the Conferment of Degrees. He has, as Senior Dean, been roped in by Hilary Price, the Dean of Degrees, to assist, and his gown has apparently been stolen.

It is already twenty to eleven; this year's crop of idlers and narcissists are gathering in Laudian Quad under the eye of Charles I, assessing the memorials and colonnades with an eye to deface and conquer. Victor's systematic excavations of the piles around the edges of his room become more frantic: scarves, an old coat, a dressing-gown, twine themselves lovingly around his ankles as he stumbles, his balance a little off, from desk to chair. He wore it to High Table only last week: the evening he heard – never mind.

And, thank God, here it is. A ragged pair of bat-wings, fading to grey-green. He pulls it on and turns to the door, and then remembers: where is his hood?

Damn Jean. She could, at least, have put it by for him, but she has been fixated on Paris for days. In his mind's eye her train enters a crumbling and dangerous tunnel: he should not have let her go. Small white teeth appear at the black mouth of the tunnel. He shakes his head and squeezes his eyes shut.

Ten to eleven. His hood, he remembers, is being mended at Jecks's in town; Phoebe, at the St James's summer garden party, stole it to be her red silk sack for the Children's Races. He will have to borrow one, without being seen: he cannot afford to look foolish with the Spenser Lectureship so close.

He will go next door to Balliol and see if Petersen is in. One-handed, with an ease borne of decades of lateness, he puts on his gown while locking the inner door and hurries down the stairs. Head down, gown barely rippling in the damp still air, he crosses the quad and flits heavily through the porters' lodge. Then, like a crow in sudden sunlight, he emerges on to the street outside: St Giles.

Despite the time he is smiling to himself: a couple of hours of dandified ceremony will be the tonic he needs. Like other dons, he has, he knows, a taste for the theatrical. The libraries and shabbiness disguise it, but it is there within him; a secret talent. He pictures himself standing before his colleagues at the Spenser Memorial Lecture: the darkened hall, the pale upturned faces. Given the opportunity, he will make the most of it. He, Victor, knows how to make a scene.

I must escape, thinks Helena. She is fizzing with nervous energy: on her desk lie a model of DNA made from paperclips, a piece of mild Cheddar stolen from her lunchtime sandwich, imprinted with neat toothy spade-marks, and a pink index card, torn into 104 pieces. Unless she distracts herself, she fears a rogue molecule, blown south from the Chemistry faculty, may ignite her and blow her secret through the roof.

She fastens her cape and descends. A straggling nervous pack of undergraduates, less obviously muscled, louder-voiced than the St Anne's stock, are heading for Front Quad in short Matriculation gowns and white ties. They do not look ready to be welcomed into the University; they look like dogs, dalmatians, perhaps – showy and ill-trained. She moves through them gingerly, like a bomber. Where should she go? There are better walks, through the deer park or beside the river, but they do not interest her today. She will go to St Giles, her favourite street for its width and light and where, with Jean in Paris, she will be safe.

The streets are full of tutors in mossy gowns and red hoods and, scattered amongst them, sleek as parrots, the doctors of philosophy, divinity and music, gorgeous in purple silk, pale blue velvet, French brocade. Gargoyles gaze down their broken noses, as if preparing to spit. Helena, horribly transported by the thought of what Jean would say if, in the Panty or her own shady garden, she were to be presented with the truth, rubs the heels of her hands deep into her eyes and is almost knocked down by a running scholar, propelling her straight into the path of Victor Lux.

'God's sake!' he growls, pulling the tail of his gown roughly free. She looks up, still half-blinded. She thinks: I have thought him here.

They are transfixed. Helena feels herself beginning to blush, mildly at first and then harder and harder, until it feels as if her face might begin to smoulder. Daylight reveals the white hairs in his ears, the shaggy eyebrows. He looks like a dangerous animal, barely tamed.

He frowns down at her, the cords in his neck working although he does not speak. His mouth is tight. Her scalp is prickling with heat.

'Oh! Oh – Victor,' she offers. He seems to be biting the inside of his lip.

'Hrrm,' he says. 'Helena.'

People stream around them, at the beginning or the end of something. 'I, I'd better—' she murmurs, gesturing in the general direction of elsewhere.

He nods, and goes on nodding.

'Well . . .' she says eventually.

'Yes,' he says, as if she has released him, stepping – with uncharacteristic thoughtfulness – past her before walking on.

A question, of sorts, has been answered. Now Helena knows that she cannot spend the next five days writhing, and waiting, and dreaming of confessions. She must work, as if there is nothing on her mind and eventually, perhaps, nothing will be.

So she works, like a demon. She thinks of nothing else, like an athlete closing her mind. It is only six hours later, as she uses her last DNA-paperclip to bind a sheaf of notes, that she remembers her son.

She cycles quickly home to Jericho: he is not a forgiving child, and expects her there for dinner. She cannot, she notes as she mounts the kerb, think of a single excuse that will satisfy him. Wearily, she rests her mother-in-law's small mauve bicycle against the dustbins and lets herself in.

For the last two years, since her husband died mid-fuck with the wife of her own college bursar, she has had nothing but his debts, and his parents' charity. Everything had been spent on women – dinners, weekends away, two flats rented simultaneously by the canal – leaving her marooned on her bemused and gentle in-laws, trying to work her way back to independence. If she could ensure that Jeffrey never found out about his father, none of this would matter. Her family, their lifelong disapproval of her compounded by her precipitous marriage to a poor Irish GP, whose flirtatiousness she had mistaken for regard, no longer contact her, so they will never know, and she is earning well now: an academic miracle. She walks over the surface of what might have been her life, counting her blessings.

It has, however, disadvantages. There is no room here for secrets. Compared to the airy ghosts of her college study, she is a giantess in their tiny house, blundering into stunted furniture.

'I'm home,' she says, and tries again, stronger-voiced, more convincing: 'I'm ho-ome.'

At least, she tells herself, she has avoided the divorced-woman land north of North Oxford, where gardens are smaller and resentments shimmer. Here in the old workmen's terraced cottages of Jericho, with their pointed chapel-windows and dragons' teeth above the doors, no one pries or offers sympathy. She passes the kitchen, in which her mother-in-law, Norah, is as usual boiling vegetables.

Norah looks up: hands wet with peelings, hair steam-damp. 'Oh, he's in the garden.'

Norah is a good woman, but she has her dead son's eyes. Helena walks on quickly, chanting 'Thank you, thank you,' straight down the hall and out of the back door. There will be a frost here tonight; the water-weed air from the canal is damply crystalline. A black and gold garden spider glints in the middle of her web amongst the ivy.

'I'm home,' she calls.

The garden is full of rustling: tiny beetles creeping through the grass-stems, the whirling rub of spinning spiders, the hustling of grubs into rotting bark. She cannot, however, hear her son; he is hiding from her.

'I'm home. Jeffrey?'

Under the honeysuckle, where her father-in-law's rusted lawn-roller and flowerpots and tiny odoriferous compost-heap lie, a brown study, she sees a section of pale flesh, blue in the twilight, sink closer to the ground. He does not know how near she is; should she give him a moment longer? If he is to prosper, despite his father's death and her own imperfect attention, he must feel successful in all things, even hiding from her.

'Jeffrey?' she calls, turning her head in the wrong direction, towards France. The next-door neighbours' cat, Aeneas, stalking for sex or food along the ivy-clouded garden wall, lifts its white head and stares at her. Ashamed, she looks away. Were her thoughts not elsewhere, she would hear the London train rumbling in the distance; she notices only that the ground feels full of life. She pulls her mind back and sees, a foot away, a horrid confusion of leaves and twigs and earth-streaked bluebell flesh, the blue-washed whites of its eyes enormous.

'Darling,' she says. 'Come to Mama.'

Jeffrey wipes his eyebrow with a muddied fist. When, she wonders, will he ever uncurl?

'No,' he says. 'I'm a maenad. We tear flesh. It wouldn't be safe.'

'I see. Well, my maenad, let us sit on your grandfather's roller and hear about your day.'

Jeffrey's knee is weeping: indigo blood shines in the

vegetable light. Her heart, which increasingly seems to float above her, an imperfect construction of helium and string, tugs back towards her first love, her son.

'How did you do that?' she asks, carefully, her finger prodding a fluorescent moss-world on the handle of the roller.

Jeffrey retracts from sympathy like salt. 'Oh,' he says airily through his camouflage, 'cross-country. We had trials for Latin Recital today.'

Jeffrey is nine. Like Phoebe, he attends the Gate, where he is reassuringly near the top of his year. His notoriously exacting teachers are, in general, charmed; he has friends; he is handsome. Yet there is something about Jeffrey that frightens her, as if she dreamt it and has now forgotten what it was. She tries to remember, but all she retains is a sense that she should be frightened, as if he is an animal that may turn.

'And how did you do?' she asks.

'*Lugete o veneres cupidinesque.* I don't know. It's all a blur.'

Physical contact with Jeffrey – indeed, with anyone – is becoming increasingly rare. At night, in his big beautiful room in the loft, she sits uncertainly on the edge of his huge bed, once hers, and is afraid to be seen to love him. Now, although she knows he will hate her for it, Helena fears she will wither without touch. She watches her son discreetly. He is stripping the pale damp bark from a hazel twig, like any other boy. She resolves to risk it. Clumsily, she rests her hand on his back.

'Please don't,' he says.

The night braces itself against questions, discovery. She smiles, unsteadily brave in the turquoise half-light. The moment passes. He shakes his shoulders angrily and her hand, like something unknown to either of them, drops back on to the matted metal.

Perhaps she should mention his father. His form master,

Doc Merwell, the headmaster, Doc Ransome, even his matron, Doc Sue, have all suggested that she should do so as often as possible, but there are problems of which they are unaware. She cannot predict her son's responses, never has, but an unacknowledged part of her hopes for tears. 'You, you don't . . . is it – is it a boy thing, this not wanting to be, you know, cuddled, or is it to do with Da—?'

'Don't talk about that,' he says sharply. 'It's not that.'

'So . . .'

'It's you.'

Helena's heart snaps shut. She knew it, but was afraid to know it.

'I'm not a child,' he says.

'Of course not, darling,' she whispers, sibilant, a monster in the half-light.

'And however much you say you didn't—'

He is crying now: star-trails are threading through the mud. She lifts her hand from the roller, and lets it fall again, afraid of the consequences.

'—you didn't know about D-dad, dad's heart, I know, I know you must have. So—'

'Darling, I—'

'*Don't lie to me.* Whatever you say is a *lie*. And now I *know* there is something wrong with *you*.'

She feels the night flare up and swallow her. 'My love, I—'

'Don't lie,' he sobs, hands dripping mercury. 'Something's happening. I know.'

This garden and the next, and next, a quiet tessellation of shiny night-green leaves, is quiet around them. His face is silver with tears. 'C-c-can you, can you *prove* that there's nothing wrong with you? I can tell there is – you're different. Can you *prove* it?'

This is it, her chance to reassure him; but what can she say? They know each other too well. Helena takes a breath, another, and still no lie comes. She must say something; her brain whirrs and does not catch, and then the night turns pale about her and she has realized why he so frightens her: he will find me out, she thinks.

The garden holds itself still. He will find her out, all of it. Until then she will be a fortress, keeping him out as long as she can, while her secret burns her from within.

'It isn't . . . I'm not ill, darling—'

'But there *is* something, isn't there? You can't deny it. *Can* you deny it?'

She cannot. She waits for his storm of crying to pass, unable to give him an answer.

Meanwhile, Eve is wrapping carrot scrapings in an old copy of the *Journal of Numismatics*, eased from one of her father's yellowing piles of papers. These sacred piles – a foot deep, tied with twine or precariously open, lying on the stairs, the kitchen table, all over the sitting-room and hall – are *essential*. They must *not be touched* – an edict recently undermined by Phoebe, who hid a postcard of a rude Indian carving from the Ashmolean Museum gift shop half-way down a stack, and found it again four months later at precisely the same angle. Eve, while shocked, had retrieved the postcard for her own purposes shortly afterwards.

Now, with Phoebe-like recklessness, she has herself disturbed a pile.

The kitchen smells raw, of sour wine and beef blood, but

this is the simplest of her father's favourite foods and he, perhaps, will be pleased. Or if not pleased, not disappointed. At least, not in her.

They will have left their cases at the hotel and gone in search of dinner. Eve knows their schedule as if it was her own – Phoebe has been lavish with the details. She has the mental version and Phoebe the actual, that is all, and maybe she will one day be someone who goes there too. This thought, which should spur her on, instead fills her with grey alarm. She is nothing like she should be, as proved by the mediocrity of her exam results, and now she is in the sixth form she must work even harder, or risk falling further behind.

She catches her reflection in the kitchen door-glass and moves towards it, like a lover. The hall is dark, which flatters her eyes. They are not blue-green, like her mother's and Phoebe's, or dark like her father's, but a strange bright yellow-brown, too pale for her skin. Her mother has sometimes called them golden; Eve, in private, calls them tigerish, or tawny, and hopes, a little disgusted with herself, that one day someone will say it for her, aloud. As for her sister – well, her sister says that they are diarrhoea. *Said* that they are, only once, but it isn't the kind of comment that goes away.

A walrus is beating its tusks against the front door. Her stomach tightens.

'Jean?' calls her father.

He is late, of course, although he works only two quadrangles away. There is a subdued metallic crash – he has knocked over his bicycle which stands, in flagrant contravention of Eve's mother's only rule, in the hallway. As a compromise, she lets it stay in the hall provided it is self-supporting, far from the wallpaper, but bicycle stands, as everyone knows, are weak and inconstant things.

Eve wipes her hands, and remembers the potatoes. Running to the larder, she shouts, 'Dad, she's not here. You know she's not.'

'Blast,' he roars, in general. 'Where is she?'

'You know. Don't you?' Momentarily she wonders whether her mother has actually walked out on him, taking only one of her daughters. Her father, however, is the most forgetful man in England. Of course he knows.

'No,' he shouts. 'I don't.'

'Pa, she's—'

'Oh yes. I do. Fool that I am.' There is a scraping, another, louder, crash, and then the long corduroy legs of her father appear at the top of the stairs.

Victor is not, tonight, a happy man. First, although he tries to ignore it, his ear seems noisily swaddled, as if by a layer of Brillo pad. He shakes his head quickly; this is a private weakness. He is an old man with a young family, and there are standards to maintain.

Second, all his attempts to promote Lewis Depuise as the new History fellow have been met with polite intransigence, like a moss-padded wall. He had begun to wonder whether paranoia, or his own bad ear, could explain what he heard on the stairs leading to Hall, the long-anticipated mention of that name. He tells himself that he is a fool, that fearing someone's reappearance cannot bring it about. Despite this he senses dread condensing, a slow drip in the corners of his mind.

He feels, this evening, like a straggly old bear pursued by wolves. He is not in the mood for this cold, shabby, noisy house, for the clinging requirements of family life or the rules of personal hygiene. He wants to be barricaded in his room in college, living on woodsmoke, rare books and digestive biscuits, moping and imagining the worst.

The worst is undoubtedly Raymond Snow, a wolf that the ancients would have recognized: bony, vicious, merciless.

Eve considers her father as he descends. He is, above all, a brain. Compared to others – Royal Astronomers, delegates of the University Press, Lucy Nesbitt's father, who will be Vice-Chancellor when the old one dies and could speak as a child in iambic pentameter ('He still does,' says Lucy, 'when he swears') – he is, admittedly, nothing. Despite his early promise, of which she has heard many rumours and no hard proof, he has never appeared on television; he is not even a professor, yet. However, she is often amazed by what he knows: his languages, his memory, the histories he proffers, like a toy, when you wonder aloud about the Congo, or runes, or the dragon forever chasing its tail on the gate of the high-walled fellows' garden, through which, on certain days and in certain moods, he lets you pass.

It also appals her. When did he learn all this? How does he, a man barely able to tie his own shoelaces, remember so much in such detail? He can act out for you Athenian maritime manoeuvres, and does so in cinema queues and busy public pathways. He can quote Heraclitus and Edward Lear, scan anything, parse anything, destroy any argument. He can describe the death of every Merovingian or the etymology of almost any English word, and there is not even the slimmest possibility that Eve will ever know a fraction of these things.

Poor man, he is disappointed in his daughters. He would, she tells herself, prefer it if Phoebe, instead of roller-skates and cameras, devoted herself to dinosaurs, or the Latin names of plants. Yet Phoebe compensates for much.

Eve, however, is lacking. The signs have always been there. At eleven she was briefly identified as a suitable friend for a lonely prodigy, before they decided that she was not, after all, clever enough. The prodigy – not that Eve had wanted to meet her, with her stupid clothes and embarrassing parents – was befriended elsewhere. She still sometimes torments herself with this, but further proofs have accumulated: namely that, despite having been educated continuously since she entered Somerville crèche at two, she is still merely ordinary. The $\beta\alpha$s and α-s she regularly receives are fine, but fine is not enough.

All of this is exacerbated by family law, under which intellectual conversations must be mocked. When her father mentions acanthus leaves or Ptolemy she must be irritated, and drolly bored, or she will be cast out by her mother and sister, consigned to the glasses-wearing regiment of square girls, whose huge hot-housed brains throb under extraordinarily dated hairstyles and horrible spectacles. Although, given her failure to learn more instruments, or to join the Thames Vale Ornithological Society, they wouldn't want her either. Every interesting conversation about evolution or potential trip to the Ashmolean has been blighted by this need to respond correctly; neither to exclude nor slight them, while they do as they please. It has made her, she knows, not what he hoped for, and their relationship a waste of what might have been.

Now, however, while the others are away, she can win him in secret. The stew bubbles like a petulant geyser. She has remembered napkins; her Greek lexicon waits upstairs, should he be moved to help her with her homework, although her desk is disappointingly ordinary for home tuition. As he enters the kitchen she puts down a half-bared potato and smiles, like a wife to a husband.

Victor Lux lifts an eyebrow.

The stew, however, is not what she hoped. None of it as she had hoped. Her father, refusing to see that this is their chance to bond, is short-tempered and opaque – as he is, to be honest, most of the time. Her plans for intellectual camaraderie are, like the food, best abandoned. The smell of burnt beef lingers.

She has been pretending to read the paper, thinking of her stolen knife upstairs, when, alarmingly, his breathing seems to stop.

'Pa?' she says.

He is writing in his notebook under the pull-down central light; his orange, peeled and arranged by her in imitation of her mother, sits before him, hardening. She needs something to break the silence. She looks at the dresser, but even the few objects that she knows are from his past – ornamental plates, a woven mat, candlesticks decorated with foreign birds and flowers in refugee colours, blue and red and brown – are sodden with history, too sad to mention.

'Pa?' she says, more loudly.

Could he die and go on writing? If anyone could, he could. She cannot hear him take another breath. Her own lungs catch.

'Please?'

He looks up impatiently. 'Yes, Je— Phe— Eve. What is it?'

'I just wondered,' says Eve, who has nothing to say. 'I just wondered, um, if you, do you have any books about, well,

French art, I mean, galleries, that, you know, that Mum and Phoebe might not have time . . .'

His ballpoint rattles in his teeth. He used to smoke a pipe, until her mother made him stop; he is still smoking it in some of their wedding photographs. He has been known to prod a pen-end with a hopeful paperclip, sometimes for several minutes. His eyes are in the light, but his folded mouth and chin are shadowed. He looks like a friar, or mad, she thinks.

'I mean, not that they're *not* interested in art and things, particularly . . . but. You know. A sort of parallel tour. Or . . . not?'

Her father slowly closes his notebook, slides it into his inside pocket, recaps his pen, peels the translucent skin from an orange segment and holds the long teardrops of juice up to the light.

'Hmm,' he growls, unknown suspicions contradicted or confirmed.

He mashes the orange slowly with his fork. Eve idly tallies the mess Phoebe has left behind her: a bowl of distended pulpy cereal on the dresser, her spare calculator, a cardigan, her roller-skates, several expensive biros with interestingly-coloured ink, a five pound note, a skirt of their mother's, damp with tea, and her old address book, all on or around the kitchen table. Also a small French dictionary, every edge labelled: REFERENCE: MAY NOT BE LENT. Eve, whose natural messiness is usually constrained by guilt, has herself tried to strew her possessions about the kitchen, hoping that her sister's violent carelessness is catching, like veruccas; it has not taken. Everything Phoebe owns looks somehow more spontaneous, more interesting, than anything of hers. Which is, of course, pathetic: all their possessions are from the same local shops. Except that now there is Paris. An urge to bite herself, to shake herself between her own teeth, passes, with effort.

After some time, Victor looks up again and sees his daughter. 'Hmm?'

It is like conversing with a snail. 'I just wondered,' she says, in a clear bright voice, 'whether *we* could look at some French art, or buildings, in a book or . . . somewhere, as they're there and we're not. If you like. But . . . we don't have to, if—'

Victor Lux strokes the unmanageably owlish eyebrow on his left-hand side 'What a curious idea,' he says. 'And where if not in a book, I wonder? Now tell me,' and he leans forward, as he must lean in his armchair in tutorials to frown at less rewarding students, 'would this be for pleasure? Or for pain?'

Eve bites the skin off an orange pip. She is uncovered. '—', she begins.

However, he will not listen. He operates on other planes.

'No, it was a silly idea,' she says, the bitter shell between her teeth. 'Sorry. How about . . . actually, there is something I wanted to ask you. A school thing.'

Victor sits back in his chair. His large pale-brown hand, which has crept to the inner pocket of his brown cord jacket, hesitates. Eve dares herself to seize the moment: to ask him something personal, appeal for help – but he is her father, and not that sort of man. She summons her resources. 'Could you . . . I'm having a bit of trouble with the optative. Is it always, "would that we", or can it be things like: "we wish that he had"?'

Her father visibly relaxes; he has been spared. 'Come here,' he says. 'I shall show you.'

By the time Eve has reached his side of the table, Greek words, longer and more alarming than any she has yet encountered, are spidering across an old envelope, and he is smiling.

THIRD WEEK

None of the taxis is big enough. After half an hour of cold drizzle outside Oxford station, Phoebe has stopped smiling at a party of French schoolboys and a rage is brewing. When, for the third time, she humphs down on Jean's blue woven suitcase, a souvenir of her own late mother's only trip abroad, Jean surrenders.

'Wait here,' she says.

In Phoebe's lovely rain-fresh face, hope and suspicion fight for precedence. 'What? You're not going to leave me – it's *freezing*. I'm getting a cold. Let me—'

However, Jean's task is delicate, and she will not entrust it to Phoebe.

'No,' she says, quite firmly. For a sliver of a second both pause, impressed. 'I'm doing it. Let me check . . . ' She sifts through the centimes in her purse, her bag, her coat pocket, before triumphantly holding up a ten pence piece to where, in a more ideal homecoming, the sun should be. 'Won't be a minute.'

Phoebe is muttering 'Pissing rain, it's not *fair*' with increasing force behind her, but for once Jean ignores it. Two minutes later, undeterred even by Victor's reaction to her telephone call, she and Phoebe are sheltering under the corrugated eaves of the station, waiting for their cantankerous new car, the world's second oldest Volvo, to grind into view.

Fifteen unexplained minutes later, he appears.

'How was it?' he asks, climbing stiffly from the car.

'Lovely,' cries Phoebe, wiping a wet slice of hair from her silky forehead. She begins to describe their adventure, with half-unpacked visual aids, exaggerations and several outright lies, while her parents load the boot. Jean pats his grey woollen elbow in gratitude as he veers out of the bus-lane.

If she could, she would keep her eyes shut until they reached home, but Phoebe would certainly notice. She has no choice but to look out of the window at the tyre-yard, the old hotel and then, inevitably, there they are: the thrusting slate and verdigris of the spires. She opens the window to feel rain on her face, to force herself back to the present, and hears, above the slurry of wet tyres, the tolling of another sodding bell.

When, parents like packhorses, sister cradling a suddenly sprained wrist, they clump and gambol respectively into the kitchen, Jean sees at once from Eve's bright smile that there is a problem.

Her elder daughter's hair has reached the chrysanthemum stage between cuts; towards the top of one creamy-brown cheek, the same colour as her father's, a spot has formed in their absence. Jean kisses her, but Eve does not respond. Jean feels her mind snap back. She waits for pleasantries which do come.

*

'Wow,' Eve begins, face turned to her parents, eyes on her sister. 'What a lot of stuff.'

Before her, like a scene from a Geography slide show, lie France's most covetable products, their allure magnified by packaging and the place of their birth. Teeth gritted with avarice, she notes four large jars of jam, a cellophane sack of meringues, a fat linen-bound notebook, a blue and white pottery bowl too big for the sink, a jacket – a jacket! – and a dense tangle of scarves, skirts and tights. No books, but she still envies every bit of it.

Phoebe, whose life seems composed of treats, is peeking into a cardboard tube and smiling to herself. Eve is ceremonially given a Van Gogh poster and a game involving Mona Lisa, but cannot help coveting Phoebe's snowstorm, her T-shirt, her amusing watch.

'So,' their mother asks her eventually. 'How was it? Did he behave?'

'Did you miss us?' says Phoebe. 'Bet it was boring.'

Their father, trained in tact by a thousand Senior Common Room disagreements, chooses his words carefully.

'Glad to have you back, of course. Is that not the case, Evie? Which is not to say we could not manage for ourselves.'

Eve smiles at him in relief and gratitude. Then, unable to help herself, she steals a glance at the dustbin.

Phoebe, sharp-eyed as a landlady, grins. 'What?'

If Eve were Phoebe – well, everything would be different. Tonight, in particular, she would say airily say 'Nothing', and the thin skin over their weekend, this illusion of rightness, would remain intact. However, Eve is Eve, and so she coughs and scratches her left shoulder with both hands and looks hard at the table and the disaster which, she had hoped, might be smoothed over, detonates.

'What *is* it?' asks Phoebe.

Their mother goes straight to the bin.

Eve looks at her father, who is picking with concentration at a smear of ink by the salt. Her mother breathes in sharply, like a fire-eater preparing to roar. Everyone holds themselves still, for different reasons. Eve's mind scrabbles for a lie.

The bin lid swings, like a saloon door before the shooting begins.

'So,' says her mother. 'Marvellous. What happened?'

In her hand, hung about with frills of burnt cheese and paper towel, is a broken teapot, its entrails bared like an egg. Seventeen years ago, already tannin-stained, this teapot was forced upon Eve's mother on her wedding day by her own mother and, since her death has been treated with particular reverence, as if it contained her ashes. Eve alone knows, having been the squirming recipient of a grandmotherly confession, that this was because 'Those Jews hate tea. Won't let her drink it. They hate English habits. The least I could do was give her equipment.'

'Well?' says Eve's mother, her voice, appallingly, wobbling.

Don't cry, Eve wills her, staring at the floor, but when she looks up from her abject cower she sees only anger, pure as passion, all for her.

'Jean, it—' begins her father, but her mother, unprecedentedly, ignores him. Very quietly, Phoebe puts down her cardboard tube.

'Right,' says her mother. Eve opens her eyes wide, with a strange sense of relief. 'I don't *care* how you say it happened, or when. As if that mattered. You know what this means – meant – to me. You knew that. It was the last good thing of hers I had.'

'I—' Eve begins.

'I don't want to hear it.'

The air is shrivelled. No one can breathe.

It is Thursday, and Helena is early. For the first time she can remember she has a moment to look around her, to prepare. She is not harried and apologizing for spilt water and trapped skirts and disarray. That is, she *should* be calm, but for the secret she has been guarding, and the coming moment when she will face her friend and have to tell her. She is smiling happily, quite beside herself.

The Panty, ordinarily a mere backdrop to their conversations, is, she sees, a sort of mini-Hall for the more extreme misfits – dimly illuminated by that peculiar Oxford light, gluey and rain-dull, filtered through oily glass. Before her Godric Nestor-Stears is smiling innocently to himself while attaching a row of paperclips to his collar. He is, Helena decides, surely the oddest of them all, but it may be that the other unkempt mutterers do not even notice him. Beside him, an island in a silken sea, lie two enormous leather books in protective tissue, a pink water-pistol and a small bird on its back in a glass box, as if its taxidermist, tiring of lifelike poses, had instead chosen to copy death. To her right Giuseppe Bowker, Latin lover, is writing a column of numbers on a crested college napkin in ant-sized writing. His goulash congeals softly beside him, like a dish of entrails. To her left, Clive, who seems to be wearing pyjamas, wipes his mouth neatly on his cuff and rearranges his cutlery. Helena, sympathetic to the obsessive habits of others – and reluctant to catch a new one herself – looks away and glimpses, in the varnished mahogany, her own reflection.

This has been a difficult week. The status quo had been

an unexpected source of comfort; in its absence certain fears have crystallized. Like a Victorian freed from her corsets, the strain of liberty has almost overwhelmed her. She has felt, at times, as if her viscera may spill out of her sides. Will Jean, her friend and never-confidante, notice the change? A small hope ignites, and is quickly suppressed.

It is still early. Helena, not usually a friend to mirrors, has a few moments to spare. Discreetly – for no one as plain as she can be seen to admire herself – she moves her bread roll to the left. There she is: big bony nose, big hooded dark-blue eyes, small mouth. Greying scrubby hair, cut by herself at the basin.

She is not blind. There have been times when her appearance has caused her distress – in common, presumably, with all unfavoured people, except for the arrogant, or Godric Nestor-Stears. When she was seventeen or so she spent the weeks before a school dance expecting romance, before spending the evening – admittedly in an unfortunate green dress, two sisters old – being so thoroughly ignored that she hid in a lavatory and pulled out most of an eyebrow. On her wedding day, putting on the dress lent to her by a charitable tutor, Mrs Balhatchet, she caught such a look of kindly pity in her tutor's mirror that she staggered backwards and cut open her foot on the grate.

No matter. She stares at her own reflection, trying to be impartial. She is probably too thin, too pale even for her, but with her height and those great sticking-out bones she will never be fragile, or soft.

Jean is soft.

Among these angular men, this grey-roofed college, Jean is an anomaly. Round face, round seawater eyes, round shoulders; even the backs of her hands are comfortably plump and, while the rest of her is not Helena's business, she has the impression of more of the same. Were a weeping child to hurl itself against Jean's body, she would say 'oof', smilingly, and go on talking; if the body were Helena's, the child would cry harder, half-impaled on bones.

The air changes. The wait is over, and Helena's private thoughts are unfurled all over the table, like a magician caught practising. Just in time, she slaps a hand over the reflection, and is reassembled. Jean will notice nothing.

However, she does.

Both are eaters, for different reasons, but this afternoon their goulash is barely touched. As Helena listens to tales of concierges and patisseries and paintings, she feels pressure building, at first in the air and then inside her, unequally matched. She clenches her toes under the table, crushes her nails into her palm, but the pressure continues to rise. What should she do? Jean is describing a failed mission to the Rodin museum, where Helena herself went on a complicated weekend, long ago, with a fellow-student. Her mind fills with marble, carved into translucency: hollows, thighs. She nods, seized by the certainty that her secret is about to fly apart.

'You don't look well,' says Jean abruptly.

'Don't I?' She tries an encouraging smile. 'I . . . I am though. Really. Just – you know. Writing. Tired.'

'What is it now?'

'Aphids. Don't smirk. They're important; when pregnant the females – oh, never mind. You're laughing.'

'It's just,' says Jean, 'the things you see. Pregnant aphids. I can't imagine – in my world nothing reproduces, or even breathes . . .'

'Still the Aleppi excavations?'

'The very same.'

'Ah.'

An awful dusty silence descends. Godric hiccups. Time seems to glide and flutter and, all at once, with an avalanche of scruples Helena knows she is going to tell Jean everything. She cannot go on deceiving her. In this long week she has forgotten how.

She leans forward. Her heart trips and falls. She opens her mouth, closes it, takes a sip of water. Her secret is baying to get out. She thinks: I cannot believe I am about to do this, and says—

Jean says, 'Dear, there's something I'm longing to talk to you about.'

Helena sees her life in sections, like a tapeworm. A stately country childhood, the opposite of her pearly well-sexed sisters; Somerville's cloistered focus, where she discovered, at last, what her brain was *for*; meeting skinny charming Catholic Simon and losing her family, all for him; Jeffrey, widowhood and the books' success all packed together. But the last part, the section she currently inhabits, is misted, hidden, distressingly unformed. Nothing, this last year, has been as she thought it would be; the tapeworm had turned out to be a skin, stuffed with gunpowder. Six seconds ago, she decided to blow it all into the open. Now, however, from the other end, Jean has taken her secret and lit a match.

'I'm desperate to talk to you about it,' says Jean. 'Do you mind?'

Helena nods painfully. She tries to think how to respond. '*Do* you?'

After an embarrassingly long delay, Helena is calm enough to speak. 'I – I don't – of course I don't. Of *course*. What is it?' she asks, but she knows the answer. How has Jean guessed? Should she deny it? She watches her friend's mouth for the moment of revelation, thrilled and horrified.

'It's awkward to say,' Jean begins, shredding her roll into doughy rags.

Helena leans towards her, the side of her hand almost touching the lip of Jean's plate. She'd imagined such lies, such battles, sometimes physical, to protect her secret and now it is coming she cannot stop smiling.

'It *is* awkward,' she says helpfully. 'I know.'

'The thing is,' says Jean.

'I know,' Helena reassures her.

But she does not know. 'It's . . . it's Phoebe,' says Jean.

Phoebe?

'Oh,' says Helena. Now safe and desolate, she has been a millimetre from telling all. She feels blood rush from her skin towards more vital places – will it favour her heart or her brain? Were she not in extremis she would make a note.

'She can be . . . ' begins Jean. Her hands tremble with the effort of confession. 'I can't tell Victor, you see. He wouldn't understand – it's not his, well, sphere. But . . . it was Paris.'

There is an expectant pause. Godric Nestor-Stears says brightly to himself, 'Is there, I wonder, any marmalade?'

Helena, belatedly, realizes a response is required. 'Was it – was it bad, in Paris?'

'Well. Not exactly – it's only relative, obviously. She can be such a pleasure, as you know . . .'

Helena, utterly distracted, misses her cue.

'—and usually, of course, the odd burst of high spirits and independence I don't mind; it's prickliness that I can't bear,' she confides, her voice lowered, as if her elder, pricklier daughter is concealed behind the hot-water samovar. 'But the point *is* that usually Phoebe – you know, I feel guilty, saying even this . . .'

Helena mutely shakes her head.

'Usually she's diluted, is I suppose the word, by Victor and Eve, so she's mainly just a pleasure – tiring, I suppose, but then pleasures are.' Despite her embarrassed fluster, Jean is speaking easily now, although theirs has never been a confiding sort of friendship. 'But in Paris, well – I haven't had her to myself for days at a time since she was a baby, I suppose – you know, that blistering love . . .'

'I know,' says Helena.

'Which is after all so hard, in its way – well, that's almost what it was like. She's so . . . herself, is Phoebe; does what she wants, expects certain things – everything, actually. She's irresistible; you can't not indulge her, but she's *unquenchable*. She wants it *all*. And if everything's a treat, you just go on and on, but . . . I took the last of my cash, and that all went, and I had to use household money I'd set aside for curtains and the boiler, and . . . and it's not so much the money as the expectation – I was just rather taken aback by that.'

'I see. Yes, I see.' With an effort, Helena ends her close contemplation of the tabletop.

'And there were a couple of incidents – this horrible embarrassing row at dinner in a beautiful brasserie, candle-lit, with these very sound-magnifying tiles, where she said her apple tart was burnt and would I complain, and you know how bad I am – sorry, am I being boring?'

'No. *No*,' says Helena, wondering if at any moment she will be borne aloft by nervous energy, over the unheeding heads of these men, above the battlements and treetops until, directly above a sharp and merciless spire, she decides to let go.

'If you're sure,' says Jean, seeming unconvinced. She rubs the back of her hand across her forehead. 'Right. Yes. So she got crosser, and started saying I would if I *loved* her, for God's sake, and when I eventually did complain she was so rude about *that*, even my *technique*, and we fought and fought, until suddenly she stormed off, and I had to follow, you know, and then she burst into tears and was sweet again and somehow it all just passed. But then it happened again on Sunday, in a market, and I know her rages here are pretty extraordinary, but there, she just let *fly*. Maybe the anonymity – but probably half of them spoke English anyway. It was . . . I was shaking, silly as it sounds. God. Anyway. That's it.'

Jean folds her hands on her napkin and glances up shyly.

'I see,' says Helena.

'Are you . . . shocked?'

'No. *No*. Of course not,' she says sturdily. 'It's quite, ah, reasonable. She's a, well, remarkable girl, but that doesn't mean she's easy. They never are.'

Jean looks at her in some surprise. Her opinion of Helena's own child, Perfect Jeffrey, is that he's a charming nightmare, but she never expected to hear it from her.

'Oh, good,' she murmurs.

There is nothing more to say. Helena's eyes are sore; she wants Jean to stand up and leave her here, so she can take stock and calm herself. She tries to smile but can't; she cannot pat Jean's hand reassuringly. Jean waits, coughs, prods anxiously at her cutlery. 'Better get back,' she says, after a time.

An air of unease, of business barely started, hangs in the Pantry, unnoticed by the men. However, as Jean crosses the quadrangle in the pale sun, and Helena attempts to unhook her skirt from her bicycle chain, each smiles a private smile, relieved a little by what was said or nearly-said, and by the prospect of future confidences.

It is then that Jean realizes what she has done – or, rather, not done. Today is the annual Medieval and Early Modern History wine-and-cheese party, postponed to unseasonably warm October because of the death of the Emeritus Professor in July. This would be bad enough, were it not also Jean's turn to play hostess: the three-yearly acme, or nadir, of her wifely duties, Victor's pastoral obligations, the girls' opportunity to show the world they can behave.

Worse still, in four hours' time twenty-six under- and postgraduates, and a grisly selection of Victor's colleagues and their wives, will arrive, and she has nothing but Phoebe's La Vache Qui Rit and some stale Swedish crackers in the house. She thinks of running after Helena, for advice or consolation, but she will only complicate things further. Complications, thinks Jean, beginning to panic, are the very last thing she needs.

Victor frowns at a pair of undergraduates as they read muffled nonsenses from their essays. His imagination – his only self-indulgence – will not stop inventing scenarios whereby Raymond Snow, just as aggressive, as sardonic and brutally ambitious as he had been at Queen's in their student days, yet less resilient, less *himself,* is definitively and roundly crushed: by appealing for the Lectureship by letter, only to have it returned with 'I hardly think so' scrawled across it in an unknown hand; by, when asked by the Lecture's Trustees, over dessert in the Senior Common Room, to bring in the Major Fruits, their favourite test, filling the bowl with oranges, lychees, dates and mangosteens – but the Major fruits are the English ones, as any fool should know; best, most terrifyingly, of all, by stuttering his way through the beginning of the Lecture, only to be removed from the stage by the President in favour of Victor, who delivers an impromptu speech to a standing ovation.

All childish, of course, all, he reminds himself, watching the undergraduates flirt as they struggle with his questions, unlikely, and close to madness. Raymond Snow will not be back. He has conjured him into the closed air of the college; now he must imagine him out again, before the golem runs amuck.

It is her double Free, and Eve has decided to save herself.

The bus stops in a cloud of fumes beside the green churchyard on Magdalen Street. Eve, a cyclist, is unused to buses, but they are, at least, discreet for escaping from school. Shyly she thanks the driver and jumps from the step, straight on to the foot of a tweedy mathematician who once reprimanded her for attempting to roller-skate outside the college gates.

'Sorry,' she says, but he merely mutters, 'Lux girl,' and stares with such enmity that she stumbles, treading firmly on his other foot. Then, before she has time to do more damage, she is caught up in a surge of pensioners and finds herself walking away, head down, neck scarlet. It is her first illegal trip through the school gates, and already she is marked.

It is twenty past two – she has so little time. Blood thumping, practising a range of lengthy and unconvincing excuses, she scurries past Balliol and along the Broad. At the last possible second she notices a woman with pale red hair in a cottage-loaf-sized bun, adjusting the Liberty-print bag in her wicker basket. It is Miss Trask, her English teacher, hoping that Boswell's, the elderly department store where Eve's father buys her mother birthday presents, still sells detachable lace collars. Deftly, Eve dodges a nervy tangle of schoolboys and an overalled old man carrying planks on a bicycle, nips up the Turl and enters the Covered Market. Breathless, increasingly maze-muddled, she passes gaping fish on ice-chips, riding crops, a dissertation-bindery, a tempting second-hand bookshop, an antiquated ironmonger's; then she rounds the corner of a butcher's and almost hits her head on a solid furry trunk. It is a deer, white tail bright in the eaves, neck dripping brown blood on to the sawdust. The market tilts; she puts out a hand and finds herself leaning against the window of Dutton's, her target: purveyor of teapots to wardens' tables, Jericho barges and the windswept Edwardian castles of Boar's Hill.

It was, at least, a good idea this morning. However, Dutton's is tiny, all crests, solo cafetières and serviceable white glazing, and despite the seductive smell of coffee-beans she knows she'll find nothing here. Disconsolate, she fingers a blue milk-jug; even if, as in fiction, she found the broken teapot's twin behind a sack of beans, it would not be enough. Her sister went to school this morning with an ostentatiously red waterproof jacket and a little rucksack; she called 'Au revoir' loudly up the stairs, and their mother answered 'À bientôt, chérie'. Even their father has been infected; as her mother produced croissants for breakfast, wrapped in *Le Monde*, the morning after their return, he headed to the freezer for a celebratory tube of orange juice concentrate. Eve, who is too fat for croissants, dropped marmalade on her school shirt, and waited fearfully to see what their tea would come in. So, it seemed, did everyone else. When their mother put an ancient tin coffee-pot on the table, eyes averted, even Phoebe shut up.

It is useless. Eve took the risk for nothing. Miserably, now certain she will be caught, she resolves to buy something anyway, and in future to do better, be better, be less like herself and more like Phoebe, whatever it takes.

The Cupboard is still locked; Hedley is lunching with the Fellows. Jean, whose conscientiousness owes everything to fear and nothing to duty, checks her watch and bites her lip. Paperless, keyless, she rushes back down the staircase to the notice-board. An old notice informs her of an inter-college tortoise race; out of sympathy for St Thomas's tortoise – which, despite having once been blessed by Gerard Manley Hopkins, came nineteenth – she rips it down. Then she goes up again to the Cupboard to write her note.

> *Half past one*
> *HG – am checking Cauldrake's memoirs in the Divinity*
> *School Lib., or elsewhere if ~~not~~ unavailable. Assuming*
> *Boris L. has returned them . . . ~~Sorry~~*
> *Hope that's satisfactory. See you later. Jean.*

Ten minutes later Jean has passed the pastel glories of Oriel

Square without being spotted, and has entered the Covered Market.

'Brie, a whole one,' she muses, passing a neighbour, Ginny Rice, looking oddly shifty in the saddler's. 'Though not a good one – not de Meaux; if only. Something blue? Gorgonzola? Too expensive, and they'll turn up their noses, but I'm not having Danish Blue. Something old – oh no, that's weddings. But Cheddar, maybe, to show I'm trying? A good one. Nothing unpasteurised – might kill the oldies. Although . . .'

This market had been part of Victor's wooing of her. When she first arrived here, nearly two decades ago, stunned speechless, her diet consisted of floury Somerville soups, brown paper parcels, shamefully protruding from her pigeon-hole, of fruit-cake and allotment carrots still cold with Lancashire air; and packets of ginger-snaps, salty with panic, on which she gorged by the river-bank. She talked in that first term to almost no one; there was a brief shy friendship with another grammar-school girl, who found a boyfriend and started ignoring her: after that, nothing at all.

Then, in Hilary term, the spring of her final year, she had entered an attic room to find herself the only woman before an audience of men. One, dark-skinned and shadowed – Indian-looking, she guessed, feeling worldly – scraped back his chair and rose, and rose. He was already older than she is now: a black-haired courtly foreign giant. In her confusion she stayed, realizing too late that the lecture wasn't on *Gawain* after all but on some impenetrable aspect of ancient shipping. The dark man at whose one heavily-accented donnish witti-cism she smiled politely was, it seemed, in charge. How could she leave?

When he met her the following week, palely loitering on

the staircase, he invited her to tea, surprising them both. His accent was as strong as the day he had reached England, a penniless ten-year-old, death snapping at his heels. He was the saddest man she had ever met, with reason. The ginger-bread, the ham (his faith had newly lapsed: he could neither afford nor resist it), the gherkins and honey sweets were new foods to her, as if invented to feed love. He bought them at the German delicatessen in the market, a place she had half heard of and vaguely feared. After that, for the year before the babies and the mist set in, she went there weekly to collect treats for him, lures and small rewards and consolations.

The sawdust-disinfectant smell of the market, its casual butchery, still reminds her of her husband, although since she discovered Grove's, the cheese shop, it has other associations. If she hurries, her excuse may hold. However, she keeps having to double back to avoid Lady Scott – who, despite being wife of the Master of Worcester, still teaches Latin at Oxford Girls', not least to Eve Lux – only to be caught by Margaret, chief scout at Victor's college, who cleans for the President and several of the Luxes' neighbours.

Margaret has her favourites. 'I see,' she says, tight-lipped, after Jean has run through tonight's guest-list. 'And will the girls be helping?'

'Oh yes!' says Jean brightly.

'And what will you be serving?' asks Margaret, red-nosed and malign.

'Nothing, at this rate!' says Jean clumsily, knowing that her husband's colleagues will now be treated to reports of Aeschylean disarray at number eleven. As she excuses herself, she thanks God that St James's delivers the wine straight from the cellars, and that the glasses were brought round by Beatty, the butler's boy, days ago. She buys two huge bunches of grapes, black and white, and discovers that, in emergencies, the nastier of the bakeries will deliver cheese biscuits and fifteen French sticks to the porters' lodge for six o'clock. She will send the girls round to collect them, although Phoebe will probably insist on using them as javelins.

In a second she will reach Grove's, a cool stinking sanctuary of gnarled mould-powdered rinds and fat pale ooze, where everything comes down to taste, to unctuousness. It is pointless to waste perfection on her guests, to give them anything other than the most unimaginative cheeses, but she has a reputation for unpredictability to maintain. At least, unlike the other History wives, she hasn't insisted on baking her own bread.

Helena, passing a telephone box as she hurries to a seminar, turns on her heel and pulls open the door. She stands on one leg, then the other; the floor smells faintly unpleasant. However, there is a ladybird crawling up the outside of the glass. She keeps her eyes on its back as she feels for her purse.

Telephone boxes are not a strong point. It takes a little while to work out where the coin should go. One of her research students passes at a run; she should have begun the seminar four minutes ago. The telephone box is filling with her nervous breath. 'Be there, be there,' she thinks, as in a not-too-distant college room a telephone rings and rings. Her heart is crushing her; she thinks: I will faint before—

'Hello?'

It is not the voice she expected, at all. Horrified, as if it had burned her, she slams the receiver clumsily into its cradle. She wipes her dry mouth with her hand and stumbles out on to the pavement, crushing the ladybird with her bag. As she silently berates herself for her rash act – the danger, her frightening lack of control – she steps almost into the path of a sparsely-laden removal van, heading for St Giles and Victor's college.

Despite the pressure of time, and unwanted guests, Jean finds the prospect of the cheese shop deliciously relaxing. Unbeknownst to her family, she comes here weekly for a quarter-pound of private pleasure, a half pound at most, which she eats standing at the kitchen table, straight from the knife. Her mind is full of Roquefort veins, of Vignotte and Wensleydale. Smiling, she rounds the corner, and finds herself staring into the disconcertingly pale eyes of Eve, her daughter.

'Oh,' they say, as one. They have barely spoken since Jean's return from Paris. Eve blushes; Jean steps back.

'What on earth are you doing here?'

'I . . .' Eve begins, vainly. 'I'm . . . looking for a book, for school . . .' Then, to her mother's alarm, she whips a carrier-bag from behind her back and holds it out, smiling hopefully.

'What is it?'

'It's yours. Look inside.'

Jean, frowning, pulls out a tissue-wrapped packet. 'What is it?'

'*Open* it,' says Eve, already looking petulant.

Jean slides her hand inside and breaks the seal. Inside is a heavy brown teapot with an off-white stripe, as if already dirty, around the lid. She opens her mouth, but nothing comes out.

'It's for you.'

'Is it? Well . . .' In its place she pictures her mother's

broken rose teapot, covered in cheese and coffee-grounds, still beautiful. 'Thank you. That's very kind. What a pretty colour.'

'What's wrong?' says her daughter.

'Nothing. Thank you. Really.' But Eve is studying her closely, and she is longing to escape. 'Oh, look,' she says, 'if you must know ... Phoebe's already bought me a replacement.'

'When? But there's been no time—' Eve scratches her head angrily; even from this distance Jean can see she needs a hair-wash.

'At the V&A – her history field trip, yesterday,' says Jean. Eve's face pinches with resentment. 'It's Wedgwood. Well, Wedgwoodish.'

'I didn't know,' says Eve, lowering her black eyebrows. Jean longs to attack them with tweezers. However, Eve responds so badly to her mother's attempts to help, unlike Phoebe, who basks, that it is simply not worth it.

Jean rewraps the teapot in its bag and glances at the cheese-shop door. 'But yours is very nice, too,' she says.

Eve is looking sullen. 'How could she afford it?' she asks.

'She spent the last of her francs. She pretended to be French. Now, I should ...' She looks at her watch. Three and three-quarter hours. 'Don't forget the party tonight.'

Surreptitiously, Eve touches the door-frame: left side, right. 'The francs you gave her?' she asks.

Jean sighs. 'That's hardly the point,' she says, but Eve is still not satisfied. Jean is patting the side of the hideous teapot, trying to think of something to say in its favour, when a tramp-like old woman tsks past them, knocking Eve's leg with her Bodleian Library bag.

'Why aren't you in the Cupboard?' Eve asks grumpily.

'They let me out sometimes, you know,' says Jean.

'You know that essay about *Bleak House*? I got an alph – I mean, A minus.'

Jean nods, not knowing whether to commiserate or praise. She is impatient for Grove's; the air outside is creamy with ammonia and goats' milk. 'You'd better get back to school.' She steps inside. Eve follows her.

'I know. But—'

'Mrs Lux,' says the older, more silky-voiced cheeseman, ignoring Eve. 'We have some Pont l'Evêque I think you'd enjoy. Shall I—'

'Does he *know* you?' Eve whispers.

Jean requires privacy. She will fight for it to the death. 'Eve,' she says. 'Thank you for the teapot. But it's very late. Now, *go.*'

Jean watches the back of her daughter's dark head weave through the crowds in search of an exit. The prospect of the party, those querulous gossips – not to mention their wives – chills her; they are dreary at the best of times, but in her own garden . . . If she is to endure tonight, she will need support. She thinks of Helena, her true trustworthy friend, and her spirits lift.

Two hours later, in her book-stacked bedroom, Eve sits on her bed, holding a needle over a match. It glows red, then gold. She blows out the match, wipes the needle on a tissue and holds it up to the window: a private spear-point. Then she jabs it, hard and fast, in the pale skin of her forearm.

No slicing tonight; she only needs a drop of blood, a small sting to keep her sane. Besides, she'll have to pass glasses and smile all evening; she must move without wincing, and her last session, the most painful and most addictively soothing so far, is only just beginning to heal. She has invented her own system for release; a private, simple, controllable pain. She mops the blood, admiring the tiny ember now blooming on her skin; then, in the open wardrobe mirror, she sees her own side, hideously creased, and only just resists the urge to jab herself again. That is not the way. Instead, gratifyingly unimpaired by her tiny localized ache, she takes a green round-necked jersey from the bottom drawer. The blood feels wet and self-conscious against the wool. Then, for courage, she takes an old paperback from the shelf above her desk, and reads under her breath from *Seven against Thebes*, a delicious story of fratricide.

In college, although he should be at home already, Victor is uneasy. He is dreading the party; this year it is imperative that all goes well. He can only hope that Jean will not let him down.

He has just spent most of a tutorial looking for his spare tie, while pretending to search for a pamphlet on irrigation. Jean was once the sort of wife who left his laundry, newly ironed, in the wardrobe ready for him. That, however, was when she was young, shocked out of her natural languor by love – a phase which lasted, on reflection, about four months. Now he unearths his shirts from piles in the boiler-room, and hides semi-clean garments in college, for emergencies such as this.

This is the stage he hates: the getting-ready. He always suspects that he is on the wrong schedule; that everyone else has other instructions, for which they are infinitely better prepared. As he arranges the brown wool into something like a knot, he thinks of the nightmare he has every May, in which he is in the wrong hall in the wrong subject for finals. This dream, bad enough, comes with an attendant palm-sweating cold fear whose origin he will not, simply will not, allow himself to consider. (Although sometimes, without his leave, a thought does occur to him: is the muffled rushing in his ear perhaps the *sound* of this thing he must try not to think of – unburiable, rising?)

He blinks and it is gone; he makes it go.

Now, to the present.

This is his thirty-fourth St James's history party, but every third year, when he is the host, is the worst. It always seems his chance to shine, to be the affable, tolerant, brilliant paterfamilias he always intended to be: admired by colleagues, revered by students, beloved, not the distant monster he has become. Victor has made himself a promise: it is not too late. This evening, in the presence of his peers – and perhaps the President himself, in whose hands the Sir Henry Spenser Lectureship particularly rests – he will be convivial and learned, beyond rebuke: well worthy of the honour. If, that is, all goes smoothly. Hope, rather than logic, tells him that it will.

Phoebe has her own plans for tonight. In the pocket of her jeans, hard against her hipbone, rests a small lump wrapped in cling-film, provided by Tamsin, an older girl who once attended the Gate. It had been so easy: Phoebe had said hello to her one evening as Tamsin collected her brother, a stutterer in Phoebe's class, and within five minutes an arrangement had been made. She chose well. Tamsin's parents teach Ethics; she has very conscientiously explained techniques and options, has even demonstrated with a green ballpoint how to hold the finished product. Phoebe has been practising with Rice Krispies and her father's Tippex-y typewriter squares.

It is weirdly warm tonight; she can feel summer dying around her. She squeezes her glowing pocketful of treasure between her fingers; it feels hard-baked, impenetrable. By the time Dorcas, her friend and co-investor, comes round, she'll be more than ready.

The party, for what it is worth, has begun. Victor's colleagues and their Guernsey-wearing sensible wives have arrived, together with a handful of eager first-years, a clump of third-years obviously hoping to curry favour, and his unsettlingly nervous research student, whose colourless hair falls in three thin plaits from the crown of her head. Someone has already sliced into the cloudy wheel of Brie, and grape-wet bread-crumbs are sticking to the lips and jumpers of the more careless eaters – who are, of course, the majority.

As he smiles, stiff-jawed, at the not at all bad Latin witticism just murmured by his research student into her glass, he half hears the doorbell. He ignores it – Eve is in charge of arrivals. Instead he concentrates on the fact that he heard it at all, above the chatter of his guests and his own bad ear. He will focus on the present, as Henry Glover, a man who knew happiness, was always telling him to do. Even he, Victor, must accept that not much, this evening, is likely to go wrong. As he begins to peel the heavy foil from the neck of another bottle, he forces himself to relax, to be quite unprepared.

'Victor?'

His ears, surely, have deceived him. He keeps his back

turned, like a child ineptly hiding, and feels a firm hand on his shoulder.

No, he thinks. He lifts his head; he is facing the wall, but imagines scaling it, escaping, leaving the future behind. He is trapped here. He thinks: he has found me.

He hesitates until the last possible moment; then, heavily, turns. The hand has tightened. He is being smiled upon by Raymond Snow, his bête noire.

'Hello, Lux. Thought I'd drop by. How remiss of you not to invite me.'

Victor grasps the table-edge to steady himself. His enemy's smirk shows that he has seen. Raymond Snow is uncannily unchanged. Neither America nor Liverpool have worn him down; despite a decade of successful punditry, he has not acquired the burnish of studio lights. Bright-eyed, bony, avid, he looks exactly as he did when Victor first saw him, two places away as they posed for their Matriculation photograph, smoothing his silky cow-lick with a white plastic comb. An outcast, even then. His smile is still as sharp. He is an invented man, pulpy with deceit and dark intentions; an unlikely Lothario, a danger to them all.

Beside him a straggle-haired woman, dressed in what looks like a faded school blouse, is smiling with the cowed expression of a recently beaten dog. She seems too plain, Victor catches himself thinking, and suppresses the thought. Raymond Snow does not acknowledge her, even when she passes him a plate. They appear not to have eaten for some time.

'So,' he says, spearing a pale slice of Brie. 'Just arrived.'

Behind him Victor can hear, or thinks he hears, an

innocent roar of playing children and polite students, but he cannot hear his wife. Is she nearby? Has Raymond Snow seen her? He turns his head a little to the left and right, but is afraid that he will draw attention to her. His heart turns in his chest: an unsuccessful radar.

'Oh?' he says, feeling his hand tremble. It may be that Raymond Snow is here for a visit, or a lecture by a colleague. Even a seminar – even a *series* of seminars – would not be too bad, if he leaves at the end of it.

'Assume you've heard?'

It is like looking into the mouth of a sleeping shark. Victor, forcing himself not to step backwards, nods his uncombed head. 'Ah . . . ' he says.

'As of Friday, this Friday. Imperative that I start at once, apparently.' He parcels Stilton between soft scraps of bread, takes a neat gulp of wine, wipes his thin lips with one of Victor's own white paper napkins. Victor waits, his ears fizzing, longing to snatch up the napkin and take it down to the end of the garden to be burnt. His brain is refusing to take in the details. Instead he observes this slowness with interest: the general state, he supposes, of ordinary people.

'So,' says Raymond Snow, triumphant, resting one foot against a heavy garden chair. His hand stretches between them: white, black-tufted, flat-fingertipped. 'Just like our first day at Queen's.'

There is a booming in Victor's ears. He glares at his feet.

'Shake hands, Lux. We're equals again.'

Further down the garden, Eve has something of a shock. Without quite meaning to, she has begun to tell two of her father's ex-students the story of when Phoebe had leapt naked from her paddling-pool, across the lawn, and frolicked through quads and shrubbery to the college garden, where she had surprised the old President and several elderly philosophers on a tour of the grounds.

Peter Dunbarbin, a depressive wraith in a long brown tank-top, blushes from ear-tips to collarbone. Athena Kouriakis, a peroxided postgraduate known as the Laughing Greek, is crying tears of mirth.

'And she was how old?' she asks, wiping her eyes with her fingertips.

'Four, I think,' says Eve. She regrets beginning this. She wants to return to their last conversation: a description of the scimitar collection of one of Athena's many exes, a college chaplain. The evening air is cooling fast; the flames inside the borrowed gardeners' lanterns are beginning to bob and shiver. Her sister has been vile all evening, openly smirking when Eve came downstairs in her school shoes and a too-wide skirt from Laura Ashley, and has now disappeared inside the yew tree to whisper with Dorcas, leaving it all to her.

Eve's head is full of weapons, broken stone balconies and laburnum. She rests her cheek against a cool ivy leaf, breathes in a soothing lungful of limestone from the masons' yard behind the wall, and finds herself staring through a hole at a huge and bloodshot eyeball.

She shrieks, although she can guess its owner: Ralph Sorelson, an irascible ex-engineer who lives two houses away, and likes to visit the masons' yard for projects of his own. 'No madder,' as her mother remarks, 'than the next man,' he talks to himself so loudly that he has a separate room in the Bodleian Library, and walks backwards through North Oxford for two miles every morning, for obscure reasons of health.

'What is it?' asks the Laughing Greek.

Eve, still gripping Athena's sleeve in horror, looks again at the wall, but the eye has vanished. Perhaps he is looking for something to poke through at her.

'He should be stopped,' says Peter thinly. Eve's father says Peter believes college houses should go to impoverished young tutors only – like him, for instance. 'You see, whether under College statutes he is merely an incumbent, or . . .'

Eve nods, to humour him, but she must stay alert. She can hear the shriek of metal being sharpened. She looks for her mother, who is smiling vaguely on the edge of a circle of pink-cheeked first-years. She cannot be trusted to keep control. Her father, equally unreliable, is standing by the table, scratching anxiously at the back of his neck. Maybe the drink is already running out. Worst of all, Phoebe, who usually would be showing-off or sulking, is nowhere to be seen.

What is she up to? There must be a sinister reason for her absence. To Eve's left, the scraping of metal seems to be coming faster. Ahead, her father is still scratching his neck, more and more vigorously, as if he is trying to remove something that has settled there. And, to her right, in addition to old wood and leafmould, she can smell cigarettes, or incense, coming from the yew. If anything goes wrong at this party, her father's colleagues will think less of him. Perhaps, as a result, he won't get to give the Spenser Lecture – the one she is not supposed to know about, but does. Phoebe is going to ruin it all.

'Why don't . . . ' she begins, noticing that Peter's fly is mis-buttoned. 'Why don't we . . . um. Have you seen my mother?'

The garden is thick with cold unknowable life. 'Come

this way,' she insists, urging Athena and Peter towards the middle of the grass. If her mother were doing her share of looking-after, if her sister weren't so unconcerned, so dangerously selfish, Eve would not be singlehandedly trying to save her father's reputation, and looking like a fool.

'Peter,' she says, desperately. 'Um. Do you, tell me . . . do you have any thoughts about . . .'

Peter blows his nose and inspects his handkerchief. Athena, without a word, leaves them and walks towards a gorgeous second year. From the yew tree, Eve hears a sly little laugh. Hot with hatred, she turns away and glimpses her mother climbing the steps from the kitchen, an unparalleled smile on her face.

Jean Lux stands on the topmost step, surveying her guests. The last unattractive student and disapproving don's wife has arrived, hungry for entertainment. Despite the scents of dry leaves and bonfires, it is a warm late-summer evening, as if God, or the President, has taken pity on them. Provided her girls, in their several ways, and her husband behave themselves, all will be well, relatively. Covertly, under her loose black shirt, she undoes her trousers' upper button. She has just eaten a large wedge of Fourme d'Ambert, neatly included in her purchases for the party, yet she still feels unsettled.

These evenings make her feel both resentfully rebellious and fatly dowdy. She is no better than when she was twenty at flirting with the boy students or talking as if an equal to the girl students, but she is – as if she could forget it – twice their age. The other wives mistrust her; the graduates, unless they are polite because of Victor, seem to see her as merely a glass-passer, a bread-slicer, a sort of gossip-free scout.

Victor, she notices, is talking to a thin man whose back is turned to her, not by the look of him someone she knows. She will stay away. They are, unusually, almost the same height, and it is this, rather than her husband's harried expression, which registers. She is thinking of height, of Helena. She is wondering whether she should have done what she has just done.

She has telephoned her. They rarely telephone each other; it felt, as she dialled, enjoyably rash but, to her frustration, Helena did not seem pleased. Indeed, she was vexingly distracted, as if something more important were on her mind. Jean is used to her friend's oddities, her tendency to drift off in the middle of conversations, transfixed by an earwig's attempts to hide beneath a tile, but this was no comfort. Helena, who can cheer her more than anyone, was stilted and abrupt: Victor's grisly colleagues remained unanalysed, the fascinating mysteries of their clothes and spouses remained unpicked. By the end of the conversation Jean felt curiously desolate.

Then, at the last moment, with the decisiveness which Jean so admires, Helena saved her. She said, quite unexpectedly, 'I'm coming round.'

'Oh?' said Jean. 'Are you – I mean, are you sure? It would be lov—'

'I have to,' said Helena, whatever that meant. 'Five minutes.'

From her position on the top step, Jean watches the historians, ill-dressed, bitter, suspicious to the last. A short while ago she was stranded amongst them, her polite smile stiffening, longing for peace, privacy, like-mindedness, a cool breath of garden air. Now it is coming. A little uncertain, faintly alarmed, she smiles to herself, while the whirlwind gathers.

Helena unleashes her mauve bicycle, kicks her leg high over the tiny saddle and is away. She ignores the outraged squeak of Jeffrey's bedroom curtains. He does not let her out in the evenings without raging and tantrums but, at this moment, she does not care.

She is going to do it tonight. Oxford ticks with promise. She has been weary with worry, a battleground, scraped dry by making decisions and breaking them all. All day she longs for night to come, an end to tutorials and lectures, the continual, increasing, pressure. Night is when she can think.

But now, light-headed with shock and her own daring, she is not thinking but acting. She is moving almost too quickly to be frightened. Night wind streams across her hands, her neck, her eyes, like mercury. Nothing, no fear of friendship lost or retribution or humiliating pity, is going to stop her.

In the yew tree, muffled by waist-thick branches, damp brown needles and adult chatter, Phoebe is supporting a puking Dorcas.

'I'm holding you,' she says, listening to the reedy voices above the sound of retching. 'I've got your fringe—'

Dorcas heaves again, but the last of Victor Lux's vodka is already seeping through the needles to the floor. 'I . . . yeah, I think I'm OK,' she says, wiping her mouth on her shoulder. 'Fuck, that was . . . Do you think it's the booze, or the . . .'

In the dense darkness of the yew tree, Phoebe's eyes glint like a squirrel's, or a snake.

'You, you look like a s—' says Dorcas, beginning to giggle. 'Like a sss, a sn—'

Phoebe presses her wrist to her own smile. 'A what?' she says. She must be quiet, but silver leaves of laughter are slithering under her feet, across her brain, and the world is suddenly unsteady and hilarious. 'A ss?'

'A *sssn*—' begins Dorcas again. 'Stop it. A ss, a sns, a sss—'

'A sssugar? A sod? A ssssausausage? You are being stupid,' Phoebe says, in her father's voice. 'What do you mean, a sssausage? Be more precise.'

Dorcas's father is a builder, now living fatly off the new English faculty library. His voice is not like Phoebe's father's, and this imitation is the end of her. 'I *said*,' Dorcas snorts, 'I *said*—' and is undone, helpless, unlike Phoebe, who has taken out a cigarette paper and is holding a match to the last chocolatey crumbs.

'I know,' says Phoebe, a warrior king in a tent full of weapons. 'Why don't we stir things up a bit?'

From where she sits, bum tight in a curved yew-bough, she can just see her weird-looking sister, sucking up to the grown-ups in the middle of the garden. Her hair looks like a loo brush. She is drinking apple juice.

This morning, although no one else knows it, Phoebe's mother told her that at the end of this year she would be going to Bocardo's, a local liberal school with a reputation for art, horses, fun. 'Eve's school isn't really your thing, is it, lovey?' she said. 'You could if you wanted, I know you could, but – well, do you want to?'

'Huh,' said Phoebe. 'Course not.'

'That's what I, we, thought. You'll love Bocardo's.'

'I know,' said Phoebe, and it is true. Dorcas, Ali Morris, who wants to dye her fringe blue, and Martha Moxon, who can hardly count, are all going, and none of the squares. *They* go to Eve's school, Oxford Girls', of course. Phoebe may only be there for a year – the headmaster is so keen to get his spotty son into Phoebe's father's college that he's given her a Temporary Art Bursary, whatever that means – but she's going to make the most of it. Bocardo's will be great, everyone says so, and it costs loads, which means there'll be stuff to do. She'd hate Oxford Girls' – even if they asked her, which they won't. Creepy place. Through the swollen pine-smelling needles, Phoebe watches her sister.

'Eve,' says her mother, 'your top . . .' She reaches out and twitches at the fabric; Eve pulls away. 'Was that all you could find? Do you want to borrow something?'

Eve's scowl deepens. She knows she is hideous, and the thick boiled-seeming wool clings shamefully to her hips and breasts, but now she has been inspected and found to be misshapen, and the heat in her cheeks makes everything worse.

Bitch.

She stamps into the house thinking comforting thoughts: the tree in which Phoebe hides is reduced to kindling by a sudden storm; her father gives a speech praising his only true daughter; her mother rushes to help Eve hand out plates, and sees her arm. Selfish bitches, she thinks, pouring juice: angry enough to spit into the jug but, like a good girl, restraining herself, wiping up, putting away. There is so much loathing inside her that she feels like a ripe fig, about to split. All it would take is a little cut to relieve the pressure. She keeps at the front of her mind, like a promise, one thought: the thinness of skin.

Jean is drifting around at the kitchen end of the garden when she encounters Victor. She seems anxious. He is not in a placatory mood.

'Is it going, you know, all right, do you think?' she asks him. Sometimes he can see that he makes her nervous, but what does she expect? That he will hit her? Other men do, he knows, but he is not that type of man. Sometimes she looks at him as if she thinks he might, and he knows that in his stormiest, most wounding mood he might seem capable, but he is not. Why not? Is it race? Or love? He has never explained any of this to her. He fears her response may surprise him.

He can see from the way she turns to him, keeping her eyes on their guests, that she has barely thought of him all evening. He begins to chew abstractedly on the edge of his knuckle.

'Don't do that, Victor,' she says, gently taking his hand. His ear feels wadded with the filthy yellow fleece that lines their loft. He shakes his head, but says nothing. She is nearly two decades younger than he and has, beneath the gentleness, Phoebe's disdain for weakness. He exhales dragonishly through his nostrils; there is a stinging, constricted feeling in his throat he does not recognize. His hand is clenched inside his pocket; he keeps it there. She gives no sign of having seen Raymond Snow, but surely she has done so – although Raymond Snow has not been near her, and seems to be biding his time. He knows he must not ask her, but the uncertainty is intolerable. Now Raymond Snow is here, there will be nothing else.

Helena decides, pedalling swiftly, not to bother with the front door; it will waste time. She can imagine herself in the garden already, in the middle of it all. She will go straight through the side-gate, she decides, as she arrives at the turnstile, and finds it abandoned. There is no gate-porter to let her through.

The fool must be at servants' supper. She wipes her forehead with her sleeve, combs at the front of her hair with her fingers, picks a little soil from her fingernails. Now she is fully groomed, and ten seconds have passed, and there is still no porter to be seen.

She is breathing too quickly to think. Slow, she tells herself, slow, but everything in her, every chemical reaction and tiny pulse, impels her forwards. She cannot be slow.

Where *is* the man?

Barely bothering to look around her, Helena clasps the rusty bicycle to her breast and half-lowers, half-drops it on the other side of the turnstile. Then, one foot, one hand, two feet, she heaves herself up over the bars—

'Hoi!'

With a beery shout, the blurry glass bricks of the gate-porters' lodge fill with the silhouette of Arthur, who will not recognize her without her gown. She hitches her other foot up on to the top bar, and jumps, high, far, on to the other, private, side.

'Hoi!' yells Arthur again, as she skids around the corner on tiny bicycle wheels. She reaches the path and pulls open the side-gate. It looks as if someone has sent up a flare to warn them: every fading flower and neon blade of grass is blurred, as if with heat haze, yet startlingly itself. Her mother-in-law's bicycle crashes against the dustbins, but already Helena is walking, swift and unstoppable, towards the garden.

'So,' says Eve wearily. 'You mean a thing is – no. Sorry. I still . . . say it again?'

Alison Williams, a fantastically ill-favoured ex-Oxford Girls' girl, now in her second year of Victor, smiles. A spot beside her mouth, unused to the exercise, begins to bleed: a bright perforation in the suety surface of her skin. Eve watches, fascinated, as the bead swells and brightens. 'A thing is either carried because it is a carried thing, or is a carried thing because it is carried. Just as a thing is either a . . . a *loved* thing' – her hand moves to the spot; Eve is unable to look away – 'because it is loved,' she blinks hard, several times, 'or it is loved because it is a loved thing.'

Plainly she has never been either. Eve's brain is straining. She thinks she follows, but it's the kind of mental test she *should* be able to follow; perhaps she only imagines that she can. She fears she is stupider than she realizes. There are assessing eyes all around her: her mother's, her father's, her sister's, glintingly, from the yew. She has run out of questions, all her father's more glamorously clever students are occupied elsewhere, with the red wine and each other. The sore place on her arm feels burnt. If it becomes infected, what could she tell a doctor? She should be enjoying herself, but all she feels is a hot, dismal anger, and a longing to return to her bedroom for more of the same.

'At least, that's what Plato said,' says Alison, with Brie-speckled enthusiasm. 'But Aquinas—'

*

'Have you ever thought,' says Dorcas in the yew tree, exhaling a plumey smoke-stream, 'that this place, like, you know, this town, is, like, a flowerbed? And everyone is, you know, really tall, or really short? And you have to be tall, or they'll—'

'No,' says Phoebe.

Raymond Snow looks up from the Stilton, towards the masons' yard.

'Funny screeching noise,' he says to Victor who is, white-knuckled, opening another bottle. 'Wouldn't want to live this close to the college, myself. Not that I'll have to. It's Park Town for me.'

The twin crescents of Park Town are, after the Spenser Lectureship, the college's greatest prize. Victor, imagining a perfect Georgian house, newly infested, tightens his hand around the corkscrew and hears footsteps.

Helena is approaching. The air in the garden appears to part before her. What is she doing here? thinks Victor. He does not want her here. He closes his eyes.

'You all right, Lux?' says Raymond Snow, peering over his shoulder for the source of Victor's distress. 'Looking ropy.' Then he catches sight of Helena, blazing past the side of the house. She is heading for Victor's wife.

'Friend of yours?' he asks, regarding her with interest. As Helena sweeps past him, he keeps her in his sights.

There, on the step, is Jean, smiling sweetly. She bites her lip and holds out her hand.

'Helena, thank you so much for coming. I—'
'We have to talk,' says Helena.

'Well,' begins Jean, but it is too late. Helena, skirt swishing, is storming through the heedless undergraduates, towards the horse-chestnut at the far end of the garden. Anxiously, Jean wipes her fingers on her grey wool trousers, tucks a silvery strand of hair behind her ear, and follows her.

Here the historians' drone is deadened by gorging insects and autumnal birdsong. The neighbouring gardens are in uproar; the air is bright with decay. Jean plucks at the fabric of her shirt and moves aside a papery swathe of wisteria. Then she steps carefully around the chestnut through the damp lush grass, towards Helena, who is waiting.

'Are – are you all right?' she asks.

Helena turns. In the thick violet light, her eyes are sepulchral.

'Helena, dear, what is it? I should – I ought to be—'

The long grass shushes around Helena's ankles as she steps backwards. Her fingers worry at a mossy ridge of bark. She takes a breath. She will not look at Jean.

'So here we are,' she says eventually. 'Are you, ah, well?'

Jean frowns in disappointment. The drama of Helena's arrival, and an obscure excitement, had led her to expect rather more than this. 'Well, I'm fine, thank you. Are you – how are you?'

'Hmm,' says Helena, picking at the tree. Her mouth closes with a faint dry click.

This could go on all night. While Jean does not want to return to the party, there is something alarming about her odd friend's particularly odd behaviour. There is, she realizes, a reason for Helena's visit.

'What is it?' she asks abruptly.

'It's not . . .' Helena says. 'It's not—'

Jean's small allotment of patience falters, and dies. 'Well—' she begins, and tries again, keeping her voice down. 'It's obviously *something*.'

Helena turns her head away. Her mouth is trembling.

Jean steps forward, suddenly fearful. 'Tell me. Tell me now. Helena? For God's sake.' Her voice will not be calm. 'You're ill, aren't you. How ill?'

'I – no, I'm not,' says Helena. 'Not strictly.'

'Oh . . . I thought . . . And Jeffrey's all right?'

'Yes. Sort of. Yes.'

If not death, then . . . 'Oh, no,' she says. 'It's not – it's not Simon, is it?' Of course: the secret misery of Helena's widowhood, the signs she should have noticed, the assurances swept aside. 'Hell. I thought, you see, that – it's been so long, I thought, but of course, not for you – you must be missing him so horribly – I really thought you were getting over it. I've been so—'

'Simon?' says Helena. She straightens her back against the chestnut trunk. 'I – I don't feel as you think I feel about him, if you want to know the truth. It never seemed like the right time to tell you, but I just don't.'

'You don't?'

'He was a lying shit, wasn't he, and frankly I feel, I feel . . . nothing but relief since his death.'

'Oh.' Jean's mouth hangs open. 'Do you mean—'

'I . . . I just didn't say so. That's why I went so quiet.'

'I assumed—'

'I know. And if you thought, by the way, that I didn't know . . . what everyone else knew. The affairs. That he died actually – of course I did. He was a horrible bitter man.'

'I thought so too ... I mean – Well, there it is. Stupid to think you didn't. Of course you did. I thought you adored him. He was so good-look—'

'Well, yes. Naturally you did,' says Helena. 'Everyone did.'

Jean nods encouragingly, but Helena's face is stony. 'So what is it?' she asks, full again of foreboding. The air seems too crowded to breathe. 'What *is* wrong?'

Helena, her revelations apparently exhausted, shakes her head.

'I need to know,' says Jean, trying to sound ready. 'Please tell me.'

Helena takes a deep breath. She looks ominously exhausted. 'I'm, I'm trying,' she says. 'Please. It's ... I can't ...'

Oh, God, thinks Jean. It's something terrible for *me*. Helena is leaving me. She snatches at an overhanging leaf and angrily begins to tear little crenellations from its spines. 'Are you ... are you moving away?'

Helena swallows. 'No,' she says, with a little twitch of her mouth. 'Unless I have to.'

What then? Jean searches for other betrayals. If not death, then, surely, love. But whom? 'It's not ... it's not Victor, is it?'

It's almost funny, but Helena doesn't smile. 'No. Not Victor. But it ... it ... it is someone.'

'I can't bear this. I don't care who – who is it then?'

'It's you.'

*

Jean stares. Nearby, almost underfoot, something begins to chirrup, as if orchestrated by Helena herself. Another noise follows, this time from Helena's throat: a sort of compressed moan. She ducks her head and, blindly, half-garrotted by wisteria fronds, walks away.

Jean stands alone beside the chestnut. 'I—' she begins.

Helena shakes her head, and keeps walking.

'Me?' says Jean.

Helena stops. Her narrow back seems turned inwards, as if she is clutching at herself. 'Don't make me repeat it,' she says in a muffled voice.

'But—'

'Just *don't*. Forget it. I can't believe—'

'But how can I forget it?' Jean's eyes are beginning to smart, with the effort of staring, or something. 'D—' but she cannot call her Dear, even for comfort; not after this. 'It's not the sort of comment you just forget—'

'I should never have said . . .'

'But you *did* say,' says Jean. 'You . . . are you . . . I can't—'

There is a heavy metallic crash and then, in the silence that follows, someone begins to cry.

In an instant Jean has crossed the dark end of the garden and streaked towards the table. Her younger daughter is sobbing on the grass, her foot trapped under the cast-iron leg of a chair. Jean drops to her knees beside her. The party has realigned itself in solemn little groups. She seizes Phoebe's hand.

'What happened?' she asks. Phoebe, crying harder now, shakes her head. 'For God's sake,' shouts Jean at the nearest students, 'are you blind? *Move the chair.*'

Sheepishly, someone steps forward and lifts it away. As her foot is released, Phoebe's face turns a shade paler.

Jean's murmurings of comfort are lost as she embraces her. Victor kneels, awkwardly, and tries to inspect the injured foot.

'Ow!' shrieks Phoebe, pulling it away from his stubby fingers. 'Don't *touch*!'

'For God's sake, Victor, please,' says Jean, her face wet. 'Don't *touch* her. You might damage it – what happened? My poor love—'

'It looks somewhat – bruised,' Victor announces.

'Can she move the toes?' someone says at the back.

'Can you move your toes, darling?' asks Jean.

'I – don't know,' says Phoebe, wincing horribly, although she is staring in the direction from which her mother ran. There is a faint smear of night along the top of her foot. She returns her gaze to her mother. 'Crushed,' she moans. Her toes, however, wiggle.

'Thank God,' whispers Athena loudly.

'What happened?' asks Jean again. 'Did you fall? Where's Dorcas? Did she—'

'*No*,' Phoebe wails, burrowing closer. '*Dorcas*? It wasn't—'

'Jean,' says Victor carefully, 'it's, ah—'

Jean sits back, her arm still around Phoebe's shoulders. Her eyes sweep across the gathered faces, her face impassive. Then she stops. Her gaze rests on her elder daughter.

'Jean—' begins Victor.

'What,' says Jean, speaking slowly and distinctly, as to an idiot, 'did you do to her?'

The students hold their breath.

'I—' says Eve.

'I'm waiting.'

From her mother's arms, Phoebe's sobbing begins again. 'It hurts,' she whispers to her mother, 'so-oo much.'

'She was . . . ' Eve begins, weeping herself now, her hands grasping miserably at each other. 'She was . . . *not helping*, and . . . and she ran out of the tree and knocked *in* to me, and – the chair *fell*. I couldn't *help* it.'

'She pushed it,' wails Phoebe. 'On to me!'

'Did you?' demands Jean. The clusters of undergraduates are beginning to disperse; several of the most cowardly slip away through the side-gate. From his vantage-point beside the garden table, Raymond Snow watches the shadows at the end of the garden, one eyebrow raised.

'Not on purpose,' sobs Eve, wiping her face with her sleeve. She looks desperately for witnesses, but no one speaks. 'I didn't mean—'

'She *did*,' spits Phoebe.

Jean nods, slowly, certainly. Eve stares at her, distraught. Then, undignified and melodramatic as ever, Eve rushes from the crowd, almost crashing into Alison Williams, tripping over the step and racing into the house. She is watched in silence by them all; even Dorcas, wobbling out of the yew tree, says nothing until she leaves. Then the chatter begins again: impractical suggestions, words of comfort, Jean and Phoebe's tears. No one present has done a first-aid course or can make a stretcher. All agree that Phoebe's toe-moving is a good sign, an excellent sign: they congratulate her, and each other. Now that Eve, the snot-faced banshee, has gone, the atmosphere is celebratory. More wine is poured, discreetly at first; the Brie is devoured ('Survival makes one so hungry,' they say, turning to the Stilton); Dorcas asks for a go on her wheelchair, if it comes to that.

*

Victor Lux, his moment of paternal manliness come at last, hoists his daughter over his shoulder. Staggering slightly, he carries her out of the side-gate and through the dusty lane, towards the masons' yard and the fellows' garages. Jean follows, supporting her daughter's feet.

'You'll be there in moments,' reassures the Rt. Hon. J. T. T. Kramer, MA, DPhil, Hon. DCL, FBA, the shadowy Pro-Vice-Chancellor and President of Victor's college. His unexpected arrival had seemed, to Victor, a good sign, until he saw him making his way through the crowd like an urbane missile, towards Raymond Snow. Even now, with Phoebe heavy in his arms, he cannot stop wondering what was being discussed, and why it could not wait.

His daughter's elbow digs into his shoulder as she waves at the students. Her mouth, he realizes anxiously, is beside his bad ear.

He pauses for breath. 'Do we,' he asks his wife, 'ah, know, precisely, the direction—'

The shining new hospital on the hill opened years ago, but Victor, happily, has never been. 'Of course we do,' she says impatiently.

They approach the comforting brown bulk of the elderly Volvo. The party is over, but not everybody seems to have noticed. A large group is standing in the lane; others, fears Victor, may be lurking behind the gate.

'Ah, Jim,' he says, gesturing helplessly with his free shoulder. 'I am afraid . . .'

Jim Kramer, blue-eyed, silver-haired, is the man for a crisis. 'Why, naturally,' he says, beginning to shepherd dons and students down the lane towards St Giles. Victor, unable to see clearly over his daughter's plait, cannot tell if Raymond Snow is among them. He prays that he is.

'I'll close the gate behind me,' calls the President, with an elegant wave. 'It will be perfectly safe.'

'Thank you,' calls Jean.

Victor, unable to prevent himself, turns and sees the President and Raymond Snow rounding the curving wall of the lane, heads close in conversation. He hesitates.

'Come *on*, Dad,' shrieks Phoebe.

They disappear together around the bend, leaving Victor alone with his family, his worst fears realized – at least, his worst fears to date.

Not all his family. One of its members is storming around her bedroom. She throws pillows, slippers, even a book, gently, across the floor. She rounds on herself in the mirror and glowers at her own lemon-peel eyes.

Her sobs of rage and self-pity which, now everyone has left the garden, cannot be overheard, have dwindled to a continual stream of silent tears. For a few dreadful minutes, Eve had thought they were going off to get the police. Then she had remembered the hospital. Even as she cursed and wept, she listened out for the telephone. Her parents, however, have not called; they are not interested in hearing her version. Now the house is quiet. Night fills the garden. She keeps away from the window: the last time she drifted there, she saw someone in a long dress creeping up the side of the lawn, well after the other stragglers had left.

She is too upset to be frightened. She is more afraid that her parents will leave her alone all night. She can imagine her mother striding angrily past hospital telephones, her father simply forgetting. Choral music, intricate and self-absorbed, drifts through the open window. She sits on the floor by the bed, looking at the place where, hidden on a bookshelf, the Finnish knife she stole from her father lies in its scabbard, waiting to hatch. She visits it often. Even at this distance she can feel its weight, its edge.

Phoebe comes home from the hospital a beautiful martyr. At breakfast she describes in hilarious detail her hobbling attempts to steal chocolates from the nurses' station while awaiting the X-ray results. Eve, now also in trouble for having left cheese and open bottles out all night, stares blackly at her Weetabix and resolves to achieve transcendence. The mere thought lightens her stomach, like hunger; she will work for an extra hour, no, an extra ninety minutes a night, becoming ethereally thin and graceful in the process. There are exams at the end of term; she will excel, overcoming the shameful prospect of failure, or boredom, or misery, and nothing at home will matter. Her future, her very survival, depends on this.

Once, Helena worked because she loved it. Today, however, it is as if an ink-cloud blocks the way to her desk, or a spider's screen laced with poison. She cannot think. She cannot move. She sits in her tutorial armchair, curled into a hard dry ball, digging her fingers violently into her hair. Like a stupid philosopher, of whom she knows several, her mind beats heavily against two basic truths:

If only she had said nothing.
If only she had died at birth.
She tries to make her mind a vacuum, to ignore or at least avoid the sickening shame which crinkles her brain and

clutches her stomach and sets her groaning aloud into her knees, eyes tight, heart tighter. Oh God, she thinks. What have I done?

She has not left this room since nine this morning, does not know how she made it here or what she may have said. She has missed lectures and a seminar, is afraid even to go to her window in case Jean, whose name she can barely think of without wanting to beat out her brains on the bookcase, is on her way to leave a letter to tell her that their friendship is over, and happens to glance up.

Fool, fool, fool, she tells herself, although it is far too late for that. She has lost everything.

Bells strike the hour, but she is locked inside her own breathing and the infinite adjustments of the armchair springs, and does not lift her head until the last note dies. Is it two, or four, or later? From where she sits she can see only a billowy square of sky above the old city wall, and the tops of the tallest trees in Magdalen Grove. She has fantasies of flight, and sudden downfall.

It is not yet dark, outside.

Gregory Forfar, her least favourite research student, is pacing and coughing on the landing. She has locked both the inner and outer doors to her rooms, in breach of college etiquette, and now sits in a tomb of her own devising while he watches for her on the stairs. She cannot fling herself about, or howl too loudly, or leave, which may be a blessing. Her body is starved and rattling, like a shell. What was she thinking? It is too late for regret, but oh, if only if only she had not spoken. She would give her soul for that.

*

Jean has spent the last seven hours positioned neatly in front of her work, her mind blazing. Unfortunately for her, Hedley (his great domed forehead lightly sweating, his small Coptic beard growing greyer by the hour) has chosen today to catalogue a collection of eighteenth-century psalters, discovered in a shoe-box in a college guest bedroom, and the Cupboard is full of dust and his mutterings, none of which are helping her think. Now that the Phoebe and Eve fuss is over she must think, she keeps telling herself, but she feels dazed. Perhaps, by fastening on an aspect of last night's extraordinary conversation, all will become clear.

Nothing is clear.

Her nails, untouched since she first arrived in Oxford, have been bitten short; the buttons on her cuff have been nibbled; she has even sucked her wedding ring – none of which has helped. Whenever Hedley leaves the room she emits strangled cries at the cornicing; she has visited the toilet so often, for muted exclamations and grimacing squawks of astonishment, that Hedley has said (he has a new young viola-playing girlfriend, thinks of himself as a man of the world), 'You know, Jean, if you're – if there's ever a, if you need a doctor's, you know, appointment, ever, don't hesitate—'

'Yes, thank you, I certainly will,' said Jean, weeping actual tears of embarrassment from which, to Hedley's alarm, she is forced to return to the toilet to recover.

She moves between confusion, alarm and a sort of amazed amused elation, so quickly: she barely has time to register one emotion before the next begins. What, she keeps wondering, is she supposed to think?

She leans forward against the little basin and examines her face in the mirror, trying to ignore the section of chapel window reflected over her shoulder. She was brought up a

Methodist; chapels make her uncomfortable. Merely peeing within eyeshot feels irreligious, let alone thinking about—

Helena. Oh my God.

Jean is not a racy woman. She has her roles, in which she is comfortable, just about, although in the past – arguing with Eve, or emerging from under the duvet beside a now-supine Victor – she has watched herself, and wondered how she came to be doing this. None of these roles include being found attractive, let alone . . .

'Jean,' says Hedley, his mouth very close to the toilet door. 'Jean? *Jean.*'

'Oh . . .' Oh God. Bugger, bugger. Oh God—

'Are you – is – are you quite all right?'

'Sorry, sorry. Yes. Sorry. Were—'

'Yes. I was. Look, if you think you're infectious—'

Am I? wonders Jean. Can this be? 'I don't think . . .'

'Well. Look. If you've quite finished . . . resting, we do need Swanson's legacy done today. If at all possible.'

Jean, lost in thick grass and birdsong, in a vision of Helena's face as she confessed, remembers as if through fog her duties, her files, the world as she thought she knew it. She emerges, averts her eyes, sits numbly at her desk. Her day's work lies in front of her on her blotter: a letter on headed college paper beginning 'Dear Helena,' ending there.

'*Jean.* For goodness' sake. Perhaps this job is a little too—'

Jean smoothes her hair out of her eyes. 'No, no, absolutely fine. Sorry. Just a . . . cold. Actually, you know,' she says, covering the letter with her elbow and turning to him, 'it's not going too badly.'

'Isn't it? Let me see.'

Reluctantly, Jean passes him the leather-bound book into which the last eight months have disappeared, and as he begins to leaf through the pages she sees, dark as a badge, a love-bite on the plucked-looking skin of his neck. An enormous blush, which has been struggling under her skin all day, swells, crests and engulfs her. She turns back to her desk and stares at the wall, feeling the heat of her cheeks with her palms.

Her brain simultaneously marvels at, recoils from and denies it; she wants to discuss it with everyone, and forget it at once. One thing, however, is certain. She can never see Helena again.

Oxford, however, is a small town. Their homeward journeys overlap, they both visit the Gate, and there are few shops where Pyrex jugs and gym-knicker elastic may be bought. They will bump into each other eventually, Jean tells herself. It is only natural. However, there is no one she would rather avoid.

I am *not* avoiding her, she tells herself, as she walks laboriously to work via the chain-store tangle on Cornmarket: her least favourite route, and the slowest by far. She is jumpily prepared for her to emerge from every jangling doorway, ten feet tall and unforgiving, a Helena she has never known. She keeps her eyes on the phallic strut of Christ Church, towering above the sweatshirt shops and chemists, to steady her mind, but it will not be steady. Helena, are you mad? What have you done?

At least her journey gives her time to think. At home it is impossible. Phoebe, whose ankle has swiftly recovered, still seems to feel shaken, despite Jean's loving but slightly distracted attempts at nursing. Eve, sulky, defensive, is spending more and more time in her bedroom, and comes downstairs even pricklier than before. Victor, Victorishly, appears not to have noticed; he is more absorbed in his work than ever, leaving Jean and her younger daughter to cheer and comfort each other – and even that, at times, is a little strained.

Eventually, on Tuesday evening after dinner, something breaks.

All I want, Jean is thinking, is a long soak in my rose bath oil, which on second thoughts was from Helena, so perhaps not that, and time to consider—

'I need a pony,' says Phoebe.

Eve, who is passing her mother a pile of dirty plates, freezes. Jean feels herself wilt. Victor does not even look up.

'Since when?' Eve asks, rather aggressively.

Phoebe, ignoring her, grins at Jean. 'I know you'd be surprised. But I've been desperate for one – you know how I've been practically living with Dorcas, and she's got two—'

'Well, yes,' begins Jean. 'But—'

'And you said I was brilliant when I had those lessons, they did too, you said they did.'

'Yes, I know,' says Jean, feeling the raging waters of her family life beginning to close above her head. 'You were brilliant. A natural, they said, didn't they? Victor? You remember.' It is true. That she, a drainage inspector's daughter, should have produced such a child amazes her daily. 'But—'

'And you know how I love animals, and I do need the exercise, you said . . .'

'You wouldn't if you didn't skive Games,' says Eve, who is herself no athlete, and has never wanted a pony in her life.

Phoebe narrows her eyes. 'Just because you don't want me to have one,' she tells her sister, 'doesn't mean I can't.'

Fair point, thinks Jean vaguely, although she is momentarily enjoying a little spurt of pride (it has flared once or twice before today, when Victor was complaining, or Eve was looking anguished about her latest almost-perfect essay). I am only thirty-nine, she tells herself. Everything is not over. I am still wantable. *Me*.

'And besides – ouch,' says Phoebe. 'Mum, can you move that chair a bit nearer? I need to rest my ank—'

Jean recovers, temporarily. 'But . . . ' she says, bringing a stool from the hall. She ignores the temptation to dump it on the floor and leave them to it. Could she go for a walk? They look at her expectantly. 'Oh, I don't know. Victor?'

Victor, sounding irritable even for Victor, says: 'Phoebe, this is ridiculous. Where would we keep it? Who would look after it? And—'

'*I* would,' insists Phoebe. There are tears in her eyes. 'You're always *saying* I need more responsibility and stuff, and I *will*. I'll *love* it—'

'Do not interrupt me,' says Victor. 'And it is "I would love it," not "I will love it". We are in the realms of the subjunctive, and *were* we to leave that realm, I *would* tell you.'

Eve has begun noisily to wash up the custard pan, but Jean can see the corner of her mouth, and she is smirking. 'Phoebe,' she says, 'darling. We—'

'Kindly do *not* interrupt,' says Victor. 'As I was saying, Phoebe, the likelihood that you would indeed look after any such animal were I to buy it for you will never be known. We cannot afford a horse—'

'A *pony*,' says Phoebe, wiping her nose with a nearby napkin.

'—or anything like one, and it is most unlikely that we ever shall. Do you have any idea how much they eat? Hundreds of pounds worth of straw a term,' he extemporizes.

Jean winces. 'And equipment? Let alone stabling costs? God Almighty.'

'Anyway,' Eve adds, 'since when did you ever—'

'This is not your business,' says Jean sharply. Her head is beginning to ache, and all this while her outside life is caving in, unnoticed.

'I thought,' Phoebe says, beginning to weep again, 'that you wanted me to be *happy*. Do you want me to be the only one at Bocardo's? Left out and, and, *laughed* at?'

Jean stares into the middle distance. Oh God, she thinks. What can I say if I see her? Did I encourage her? How could— Oh *God* . . .

'No one is laughing at you, Phoebe,' says Victor.

Jean, half-registering Victor's tone, returns to save her daughter. 'Look,' she says. 'I know . . . I know Bocardo's might be . . . hard. It *is* a – well, well-off school—'

'Stinking rich,' says Eve. 'It's ridic—'

Jean shakes her head at her and smiles at Phoebe, feeling her heart sink. 'I suppose—'

Phoebe's face changes. She takes Jean's hand and grins. 'And anyway,' she says, 'we . . . there is *somewhere* we could keep it.'

'Where?' asks Victor. 'Tell me that.'

'On Port Meadow?' suggests Jean. 'People do keep them there, I think. It *is* enormous. And very green. Though where—'

'I know!' says Phoebe. 'I have a place!'

'Do not be ridiculous,' says Victor.

'In the college stables!' says Phoebe triumphantly. 'In Binsey!'

Eve, disgusted, turns away. Victor blinks and shakes his head, a gesture Jean feels she has seen every single time she has ever made a flippant suggestion, or expressed a desire for anything out of the ordinary. She strokes Phoebe's bare toes as Victor says: 'Highly unlikely. Those stables are disused. How were *you* planning to change that?'

Phoebe takes her time. She blows her nose imperfectly, puts on lip salve, gingerly prods her ankle. 'They are used,' she says eventually. 'Actually, they are. The President keeps his hunters there.'

'How do you know?' asks Eve, with a sneer.

Phoebe lifts her chin and stares at her through half-closed lids. Jean, whose mind has veered back to Helena, and the question of what will happen on Thursday, their usual day for lunch at the Panty, returns to her daughter. 'Phoebe,' she says, warningly.

'I asked him!' Phoebe says.

It appears that Phoebe, who is after all the President's god-daughter, had been sent a Get Well card, and had decided to telephone to thank him. Despite remembering his surname only imperfectly, she had persuaded a porter to put her through to his lodgings.

'I thought he'd want to hear about our problem,' she says. 'So I told him.'

'You told him *what*?' asks Victor. Even with his muffled ear, he knows he has begun to shout. '*Our* problem? What will he think? You idiotic child, what have you done?'

Jean's attempts to calm him only make it worse. Perhaps, as he knows she suspects, he is upset for other reasons, but he cannot discuss them with her. He might, in all honesty, conceivably be able to afford a horse – a small, or perhaps merely old, one. The college owns his house; the girls' education requires only a nominal input from him; they take depressing summer holidays at Jean's father's cottage. His income may be small, but their outgoings are, thankfully, smaller. However, the very idea of it, and the President's involvement, has alarmed him. He has, moreover, a possibly groundbreaking article on feudal justice to finish. He cannot bear to stay at home any longer.

Yet even as he enters the college he knows he cannot work. The peace has gone. When he stands still he can hear, under the heavy quiet and the organ-practice, the hum of an unknown motor. Raymond Snow is all around him: in the dark eyes of Lenin, flyposted for a student play in almost every doorway, the glossy crests on the chapel roof, the gaping mouths of the drainpipes, the shadows behind every leaded pane. Like a ghostly groom on his way to the altar, he walks alone past the grey statues of Laudian Quad towards the gardens.

He does not want the gardens themselves tonight. They are too full of life. Instead he stands at their gated entrance, trying not to think of the contamination at his back. He imagines himself before an audience of his peers, worthy of their respect. He could, he knows, deliver the Spenser Lecture just as well as Raymond Snow. With the right subject he could lecture gloriously. He did in his youth – he was famous for it – but lately age and embarrassment have made him lose the knack.

He trails his fingers over the panelling in the archway, listening to the whisper of rare trees in the moonlight. His fingers reach further and further back, until he finds a favourite spot on the panelling, a smooth egg-shape among the carved lozenges. It has seen him through difficult times: with Jean, with the girls, with Raymond Snow the first time round. He touches it to remind him of his luck: that there is a place where learning is all, and it has welcomed him. He might have lived like his poor sister, too grateful for having a life at all to admit to being book-starved, beauty-starved. He, Victor, feasts. His hungry frightened past is behind him. And yet – because no Jew has luck like that, or because he was not sufficiently thankful – his other, more recent past, like the dragon on the fellows' garden gate, has come back to devour him.

'I may be ill,' says Jean.

'Where is my blue shirt?' Victor asks.

Jean rolls over and closes her eyes. It is Thursday. In four hours she is supposed to be meeting Helena in the Panty, and at this particular moment she would rather walk naked into town than face her in front of the fishy eyes of those men. Her embarrassment seems to have expanded. It pushes against every pore, growing ever hotter, fed by an underground spring of what seems to be anger.

She had not expected anger – but then she had neither expected nor asked for any of this. Did Helena not know what they had? Did she think that friendships like theirs were easily won? And how, having produced a stick of dynamite from behind her back, does she expect it to recover? She hasn't written, or telephoned; is she expecting Jean to turn up at lunch to offer comfort? Well, she'll damn well have to think again. If they are to rebuild their friendship, she is the one who should make the next move.

Jean clenches her fists, determined not to weaken, and thinks of the worst outrage: Helena's irreplacability. With whom is Jean supposed to discuss all this? Who else will help her decide what to do? Thanks to Helena's insane idea, Jean has only two options: bereavement, or the unimaginable awkwardness of a meeting. She wants neither.

Damn you, Helena, she thinks. Damn you. Confusingly, however, she has begun to smile into the pillow, and cannot stop. She, who had begun to feel fly-blown, dust-furred, is wanted. Wanted! She snorts through her nose into the feathers.

'You are not ill,' says Victor.

For the second time this week, Jean wears her favourite white shirt. She cycles to the Cupboard like an extra in a crowd scene: straight back, clear hand-signals, her body merely a surface to be seen. She must, she decides, do something; if not for Helena's sake, then for her own. She spends the morning steeling herself either to turn up for lunch or send a note. By ten, she commands herself, or eleven, or twelve, I will act.

Lunchtime, however, finds her standing in the academic section of Blackwell's, no note sent. It had seemed like a refuge, but she has known some of the assistants by sight since before she was married. In every alcove she encounters Gate mothers, St Thomas's tutors, Victor's students. She is not safe here.

She cannot, however, tear herself away. Barely breathing, entirely failing to maintain an expression of bland curiosity, she reads two horrendous pages of *The Well of Loneliness,* an essay on vampirism in the art of the Weimar republic, poems about petals in the juvenilia of an Oxford poet, and a frankly extraordinary discourse on butch/femme self-allocation in a psychology manual from the University of Nantucket. Each leaves her more confused than the last. Everything – her shoes, her mascara, the fact that she rides an old bicycle of Victor's – seems laden with unwanted significance. She leafs through the Ls in a medical textbook, and is horrified.

It is only when she finds herself looking for Sappho that she manages to stop. Bewildered, blushing, increasingly plagued by guilty thoughts of Helena alone in the Panty, she forces herself outside and pauses for breath on the pavement. A man in a brown shirt and kipper tie is admiring the Byzantium window display. Behind him a thin woman pinches the tyres of her enormous tricycle, watched from their seat on the back by a pair of solemn children, their pudding-bowl haircuts unruly versions of her own, scuffed T-bars swinging in secret syncopation. Jean smiles reassuringly at no one in particular and smoothes her hair from her eyes. I have nothing to be ashamed of, she tells herself. I am merely engaging in research.

She crosses the road, looking particularly carefully to her left, towards Helena's college. There is no one she recognizes outside the art bookshop. She seizes her chance and hurries upstairs.

However, after twenty undisturbed minutes of female flesh she feels no better; she doesn't even know what she feels. She gazes upon the monumental thighs of Roman goddesses, Ingres' beautiful bottoms, saints' repellent squirting breasts.

She feels nothing.

Really nothing?

Curiosity. Envy, perhaps; occasional relief. Is she drawn to any of them? No. Not in the slightest. She picks up another book, this one on Modigliani, and hesitates. There is something about these stretched women, their narrow, modest, flushed faces, that she has always liked, but they *are* art: she is supposed to like them. Moreover, other images, unwanted ones – Helena's bony shoulders, her wrists, her . . . well, body, as she guesses it might be – have begun to assail her. She turns away. This is not for her.

A few streets away, Helena is writing.

~~Dear Jean,~~
~~Jean,~~
~~Dear Jean~~
~~Jean, I~~

There is no question of meeting Jean for lunch. She has said nothing, has sent no indication that she can accept or forgive what Helena has told her, or that she ever wants to see her again. Helena's impulse is to write, but every attempt becomes either a downpour of explanation and self-analysis, or a stiff cold note, and she can send neither. It is for Jean to indicate that she wants further contact, and her silence shows quite clearly that she does not. Helena must accept it. She must.

Half an hour later Victor, crossing the road beside the Bodleian Library, is almost run over by the pigeon-post delivery boy who bears a letter sent by Helena – written to his wife but addressed at the last minute, under the curious eye of a porter, to herself.

'Fool,' he growls, but is shaken: only last year an ex-tutee, jilted and drunk and Lord knows what else, stepped naked in front of traffic only yards from here. The press was everywhere, of course. He should be careful, particularly with his ear, but even before he has reached the other side carefulness is forgotten. He is distracted; saving himself is not a priority.

The last experience Victor had of Raymond Snow is one he has repeatedly tried to forget. Raymond Snow was elsewhere – that was the point. It was just Victor and Jean, walking through the wild wet grass on the far bank of the River Cherwell, seventeen years ago.

'Where did I leave this?'

There was a cigarette case protruding from Jean's bookbag. That was how it began. His words can still return without warning; they leave him tight with shame. In the second before he reached out and took it, his mind had squeezed full of love: because she had thought to bring it for him; because she was walking with him despite the weather; because, after half a year of courteous restraint by Victor, they had been sleeping together for two weeks today, and her soft calm Englishness moved him almost to tears. He snapped open the catch.

'What is this?' he asked.

On the right was a row of cigarettes, each printed with a tiny Queen's College crest: all as it should be. On the left, however, stamped on to the cheap vaguely-gold metal was a pattern new to him: a streamlined herringbone. It was not his case, after all.

'Jean?' he said, as a boatload of wild-haired undergraduates shot past, rowing to the croak of a boy in a blanket. The moorhens scattered. 'Whose is this?'

'Oh,' she said airily, looking up at him with her lovely eyes, 'a friend's. Just a friend's. I'm . . . returning it.'

'I see,' said Victor as she walked on. He felt his senses slow. 'Which friend?'

'Um,' said Jean. 'Um . . . Victor.'

Her face was solemn, as if a mask had been removed.

'Oh hell.'

'What?'

'I . . . I *should* tell you . . .'

'So it appears,' said Victor, his face stiff and cold.

'I didn't know how to tell you—'

'I think you must.'

'Jesus. Where should I . . . Raymond,' she said suddenly.

Victor sank on to a tree trunk, head bowed, hands between his knees: the opposite of prayer. He listened to how, a mere three months into his careful courtship, she had had sex with Raymond Snow, 'five or six times'. It had begun in the bushes at a ball just after her finals, and ended – well, she said a fortnight later, but was he to believe her? Misery rose slowly in his gullet. He thought of putting his face in the rain-swollen river to wash the taste from his tongue.

He said: 'I am . . . astonished.'

He closed his eyes, then covered them with his hands. Her pale flesh, whose curves and folds he had not then touched, had barely dared imagine, violated by this man—

'I don't see why you're so upset,' she said. 'It's not as if we – Raymond and I – are doing it *now*.'

'But . . . but that is not the point.' The bitterness was biting at his nose and eyes. 'It is Harvard, merely, which ended it: geography, not choice. Not loyalty. That you *started* is the point. I thought—'

'I know what you thought. That you'd be the first – well, you would've been the first. If you'd hurried—'

'*Hurried?*'

'Well. You know what I mean.'

Victor fought the urge to punch the tree-trunk to splinters. Only the thought of Raymond Snow's distant satisfaction, malign and splendid among the golden clouds of New England, prevented him.

'But I—'

'Oh, Victor.' Jean took his big hand in both of hers, and smiled at him, like a woman twice her age. 'I know you were . . . doing what you thought was best. Being, well, gentle. But, you know, I was – by then I was *longing*—'

Was that what it was? Victor wondered. Gentleness? Perhaps that was not – perhaps *he* was not – what was needed. He had assumed that other men felt, like him, less ardent at forty.

Not, it seems, all other men. 'But why on earth did you not say so?' he asked. 'You seemed to *enjoy* the, the . . . talks, and so forth. It seemed to be . . . appropriate.'

The acts themselves barely upset him, then as now; it was the protagonist. He would have preferred anyone to Raymond Snow – which was why, presumably, it had to be him. He tried to tell himself that it was merely a coincidence, that Raymond Snow, the most competitive man he knew, had not known of her connection to Victor. However, he had no obvious alternative route to Jean; he was teaching History at Queen's, drank with members of the Philology Society, and lived in a small grim room off the Cowley Road above a fish shop (Victor derived much private pleasure from this fact). Moreover, he would have been about to leave for America when it happened; he must have known this was the last chance he would have.

'Well, yes,' Jean said. 'I did enjoy them, and the walks, and everything. Of course. But it was all so *courtly*. I wanted to . . . begin.'

'I wish you had said.'

'How could I have said?'

They left it there. However, while Jean seemed uncon-cerned, for Victor it lived between them, like an ugly infection they were pretending not to see. He would sit at his desk in college, his feet in a drawer, unravelling those endless afternoons of inexpert punting, the tea-rooms, the cycle-rides, while all along Raymond Snow had been there, on her milky body or in her mind.

Now, just when Victor has begun to look forward to a little calm – the Spenser Lectureship, perhaps, and the kudos that would follow; even, now the girls are older, a little time with his wife – Raymond Snow is back. Did he ever leave? Or was what appeared whole merely hollow, sheltering spores whose time has come? I cannot bear this a second time, he thinks. I will not bear it. If Raymond Snow puts a foot wrong, I will have him. The world will see.

FIFTH WEEK

What can they do but find Phoebe a pony? Jean meets the President himself coming out of the porters' lodge; when he asks her how the preparations are going, she has to pretend they are still looking. My pony, as Phoebe calls it, has been so discussed that it seems to live amongst them already, neighing for attention. In the rare moments when Jean is not fretting over the growing problem of Helena's silence, or imagining their eventual meeting, or noting the extent, most worrying, most surprising, to which she misses her and longs to talk to her: the observations wasted, the questions unexpressed (she had not noticed before how much she relied on her – is it healthy? she wonders, could I have stopped it if I'd known?) – despite all this, perhaps once a day she rather enjoys the diversion.

Eve, of course, is trying to spoil everything. One morning she delivers a bizarre speech about the impracticality of keeping a horse. It sounds as if it has been lifted from Trollope; knowing Eve, it is. This, and a sulking-fit because, as she put it, '*I* don't want a sodding horse, but you could have *asked* me,' and the fact that on the day after Phoebe is told she's moving down to the Gate's third stream for all subjects, 'due to profound inattention', Eve gets up at five to revise for a test, goes on all through breakfast about how she is certain to fail and that evening, at a special dinner designed to make Phoebe feel better, insists on ringing a friend to discuss who'll get ninety per cent and who'll only get seventy-eight – all these elements and a thousand more together convince Jean that a pony is exactly what Phoebe needs. Fresh air, and responsibility, and something to excel at: these will be the making of her younger daughter.

There is not, of course, enough money. How could there ever be enough? So she begins a secret cheese fund, comprising all next year's Taleggio and Chaumes and as yet untasted local specialities. She sells some old set texts, and an amethyst ring, but there is still too little. Absorbed in the contemplation of further money-making schemes, she trudges absent-mindedly through the drizzle to the Gate for the annual winter play, *Dido and Aeneas*, and there, at Hun One, the main entrance, she meets Helena.

'Oh!' says Jean, who has clearly forgotten that they both bought tickets.

'Oh no,' says Helena, who had not forgotten, but had simply assumed that Jean would stay away. Despite all her plans for where and how they will meet, and what she will say to save their friendship – the friendship that Jean plainly now regrets – she is entirely, disastrously, unprepared.

'I . . . ' she begins. 'You—'

'We're standing in the way,' says Jean shortly. 'Let's—'

She moves to a part of the path a little less in the way of, and audible to, the procession of sensibly-bobbed family doctors and chaplains' wives with dangly earrings who flow around them, entirely unaware.

Helena balances uncomfortably on the edge of a rhododendron bed, clods of earth clinging to her feet. She is dazed with self-loathing. She waits to hear her speak.

'Helena,' says Jean, twisting the end of her scarf around and around her fingers, 'I didn't—'

Fraught with wishing and unwishing, Helena closes her eyes. The joints of her fingers seem swollen with tears of regret; her other bones feel fragile, as if with one word from Jean she will atomize. I cannot eat, I cannot drink, she wants to tell her. Please be careful what you say.

Jean, who looks slightly embarrassed but otherwise untouched, smiles enchantingly at the wife of the Yugoslav dry-cleaner, fiddles with her watch, frowns, and turns to Helena.

'So,' she says, 'how have you been?'

'Fine,' mumbles Helena.

'I see.'

Helena waits, her mind flat and dogged. The past year and a half of distraction, of constant daydreams and disbelieving slow desire, are sinking into the ground before her, sucking the future with it. Jean, barely able to produce a half-smile, coughs nervously and looks at her feet. Were Helena blind – and increasingly she wishes she were, and deaf, and frankly dead, buried twenty feet down head first under boulders – she could see how much Jean does not want this. She clenches her jaw and her fists: her mouth, she knows, is a hard bitter line, but it hardly matters now. With the last bit of self-possession she can find, she draws herself upright.

'It was a mistake,' she says. 'I'm sorry. Please forget it as quickly as, as you can.'

'Right,' says Jean, with a tight little punctuating smile. 'I'd better—'

She motions vaguely towards the school hall, although Phoebe won't be on for fifteen minutes. Latecomers in fluorescent cycle-bands and kagouls still hurry through the gates.

Helena nods, her social faculties drained dry. The flames are gone; there is only ash. Her burning eyes averted, she steps off the lead-coloured wedding-cake edging of the flowerbed and strides towards the hall.

They are not sitting together; they had both left their ticket-buying too late for that. They are, however, both in the right-hand half of the hall: twenty across and seven down apart. Jean is behind, to Helena's left, and so it is easy, particularly in the intervals between songs, and during soliloquies and set-pieces and, occasionally, at other times, to lean minutely forward, turning her head a little to the right, and see, through the ill-combed hair and bushy beards and spectacle-arms, Helena, in pale Imperial profile, looking straight ahead.

On stage Phoebe, her black dress flatteringly draped – 'I'm the Sorceress,' she had said, 'not a bloody *bag* lady' – is plotting someone's tragic undoing in a warbling monotone. Helena's face does not change. She gives no sign that she knows Jean is watching, so Jean can simply sit and stare, retelling what has just happened. If only she had—

'For God's sake,' whispers Victor, too loudly. 'What is *wrong* with you?'

Jean abruptly sits back. Now, however, all grizzle and big knees, Victor himself is craning forward, and while he can see – *surely* he can see her – Helena from here, he keeps on swaying and fidgeting, apparently unsatisfied. Some minutes pass before he settles. Then, although uncharacteristically he stays awake, she is again free to sidle forward, waiting anxiously until a section of Helena is once again revealed.

She does not know what she should have said, only that she handled it all quite wrongly. She has decided that Helena's recent silence is due to anger, which in turn makes Jean angry: why *should* she know how to respond to something like that? However, she also worries that she has misinterpreted the whole thing. Is it possible – oh God, let it not be possible, although the alternative hardly bears considering – that Helena meant nothing of the sort? Whatever she meant, Jean's embarrassment and, frankly, alarm, has made it all worse. If there was any chance of their friendship recovering, Jean has blown it. Not that she's sure she wants it to recover. Not that she can imagine the future if it doesn't. Besides—

'*Jean*,' stage-whispers Victor, 'What has got into you? At whom are you staring? Stop it, will you, please?' Again he cranes forward, and Jean smiles a magnificently apologetic and soothing smile, as if she had been merely in a daze, and he stares angrily across the audience but still does not see Helena, although it must be so obvious that Jean is looking at her, where else but at her, and eventually he subsides, but simmeringly, so Jean must be wary.

'Deprived,' announces Phoebe to the less attractively-costumed witches, 'of fame, of life, of love.' One of them looks a little like Eve, who is sulking at home, casting spells. Whatever the result of Jean's initial, understandably surprised, reaction, Helena evidently no longer feels what she said she felt. Whatever that was. What's more, now Jean will never know because, when given a second chance by the gate, she again failed to respond correctly, to save whatever could have been saved, or, at least, to find out what is, and has been, going on.

Well, if Helena is angry, Jean is furious. It's all right for her: she *knows* what she meant and what she thinks now. While for Jean – and it must be written all over her face, if only Helena would turn round and see it, instead of sitting there so calmly – there is nothing. No explanations, no friendship, nothing. She may not want what Helena wants – wanted – but she does, at least, deserve an explanation.

I am besieged from all sides, thinks Victor. He shifts heavily in his chair, turning his muffled ear to the cacophony on stage.

First is his daughter, the wheedling, charming one. He does not want to buy a horse. Not only is the cost prohibitive, when he should be thinking of Eve's university (not to mention the shocking cost of hearing-aids, which he happened, by chance, to notice in a newspaper), but there is no point. He knows Phoebe. Next month it will be something else – a record-player, or diving lessons, or a microlight, and she and Jean will beg and, increasingly, mock him, until he gives in. Moreover, there is a part of him – the East London schoolboy, the pin-seller's son – which is a little too drawn to having a horse, a horsy daughter, and he does not want to be that kind of man. He owes it to the memory of his parents, *olam le-shalom*, to the small hopes of his ancestors and the honest poverty of the English working class, who saved him, not to succumb to the fantasy of the country gentleman.

Second is Raymond Snow, the polluter, who has already sat once beside the President at High Table. He has seen him working on the other senior Fellows, sidling ever closer to the

Spenser Lectureship. He will magic them all, smilingly, and Victor's hard work and hopes will be undone. Victor's mind turns and turns with ways to foil him, but powerlessness is upon him. It feels like death.

Third, the worst, is Jean, who is writhing and sighing in her chair. Victor knows why. He is too clever for both of them. However, maddeningly, he cannot quite see his quarry. He leans forward again, but his vision is blocked by the extraordinary turban of the woman in front, and so he subsides, with a harumph audible several rows away. Let Jean sigh and stare. He knows the reason – only not, thank God, exactly what has taken place. The fact of it is sufficient; he does not need to see. He knows his enemy.

All eyes are upon Helena. Although her face and body are turned to the stage – and with what longing she stares at the props cupboards beneath it, just the size for a tall woman to curl up and quietly expire – she can feel, like a rain of fiery pinpoints, that she is being watched.

Steam seems to be rising from the front of her dress. The insides of her knees, her breastbone, the all-too-visible back of her neck, are slick with sweat. The hall reeks of her. She has never believed in spontaneous combustion, but at this moment she would welcome it.

If only she had not said what she said, and made everything so much worse. Instead, she knows that every member of this audience has seen her face as she stood by the gate; they know her private thoughts as clearly as if her brain were sliced and mounted on a slide. She has left herself with nothing: no pride, no way out, no Jean, her true friend, her soul's companion.

The eyes behind her slither through her hair and down her spine, but one person is not looking at her, will not look at her again. Everything is over. The moment the interval begins — it will be a miracle if she can wait that long — she will escape.

As the curtain closes, Jean springs to her feet.

'What are you doing?' asks Victor crossly, as around them parents shuffle and stand and call over each others' heads like giant ridiculous birds:

'Is Sven going on the A Form trip to Knossos?'

'Jerome does all his prep at breakfast; he likes to spend the evening playing mathematical games.'

'There's the most *super* shop on Pusey Lane — basically nothing but abacuses. Abaci.'

Oh, for God's sake, thinks Jean, trying to tiptoe between her neighbour's shopping bags to reach the end of the row. Her route to the wide central aisle, however, is blocked by an extremely old man in two pairs of glasses, asleep on a camping stool. She can't barge past because beside him sits a woman who hates her: a neighbour who, years ago, was asked by the mother of a local prodigy to find friends for her weird daughter. She approached Jean about Eve, and Jean said no, to great offence. Of course she said no — the family was barking and would have made Eve feel miserable. It was the right thing to do for her, if nothing else.

Now, unsuccessfully trying to avoid the neighbour's eye, she is forced to turn the other way, to Victor.

'What are you *doing*?' he demands again.

'Nothing — I . . . do you want an ice-cream?' asks Jean,

although there is nothing on offer but muesli bars and Russian tea.

Victor lowers his eyebrows and opens his mouth, but Jean has already waded through their collective jumble towards the side of the hall beneath the windows, where Helena had been.

Her place, however, is empty. Jean edges nearer, hoping to spot her in the clouds of familiar faces moving towards her away from the stage. She presses through narrow gaps in the growing crowd, surprising several pensioners and one meek mother from Phoebe's class, who had hoped to have a word. She feels alarmingly agitated, as if at any moment she might forget to breathe. She holds a hand to her hot neck. Everything now depends on finding Helena quickly, before the embarrassment becomes impenetrable. She must, she realizes, at any cost see her tonight.

Already, however, most of the audience is on its feet and Helena, despite her height, seems to have disappeared. Jean reaches the front of the hall and decides to try the central aisle instead. She trots quickly along the stage, ignoring Victor's gesticulations, and catches up with a throng of parents heading for the exit in search of orange juice and gossip. Already more flushed and breathless than she would like, Jean hurries behind them, practising:

> Helena, I don't want you to—
> Helena, don't think I didn't—
> Helena, I'm very—
> Helena, I think that I—

'Jean?' says a voice behind her.

*

Jean turns round, so quickly that she almost treads on her own feet, and looks up. Her mouth falls open.

'How *are* you?' asks Raymond Snow.

Jean stares wildly at his mouth, his eyes.

'Are you all right?' he asks.

'I . . . I . . .' She is trapped; with every second Helena may be lost. What is he doing here? 'I'm, ah, fine,' she says. 'How, how are you?'

'Very well.'

Bound by etiquette and lost virginity to a man she has barely thought of for seventeen years, Jean forces herself to respond. She must, she realizes, have seen him quite recently, because his weirdly well-preserved appearance, as if he bathes in formaldehyde, does not surprise her, although she does not ever, consciously, think of him. But when can it have been?

'Aren't you in America?' she says. 'I mean . . .' She scans the crowd with growing panic. 'Do you, do you . . . what are you doing here?'

Momentarily his sharp white smile, the disarming focus of his dark-lashed eyes, reminds her. She remembers, as clearly as if he handed her a photograph, the stretch of his hard back behind a drinks marquee; the grass scattered with wine bottles and dishevelled virgins like her. Then she blinks, and returns to the present. There is a shoulder that may be Helena's only a few rows away. 'I'm afraid—' she begins.

'No, not America. Not even Liverpool. I'm back at St James's now, visiting fellow; in the President's gift. With your husband. He said nothing at all? And I was at your party, although you seemed a little . . . preoccupied. Remarkable.'

'Well, no,' says Jean distractedly. 'I didn't notice.' The shoulder is moving quickly; if she can just—

'How fascinating.' Raymond Snow leans forward. 'Now tell me—'

Jean, whose comments are rarely met with such interest, steps back. 'Raymond, I'm really – I must—'

He touches her arm, a little too firmly to be reassuring. As she half-turns from him, in search of Helena, she finds her path blocked again: this time by her husband.

'Oh!' she says guiltily, now entirely flustered. 'Oh – Victor. Lovely. But I must—'

'What are you *doing*?' he asks. Above the hum of voices they hear the first interval bell.

Raymond Snow grins. 'Victor. How—'

'Quite, quite,' mutters Victor. 'Jean, we must return to our seats.'

'I can't. I—'

'What? Yes you can. Ridiculous. Just—'

'I shall leave you both to it,' says Raymond Snow. 'But I look forward to having the pleasure . . .'

With shocking dismissiveness, Victor turns his back.

'Really—' he begins. He is so much stronger than Jean, and so oddly angry that it takes real effort to twist away.

'Love,' she says, to soften it. 'Just one second. I have to—'

'Can you *leave* him, please,' he hisses.

'What? I'm not – Look, I'll just be a second. Go back to your seat,' she says, dodging behind him. Now the crowd has turned back to face her, but she begins to force her way through them, ignoring Victor's glower and Raymond Snow's smile, her mind fixed on Helena.

She emerges in the bright entrance foyer. There is no sign of her. Perhaps she has gone to the toilets, or slipped back past Jean while she wasted time with Raymond Snow. Perhaps she is sitting in her seat already, reading her programme notes, distressingly composed.

A small boy in cupid's wings begins to toll the second interval bell. Jean peers back through the doors, unable to see Helena's row. There is still time. She crosses the foyer and finds the stone staircase leading down to the women's lavatory. Her footsteps echo; she knows already from the silence and the monastic chill that there is no one there.

'Helena,' she says, nevertheless, then calls more loudly: 'Helena?' One door at the end of the row is closed; she hits it with her hand. 'It's me,' she says. The door swings open to reveal no one, as she knew it would.

'Fuck.' The word bounces satisfyingly off the cubicles. 'Fuck. Fuck fuck.' Then she hurries hotly back up the stairs, towards the sound of the musicians tuning their instruments and the roar of two hundred adults discussing Purcell.

The hall doors swing shut as she approaches. The little cupid has disappeared to learn the subjunctive in the Green Room; there is no one left in the foyer. Jean grasps the great bronze handle to the outer door and pushes it open. Behind her, the scene in the grove begins. Before her is the beginning of another scene.

Ten more seconds and all would have been lost.

She catches sight of her beside the rose beds. 'Helena,' she calls softly. She walks on a little further. 'Helena. Please stop.'

Helena does stop, silhouetted against lamplit gate-posts, but she keeps her back turned.

The air is misted with drizzle. Jean can see from the set

of her head and the way her hands do not move that she has lost her. There is nothing left to do but apologize.

'Listen . . .' she begins as she comes nearer. 'Please. Please listen.'

Close up, however, it is less easy. She steps around Helena and looks into her face through a shower of tiny diamonds. 'I don't know what to say,' she says sadly. She opens her empty hands.

'Neither do I,' says Helena.

Although there is nothing to smile about, Jean smiles. The gold-lit hall behind them now seems ridiculous: a hothouse of steaming hand-knitted jerkins and nasty hats. Helena's declaration seems ridiculous; *this* seems ridiculous. Helena, however, does not smile back.

Now Jean begins to feel uncomfortable. This seems hardly fair. Her amusement dissolves; she is angry again, and amazed that Helena could have this effect.

'I—' they both say.

'Go on then.'

'No,' says Helena suspiciously. 'You go on.'

'I don't want you to think—'

'I don't,' Helena interrupts. 'Look, you don't need to, you know, say anything. I should . . . I have to apologize. I'm sorry I haven't already. It's all a ghastly—'

'Oh!' says Jean. 'Is it? I . . . I thought—'

'Truly, I'm sorry about all of this. I really am. You must . . . what must you think?'

'No, no,' Jean says. 'I didn't mean that. I only meant I – God, this is . . . I didn't want you to think . . . You see, I was – well, horrified.'

Helena hangs her head.

'No, sorry, God, I don't mean *that*,' says Jean. 'I mean –

I mean I should be flattered. I *am* flattered. I just didn't expect—'

'Of course you didn't,' says Helena abruptly.

'I never knew – I never *imagined* . . . ' She would like to touch Helena's arm, to prove that she is *not* horrified, but fears that this would be too intimate. Too . . . encouraging. Every question she would like to ask her seems vain, or crude. 'Are you . . . upset by me?' she asks carefully. 'You know, you must know, that is the very last thing I'd want – I hope you know. I really want you to see that. It's important, it's – no. Never mind. I think, I think—'

But whatever it was dissolves on her tongue and vanishes. For running down the spotlit drive towards them, her black dress shining, is Phoebe, and she is raging.

'—as if you couldn't see me, which of course you sodding could if you'd just *looked* – and what will people *think*?' demands Phoebe, hands in the air, as she stops neatly in front of them. She stares furiously at Helena, who forces herself to stare back. Go away, she wills Phoebe. *Go away.* Give us this one moment.

Phoebe, however, is unmoved. She sniffs and steps between them, her back to Helena.

'What were you *doing*?' she asks. 'Every single time I looked at you – and I tried *not* to, I was so hurt – you were looking everywhere – *every*where – but at me. It was *horrible*. It was impossible not to see it – you looked like a *duck*, bobbing away. And you're my parents – it's disgusting. How could you—'

'Phoebe,' says Jean, surprisingly firmly.

Phoebe appears not to notice. 'And other people saw it

142

too – I was backstage and I was crying, and even *Dorcas* noticed you were being weird. I'm so, I'm so ... I mean, what's the point of learning all those crappy lines and trying and trying—'

Now Phoebe is sobbing loudly, wantonly, with a freedom Helena has never had. She looks down upon Jean's daughter's sleek head, sparkling grey-gold in the drizzle; the sharp curves of her full upper lip; her long arched eyebrows and the slightly swollen-looking lids of her long sly eyes – all Jean's, unmistakably, and thinks: you cannot be her child.

'Phoebe.' Jean puts her small soft hands on her daughter's shoulders: almost the same height as her own. 'Listen ... why are you crying? I still don't know what I've done.'

'Done?' shrieks Phoebe. 'Are you *mad*?'

'Don't—' begins Helena, stepping forward, to absolutely no effect whatsoever. Jean does not even look up. Think of pupae, Helena tells herself; think of shells and carapaces and silken walls.

'What you've *done* is *ignored* me while I was on *stage*. I was only doing it for you! I'm not interested in stupid Dildo and Anus – why would I be? And then I looked out in the interval and I saw you leaving. Just ... leaving! Like you didn't even care ... How do you think it felt? Am I not – I'm not enough *fucking fuck* – ohhhhhh—' she wails, burying herself between her mother's arms.

'Oh, love,' says Jean. 'It's not—'

Helena looks at the road, and the forest of bicycles parked beside the main gate. She presses her mind against cool rusted metal.

'I'm sorry,' says Jean. 'I – I felt ill. I needed some air.'

Phoebe continues to sob. Oh no, let her not be ill, thinks Helena, forgetting she is the cause.

'All right. All right,' says Jean, rubbing her daughter's back unselfconsciously, comfortingly, as Helena would never think to do. She is theirs, Helena thinks, as Phoebe snorts enormously against Jean's breast. 'I'm sorry. I'm so proud of you. I'm so proud of you. My wonder girl.'

Phoebe shudders, recovers, grows still. She lifts her head. 'C-can we go in?' she says. 'I'm nearly on – there'll just be a scene change, and then . . . if you want?'

'Of course I want,' says Jean. 'You're my girl.'

'Good,' says Phoebe forcefully, a smile in her voice. She puts her arm around her mother and pulls her from Helena, one step, two, until Jean is walking slowly back to the hall, bound to her.

Helena stands uselessly by the gate, and watches Jean's back receding: five, six steps. Then, on the eighth step, Phoebe stops. She looks over her shoulder, lifts her chin, and sends Helena a hard cold look: a warning. Then she turns back to her mother.

Helena should, of course, walk away. She does try to, but she is rooted here, aching, suspended in drizzle. And so, for once in her life, she is in the right place at the right time, because Jean stops at the edge of the lantern-light outside the hall, and turns back, and there is Helena, waiting.

Jean's face is bright: gold and silver. She opens her mouth. Helena waits for the sound, but there is no sound. There is only the shape of a word on Jean's tongue: 'Letter?'

Helena nods once and looks up at the sky. Her entire body is smiling. It is all about to begin.

They buy her a horse. They actually do it.

Eve — who, since the wine-and-cheese party, has been striving to reach new heights of attainment — has had a horrible week. Her coccyx is bruised from falling on a slippery netball pitch; she slammed the piano lid in a fit of frustrated perfectionism, leaving a conspicuous crack; her eyes are sore from hours of vocabulary and split-end picking. Now, at the end of it all, there is a row of cuts on her forearm from the edge of her mother's sewing scissors: the most she has ever done at once, each thinly enamelled with blood and beginning to pucker neatly beneath the scab. As with all her bad weeks, she has decided that the solution is to try harder, to work until her many failings are barely visible and she becomes the Eve of her dreams. Her sister, it seems, exceeds everyone's dreams already.

And now there is this.

She had not, of course, forgotten about the horse. However, she had hoped that, by refusing to think about it, she could somehow force the thought from her parents' minds. The horse would remain unbought and, in its absence, their family would miraculously attain that state of loving happiness which still eludes them.

With a horse, however, the balance will be wrong. Balance, she has begun to realize, is so important. There is no thought, no action, no tiny accidental event which does not require other objects to be touched or seen or thought of, perpetually edited and double-checked, endlessly repeated. She is starting to see that all things are connected – their individual and familial wellbeing, her past and future exams, her mother's mood, Phoebe's future – as if by spiders' webs, or glowing fibres, whose ends she must continually feel for because she alone knows they are there. The necessary rituals, like the contaminants and dangers they keep at bay, she knows instinctively. They multiply constantly. The horse could not happen, because she would not know what to do.

However, it does happen, and her parents drive Phoebe somewhere in the country and come back happy, smelling of mud and bearing leather and plastic devices of which she has never even heard. They have chosen the horse, Bilbo, for whom, out of nowhere, they all seem to have conjured the most enormous love. Bilbo is a Lux too, it seems.

'What colour is it?' asks Eve.

'Why are you shouting?' says Phoebe. 'It is a he, and he is a grey.'

'Grey?' says Eve. 'Ugh. Doesn't sound very glamorous.'

Phoebe smiles, about to release her secret weapon. 'No, stupid. Grey means white. It's a white pony.'

Eve takes this information into the garden, the only place still uninfected by smelly blankets, curry combs and lifetime subscriptions to *My Horse*. She goes to the patch of earth beyond the yew tree where, as a child, she devoted herself to archaeological digs, flint-tool manufacture, and the creation of natural paints from sandstone and brick-dust. Here she is entirely secluded. She used to look at this wall and this earth and imagine herself a Victorian don's daughter, or the child of an Elizabethan college gardener, looking on the same wall and earth but being happier.

OK, thinks Eve. So they gave her a horse. I don't care. I don't care.

I definitely don't. I don't want a bloody horse. She must be more babyish than I think.

Why am I crying?

She thinks of horses with wings, with horns, cut into hillsides – the kind with which she is familiar. No one she knows has a real one, and even if they did, this horse, Phoebe's horse, could not be made public. Her parents' oddnesses, the rows and lopsidedness, her mother's feelings about her: these must at all costs be kept from her friends. Everything is tinged with shame.

She is too old to need the resinous darkness of her yew tree, crying over unwanted horses, but she ducks inside it anyway. She wipes her nose unhappily on her cuff and reaches for a thin branch to strip the bark from: the third most satisfying activity she knows. This was her house, pegged and dovetailed like the Little House on the Prairie: a Phoebe-free pure place. She glances at the scented springy floor and there, among the innocent brown needles, lie dozens of cigarette ends, twists of gold foil and cellophane, miniatures of brandy and Drambuie immediately identifiable as their father's, and two empty vodka bottles.

All at once she remembers another tree: the mulberry tree just inside the college gates in which, every September, she and Phoebe and her father would sit, harvesting berries, pretending not to notice the tourists taking photographs as they passed. One year in particular, when she and Phoebe had been trapped in the tree all afternoon – they had been banned from their father's rooms after an incident involving ink and examination papers – he had gone to his study to fetch a groundsheet, leaving them there. They had been squabbling for hours; unbearably irritable, stuffed and sick with berries. The hot green shade buzzed and sang. Turning, Eve had caught sight of Phoebe through a frame of leaves: smeared with purple juice, she looked like a child reared by lions. Her gleaming skin seethed with life. She is dangerous, thought Eve.

Now, squatting on the desecrated floor, she knows she was right. If anyone were to find out that Phoebe has been smoking and drinking, under-age, at a college party . . . She feels like a boiler being stoked with coal. There is nothing left that Phoebe has not ruined. Sick with alarm and unwanted responsibility, Eve trudges back to the house.

Victor, meanwhile, is standing at the pigeonholes, going through his post. As of this term he is Senior Dean, responsible for disciplinary matters for the next two years. He now has to waste time on infantile crimes: nude punting, late-night tower-climbing, pill-popping during exams. He sifts irritably through his other letters: a sentimental note from the President of France, who once babysat for his daughters, and a polite reminder from the Ashmolean Library, requesting the return of a pamphlet borrowed in 1973.

Raymond Snow's pigeonhole is fat with envelopes. Premature dreams of the Spenser Lecture weighing on Victor's mind, he begins the climb to his room. The last thing he needs now is the Senior Deanship; it will weigh him down while Raymond Snow is free to fly. He takes out his key and jabs it angrily at the door. Raymond Snow, quite clearly, is intending to win both Victor's Lectureship *and* his wife.

It is evening. Her arm tender and hot to the touch, Eve emerges from her bedroom. She has slashed the underside of her mattress with the stolen sewing scissors, whose disappearance during the holidays caused an immense argument in which her sister was first blamed and then, after a heated defence, exonerated, not only from this theft but from other recent crimes for which she is in fact responsible. This makes Eve, in whom the scissors' disappearance have inspired hours of sweaty guilt, the family's chief criminal, while in her sister's room teaspoons, scarves, dice, bracelets, matches and candlesticks accumulate and fester.

There were times, once, when the Luxes could still achieve harmony at table: a perfect combination of food and mood and frivolity. The horse, however, has ruined it.

'Oh, Eve,' says her mother, 'don't look so fed up. Aren't you pleased about Bilbo?'

'Yeah,' says Phoebe, who until two minutes ago was raging at her parents for denying her a numnah, and now is sitting on her father's knee. 'Why do you always want everything I have?'

'I do *not*,' says Eve sullenly. 'That's stupid. Why would—'

'Eve,' says her mother abruptly, throwing down the dishcloth. 'Come here. I want to talk to you.'

Eve jumps. For a fantastic moment, it seems as if her soft slow mother might actually hit her. Instead she stalks right past Eve and out of the kitchen door into the hallway. She stands on the bottom step, waiting.

Eve, dazed, follows.

'Shut the door.'

Through the glass panes her golden sister, posed like a Renaissance bambina in her father's arms, watches them with interest.

'That pony was old and cheap,' her mother whispers fiercely, 'but it was the best we could do, and your sister needs encouragement. And interests. I'd have thought you were old enough to understand that.'

'I *am*!'

'Does it never occur to you,' she goes on, 'that you should set her an example? Why does everything have to be a competition? Don't tell me you want a pony too?'

Eve begins to cry.

'You haven't even asked to see it. Him. You never think about how she feels.'

'I'm, I'm *trying*,' says Eve. She knows that she is snivelling. 'But—'

'I have other things to worry about. Please, Eve, try. I don't want any more trouble out of you.'

Later that night in the University Museum, home of the dodo's bones and other, less famous, corpses, all is still. The carvings of pineapples and flying fish above the pillars exhale tiny pockets of spent breath. The air smells of cold. Flagstones, dense with geological secrets, lie bare to the moonlight. Nothing moves – much.

Then something scrapes across the floor. A handle is released. With a click, like the tapping-open of an egg, a single light is switched on in the entrance. The blunt bones of nearby dinosaurs, the enormous blue butterflies suspended in glass, the stony cells of ancient life, horned and tentacled, retrieved from the mud of Oxfordshire, all begin to gleam with faint reflections, quietly phosphorescent, as if communicating privately in the night.

Helena, in the doorway, pockets her key. She has obtained it slightly illegally, although her researches justify it. If she is caught, there will be hell to pay.

Hell, however, is relative. She walks calmly across the main room, past darkened crocodiles, a ghostly albatross, the barely-visible thighs of mastodons. Her back to the light, she extends her fingers until she touches wood: the door to the Pitt Rivers Museum, to which there is no other entrance. With a small brass key she stole this morning from a colleague, she opens the door.

At last. She closes her eyes and leans against a wall. She feels fossilized already, all her soft tissue rotted to clay. This was a mistake, she thinks, trying to ignore the tiny fibres of excitement which quiver through her, dangerously close to the air.

She dares not turn on all the lights, but the few she does produce an unsettling effect. The narrow pathways and cluttered walls remain in darkness, but the cases are illuminated: some bright, others shadowed with antlers and raised spears, the remainder merely glinting as sharpened metal or polished stones catch the light.

Nervously, checking her watch unnecessarily often, she begins to walk about between the cases. They are typologically arranged: banjos from New Orleans and stringed drums from the Kingdom of Benin; a feathered cloak and rhino-horn lip-plugs; Noh masks and canary head-dresses; a shogun's lock, a French courtesan's key. There are hundreds of them, each layered with shelves and extensions and glazed drawers, their contents labelled in brown Victorian ink: cursive, italic, minuscule, deranged. Above her float sections of dhows and junks and faerings and the beaks of totem-poles. At knee-height, barely noticed as she passes, tiny canoes and Viking buckles and toys made from eagles' underfeathers cluster in the dark. She is so nervous she can barely stand. Her sighs add to the air's dampness, the museum's decay.

How long should she wait? Ancient trees breathe, leather flexes, bell-clappers shiver all around her and, for the first time in her life, nothing is merely cells or molecules, an interesting evolutionary model, a parallel of something else. Instead, she thinks: would she like this? Is she interested in this? What, precisely, did the shrunken heads, the Buddhas and Victorians, know of love?

She passes a cabinet of writing instruments, a narwhal-horn plaque inscribed in black eighteenth-century letters: *Before thee I bow my head, o my Queen*. She pauses beside a small case of jet brooches, bracelets woven from human hair, cameos, and hears a noise behind her.

She looks over her shoulder, and there in the light stands Jean.

The complete works of the Doors, Eve's least favourite band, thud heavily through the wall as Eve paces her bedroom, looking for surfaces on which to find relief. Phoebe is probably trimming the top of her riding boots into ornamental fringes, or unwrapping velvet browbands bought with their mother's credit card, or persuading a friend to write 'Bilbo' in embroidery silks on the back of her hacking jacket. Their mother is out; their father might as well be. They have been left to their own devices, and Eve cannot trust herself.

She has, for her own safety, hidden the sewing scissors in the bathroom cupboard. Their uncomfortable orange handles and brushed steel blades are becoming irresistible. There is, in addition, a new problem to deal with: Phoebe is going off the rails. Eve does not know how much their parents have realized: whether cigarette smoke seeps into their bedroom; whether they have memorized, like her, the symptoms of drug use; whether they know what people say about Bocardo's and what happens there. Both her mother and father are so weirdly absent at the moment, so touchy and preoccupied – they might as well be taking drugs. Would they notice if she, Eve, given the chance, did too? Impossible – she lacks the courage. Phoebe, however, has the courage for anything.

She has recently begun to find silverfish on the curtains; even, once, on her sheet. She knows the cause: her sister's squalor, spreading from her bedroom into the hall. Tiny brown beetles, moreover, are appearing everywhere. Their dead shells stain her shelves like toxic droppings. Sometimes, if she lets her eyes rest on a point chosen at random, she sees one moving quickly towards her, or moving away, back towards Phoebe, its eggs laid, its contagion spreading.

If it wasn't for her, thinks Eve, I could manage. I could be myself, not the skulking shamefaced person her scowling friends, her slyness, her beetles have made me. I can't bear this any longer. I hate it.

I hate her.

There – it is said.

'So,' says Jean.

'So.'

They are sitting on a bench in a corner: a relatively well-lit corner, to which they both instinctively moved. The eyes of a golden Buddha, trapped inside a huge Malaysian dolls' house, rest upon them. The shrunken heads stare through glass sticky with schoolchildren's fingertips.

Apologies have been made and accepted; Jean has tried, at length and with little success, to explain her feelings, then and now.

'I see,' Helena says. 'If you're sure.'

'I am sure. I've thought and thought – I mean . . .'

'It's fine. But really, only if you're sure you don't—'

'I'm sure.'

'Really? It doesn't – I don't expect you to . . . to be honest I thought we, I thought I . . . I really thought we wouldn't speak again.'

'Yes. I know. It was horrible. That's why I came.'

'And if you . . . well, can still stand to—'

'I *want* to talk. I want to talk about it, and understand – I'm sick of all this not-talking. No one can articulate anything; it's just this lowering and frowning and mumbling. At least you talk, Helena.'

'Well, yes.'

'And you're . . . you're brave. I mean . . . you know, at that bloody party in the garden, while that . . . while you . . . while we were, um, talking, they were all terrified – you know, scared of saying anything that would jeopardize a post, or make them stand out, or challenge anyone.' She pauses, catches Helena's eye, looks away, looks back. She is shivering.

'Are you cold?'

'Scared and cold.'

'I'm sorry about all these . . . you know. Items.' Helena gestures at the muskets and masks.

'It's fine. You're clever to have thought of it. I mean, at least we can't possibly be seen.'

'Well, for privacy, yes, but, you know, it's not *illegal*,' says Helena, light-headed now with relief and disbelief.

'Isn't it?' asks Jean. From the depths of the shadows behind her, a clock strikes and goes on striking: thirteen, fourteen, fifteen, its tone silvery as struck glass. They look up, but only at the light before them: not, for example, at the case to their right where, among the votive offerings, a silver heart with perforated sides glints on a velvet bed. Nor do they look at the case to their left, a mere yard away, in which, almost hidden from view by other magic objects, lie a pair of rings, carved and interlocking, made from jade. They are, according to the card beside them, a gift from a ninth-century Japanese princess to her lady-in-waiting: a lock for souls, extremely powerful and, what is more, its case is unlatched.

'Do you think,' says Helena cautiously as, a little later, they prepare to leave, 'I mean . . . so this wasn't just a . . . a smoothing over?'

'What do you mean?'

'I mean. I mean . . . I can't just go back to . . . you know. Not.'

'Not?'

'Not.'

'Right,' says Jean. 'No. I understand that.'

'So . . . so if we carry on, you know, meeting, you know that I—'

'Listen.' Jean puts down her bag and pauses, one hand resting on the light-switches by the door. Helena watches it: the little cloudy outline on the brass. 'I don't . . . You know me, Helena. I'm married – I've always wanted to be married. You know I'm not – I've never been—'

'I know,' says Helena.

'We're friends. I want to carry on being friends. Don't ruin it now.' And with that she pushes up the remaining switches, and the lights go out.

Phoebe escapes. It isn't easy, but she does it. She tells her form-master that she has a urinary infection that prevents her from swimming, which conveniently frees her to help her father move a coffer which he is identifying for the Ashmolean and about which a letter is sitting at this moment in the headmaster's tray.

'Be good,' says her form-master.

'I will,' says Phoebe.

She freewheels most of the way, deciding, as she rattles to the college gate, to ask for a moped for Christmas. There is a sign on the studded doors forbidding something; she leaves her bike propped against it, and goes in.

That porter is on duty. The last few times she's been here, his smile has changed. She can feel his eyes on her as she crosses the lodge. She gives him a full-on grin and, skipping past him, enters the bright centre of the college to reclaim her mother.

She hasn't been inside a college since she went to Tamsin's. Tamsin used to live in a depressing house past the ring-road, and Tamsin was ordinary. Then her mum was made head of a college on the Turl, and Tamsin lost it. It was her last year at the Gate, and Phoebe and Dorcas used to find her discreetly passed out in the coat-room, her bleached hair bluish, the corners of her smile sparkling in the strip-lighting. Her new home, a wood-lined palace, suits her chemical glamour perfectly. When she first visited her there, a couple of months ago, Phoebe felt like a lucky worm in the middle of an apple. Her eyes stinging with beauty, she watched Tamsin drop pills into a bag like penny sweets and felt blessed, gifted, as if the world was about to start.

Now she, Phoebe, is different – braver and stronger. With a pill under her tongue and little time to spare, she knocks on two wrong doors. The first, which she'd have sworn was the right one, doesn't open, and she's about to write 'Bum' or 'Hi' or 'Piss off' in the drawing pins stuck all over it when she notices a little notebook nailed to the wood, and a pencil on a shoelace.

> *Dear Dr Shale, Regretfully I have double pneumonia and will be unable to meet you at 10. Hannah Kaufner (St Peter's)*
>
> *Dr S., As per yr note of 17/10, W. states $\varepsilon\{\varphi\chi\}/\varepsilon_2$, which = compelling. However, Strothcutt surmises ε cannot $\therefore$ be $< \varphi\chi$. I suspect both are wrong, and ε is as is.*
> *Pls. ppost soonest. Arnold P.*
>
> *Dear Dr Shale, I love you pasionately but am anothers, yrs. The Bursar'*

writes Phoebe under the last message. She returns the pencil to its noose, on reflection slips it into her pocket, and thunders as noisily as possible, school kilt flapping, to the floor below. Her second choice of door is answered by a whiskery-chinned old bag who calls Phoebe a 'ragamuffin', and claims not to know who she means.

'Try Gillette,' shouts Phoebe as she bounds down the stairs.

She cannot, however, find the right door, and if she tries other staircases she will waste time. So she tries something else – not subtle, but effective.

She opens her mouth and tips her head back. Above her are spindly turrets and baby spires, mouldy slate, dingy battlements. It is a miniature castle for frightened self-punishing weirdos: people far too mad to reproduce. She fills her lungs. The turrets reel.

'*Mum,*' she bellows.

The walls of the courtyard, grey-yellow and stained by centuries of brains, ring satisfyingly. Pasty spectacled faces stare anxiously through mottled windows. Phoebe takes another, deeper breath.

'*Mum! Jean Lux! MUM!*'

Feet scamper down the stairs behind her. '*Mum!*' she yells once more, for good measure, as her mother, not looking nearly pleased enough to see her, bursts out of the doorway and grabs her arm.

'What are you doing here?' asks Jean.

Phoebe sticks her bottom lip out. 'I thought you'd be pleased.'

'But . . . ' begins Jean fearfully. 'I am pleased, love, of course I'm pleased, but why aren't you at school? Are you ill?'

'I'm not *ill*,' says Phoebe disdainfully. 'We've got a free period to look at colleges. For history. Local history.'

'Oh. Well. It's lovely to see you, but you know, we're, I, we're supposed to be quiet here. People are working . . .'

Phoebe pulls a disgusted face and stamps straight up Jean's staircase. Full of trepidation, Jean follows. In the best of circumstances, a visit here from Phoebe would be unwise. Now, however, it terrifies her.

'Come in,' she says, opening the inner door of the Cupboard. At least, for the time being, Hedley is absent. She begins to clear a chair. 'So,' she says, attempting to hide an infinitely doodled-upon compliments slip under a note about commentaries upon the Epistles, which she should have finished this morning. 'How are you then?'

'I *said*,' Phoebe tells her. She has, it seems, entirely forgotten her infantile biscuit-fuelled games behind the curtains; her improvement of an immensely valuable bust of Seneca with crayons; her baiting of Hedley, to Jean's intense pride.

Half of a letter from Helena, a dumbfounding, beautiful letter, just arrived by afternoon post, has floated on to the floor and is lying beside Phoebe's foot. 'Oh,' she says. 'Oh! I – um. I must – um. I must – Good God, what's that sticking out of Hedley's drawer?'

Phoebe's head whips round and, before she turns back, eyes narrowed, Jean snatches up the letter and crumples it in her hand.

Hedley will return any second. The air in the Cupboard is shadowy with dust. She thinks of the picture that was forming in her mind just before Phoebe shouted, and feels herself tighten with excitement.

'I just wanted to see you,' says Phoebe.

'Oh, love,' says Jean, patting vainly for a pocket in which to hide the letter. There is no pocket. With a curious sidestepping gait she sidles over to her bag and pushes her letter in. Then she sees that Phoebe's eyes are, unmistakably, on the letter's envelope which still lies on her desk, marked 'Jean Lux – private' in Helena's unforgettably sprawling hand. Spots of rain are appearing on the Cupboard's little window, but inside it has become unbearably hot.

'There was something I meant to say to you – now, what was it?' says Jean, as she always finds herself saying at difficult moments. She shoos her daughter out of the way and pretends to look through the papers on her desk, pressing her elbow awkwardly upon the envelope from Helena. 'I wrote myself a note . . .'

'I've got to go,' says Phoebe. 'But – let's go shopping at the weekend. In town. I really want to.'

'Ah,' says Jean.

'*What*?' Phoebe stands, scowling. 'What are you doing? Why are you so busy all of a sudden?'

'I'm not exactly . . . no, I'm not. I'd just . . . well, I'm sure we can.'

'Why's Helena writing to you at work?'

Jean's brain dissolves. She digs her nails into her knees. 'I . . . she—' she says.

Phoebe waits.

'She . . . wanted to ask me something. Now, she . . .'

'What?'

'Ah. Noth—'

'What was so important that you had to leave my play for? What's going on? Are you giving her money?'

Jean's hands unclench. 'Oh, *no*,' she says, stupid with relief. 'Oh no. No. No! You're not . . . is it . . . is it that crop? The blue one? I said you deserved it, didn't I? Well, you do. Listen, this weekend, just you and me, let's go to that saddler's in the Covered Market, and get it. It can be our secret. OK?'

Footsteps are climbing the stairs towards them.

'OK?' she says again, resisting the urge to leap up and fling the door wide.

Phoebe frowns. Jean waits, strung tight with nerves. The door opens. Hedley, in drip-dry white shirt-sleeves, his string vest clearly visible as if beneath peekaboo chiffon, enters the room, an ostentatiously large pile of grubby folders in his arms. He looks at Phoebe.

'Jean?' he says.

'Hello, Hedley,' says Phoebe. 'You seem to be sweating. It's bloody hot. Shall I—' She picks up a booklet from his desk and, holding it by a crumbling corner, begins to flap it at him.

'Do you mind?' he snaps, snatching it from her. 'This is an important chapbook.'

'Do you want to use my chapstick?' asks Phoebe solemnly. 'It's just—'

'Jean,' he says. 'I don't know what's going on here, nor do I intend to find out. We have work to do, and these objects are under my protection. Could you kindly . . .'

Jean orders herself not to laugh. 'Love, we really should go . . . *you* should. Which, which college is next? For school.'

For a fraction of a second, Phoebe pauses. 'Oh,' she says, 'Keble, I think. You know, the ugly one. We're just going to laugh at it. Anyway. Seeya, Hed.'

Hedley is pretending to write, but his lashes are beating quickly against the dirty plastic of his glasses.

'So we'll go to town then,' she says to her mother as she leaves.

'Good. Lovely.' Smilingly, Jean sighs. The crisis is over. 'Just us. I mean it. Tell Helena to keep away.'

Several days pass smoothly. Everyone is in their rightful places. Phoebe and Jean spend as much time as possible together, shopping and making amusing plans. In the dark depths of the Bodleian at closing time, as ordinary people are going to bed and only the most socially autistic monomaniacs remain, quietly twitching, Victor writes notes for his over-ambitious Hilary term lectures (Burgundian Administration: Thegns to Drains), refusing to consider why his wife has taken to telephoning from their bedroom, or posting letters after dinner. She says a friend of hers is in trouble. Victor does not question her, but the signs of Raymond Snow are everywhere. He breathes him as he sleeps.

Eve, whether drinking Saturday-night cider with friends in murky medieval pubs, or contemplating alone the likelihood of exam failure, orchestral disaster and being dropped from the Swimming B-squad reserves, has begun to gouge deeper and deeper into the skin around her cuticles, unable to stop herself, as if her mind is trapped on a wheel. Then, on Sunday evening, she discovers that her eight-page essay on Life's Little Ironies has received a β+ ?+, not because she has failed to provide adequate examples, or because she has not understood the more obvious subtleties of Hardy's morose sentimentality, but because Phoebe has Tippexed 'Tess' to read 'Toss' throughout.

The time has come to act. Phoebe is at the stables; her father is working in college; her mother, murmuring something about museums, but probably intending to find Phoebe a platinum snaffle, has left the house. Eve goes to her sister's unspeakably squalid room, her eyes half-closed. Breathing through her mouth, she copies down the address of the President's stables from the back of a scrap of misspelt French homework, left conveniently on a bongo drum.

It is a cold night. Back in her room, she puts on a black polo-neck, her navy school cords, her dirty brown trainers, stained dark red from last year's mulberrying. Then she collects her jacket from among the duffel-coats and mittens by the kitchen stairs – an area known as The Tabards. As a child, Eve remembers, she would occasionally look for heraldic equipment there, a halberd, perhaps, or a Children's Crusader's breastplate. In the end it had turned out to be some kind of joke to do with Iris Murdoch, yet another author whom Eve has not read.

She is entirely calm, as if there is cool water running through her veins, or oxygen. She has never before dared to confront her sister like this, but now her anger feels useful, and that excites her. She is, finally, in control.

There is, as she wheels her bicycle up the path, a whiff of stone-dust from the masons' yard – meatier, more bodily than the smells of cobbles or slate. *Jude the Obscure*, however, is avoided by all the local schools, and there is more than Hardy on her mind. It is some time before she registers the dull flump-flump-flump of her back wheel on the concrete. The tyre is soft, and the bicycle pump is with her father in college. She will have to collect it from him and then go after Phoebe; she must not let her get away with this.

Young Arthur, Arthur's son, nods her through the turnstile. He, at least, makes her feel better: his stomach spills in heavy folds into his lap; his calves are like melons. He ignores her, as ever, but Eve blows her nose and smiles at him. Depending on what happens tonight, she may need witnesses.

There are students everywhere: show-offs in cricket jumpers, plain girls in dresses singing plainsong on the lawn, a small group of drinkers huddled matily against the cold. Eve, already fired up by a few swigs of her father's mulberry gin, imagines walking up to them and asking for a glass. However, she is not her sister. Trying to look knowing and self-contained, she wheels past them into the next quad, towards the chapel and her father.

He is there already. He is coming towards her through the hazy chapel lights: taller than the rest of them, dark-haired like herself. She can almost hear his breathing. He is fifty-six: fourteen years till seventy. She thinks about death all the time, and he is the only one she would want to save.

Just being near him lifts her spirits. She has, she realizes, been waiting all this time to *be* saved, and here he is; her reward.

'Pa?' she says, and then sees that his smile is not her father's smile. This man is thinner and sharper and paler than her father. Confused, a little embarrassed, she is about to push her bicycle past him and leave him behind in the chapel shadows when, for no reason, she hesitates. She hears him say, very quietly:

'Eve.'

She does not know this man. However, he looks as if he knows her, and she has, even now, a terrible compulsion to be polite.

'Eve,' he says again.

'Sorry – are you, um . . .' she begins; she has probably met him with her father in the University Parks, or been forced to play with his children. The silence lengthens. Eve's smile beginning to prickle. Then, to her surprise, he grins at her.

'You haven't a clue who I am, have you?'

He is staring into her eyes, right into her soul, and he doesn't seem put off by what he sees. The air is sharp with frost and mulberry gin. I could be brave, she thinks, feeling for a moment as if the real Eve has finally ousted a weak and shameful impostor.

'No!' she says, and his grin widens. He is still staring at her. Her skin is hot and full, like bread. Because he is still smiling she smiles too. 'I – sorry.'

He takes a step towards her. Her hands tighten on the handlebars; she sees them, and makes herself relax. Students are passing all the time. Besides, what could happen to her in her father's college?

Now she sees why she had mistaken him for her father: he is old. Oh – disappointingly old. Her skin, however, will not cool down.

'So,' she says, like a much braver person, 'who are you then? I'm sorry, I've—'

'Not to worry,' he says, enclosing her knuckles with his big hand. 'It's been a long time. I'm a friend of your father's. I've been away, but I always hear so much about you. Though I hadn't expected – well, you're quite . . . you're a woman now, Eve. Aren't you?'

Eve's head fills with a high-pitched hum of embarrassment and glee and disbelief. His comment makes her want to run around, grimacing. Instead, she mumbles: 'Oh. I . . . um, well. I'm sixteen. And, um, a half.'

He grins again. He is holding her with his teeth, his eyes.

'I'd really better—' she says, waving her fingers weakly towards the chapel.

'Just a second.' He takes the end of her handlebar in his hand, not touching her but very close. 'You know,' he says, 'it's lovely to see you. You're so different – not at all the girl I remember. But you're not . . . you're not quite yourself, are you? Is something wrong?'

Eve begins to cry.

Incredibly he is neither alarmed nor disgusted. He touches her sore arm with his fingertips – as if he knew, she will think later that night – and then steers her and her bicycle off to the right into deep darkness, and out again into a pool of light.

They are standing in front of a doorway. 'Up there,' he says and, with one hand, lifts her heavy rusted bicycle up on to the step. She can barely see for tears upon tears, and the black light in the doorway, and the confusing shape of this man with her bicycle on his shoulder. 'This way,' he says gently, and what else can she do? She follows him upstairs.

Part Two
Hilary Term,
January, 1987

Eve has been deified. She sits alone and splendid, her gold-sprayed laurel crown pinching her temple, testing the sharp end of her thyrsos with her thumb-tip. Moments ago she was among the other chorus-members on the gym-mats, declaiming about Zeus's birth from smelly mimeographed sheets. Now, because the real Dionysus is having her warts removed, she is having a taste of Olympus.

Dionysus is not really her vocation. She understands Athene, would secretly prefer to be Aphrodite, but Dionysus, with his deerskins and revelry, frightens her. She is, she suspects, closer to repressed King Pentheus: more likely to be ripped apart by drunken Bacchae than be their leader. She knows who *that* would be.

In Greek, to a tune devised by the deputy head girl, the Messenger tells of the mission to rescue Pentheus's mother from her wild life among the Bacchae. Eve's Bacchic friends cannot see her up here. Her mind is free to wander. It settles, after a prolonged and exciting daydream, on thoughts of her own mother.

Jean Lux may not be eating live goats on a mountainside, but something is amiss. Eve's father, of course, has noticed nothing. Her sister, however, has. She is behaving worse than ever: this morning, for example, she went into the garden completely naked, despite the fact that she could be seen from forty-six students' windows. Eve's idea of relaxing nudity involves locks, bubbles and the knowledge that her family is at least two floors away, but this was extreme even for Phoebe.

Through the sink window, her apricotty bottom bared, Phoebe was pretending to search the rose bushes.

Eve thought: should I tell someone? Should I go and get her? She gave an involuntary whimper of embarrassment, and noticed a papery rustle from the table behind her. She jumped, and saw her mother, calmly reading.

'Um?' said Eve. Only a couple of minutes ago, coming down the basement stairs, she had seen Phoebe taking off her nightie and leaving it on the table. Their mother must have been sitting there all along. She must have noticed.

As Eve stared at her mother, the older boy in the next-door college house, whose father has forbidden television and who is rumoured to have half-blinded a college gardener with a home-made longbow, began to play the trombone: BA ba ba, ba BA ba, ba ba BA. Eve does not trust this boy. He wins chemistry competitions nationwide. What's more, when thrown together by St James's, which owns both their fathers, she has seen him being sadistic to smaller children. At least, she thinks it is sadism, although her attempts to look it up among her father's books have led her down disturbing paths.

'Mum!' called Phoebe from the herb patch. 'For God's sake. I said, have you seen my gym bag?'

'Mum?' said Eve.

Their mother – who was, Eve noticed, looking well and, perhaps, a little thinner – continued to read something with enormous concentration. It was a copy of *Oxoniensis*, a drearily

detailed newsletter about the glories of people other than their
father. Eve craned across the table to see what was transfixing
her:

Recent Music Appointments

Russian Accolade for Lincoln Master

Royal Society Honours Entomologist

'Mum,' yelled Phoebe. 'This is an emergency. I'm freezing
my tits off. Can you come OUTSIDE!'

Medieval Historian at St James's

Eve gasped. There, in grainy three-quarters profile, were
the black eyebrows, extraordinary cheekbones and deep whirl-
pool eyes of Raymond Snow.

At the sound of her gasp, her mother looked up, eyes
glazed.

'Oh!' she said.

'Oh!' said Eve. The truth was all over her face, but it was
her mother who jumped back, slamming shut the magazine
as if *she* were guilty. Eve's mind refused to work. She knew
from the way her entire body was blushing and her eyes
were being drawn to the photograph, that her mother would
know what was going on. Perhaps she had known for weeks.
However, her face revealed nothing. She looked instead
embarrassed, and faintly defensive: a Phoebe-ish look.

Eve glanced nervously towards the garden window, which
showed Phoebe's approaching thighs. The utter secrecy in
which the last six weeks had passed seemed, for a second, too
heavy to maintain. If she were to tell her mother the truth,
might it bring them closer?

'Mum . . . ' she said, imagining peeling open a corner of
her private world. At that very moment, her mother, with

uncharacteristic briskness, jumped up and began to pack her bag.

'Right,' she said. 'I've got to, um – I . . . must go. Are you all right, Eve, love?'

Oxoniensis lay between them on the table, only an arm's length away. Looking with interest at her shoes, Eve reached out towards it. So did her mother.

'Did you need it?' asked Eve, hopelessly flustered.

'Yes,' said her mother, very firmly.

Eve gazed stupidly at her, dazzled by her half-bared secret, unable to imagine what she'd want the magazine for. 'Is it for Phoebe?' she asked.

'No,' said her mother, unaccountably lowering her lashes and blushing herself. 'It's . . . for work.'

With a crash Phoebe was upon them, flouncing nakedly across the kitchen. 'I am cold,' she stated. 'No one helped me. I may become ill. If I am, don't bother to visit.'

Eve's mother bit her lip. She sighed. 'Don't slam the door, love,' she said, continuing to pack her books and pens. 'You're flaking the paint off the door frame.'

Eve stared. Phoebe stared.

'Oh,' she said. 'God, it's time I went. Phoebe, where's your uniform? Hadn't you better put it on?'

Now Eve, splendid and alone, tries to think like a god. Theirs has never been a bustling, vigorous sort of mother, but she seems to be caught in treacle. At the thought of her sister's slighted face, Eve begins to smile, and cannot stop. To her immense relief, whatever is distracting their mother is not the obvious: Eve's own fanfaring, prancing, spotlit secret. What *would* it take to attract her attention? Eve, for once in her life, can think of a thing or two.

January, thinks Victor Lux, is the cruellest month. Eliot had obviously never seen North Quad in First Week. Here, everything seeps: the lead drainpipes, braced against the wall with studded bands, the casement windows, the dark gate to St Giles. Damp spreads across stone the colour of dirty butter, already mottled with darker sand and soot; dreary flowers of lichen bloom; rust bleeds from spear-head window latches. The college is ominously still.

It is horribly cold. His fire has gone out, and so he sits in his gown and fingerless gloves, scribbling amendments to his Burgundian lectures in cramped copperplate, his left hand clamped over his ringing ear.

The lectures begin this Thursday, and the idea that these eight discussions of ditches would bring the Spenser Lectureship, the one that matters, within his reach now seems vain and absurd. He twists in his seat and looks once again out of the window. The arrangement of his rooms discomfits him. He must sit with his back to his vantage point, an expanse of mottled glass on the western side of Front Quad, which means that his foe may approach him unobserved, creep up the stairs with his long black legs and knock on the door. At any moment his sanctuary may be ruptured.

It has happened once already, on a filthy evening early in the vacation. He had been gathering up books for home when he heard a shifty shuffling in the passage, and there on the step he found Raymond Snow, tucking something quickly into his jacket pocket. The idea that he may have a key turns Victor's stomach. He gave his loathsome smirk, and asked for a drink, which he then refused, as if testing Victor. Victor was tested to his limits. Throughout their brief conversation, in which Raymond Snow expressed concern that Victor's lectures would be sparsely attended, his eyes swept the room. He is a rat, not a man.

After that, everything was sullied. Victor cannot enter his rooms without self-consciousness: does the shabbiness of his furnishings suggest poverty or high-mindedness? Are his visible books too old-fashioned, not old-fashioned enough? Everything is a trap – but it is not he who should feel trapped, he reminds himself. He is not the lecher, the charlatan.

This is bad enough, but the situation has worsened. The last two times he encountered Raymond Snow, once lamplit in the library, once walking through Laudian Quad in icy morning mist, there was something new behind the sharp white smile, his confiding air, his extortionist's offer of friendship. He had a look about him, as if – no, it is ridiculous. Victor clears his throat, blows his nose and, after a moment of indecision, stamps downstairs towards the library, only to glimpse Raymond Snow in the next quadrangle, leaving the chapel passage. He is like a spot on Victor's eye; wherever he turns he sees him. Dreaming of destruction, he watches him walk away, and there it is again, even from behind: that look of self-satisfaction.

Eve steps up to the doorway of staircase VI, North Quad, and closes her eyes. Even the air seems warmer. She extends her fingertips into the golden light of the stairwell and feels pinkness spreading through her skin. She is so alive she feels she might die.

The worn stairs and ancient panelling magnify everything.

By the time she reaches the top her body is not her own. Be calm, she tells herself. She is pink all over, a teenage changeling, herself times a hundred, wonderfully enhanced. She could bound across the rooftops if called upon, and it seems possible that she might be. Anything could happen. She wants it to.

'Come in,' he says.

She has not even knocked. She does not need to; she is profoundly, entirely known. She tries to amend her expression, squash herself down somehow, but hers is not a concealing kind of face. The door opens wide at her touch, but she walks in slowly, ready for anything. It's as well that she is. Raymond Snow is sitting in his armchair, and the look on his face is not what she expected at all.

Victor cannot concentrate. This is most unlike him. He has read during dinner parties, while climbing the Acropolis on donkey-back. The niceness of his written arguments is undisrupted by seasickness, funerals or despair – usually, that is. Now, however, he sits below a gloomy stained-glass window, frowning over the flower of his college's manuscript collection, and his mind will run in one direction only. He is enslaved.

Jean dresses with particular care.

She has bathed; she feels hot and strong, like a flushed goddess. It is January, she reminds herself. She will not feel this warm outside. It is also dark, but the shining, promise-filled dark of early evening. She should still be at work among the codices. Hedley, however, is examining fjords until Wednesday of Second week, and she can do as she pleases. Her earrings, icy silver shells, softly bite her ears. Her silver bracelet is misty with mineral sweat. Her thick silk shirt, washed soft as driftwood, sticks lovingly to her breasts. She is almost ready.

Victor, of course, is at college. Eve is rehearsing something in Greek. There is only Phoebe here, and she has not been downstairs for hours. One shoe dangling from each small hand, Jean edges across the carpet into the hall. Her daughter's bedroom door is shut; there is nothing but a musical murmuring, a pulse in the banisters. Treading stealthily on the outer edge of every stair, a trick she learnt in childhood, she creeps down to the kitchen to leave a reassuring note, a faint perfume of roses.

If Victor went there now what would he find? The nib of his pen feels full of fibres; he digs at the page, but no ink will come. It is possible, of course, that Raymond Snow would be working, doubtless on some Lectureship-winning article, or a sycophantic suggestion for the smooth running of the cellars. He may be giving a seminar, in which case Victor would like to hang like a clumsy bat from his windowsill and watch his technique: that way he had of appearing to play to the groundlings, while shooting learned references at his protégés over their heads. Victor, tormented by curiosity and fear, has not yet visited him in his rooms. However, he can visualize quite clearly the desk, the chair, the exact incline of Raymond Snow's white neck and skull as he bends over his poisonous page.

The rustling in his ear is growing louder. Sometimes it seems that it might contain an earwig, or that he is playing host to another, more mechanical, type of bug. There may well be devices for listening to thoughtwaves. For all he knows, they are for sale in the Covered Market. Resisting the urge to ram his pen nib through his eardrum and let it all out, Victor begins to remove papery wisps from the metal. His lecture notes are open on the desk, as a kind of deterrent. He could not possibly rush out after Raymond Snow and leave them lying here; he would have to pack them up and, in that time, he hopes, he could stop himself.

He must stop himself. The mere suspicion of what he might find up there if his wife and Raymond Snow have abandoned all caution, or if the room is empty, save for *billets-doux* and a list of dates and times, is one thing, but actually finding it would be quite another. It would kill him, and perhaps not only him.

He could, of course, go home now and wait for Jean to come back from her office at the usual time, as if nothing is going on. She has promised to make him hunter's stew tonight, full of onions; he has claimed he is developing a cold. He will wait here and work for another half-hour, so that by the time he reaches his house the air will be full of bacon and garlic, and she will be waiting for him, strange and sleepy but his alone, and he can close the door and keep her for another evening.

His pen is mended, but there is ink all over his fingers. He forces his rolled-up lecture notes into his jacket pocket and stamps downstairs to the unlit fellows' lavatory, hoping that activity will calm him. It does not. He washes his glistening hands in the half-light, watching the water darken.

His daughter, meanwhile, on the sofa, is trying not to ignite. All around her is evidence of perfection: sensitivity, originality, and the rigorous intellect to which she aspires. The minutes pass slowly; he has asked her to wait. She doesn't mind. She can gorge herself on his possessions, learning everything.

He is typing hard. The keys on his beautiful typewriter rattle like hail: a lovely sound. A newly-discovered superstition dictates that she should keep her eyes from him until he speaks. It is almost impossible. He is the leanest man she has ever encountered; thin, like an arrow, with the same packed power. His forearms are muscled, somehow like snakes: the comparison delights her. She does not care in the slightest that he is quite old: at least as old as her mother, although he does not believe in comparisons. Her mother adores comparisons. They are worlds apart.

He has stopped typing. Her blood booms.

'Eve,' he says, turning his bright brown eyes upon her. He holds her with them, hot and still.

Victor bursts out of the door, passing the front desk so quickly that the graduate on night duty, noting the book-borrowing history of his favourite second-year, jumps with fright and spills hot chocolate into the card index.

Victor can move fast when he needs to. As he runs, he growls, but he cannot hear it: only old men go to doctors. The sound is masked by heavy footfalls and heavy breaths and incidental grunts of anger or pain. He appears a man pursued, but he is the pursuer. Grey shadows watch as he races to his goal.

'We have to talk.'

He has been serious with her before, his voice low with understanding as they discuss the awfulness of home and school, his hand on hers. However, these times are brief. Usually they just amuse each other, deliciously, chastely. He has a beautiful mind.

He flexes his fingers and brushes his fringe from his eyes. Everything he does makes her feel both restful and alive: her mind slides gratefully towards him all the time now, wherever she is. She is amazingly lucky. Whatever he asks her, she will do.

'Um . . . yes?' she says. He is looking at her so intensely that she can barely breathe.

'You know that I know your father?'

In Front Quad Victor encounters Potson, now a celibate Theology fellow who regularly hears from God. 'Oh, Victor,' he says through a cloud of port fumes, as Victor squirms. 'Victor, Victor. Victor, Victor, Victor. Vict—'

'Look, ah, Walter,' Victor says hurriedly. This is not Potson's name. 'Could this wait? I'm in a terrible hurry.'

'Do you know, I don't think it can. *Vita brevis*, etc. Just a word, just a word. A word in your, hem, ear, if I may. A little, hem, word, in your—'

'I'm so sorry,' says Victor but, as he edges past him, he catches his heel on Potson's robes.

'Steady,' slurs Potson, lurching towards him. Victor angrily dodges his groping arms.

'Urgent . . . something,' he barks, trying to untangle himself.

'What?' asks Potson. 'This late?' His face changes; he gives a horrible leer. 'Victor, old man, I never thought—'

Victor has had enough of dissipation. 'Dreadfully sorry,' he says, not concealing his distaste and, a little too forcefully, pushes past Potson and rushes away towards the chapel, his face gilded by the stained-glass windows, his eyes bright with revenge.

Eve stares at Raymond Snow.

'Dad? How do you know him?' He must mean that her parents have found them out. While Phoebe does whatever she wants, they will keep Eve and Raymond apart. She is smoking with indignation. 'What does he, why does it . . . It doesn't—'

'Hold on,' he says, stretching his long legs towards her. She can see how he'd be in a tutorial; commanding, at ease, magnificent. She knows her brain would flourish under him.

'Tell me,' he says. 'Why should that be a problem?'

'Oh. It's not – isn't—' In the heat from the fire her arm is beginning to smart

'We're doing nothing wrong, Eve,' he says. 'What's wrong with this? We enjoy each other's company; it's perfectly natural.'

'Oh,' she says, looking at her fingers. 'Yes, it is.'

'And of course, while it may not be *usual* for a man of my age and a young woman of yours to meet in this way, it's quite reasonable. I see undergraduates barely older than you every day—'

Her fingers curl into her palms. She is not the only one.

'—although they are not, obviously, quite so intelligent. Or mature.'

Suddenly Eve knows what he is going to say. The room explodes in a blaze of happiness. Tonight – it is going to happen tonight.

*

For all he knows, he is being watched. As he hurries on through North Quad, gargoyles smirk maliciously from shadowy patches of lamplight. One could lean out of a window here and not know that, above and below, open jaws wait.

His ear is hammering. He cannot catch his breath. The staircase, however, is in his sights. The gargoyles have a single face. Rain dribbles over the crumbling sills and down gullies; it drips from archivaults and spandrels noted and dated unconsciously, even as he pounds on through the rain. He will take the stairs slowly, and in that time he hopes his lungs will clear. When he reaches the top he will have to be steady.

II, III, IV. In every doorway, enormous lamps swing like the sword of Damocles in the wet wind.

Eve waits patiently on the sofa, and is rewarded with one of his unsurpassable smiles.

'Which is, of course, my point. You're much too clever to need me to explain this, I know, but I do feel I should clarify the situation. Which reminds me, I'm going to have to ask you to leave in a couple of minutes.'

Eve winces. He always does this; she hopes it is to protect her. She decides, as usual, to linger until the last possible minute, to give him the encouragement that he so touchingly needs.

'No one knows that you've been visiting me, I assume?' he says.

'Well, no.' Her other secrets are merely dark and shameful; this is like the door to a glorious underworld. Instinct keeps her quiet. 'Should they?'

'I see no reason for it. Where would Plato's Academy have been if *hoi polloi* had trotted along to join in the fun?'

'Exactly,' she agrees, mentally updating her burgeoning reading list. Who cares if Phoebe gets a new martingale every time she brushes her pony? This is what Eve wants – the life of the mind.

'Good,' he says. 'You know, your father is a strange man. Remarkable, in his way, but very . . . defensive. Don't you find?'

'Um. Well. He's quite prickly, if that's what you mean—'

'You mean easily annoyed, even when you're trying to be helpful, for example, or interested?'

'Yes!' says Eve, delightedly.

'He's a strange one,' Raymond muses. 'When I knew him—'

'When *was* that?' asks Eve.

'When I knew him, everyone said . . . he was going to be great. He was a brave man, in his way, and maybe he could have been. But that depends on whether you master everything else inside you. Do you see?'

'I think . . . no,' says Eve.

'All the unhappiness, the bad things. Your father wallows in the past, more fool him. He doesn't dare – well, dare *anything*. You're not like that, are you?' he asks.

'Oh, no!' says Eve.

He has made it. Rainwater drips from his brows; it has entered every buttonhole and seam. He is, however, hot at last, his mind burned calm. Indeed, at the thought of action, of refusing to sit patiently as his life is destroyed, he is almost happy. As he stamps up the sagging staircase, he whistles part of the finale from *Don Giovanni*: '*Che strazio! ohimè! che smania! / Che inferno! Che terror!*' His breath is quick; his mind is racing. Dark drops stain the steps behind him as he climbs.

'You know, he was exactly the same when I first knew him.'

Her eyes dart to the clock on his desk, and back again. Despite her list of facts about Raymond – his opinion of the College President (excitingly irreverent), his interests when her age (remarkably like hers) – she still has no idea why he knows her father.

'When was that?' she asks again, too eagerly.

'Before you were born,' he smiles. 'So. I don't think he'd necessarily understand these . . . conversations. I'm glad you understand.'

'Oh, I do,' she says.

He jumps to his feet as if released, and crosses to the far window. Outside, the shrieks and boastings of the students carry far in the cold air. 'It can be lonely, can't it, when the parent you have most in common with intellectually is a little – well, caught up in his work. Particularly given the difficulties with your mother.'

'God, yes,' she says. Talking about this calmly, with a grown-up, is food for her hungry soul. 'And you know, she's getting even worse. Even . . . weirder!'

'Really?' says Raymond, Dr Snow.

'Yes! She's . . . well, when she's not dancing round Phoebe, she's – she's not even doing that so much, to be honest. She's so – God, she's in another world. It's like she's . . . she's so dreamy . . .'

He begins to walk towards her. His eyes seem to have locked to hers; she is being submerged.

'In what way?'

He is crouching on the rug beside her. His lashes are so dark. He looks half like a dangerous boy, and half a hero: an explorer, perhaps, not an ordinary man at all. Staring at his bright eyes, something new seems to pass between them. His hand is on her arm. 'In what way, exactly?'

Only a few moments have passed, but it seems like the past is a pellet of nothingness, and everything that counts has just taken place.

He has kissed her. She is transformed.

And now she has been dismissed, but sweetly. Her hand is resting on the handle of the inner door. She can take her time.

'So,' she begins. 'I . . . thank you. It was lovely to—'

He puts down his bag and comes towards her. Her skin unfurls.

'Don't thank me,' he says. 'Really. I'm longing for next week. Aren't you?' He puts his hand on her hand and opens the door, squeezing her fingers hotly against the brass, and looks into her eyes. 'You are extraordinary, Eve. I can see it, even if – for whatever reason, their weird preoccupations, I don't know – they can't. You're safe with me, you know,' he says.

One more flight, thinks Victor. His heart is racing; he should be careful but, really, why be careful now? He heaves himself up past the landing; there is the landing, Raymond Snow's landing – but the outer door is shut, and there is a nameplate saying:

PROF. D. H. R. FOALE

and his trail is cold.

The staircase is silent, but for the sound of dripping, and the scratching of his jaw as he lowers his head to think. He rubs at his temples, listening to his heaving breath, and suddenly understands: he is on the wrong staircase. Fool, he tells himself as he charges back towards the bottom. He will make it if he hurries. It is not too late.

Pieces of her old self lie on every landing. Her blood crackles as her feet fly over the stairs. She hits the bottom and springs off the step into the dark quadrangle, squealing with life. She does not notice her father, standing stock still at the sight of his beaming golden-eyed daughter. She tears past him out of the doorway and into the cold wet night.

SECOND WEEK

Jean is horribly, unbearably late. She has spent the afternoon incarcerated in the Cupboard, counting the minutes until her release. Then, when there was barely enough time left to visit the toilet, Hedley leant back in his chair and insisted that they go through every single entry of the Stewart Family bequest since 1925.

She sat violently still for five minutes. 'Hedley,' she murmured at last, but he ignored her. She began to pick unhappily at the gold leaf on her desk-top. After several long seconds she tried again. 'Hedley. I really . . . I must – it's nearly—'

He looked at her over the top of his spectacles. In the light of her stolen Anglepoise, the side-parting in his bushy hair shone indecently bright. 'Do you have an urgent appointment?' he asked.

'Well, no, it's just this . . .' It was impossible to lie convincingly; the very subject makes her stumble and stutter. She felt like a smuggler with gold on her tongue. 'I'd said— I'd told a friend . . .'

'That's hardly a reason to leave early,' Hedley said. 'I'm a generous man, but don't take my leniency for granted. We have a great deal of work, you know.'

The chapel bell struck the half hour, the three-quarters hour. When she heard the first note of the hour peal, she pushed back her chair. Hedley pursed his lips.

'I'm sorry,' she said, looking over the top of his head towards the rooftops. 'I really do have to go. I'm very sorry.' With that, as Hedley took breath to object, she smartly stepped past his desk and released herself.

Five minutes later she has crossed the High Street, and is hurrying past Queen's. The icy cobbles in Logic Lane have slowed her, but now she is racing, her long skirt snapping against her boots. The dark streets are full of undergraduates, reacquainting themselves after the vacation. Out of my way, she commands silently: I live here. She marches between them down the high-walled lane towards All Saints', and straight through the black gate. Everything seems crystallized. The sky is shameless. Please be here, she thinks, jog-trotting around the monastically bare quadrangle, and then almost running through the great archway into the garden. The gates are wide open; the sandy gravel sings as she stamps across it to the grass. Please be here.

She is too late. There is no one.

Violently disappointed, imagining throwing herself on the damp grass and bellowing and kicking like – well, like Phoebe, she walks slowly around the Mound, a deranged hillock in the middle of the lawn, unable to think. There is a white butterfly on the arm of the empty bench, she thinks: perhaps an omen? She comes closer, and sees it is only paper; and then she is running. It is for her.

Can't stay here – there's a groundsman in shed at end.
Come to ~~my ro~~ the cloisters – front quad by chapel.
What happened? I'm waiting.

The white butterfly has flown to her stomach; it shivers as she moves. If the groundsman saw the note being left, and then saw Jean picking it up, whom would he tell?

Hurriedly she retraces her steps, although now, of course, she imagines curious dons in the upper windows, watching her. For all she knows everything is already common knowledge, and the porters and dons' wives she meets are secretly—

She must not torment herself. She will fix her mind on what awaits her. She walks purposefully through a black-and-white-tiled passage at the far end of the quad, ignoring the excited youthful voices and pew-scrapings from the chapel which runs alongside it. At the entrance to the cloisters, she pauses. Ahead, and to her right and left, are utter blackness: almost palpable. She could eat it. She could turn back. Eyes wide, lips parted, she steps inside.

On her first holiday with Victor, in wet Wales, they visited caves – as often as possible. The guide turned off his torch and, at his command, they each held a hand in front of their faces to marvel at the dark. It had obviously been his favourite part of the tour. That darkness, however, was nothing compared to this. There are lights behind her, and presumably stars above the central courtyard, but she might as well be blindfolded. She could be a disembodied mind. Only the swooping feeling in her guts, and the tap of her feet on the flagstones, tell her that she still exists – that is, assuming they *are* her feet.

She turns the first corner. There is a tall pale shape by the wall.

'Is that you?' she whispers. 'Are you there?'

The shape says nothing. She comes closer.

'Is that you?' she says.

A tall rotten-faced man looms above her, holding another man's head in his hand. Jean screams, but quietly, too terrified for noise. Darkness chokes her; she looks away, wildly, but has no idea in which direction to run. Then she glances up, and sees a crown, pale eyes: a statue. Stupid Jean.

She moves away and can again see nothing: not her hand, not the stars, not the place where, two or twenty steps away, another mind is waiting, a little point of pulsing heat. She sets off again around the invisible central courtyard, trying to return to a more manageable level of delirium—

'Jean.'

Her foot is resting on nothing. She could end this all now, she thinks, listening to her booming heart: she could keep walking until she reaches the exit and run out into clean familiar air. She never wanted this. She has a husband who is, at least, reliable; she has a home and a job and daughters; she has a place in the world. She cannot even imagine – although she has begun to try, just to shock herself – what her mother's friends or the girls from school would make of this. Her mind spins around itself; she decides to continue seeing Helena, or stop seeing Helena, every hour, every minute. She even, to her shame, makes lists of pros and cons – they do not help at all, but how they satisfy her. Two or three times a week she rings Helena, resolved to resist her, but the truth is that she cannot keep away.

But, she tells herself. I do not want this.

'Jean,' says the darkness.

They are sitting very close, the sides of their heads pressed together, their backs to the glassless window of the inner wall. Somewhere in the dark courtyard a tree is moving in the wind, and the sound merges in their temples and their ears, as if they are twins in embryo, or drowning together.

Jean is worrying. Helena can feel it. She forces herself not to move her head, or to change the position of their hands. It has been this way every time since . . . since they . . . since it started. They meet, in the All Saints' garden or a dark lane near St Thomas's; one evening they met on Port Meadow, with the wild men doing t'ai chi and the travellers' buses, but it was too frightening to try again. There are no words for how wonderful it is each time they meet. And then the worrying begins.

The first time they kissed was . . . it felt like . . . Helena is always trying to define what it felt like. It felt as if everything extraordinary and desirable had been distilled and was there on her lips: a hot soft reflection of herself. Since then the shock has only slightly abated, and the kissing **kissing Jean** my God has grown more astonishing.

But there are problems. They cannot meet indoors, not even in Helena's rooms. Particularly not there.

'Why not?' Helena always asks. 'Really, can we not?'

'You . . . I, I'm afraid, I—'

Helena knows why they cannot. Jean is afraid of the next stage, for reasons Helena can understand, and for others that she cannot bear to consider. She is terrified too, but she knows she wants—

'I'm afraid,' Jean says, 'of . . . you know. Being alone. Us, alone. You know. I don't know if I want . . .'

'What?' asks Helena.

This keeps happening. It isn't as if there are a great many other places that two women, both unmistakably women, can meet, if they can't be in private, and yet mustn't be seen. The cloisters seem the ideal solution, although it is so very cold here, and there is always the risk of someone arriving, another couple – there may even be people in here now. If they were caught, of course, it would be terrible. Jean, however, is so warm, and so close, and smells so heavenly, that Helena is not at all sure that she cares.

Above them, unnoticed in the rafters, a tiny red light blinks on again, and off. Jean lifts her head; when the light goes on again she will see it, but in the interval Helena's head dips back down and, as they kiss, she misses it.

They are kissing again. Jean has never known anything more strange. After a short lifetime in which men were what one kissed, one hard stubbly bear-like man in particular, this, the soft skin, had felt at first like a mistake: almost repulsive. Besides, the kissing itself was all wrong. She has been used to being kissed, to being the soft place, but again this was different, like flowers, carefully, kissing. Sometimes not so carefully. The strangest thing of all is that after the first time – presumably even during the first time, because she did not pull away, indeed came back and back – her brain began to withdraw, like a light slowly going out, as the physical sensation took over. And then her brain switched back on and began to enjoy itself too. She became addicted. She is now. She cannot get enough of this.

Part of her wants them just to kiss for ever, so she can concentrate on the touch of lips and tongues, or to do nothing but close her eyes, inhaling Helena's familiar lovely smell until she can inhale no further and has to waste time by breathing out. Part of her does not. She is starting to dare to use her hands, to put her mouth in different places. She cannot stop thinking about Helena's collarbone, even in Sainsbury's.

Helena, however, is a woman. Incontrovertibly. Jean is afraid that, if they try to take this further – even a millimetre further – she will not be able to go through with it, let alone actually go to bed. She has a horrible phrase in her head: when it comes to the crunch, I will not be able to do it.

It may be something to do with Helena's hipbones. For Helena is thin, there is no escaping it, and while real curves, like Jean's own, would be worse, she fears that worse still is boniness.

However – it's as if her brain is sitting on the stone bench beside them, now that they are not kissing – she has a growing suspicion that she could even like Helena's thinness. Besides, she has touched, in passing, what seem to be proper curves: her hip, her thigh, the side of her breast, and they thrill her. That is the truth. Whenever she recalls these tiny touches, she contracts with excitement. And, she reminds herself, the thinness has never bothered her before. She was not repulsed by Helena as a friend, as aspects of other people can repulse one. And after all, she loved her. After all.

THIRD WEEK

Eve sits in Latin, drawing profiles. Her body is smiling to itself. No one else in the class is quite themselves, even the undistractable girls, the hardest working in the cleverest class in the year. Yesterday afternoon Bryony Hirsh, who when they were twelve or thirteen would get all As as a matter of course, was found weeping behind the changing-room wire lockers and has been taken to hospital. No one knows which hospital: rumours about unborn children circulate. Eve, however, can guess. It is common knowledge that Bryony got mostly Bs in her O levels, and the school is trying to put her in the second division because of results tables, and her father has been in and has stopped them. Eve has seen scratches on Bryony's wrist, which struck her at the time as odd: that kind of ostentatious minor wounding is favoured by the rebellious girls, the ones with biro spider's-web tattoos and three ear-rings. The idea that little scratches could lead to hospital fills Eve with excitement and alarm. What would it take for her to be hospitalized? Which teacher found Bryony? She begins to imagine rolling up her sleeves and waiting to be saved.

However, all this has come a little late. She *has* a saviour. At break she forsakes her friends, who are having heart-to-hearts in the crush hall and selling peppermint creams for Russian refugees, and walks about the school, communing with her inner – and increasingly outer – life. She wants to think about her body: not her arm, which is currently convalescing, but everywhere else.

Today she goes to the marbles pitch, where ten- and eleven-year-olds are setting out complicated stalls around the ruined markings of an old netball court. Cat's-eyes, navy and amber and green, glint temptingly in the flat grey light. She knew all the rules, the formations in which to lay favourite marbles, the baits and tricks, but now she finds she has forgotten them. She has more important matters to consider: this extraordinary adult world she is entering, this life of the mind.

Except that their minds are not the main thing any more. He is being gentle, she realizes, because he knows or has guessed almost everything, her most shameful secrets and fiercest desires. Because of him the arm business has abated: she has decided never to do it again. She no longer wants to; what she wants is him. She suspects that he is waiting for her to say she is ready. She is ready. Tonight, if she dares, she will show him how ready she is.

Helena cannot stop smiling either. There is work to do: a rare caterpillar has arrived from Chile and is eating through its small supply of casca leaves unobserved; she must decide, as every year, whether or not to send her silent mother a birthday card; she has promised to help Jeffrey build a drawbridge; she has a book to write; she has a newly-acquired tube of moisturizing cream to apply to her dry elbows.

In her new world, this last task has priority. She squeezes

a drop of cold cream on to her hot fingertip and rubs it thoughtfully into the skin, thinking of elephant knees, of human knees, of Jean's knees. The cream vanishes; her skin is thirsty. She smiles and smiles and smiles.

Later that evening, as Jean walks towards the back gate of Helena's college, stroking her own wrist with a dreamily surprised expression, she half notices that, for the first time, there is a porter at the desolate little desk by the entrance. He is, however, too absorbed by something on a screen before him to look up.

Thank God, she thinks, a close escape. She hurries through the gate, hugging herself with relief.

The porter, Jimmy, is indeed preoccupied. He is actually an underporter: only nineteen, he has been apprenticed to his uncle the deputy porter, whose alcoholism means that Jimmy is learning fast. As well as supervising the scouts' tea-break, and evicting pissed students from the bar, he has the laborious task of fortnightly checking and deleting the pictures taken by the new infra-red cameras, designed by a physics don after someone tried to nick the El Greco in the chapel. Infra-red, or ultra-violet, or something. There's only three – in the chapel, the cloisters and the lodge. It's a job so boring the other porters won't do it – there's never anything to see. Until today.

FOURTH WEEK

On Sunday evening, Victor sits alone at the kitchen table, revising the notes for his next ill-attended lecture, and allowing himself, for once, not to worry about Jean. He knows where she is.

She is, at this very moment, gorgeous in old but extremely flattering black velvet, climbing the stone stairs to the All Saints' hall, and Helena.

They have agreed that this is a risk worth taking. Fellows can invite anyone they choose to dine with them in formal splendour at High Table. It need be no secret that they are friends; least of all here, where Jean is of interest to no one. Besides, they have no choice. Family duties – visiting relatives, unwelcome social events, violent demands from both Jeffrey and Phoebe for attention and interest and gifts – mean that they will be unable to see each other any evening this week and the Panty, to Jean's considerable but delighted surprise, is no longer enough for either of them. Nothing like enough.

What is more, the dinner tonight, for misty reasons connected with St Edmund, is a minor Feast; it starts later than usual, and will go on into the night. Usually their time together is limited to the early evenings: they have families who will expect, if not miss, them; dinner must be sat through, regardless of body or soul. Because of the Feast, however, no one expects them until very late. The evening is theirs.

Jean reaches the top of the stairs and enters the hall. It is cavernous, candle-lit. The undergraduates have already left their benches after a supper of grapefruit and watery shepherd's pie. On a platform at the other end of the hall, a good twenty yards away, the dons and their guests bob and chatter, settling themselves in clusters around High Table. She walks like a lone bride towards them, her heels clattering, keeping her eyes on the back of Helena's head.

Everyone else has a gown. Smiling incredulously, Jean takes her place at the table. No one tries to stop her. Helena is talking to a liver-spotted mound of gown on her right, but turns mid-sentence to give Jean a narrow-eyed and sexy smile. Then, apparently unruffled, she turns back, and continues with her description of the ecological function of wasps. Jean, dazed, attempts to unfurl her napkin. Helena's nerve, the reserves of strength and daring which, when they were simply friends, Jean failed to notice, are terribly exciting. Her hands tremble as she plucks at the linen folds.

'How are you?' whispers Helena eventually.

'Wonderful. Glad . . . it's amazing to be here, like this. You?'

'The same.' They smile at each other, then at their plates, as the heavy chairs stop scraping and the pinched voices still. A lengthy Grace begins, in Latin. Under the table, their ankles touch.

*

Eve gets up off the day bed. While she is just as sore and stunned and reeling as last time, there has been no blood. She almost, she tells herself, enjoyed the feeling.

Her world has shrunk to this dark room; the face of the man striding across it to open the window. She still does her homework and her music practice, but she cannot write a word or open a page without looking for his initials, inventing his preferences, seeking out good omens. With her friends she is virtually silent; the romantic future, once a neutral subject, unlike home or emotions or her fears and secret rituals, is now private and closed. She does not need friends, other than him.

She joins him at the window: a little to his right, because he does not want them to be visible from outside, but near enough for their breath to merge in the cold night air. Behind her, on the day bed, a small wet patch seeps through the blue coverlet. He is careful to adjust the cover before she lies down on it; just one thoughtful act of many. She lets him do it and so has not noticed that, on the fabric of the day bed, there is a galaxy of hidden stains.

Helena has been trapped by the person to her right: a professor of Anatomy, despite his appearance. 'That sounds fascinating,' says Jean to the man to her left: a nonagenarian international lawyer with far better table manners than his neighbours. He has, moreover, small talk, and entertains her, relatively speaking, with boundary disputes, college gossip and his own unusual personal circumstances, which seem to involve his scout. He speaks with an accent which sounds oddly like Victor's but is, she decides, unable to concentrate on what he is saying yet trying to maintain a semblance of attention, probably, yes, almost certainly, Portuguese.

Now, however, she cannot ask him. She is unable to formulate a single further question, because Helena's knee has just come into contact with her own. The wood-polish scented air is suddenly too pure to breathe. She is floating, moored only by Helena's kneecap. At any moment she may be lost.

'So,' says the lawyer courteously. 'May I ask what brings you to this dinner?'

They are already half-way through the second course, but by donnish standards this is almost indecent interest. At that moment, Helena turns. Jean tries to answer, but she can feel Helena's attention hot as sunlight on the side of her face.

'Forgive me, José,' Helena says and the lawyer holds up his creased brown hand and smiles, charmingly. 'Forgive me. But I must claim my guest.'

Phoebe is on her second joint. Her mother is out, but she is hanging out of the window anyway, watching the students in their college rooms. She could be seen; she is going too far, probably, but too far keeps getting further away.

The turnstile squeaks. Phoebe takes another drag. The person coming this way is still in the shadow of the college, making their way along the path. Then the front gate squeaks, and Phoebe grinds her roach into the windowsill, taking her time, but with an unpleasant feeling of having been caught off guard. Entering the garden is the last person she'd expect to see out so late: her sister.

Phoebe, in darkness, holds her breath. There is something wrong with Eve's school skirt – she is twisting it round, as if she can't find the front. Now her fingers are running down the buttons of her shirt, counting them or checking them. She's tucking it more neatly in. Whatever she's been doing, she hasn't been swotting in her room.

Then, just before she disappears into the porch, she turns. Her face is lit up by the outside light, and she looks – well, hardly pretty, but more like their mother than usual. She's looking over her shoulder, back the way she came, and there is something in her smile that Phoebe's never seen there. She is the last person in the world Phoebe would expect to have that look, or want to have it. But she does. It is a look of sex.

'And so you see,' says José Ramos, twinkling at Jean across the crème caramel, 'my position is somewhat ... well, complicated.'

'I do see,' says Jean.

In another life – if she were, say, sixty and Brazilian – she would, she thinks, be in love with Professor Ramos. He is quite the most attractive old man she has ever met: the whitest-haired, the most courteous, the most charmingly-accented. He is also the happiest. After seventy years of human rights work and a loveless marriage in the suburbs of Rio, he tells her, he came to Oxford on sabbatical and met Fay, a college scout, with whom he now lives in a lock-keeper's cottage in Jericho.

'Oh,' sighs Jean. She looks at her plate. 'How incredibly romantic.'

Professor Ramos bends his head a little closer. 'You are almost the only person,' he says, 'who has not taken the side of Mrs Ramos. Even my friends, to whom I lend my college flat with the greatest pleasure, even they think, "This scout, she is young, you are an old fool." My son, only, was kind.'

Under cover of the table, Helena's fingertips are gliding up and down Jean's forearm.

'He is,' says Professor Ramos confidingly, 'an 'omosexual.'

Horrified, Jean snatches her arm away. Sick with dismay, she glances at her neighbours, but no one seems to have heard. She wipes her hot hand on her skirt, stares at the table, the candlestick, crumples her napkin and finally looks up at the old lawyer, who is watching her.

His smile is serene. 'It is merely an observation,' he says.

By the time the Feast is over, they both know they are going to Helena's rooms. It is not just that they have drunk enough for courage, or that they have been holding hands under the table for the last half-hour. Jean has known it for some time. Comprehensive as her doubts are, nervous as she is, she wants more – at least, she thinks she does. At least, she thinks of little else.

As the great wooden thrones scrape back and the old dons rise, Helena stands in front of her, her eyes knowing and amused. 'Would you like to come back,' she says, as if merely out of politeness, 'for . . . for—'

'Yes,' says Jean. 'I would.'

The night is sharp; their breath smells of every grape imaginable. As they climb Helena's staircase, high up in Garden Quad, Jean misses a step. Helena fumbles for her key. They fall into her room in a snort of compressed laughter.

Then there is quiet.

'So, this is it,' says Jean. All the times she has not dared to visit hang thickly in the air. 'It's much more grown-up than your last one.' She turns around slowly, taking in the mantelpiece, the floorboards, the long bare shivering windows. 'More . . . civilized.'

Helena begins to walk towards her. 'Not for long,' she says.

Her attraction grows by degrees. To talk to, vertically, she is still Helena: thin, strangely dressed, somewhat nervous. It is only on stepping closer that the pheremonal rush begins: that Helena's faint golden fragrance becomes intoxicating, an impediment to thought. Then Jean looks at her hooded eyes and her secret smile and feels herself fall. None, of this, however, is anything compared to Helena on her back on the rug, where she is a long silkily-curved woman, fantastically herself, and all Jean's at last. Jean is above her, kissing, in charge, and then beneath her, and the heat of the freckled skin under the fabric as Jean undoes one button of Helena's shirt, then another, and feels the swell of her breast begin — such surprisingly female flesh, such a delicious curve — is a pleasure she will remember until she dies.

Hours later, still smouldering, Jean steps back into the Garden Quad, alone. There is a frost tonight: pulverized diamonds lie beneath her feet. She has no idea where she left her bicycle; it is extremely late. However, she cannot leave quite yet. She will take a turn around the garden and force her liquid limbs to solidify, her lungs to reacclimatize to air. Then, if she must, she will go.

She walks through the gates towards the garden. Helena's window is dark: just looking up at it, just feeling the muscles in her neck prepare to look, gives a slipping feeling in her stomach, a tightening of the skin inside. At night the Mound is enormous, dark and tangled; the black grass shines. Demented birds flurry in the tree-tops.

Her hand moves to her own breastbone: the same beating skin, the same stiff bra-lace, the same hot womanly swell. As she moves, the cold air heats around her: she leaves a wake of steam. Everything is illuminated. Now she understands.

'I just can't,' Jean says.

They are at breakfast: Valentine's Day, Phoebe's birthday. There have been croissants and orange juice, lavish presents, although perhaps slightly less thoughtful than last year's, and a certain amount of misbehaviour.

Phoebe takes off the red jumper, the silver ring, and drops them on the floor. She waits for her sister, at least, to glare at her, but Eve cannot even be bothered to look up from the Swedish Institute of Medievalists' Annual Bulletin. Their father is reading a dictionary: he is no use either. Phoebe lets the beautiful riding boots fall from her chair.

'You said that,' she says. 'You already said that.'

Their mother, who is beginning another croissant, stops smiling to herself. 'I know,' she says, quite sharply. 'But you keep asking.'

Phoebe goes absolutely still. When she speaks it is with effort, as if it involves a thaw. 'What are you doing instead?' she asks. 'I bet I know.'

'Eve?' says their mother, ignoring her. 'You look a bit . . . stunned.'

Eve smiles happily at her, forgetting to answer. She is lost in a fantasy of the days they served turtle soup at Christ Church banquets, when the college children were allowed to ride round the kitchens on the turtles' backs before the killing. She is imagining herself and Raymond, King and Queen of the Feast, riding on gilded shells to their place at the head of the table.

'Hello?' says their mother.

Eve blinks. She sees her sister's scowl and thinks, quite calmly: not even Phoebe can make me unhappy now. She is awash with sisterly love. 'Come on,' she says, picking at a spot on her arm, 'don't be sad about tonight. We can celebrate . . . well, tomorrow.'

Phoebe's place is strewn with croissant. With a sweep of her elbow she whisks it to the floor. 'Fuck's sake,' she says, but Eve, full of sex, cannot shut up.

'I mean,' she says, 'if Mum's got some special maternal activity, then let her. It's no big deal. You—'

'Fuck's *sake*,' Phoebe shouts at her sister. 'You are all so *fucking* stupid. Can't you . . . she's just—' Everyone is staring at her. 'You make me *sick*!'

She jumps up, her chair crashing to the tiles, and storms out of the room.

'Well,' says their mother mildly, 'there we go.' She sweeps a selection of crumbs into her palm and throws them at the sink.

'Where *are* you going tonight?' asks Eve curiously.

'Don't you start.'

Eve frowns. Her father shuts his dictionary with a soft whump and lowers his eyes to the cover, his fingers caressing the spine.

'Where, though?' Eve says.

'For God's sake,' her mother snaps. 'I'm tired of explaining myself. If you must know, it's Hel-Helena. I'm going to, um, see Helena. She needs some . . . support.' She looks at Eve's father, nervously picking a bit of fluff from his shoulder. 'I'm sorry about tonight,' she tells him. 'I'll make it up to her.'

'Where will you be if I need you?' he asks quietly.

Helena is in the middle of a lecture when her mind folds. She looks from her notes to her audience; then upwards, to the blind eye of a ceiling-rose. Fingertips trickle up her spine. Her thighs are melting. There are electric filaments where ordinary nerves should be.

Sixty pairs of eyes watch her, unblinking.

'And so . . .' she says. The bare knees of Jean Lux, hot, rounded, like satin billiard balls, press into her palms. She blinks, enraptured, opens her eyes, and sees her audience, staring at her. No one is writing.

'And so . . . and so,' she says, rearranging the yoke of her gown. 'Where were we?'

They are waiting for her to return to normal. Her mind is blank.

'To continue . . .' she says.

Phoebe has begun to watch her sister. The change is obvious: a new self-conscious unselfconsciousness, pitiful efforts with her clothes, once some lipstick, subtly awful, which Phoebe just laughed at until she took it off. You'd have to be mad, or dead, to miss it, which is her parents covered. Phoebe's neither. She can't tear her eyes away.

She always thought that Eve would just get older and older and more frustrated and unshaggable. Or, maybe, she'd end up being a lesbian with one of her weirdo friends from school, since they're all the same height, all brainy and awkward, all as unwantable as each other. Yuck. But she'd never have thought this – not Eve *first*.

So what she wants to know is: who?

About an hour after school, usually, Eve gets back with that look. But twice it's been much later, more like twelve, and although she sometimes stays for hours with Janey and Gemma and the other speccies, they're in North Oxford, and you get back from there through the side-gate from the lane. No; if she's using the front gate, Eve's been in town.

Now, none of her friends live in the colleges, though you'd think they'd all be Presidents' children. If she knew anyone down Cowley way or St Clement's, she wouldn't dare cycle back from there this late. The only answer Phoebe can think of is that her sister is shagging a student. Which seems incredible, because students have got each other, and if you're going to shag a sixteen-year-old you really wouldn't choose Eve. But if she has actually found someone mad enough to do it to her, then Phoebe wants to know who. She wants to see how hideous he is, to make her feel less crap about it. And she's not going to let Eve keep it a secret. There are far too many secrets here already.

Jean, scraping carrots, tries to calculate the greatest good for the greatest number. How, if in the unimaginable future it were to come to this, can she weigh up Victor's needs versus

Helena's, or the girls' versus Helena's? Would ostracism by her acquaintances be worse than mild disdain? All that seems quantifiable is what she wants and what she doesn't want, and here is the problem. She wants it all – or rather, she can't imagine giving up any of it.

She watches the orange-brown ribbons sink into the water, thinking of Helena in the garden, beginning it all. She thinks of Helena's hands and a cloud of butterflies lands in her stomach.

Is this, she wonders, what I felt for her all along, only slightly changed?

She thinks: on the one hand the signs – of which the bond with Helena was one – were always there. On the other, it never crossed my mind. She thinks: obviously it's not just that I've had enough of Victor. This, she has realized, happened long ago, but it was easier to stay. And staying is much, much easier than leaving him for . . . well, all *this*.

She has a dreadful vision of cigarillos and women in ties and squashes it, feeling slightly sick.

Then her eyes flutter open. She stares at the tap in shock. Where does that leave me? she wonders. What does that make me? Who does it make me leave?

'Helena,' says Norah, her mother-in-law, that evening, as Helena strokes her own knee absently and smiles at the kettle. 'We're a little concerned.'

The boiled potatoes goggle. 'I'm sorry?' says Helena.

'We're a little concerned, Hugh and I.'

Helena tightens her hand around the serving spoon. Now they are both gazing at her, napkins neatly returned to their napkin-rings, cutlery together. Her father-in-law's veined hand shudders against the tabletop. The air is like china, waiting to be scraped.

'It's Jeffrey,' he says.

'Ah,' says Helena, watery with relief. It is difficult, always, to believe that she and Jean are getting away with this, but every day that passes undiscovered seems to suggest that they will. There is a J in fishbones on the side of her plate; she does not remember putting it there. 'Ah,' she says, more seriously, concealing it with the tip of her knife. Hugh and Norah are the sweetest, least interfering parents-in-law imaginable: nothing like her own parents, and nothing like that genetic anomaly, their son. She is lucky to have them. She loves them both – until the minute they try to stop her.

'We wanted to have a word before, but – well, now he's upstairs. You must have noticed: he's not himself,' says Norah, fiddling with the salt. 'Really. Not at all himself. And – well – neither are you. Forgive me for saying so.'

Helena is, despite herself, curious. 'In what way?' she asks.

'He,' begins Norah, which is not what Helena meant at all, 'just isn't. I'm sure you've noticed,' she says, encouragingly. 'Yesterday Hugh said' – Hugh nods – ' "why don't you read me a bit of your *Iliad*." Which is, isn't it, usually the sort of thing he loves, Jeffrey, doesn't he? But, Hugh says' – Hugh nods – 'he just looked at him, a very cold look, and said, "Grandpa, frankly, stick it up your bottom," and slammed out of the room!'

Helena frowns. She cannot immediately come up with the right response. Her body is distracting her. 'And,' she says, 'you're worried?'

Norah, not prone to annoyance, clicks her tongue. 'Of course I am,' she says. 'He's difficult, and sullen – not like himself at all. And there was that business at school only a few weeks ago, when they said he'd bitten that other boy – I mean, *bitten*! He's not happy – maybe it's, you know. His father. But why now?'

'Well,' says Helena, staring fixedly at the tablecloth.

'And we're worried about *you*.'

'Ah.'

They wait.

'Please don't be,' she says. Her parents-in-law, these kindly innocent people, are already stiff with embarrassment. She feels as if she is standing over a millpond holding a boulder, and wants to let it fall. Their muted paintwork, their serious shabby furniture, their wistful emigrants' paintings will curl and disintegrate when they hear what she has done. What she is doing. She pushes her anklebones tight together. She fears she will explode with love.

'You know we are. How can we not be? Is something wrong?'

'Oh no,' she says.

'Is something going on?'

Helena stares hard at her glass. Everybody waits. 'No. *No*.'

'Because if it is, and it's upsetting him,' says Norah, still very sweetly, 'Jeffrey is still our grandson. His emotional welfare is our concern, as it is yours. As I'm *sure* it is yours. We have always trusted you to do what's best for him—'

'I am his mother,' says Helena, as stiffly as she dares.

'—and we know you will. But if some . . . if something is preoccupying you, then we're afraid—'

'Thank you,' says Helena, standing. She clears the table, listening, as they all are, to the trembling of dishes and knives, Hugh's whistly breathing, and the sound of foundations cracking.

'Mum,' says Phoebe, the next morning. 'You know there's a bug?'

'Hmm?' says their mother, apparently busy with her diary.

Phoebe sighs enormously. Eve, who has been staring at her muesli, wondering what awaits her after school, barely glances up.

'You know there's a bug?' says Phoebe. 'Well, I've got it.'

Eve is thinking about the town at night: the permanent wet beneath the street-lights, the couples returning home to warm bookish rooms, the sense of promise. This evening, after she's seen Raymond – and assuming he can see her, which, given the secret project he's working on, she can't assume – she may go for a cycle ride, just to feel a part of it all. She looks at their mother, who is gazing absently at her nails with a hint of a smile and, just for a second, Eve thinks: she looks like I feel. Then, because the thought makes no sense, she sweeps it away.

'Mum!' says Phoebe.

'Yes,' their mother says. 'Sorry. What sort of bug?'

'Just a bug,' says Phoebe irritably. 'Probably bacterial.'

'You're not ill, Phoebe,' says their mother, still rather distantly. 'Are you?'

Phoebe, all at once, is in a rage. 'How would you *know*?' she shrieks. 'You wouldn't *know*. You wouldn't know if my fucking *head* fell off.'

Eve automatically looks at her father. He isn't there. 'Um,' she says, generally.

'I *am* ill,' says Phoebe. 'I feel awful. My head – my throat. Ow.'

'Well,' says their mother. 'Poor love.'

'She's not ill,' says Eve.

She almost expects their mother to agree. However, she merely rubs her neck distractedly, and lays her small hand across Phoebe's forehead. The contact seems to rouse her.

'It was probably all that long-distance business you had to do yesterday,' she says. 'Maybe it was too much. I really think you might have a talent for it, though. I am *proud* of you. Does it hurt, poor love?'

Eve bites down hard on her spoon. Yesterday she brought home the news that she was one of the twelve Oxford Girls' Distinction-winners in the Thames Vale Creative Writing Challenge and, when Phoebe dropped ketchup on the certificate, their mother's only concern was for Phoebe's skirt. Three days before, on handing her the application form for her next clarinet exam, Eve, a little overwrought, had burst into tears. Even as she left the room she could hear her mother wondering aloud whether the time was right for Phoebe to learn the saxophone. She is beginning to buckle under the strain of keeping her alarming secret. She wants love and understanding, and instead has to watch their mother growing more and more fixated on Phoebe, praising her for her constant biscuit-baking, her adventurous hair-grip selection or, once, unforgettably, her skill in recording a tape.

She is making Phoebe a hot lemon and honey. Eve tells herself that she could, at least, tell Raymond about this tonight, but she has to make the best use of their time. Her need for him is terrifying.

'Do you want to go to bed?' their mother says. Yes please, thinks Eve, before she realizes who she means.

'But,' says Phoebe. She hasn't even bothered to get dressed: she is transparent, thinks Eve, feeling her bones miserably tighten. 'But. What will happen to Bilbo? I didn't go yesterday, and he'll be hungry – it's freezing. Poor Bilbo. Maybe I'll just bike over—'

'*No*,' says their mother, as if Phoebe, who usually begs a lift, might actually need restraining. 'You can't. It's ridiculous – much too far, and too cold. And . . . well, I can't.' She is beginning to sound irritable. 'I'm sure your sister will go for you.'

Eve takes a moment to register. She keeps her head down.

'Won't you, Eve? After school?'

'Sorry?' she says eventually. The basement air is suddenly glassy. 'What?' she says. '*What*? I'm not . . .'

Phoebe's mouth is a small pleased line.

'Please,' says their mother, shoving her diary into her bag

and standing up. 'I don't have time for this. I need you to go to the stables tonight after school.'

She looks different, Eve thinks suddenly: not the familiar fretful vagueness, but tenser, hotter, as if she is waiting for the door-bell, or afraid that if she moves her skin will split. She is looking at Eve as if Eve is an obstacle between her and the outside. Eve thinks: if you side with her this time I'll never forgive you.

Their mother snaps shut her bag.

Eve is not Phoebe. She cannot just say No. 'I . . .' she begins. 'Why? *Why?* That's not, not *fair*. I don't – he's not *my* horse. Anyway, I can't. I'm – busy.'

'You're not busy,' says their mother. 'You've got homework to do – that's all. Do it later. And you need the exercise. You never help your sister. Just be charitable for once.'

Something has been crossed. Eve sees her evening crashing before her. 'I'm *not* not charitable,' she shouts, already crying, hearing herself grow more and more repugnant. 'It's not *me* . . . you can't make me. N—'

'*Listen,*' shouts their mother, and nobody moves. There was a wire across the road, and no one warned her. 'I am *sick* of your selfishness. Both of you – but Eve, I *rely* on you. Some of us have lives to lead, and I do not have time for your whining. What've you got to do? You've got nothing to do. You think you are above everything, everyone else's problems, and you are not. I've had enough.'

Even before their mother has reached the top of the stairs, Phoebe, half singing, is piling gherkins and cheese and biscuits on a plate to take upstairs. Eve looks at her aching hands, yellow, bitten, ugly as the rest of her. Everything has come loose. She can feel the longing for pain returning; she believed it had gone, but underneath it has been growing. Nothing can be right. She had thought love would release her, but now she sees that blood is stronger. Blood will have to do it in the end.

EIGHTH WEEK

'There is,' says Victor sternly, looking down on to his daughter's grubby-looking hair, 'only so much of this bad behaviour I will tolerate.'

'But what bad behaviour?' Eve is screaming. 'What? I haven't done *anything*. You're all doing it to *me*.'

He slams his hand on her desk so hard her fountain-pen jumps. 'Listen to yourself!' he shouts. 'It is your only concern: how wronged you are. I have other things to worry about than your sense of justice!'

She is crying too much to speak. Great hot tears, gouts of snot and self-pity, are muffling her words and Victor, who is frankly too angry to sympathize, is finding it difficult to hear.

'For the love of God,' he says. 'Stop this. Now.' He is exhausted. He leans against the end of her desk, his broad back to her, and rubs his eyes. 'You say that once again it was *Phoebe* who started it, *Phoebe* who got away with it, *Phoebe* this, *Phoebe* that.'

'*Yes*,' Eve says, still snuffling and weeping and wiping her eyes. Her old habitual expression of anxious crossness has returned, unchanged. '*Listen*. I keep telling you. She just keeps baiting me, and Mum lets her. She helps her. She feels sorry for her, and it's me she should feel sorry for. I *said* this.'

Eve treats him like her mother does. Treated him. The desire to barricade himself in his room and forget all about the present is growing stronger, but now is precisely the time he must exert himself: the Spenser Memorial Lectureship depends on that. He has committees and seminars to endure, an article to write for the college magazine about recent archaeological finds in the Fellows' garden – thank God they asked him, not Raymond Snow – and it was even suggested, by a non-historical colleague to whom he gave a hint of his concerns, that he find time to charm the President's house-keeper, an *éminence grise* renowned for the elegance of her dinner parties. In truth, however, there is nothing to do but wait and hope that the best man wins.

Jean, he fears, will truly believe that the winner is the best man. If Victor loses, he will lose her too, to that persecutor, that gargoyle, that excuse for a don.

He stands straight again, as if pushing against a great weight of air. He resists the urge to press his hand against his ear; instead, to his own and Eve's surprise, he rests it on her head.

'So,' he says more gently, if only to calm himself. His flat soft fingertips are right in her eyeline: not only cracked, as they are every winter, but baby-pink and burnt-looking, where he has nibbled the skin away. He puts his hand back in his pocket. 'You feel hard done by, yes?'

'Well – *yes.*'

'I know. We all do.'

'Do we? Do you?'

He has, evidently, gone too far. 'It is hard,' he says,

'sometimes, family life. This is perfectly normal. All will be well in the end.'

'Will it?' says Eve.

'I think so.'

'How?'

Victor looks at his daughter's bed; her creased pillowcase, faintly, saltily stained. He cannot meet her eye. He lifts his voice artificially, allowing himself to believe for a moment that he has already won the Lectureship. 'I do not know,' he says.

Right then, thinks Eve. It's up to me.

That evening Pam Rook, wife of a porter at Helena's college, meets Margaret Prickett, scout of St James's, for their Wednesday gin-and-lemon in Binsey.

'So, what's new?' says Margaret.

Pam sucks on her lemon slice. She has a dilemma. There is one piece of news she could offer Margaret, but Margaret gossips so much she is known as Radio Jericho, and this is a secret Pam has promised not to tell.

'Come on. There is something, isn't there.'

'All right,' Pam says. 'There is something. But I shouldn't say.'

'Who's it concerning?'

'No one you know. One of Reg's.'

'Murder?' says Margaret. She's been scouting fifty-four years; the things she's seen.

'Oh no. Do you get that? We never get that.'

'Sex then. Single or group?'

'Look at you. No, two of them. But not what you think.'

'Two. I see. And only one of them Reg's. So, who's the other?'

Part Three
Trinity Term
April 1987

Eve keeps moving her diary. If her nerdy boyfriend writes her letters she's keeping them in her knickers, because they're not here. There's only a book of Latin love poetry, and he's written in it: 'To my ardent student, from RS.'

Then, on Saturday morning, Phoebe gets up early. Eve's out. Phoebe wanders into her room, not even dressed, smoking the first fag of the morning to help her concentrate. She finds, behind the back of Eve's desk drawer, two blank postcards embossed with the St James's crest, and an empty crumpled envelope with 'Raymond' written on it.

Raymond! thinks Phoebe. Raymond!

Right, she tells him. I'm coming to get you.

She goes to the stables for her pony, and rides him into town. She is wearing her boots and hacking jacket and jeans. She looks fantastic. They cross the water into Osney and go all the way to Beaumont Street, quite slowly. Bilbo is good with cars, but not that good.

At first, no one seems to notice them. She squeezes her tight denim thighs against his pale sides. Soon they will. As they get closer to town, people start pointing. Everyone has to wait as she crosses the traffic on St Giles. Everyone stares as she walks him on to the pavement outside her father's college. She ignores them. She just tugs on the reins to dip his head, and walks him straight through the main gate to the porters' lodge.

There's someone new on duty, which is perfect. She hasn't quite worked out what to do next, so she lets the new porter stare at her for a minute, along with a couple of amazed tourists and some droopy students in attention-seeking hats. She smiles down on them like she does this all the time, deciding what to do. There's no point getting her father, who'll just shout – her mother would have been better, but there's no way she'd get into her college like this. She's stuck out here among the pigeon-holes, unless she does something.

'Can you get the President?' she says.

Unbelievably, he does – at least, he disappears. For a second she wishes she wasn't on horseback, so she could nip behind the desk and find stuff: keys, or Eve's handwriting on a letter. But since she is, and Bilbo's getting restless, she turns him round carefully and walks him on a bit into the sunlight of the front quad.

The forbidden circle of lawn in the middle looks very tempting. It reminds her of coming back from the college Christmas party when they were little, after a huge tea in the Hall with the scouts' and gardeners' children and all the dons'. By the end of the tea they'd be frenzied with sugar and mulled wine fumes, waiting for what they knew would be unbelievably fantastic presents, and their parents would be frenzied too with the effort of socializing. They'd wait and wait, and then suddenly they'd have to line up in front of the President to get their present from his sack. And then, exhausted, they'd troop back through the empty college and around the frosty grass, clasping their enormous plush hippos and multi-accessorized kites and wooden paintboxes to their stomachs, and everyone, even their father, would be happy.

Bilbo shifts from hoof to hoof. His clopping echoes all round the quad. She's hoping Eve will suddenly appear with her half-shagged boyfriend, or their father will come down and see them. Instead it's the President who sticks his head out of a window – right above her, where the sunlight is most dazzling. He looks like he can't decide how to react. She grins at him, half blinded.

'Miss Lux,' he says. 'Phoebe. What in God's name are you doing here?'

'I've come to see you,' she says. 'I . . . thought you'd be interested to see your stable-ee. Bilbo, snort at the gentleman.'

Bilbo is trying to steady his hooves on the cobblestones, and ignores her. His mane shines like nylon in the sunlight. She tightens her fists around the reins.

'Very kind of you,' says the President, 'but I'm sure there are bye-laws—'

'Maybe,' she says. 'But still. He's a guest of the college. You can't ignore your guests.'

'Your premise is correct, but not your conclusion,' he says, nearly smiling. 'Some of our guests can only be ignored. It's a pleasure as always to see you, but I must ask . . .'

Phoebe panics. She needs more of a reaction than this. 'Shall I take him for a quick canter around the garden?' she says, reversing Bilbo towards the forbidden lawn. 'Or feed him a rare specimen? Or—'

She feels Bilbo shift beneath her. He lifts his tail. 'Miss Lux,' says the President as, with a wet splat and a gust of the farmyard, Bilbo drops four fat dollops of horse-shit on the grass. There is a horrible silence, broken only by the beginning of a great jet of pony-piss that bores into the perfect lawn, on, and on, and on.

'Whoops,' says Phoebe, in the quiet that follows. Every tourist in Oxford seems to have gathered in the entrance to the quad. Bilbo lowers his tail, whickers gently and sidesteps on to the grass, right into his own droppings. The President slams the window shut, spilling pre-lunch Amontillado all over a desk so old it has visitors of its own, and races towards the stairs.

She nudges Bilbo towards the edge of the lawn. He has been recently and expensively shod; his hooves bite satisfyingly into the turf beneath them. A tiny door swings open and the President runs into the quad. He grasps Bilbo's drooly nose-band and jerks him, and Phoebe, over towards the lodge.

'Hey,' says Phoebe.

'Don't "Hey" me,' says the President. 'Listen, child—'

'Don't "child" me,' says Phoebe teasingly.

For once, she has pushed it too far. The President's face goes extremely red. 'I have had enough,' he says, 'of your imprudent impudence. This foolishness must stop. Take this filthy animal away – I do not wish to see it again, or to have to deal with you again. You must find somewhere else to keep it.'

The tourists are gaping. 'But—' she begins.

'Your father will have to answer for this,' he says.

Sunday, they have agreed, is the best night. Eve's father is never in college, and there's hardly anyone to bump into on the stairs. What's more, she can come here straight from Janey's or Kate's or Gemma's, so no one can possibly guess what she's been doing. Raymond knows this, they have decided it together, but when Eve arrives she finds the outer door closed, and a note saying 'Called away – apologies.' She waits for nearly an hour, growing more ready for him with every minute, and more anxious. Increasingly there's only time for either talking or sex. When she chooses both neither works, but she *needs* both. How can she choose? Tonight, however, he does not come at all.

If he finds her here, after all this time, she realizes, it will be worse. What is she *doing* here? Obviously she must leave right away.

She steps right up to his door to kiss the handle. That way, at least, his hand and her mouth will be connected when he reappears. It is only as she straightens up afterwards, the cold sour taste of metal on her lips, that she sees that the door on the other side of the passage is ajar. From a desk inside a white-haired don is watching her.

'Oh!' Her voice resounds round the stairwell.

The don shakes his head angrily. It's as if he knows who she is, but she does not recognize him. She turns her back to him very cautiously, feeling as if her head is made of glass. She cannot ask for paper to leave a note; she cannot stay if she's been seen. She will come by tomorrow and leave him a note in his pigeonhole, and hope that she meets him, or that he comes for her.

However, tomorrow is May Day, the day on which self-control goes out of the window. You are supposed to get drunk and meet boys by the river and turn up for school blurry and damp; nothing is predictable or entirely safe. It's not a day any Oxford child would pin its hopes to – but Eve has no choice, and does just that.

Much later, towels in hand, Jean and Helena sneak down Helena's staircase towards the fellows' bathroom.

'Is this mad?' Jean whispers.

'Of course it is,' says Helena, touching the back of her neck. 'But where else is there? It's not as if we can just jump in at one of our houses, is it?'

'Well, no.'

'And lovely as it is being up there in my study—' Jean smiles at her over her shoulder; the air between them fizzes, '—it doesn't feel normal enough. I want the normal things with you.'

'Like baths.'

'Exactly.'

'So do I,' says Jean.

She hears Helena's footsteps stop. Christ, she thinks. Keep

walking. Neither of them breathes, but Helena's body tenses behind her. There is one question in both of their minds.

Oh God, thinks Jean. Do I? Want Helena, all the time, at the expense of everything? This is not at all what she had imagined for herself. The sort of person, the – well, *couple*, they would have to be, is alien to her, and unappealing: she does not know how to live like that. She doesn't want to. She would lose all she has.

Helena stirs behind her, and silently they walk down to the bathroom. Water roars through ancient pipes and fills the room with steam. Together, in the liquid darkness, they take off their clothes and hang them in a thick rope on the back of the door. Then they stand, Jean leaning against their still-warm clothes, in each other's arms.

Helena is waiting. Jean keeps her hands flat against Helena's back, careful to keep the pressure constant: neither hope nor the end of hope. She opens her mouth and waits for the answer to roll on to her tongue like a pearl.

It is coming. Helena's blood is beating against her; her chest is full. She has both their hearts. She thinks: I am not ready for this.

However, she gives an answer. The answer is: 'Yes.'

The following morning, as their parents lie sleeping upstairs, Eve and Phoebe collide in the kitchen. It is five o'clock.

'What the fuck are *you* doing up?' Phoebe takes a casserole out of the fridge, and dumps the lid on the draining board. The kitchen resounds. She sticks her finger in the butter and rubs some on to a piece of bread.

'Shh,' whispers Eve, shutting the fridge door. 'Can't you stop that?'

'No,' says Phoebe, sucking her finger.

'For Christ's sake, be *quiet*. What do you *think* I'm doing? I can do this too, you know. I'm not as square as you think.'

'No, you're squarer. Squarer than *you* think.' Phoebe takes a bite from a chicken leg and puts it back in the pot.

Eve hangs about by the hall window, waiting for her sister to find her bike and go. She cannot bear even to stand beside her. Nothing has changed since she spoke to their father. It is, if anything, even worse. Their mother's indulgence of Phoebe grows both more erratic and more lavish. It is impossible not to be hurt by it. Eve's misery gathers, unexpressed, like hidden water growing deeper.

Phoebe's bike is new but, like the last one, she hasn't bothered to lock it. Every morning Eve expects to find it stolen, and braces herself for the fuss. A musty smell lingers behind her sister in the hallway. Eve steps closer to the window, afraid that, by going to May Morning, she's sanctioning whatever Phoebe might choose to do. She stares down at her, tight with loathing, and at that moment Phoebe glances up, a smugly calculating expression on her lovely face.

By the time Eve reaches St Giles, she's beside herself with superstitious fury: the worst possible mood for May Morning. She should have opted out this year. It's supposed to be so beautiful for the tourists, and so great to be drunk for school, but the voices of the choristers on Magdalen Tower are always washed away by the wind, and the morning always ends headachey on cold stone steps, a feeling of uncontrol and danger in the air, someone crying about something, bottles all over the grass. It's all so Phoebe-ish. Don't let her do anything bad, prays Eve.

She sits on the steps of the Martyrs' Memorial and waits for Kate D. and Janey and Nancy, the new girl, to appear. She won't drink, she decides, although this was going to be her last indulgence before the end-of-year mocks, which will determine everything. It's worth not drinking for Raymond; it will make her want to tell secrets, or go straight to his rooms after school, and she mustn't. He does not like surprises. He will turn her away.

They're pedalling towards her, shivery and pleased with themselves in the new air. Nancy has an enormous bottle of cider in her bicycle basket. I can't *not* drink, thinks Eve, waving unhappily. They'll notice. A little bit drunk won't hurt.

It's first thing, like they agreed. She should be having a cup of tea and resting her veins, but Margaret Prickett is a busy woman. Jimmy, the new underporter at Pam Rook's husband's college, young boy, very shy, is waiting for her at her convenience. She told Pam it was she was curious, that's all, and went on and on at her until Pam said she'd ask Jimmy to show her the tape. But really Margaret wants to see it for a reason. She's heard rumours, and she wants to see if her theory is right.

Jimmy looks up from his desk inside the back gate of All Saints'. Bang on time, a fat old woman appears in the entrance to his wooden room.

'Mrs Prickett?' he says.

'Got it.'

He tries not to look at her face. 'Sit here?' he says. His

voice is a squeak; he still doesn't know why he's showing her this tape. Mrs Rook said it was a matter of college security, but he's not sure. It's so hard to know who to obey and who to obstruct – last week he saw off a tramp, and then got told it was a little old pissed professor. You're supposed to have an instinct for this work, but he's not sure he's got it. He adjusts his hat anxiously, and hopes for the best.

'What do I press?'

'Here,' says Jimmy.

He stands behind her and to the side, his back hard against the wood. He tells himself he's not going to watch again. He looks hard at the swollen knuckles clasped in front of the monitor. He looks at the monitor's metal casing, and the grey box beneath it. Then, unstoppably, his eyes drift to the screen.

In this shot you can only see them if you know where to look: two shapes against a slightly lighter patch. He's been down there himself at night, and looked up at the winking red eye, and he knows how hard it is to spot if you don't know it's there. I was only doing my job, he tells the shapes, but he knows he has failed them. He thinks about what something like this would mean to someone like him.

In the next shot the figures have merged. The air leaves his little room, as if sucked out by bellows. You can just see one of the faces. It's Professor Potter, instantly recognizable, even at night, from the side. The old woman at the desk takes a breath.

'Who's that? One of yours, is she?'

'Yes,' says Jimmy regretfully. 'She is.'

He watches the side of Margaret Prickett's jaw: the soft collapse of muscle as she presses her lips together and frowns at the screen. He imagines the sliding-together of limbs, the tiny burning mouths, the drugged shock of flesh. With a click, the next shot appears: his eyes flick to the screen. He sees a black head and shoulder in the corner, leaning towards a pale streak of blue-grey. It's only when you've stared for a second that you can make out what it is: a bare shoulder and collarbone tipped back towards the window. One end, where the face should be, ends in darkness. The other curves away, at an angle: a soft slope, a breastbone, a breast.

He lowers his eyes. There is nothing else to look at, so he stares instead at the wide knee under his desk as he waits for the point he knows is coming. At the next click, the paler figure has turned to the side: you can see her face.

Margaret Prickett gives a nod.

Jimmy blinks at her, startled. 'Do you know who it is?' he asks.

'I do,' she says. 'You bet I do.'

Later that morning, as Eve, drinking cider on the banks of the Isis, thinks about jumping to her death from bridges, and Phoebe, thanks to Tamsin's pills, actually does jump off a bridge, just missing a punt-load of chilled tourists, and Jean, on whom the strain is beginning to tell, begins to cry while buying a colander, and goes instead to find Phoebe an enormous present to assuage her guilt, Victor has an epiphany.

He has been unable to bring himself to teach today. He has spent the earlier part of the morning striding around the college gardens, gown flapping at the wet rhododendra, hoping that none of his students spots him from a window. He is very cold and very morose. Woodsmoke hangs in the damp air. Then, as a huge crow or raven flaps slowly over the lawn towards his house, Victor finally realizes that he has been a fool. He has not discussed the Lectureship with Jean.

He assumed that she would despise him for wanting it. He does not like to be so scrutinized. However, it occurs to him now, as suddenly as if he had walked into a tree, that by hiding his longings and fears to this extent he has kept from her the most important fact: that the cause of his diffidence is not grumpiness, or disdain, but love. He adores her. All that seem to matter – status, reputation, the Lectureship – matter only because they may help him keep her, his small plump difficult prize.

He must explain this all to Jean. He will do it tonight, if she is in tonight; whenever he can find her to talk in person. As soon as possible. Love, not the Lectureship, will change everything.

School passes sluggishly, in a haze of alcohol and indecision. As Eve wheels her bicycle unsteadily towards the gate, hoping to avoid her friends, she finds Nancy and the others. They are blocking her way unless she goes right beside the fence, but someone on the street once spat on her through it from a knot-hole, and now a sort of dread of exposure means she cannot go that way. She heads towards them reluctantly, pretending to smile.

'We're thinking of going punting,' says Nancy.

Eve takes her foot off the pedal and rests it on the pavement. Her desire to see Raymond is so strong she cannot balance. 'Hang on,' she says. 'I'm not.'

'Come on,' says Nancy. 'You know I've never been.'

'I can't punt,' says Eve, thinking of the emerald algae

which sways against the banks down there, like giant petals breathing.

'Well, you can steer. Is it true there's a place with naked men?'

Eve frowns discouragingly. There is such a place: Parsons' Pleasure, where elderly dons go to exercise in the nude. Eve and her friends have sometimes drifted that way on birthday punting parties, but if you know they're there you can just rush past them, looking very hard for water-rats among the reeds.

She is squeezing her thighs so tightly against the bicycle saddle that her body rises. She is too excited to think. 'Yes, I suppose . . .'

'Come on then,' says Nancy.

Eve looks at the others for help.

'Don't be ridiculous,' says Gemma nervously, flexing her piano-strained thumbs through the holes in her cuffs. 'Why would we want to see them?'

Nancy, Eve realizes, isn't going to be their friend. She's too curious, too willing to talk about the subjects they don't talk about. If she sticks with her true friends, she will be safe.

It's already four. Every minute away from him is time wasted. 'I've got to go, anyway,' she says, bouncing nervously on her saddle-springs, picking at the chrome on her book-rack. 'I've got to ask my dad about – Keats.'

Gemma turns right round to face her, disbelievingly. None of the others seem to notice, but the cold chrome bites warningly into Eve's fingers. 'Have you, really?' Gemma asks. She stares at Eve.

Eve glares back. 'Um,' she says. 'Yes. Why?' At the thought of anyone, even unwittingly, coming between her and Raymond, she feels capable of violent rage. She returns her foot to the pedal.

Gemma closes her hand around Eve's handlebar. She is looking at her fiercely, as if she is a particularly hard-to-place poem, or a floating gerundive. 'Is something going on?' she says.

The others are watching now. Eve does not care. She grips the handlebar's other end more tightly, and tugs it away. She sees Gemma's pale face turn paler. Gemma assumes she knows her, and she is wrong.

'Listen,' Eve says, 'can you just stop interfering? It is *nothing* to do with you. You don't know anything about it. I'm sick of it,' she says, slamming her foot down on the pedal. The bicycle moves forward, releasing her. 'Just leave me alone,' she shouts over her shoulder, but they have already turned away.

Eve is standing in the front garden, dithering. If she just dumps her bike and dashes to Raymond's, they will have more time together. However her skirt is creased and cidery from the damp grass this morning, and she is hot-faced after her row with Gemma, and she wore her worst bra on purpose this morning to make her keep away from Victor, although now she's sure he won't mind. She knows he'll want to see her. She won't let him down.

There's no time to park her bike. She just drops it, bell reverberating, on to a patch of grass already scarred by Phoebe. Then she runs into the house.

From her vantage point over the front door, Phoebe stubs out her roll-up and spits down on to the step. If she hadn't had this fag she'd have missed her, but the chance has just landed in her lap. Smiling to herself, she prepares to follow.

Jean is having second thoughts. Back to back with Hedley, she sits at her desk pretending to write a letter about the copyright to a St Thomas's carol, and wondering how it came to this.

Perhaps it was sex. It's different for her daughters: Phoebe will be a hit the minute she's old enough; Eve, if she makes an effort, would find someone right for her, although it doesn't help that the clever boys are at home programming their BBC computers, not at parties. But Jean was so *old* by the time it happened, with a great store of longing that remained untapped. Was the problem that Victor was so much older? Would this have happened if she'd married another man, or settled somewhere less stifling?

Under cover of the desk she retrieves an old cheese shop receipt, on which she has written a poem she found in Blackwell's:

> *She asked me to luncheon in fur. Far from*
> *the loud laughter of men, our secret life stirred.*
>
> *I remember her eyes, the slim rope of her spine . . .*

'Jean,' says Hedley, far away.

> *As she undressed me, her breasts were a mirror*
> *and there were mirrors in the bed . . .*

'Jean?' says Hedley sharply. 'What on earth are you doing?'

She jumps, transparent with panic.

'I . . .' she says, 'I – um—'

He taps the side of his desk. 'Could you please come to my office?'

'I'm sorry?' says Jean, trying to shove the receipt inside her non-existent trouser pocket before, in desperation, wedging it between the chair and her thigh. 'Your office?'

'Yes, yes,' says Hedley impatiently.

Jean looks from her desk to his: a distance of about four feet. The poem has left her worryingly energized. 'Are you joking?' she says.

'I am quite serious, thank you. Must I ask you again?'

'Very well,' says Jean, and goes to stand beside him. 'What can I do for you, Hedley?'

He is, she realizes, blushing. 'I have – ah,' he begins, taking a sip of water. 'We have had increasing cause for concern—'

'Not with me, I hope,' she says, with dizzying boldness. 'Everything's under control. I gave you the armour inventory yesterday, didn't I?'

'Quite, quite,' says Hedley, 'but that is not my point. There have been concerns – that is to say, questions, ah . . .'

'Yes?' says Jean, gazing light-headedly at his bushily parted hair.

'I have been asked by Mr Crushard to remind you—'

'Oh, is that all?' Crushard, the dourly puritanical head porter, manages to tell off all but the grandest reprobate dons at least once a week. Jean is glowing inside; she has no interest in Crushards. She looks out of the window, over the roofs.

'—that, as a non-tenured member of the college staff, in a place of education, you have certain moral obligations.'

Jean's smile fades. 'What do you mean?'

Hedley lines up his pencils in order of size. He will not

240

meet her eye. 'I am not prepared to speculate. I understand that he has received . . . information. He—'

'I'm sorry?' says Jean, holding on to the corner of his desk for support. 'What on earth do you mean? What information?'

'I can't tell you, I'm afraid,' says Hedley peevishly, still refusing to look up. The back of his neck almost matches the red leather of his desktop. 'I . . . I don't know. I think it – never mind.'

'*What?*' she asks, her voice rising in fearful indignation. 'Tell me. What did he say?'

'Just that – ah. You'll really have to ask him. Ah . . . something on the grapevine, as it were. The servants,' he tells her. 'They always seem to know.'

Eve is only up there for twenty minutes. Phoebe, who knows a lot about sex already, and can guess the bits she doesn't, smirks to herself as she sees her coming back down the poky stairs. She isn't impressed.

Eve looks around her before she crosses the quad. She doesn't see Phoebe peeping out from the entrance of the next door staircase, hoping she isn't just nipping home to get an interesting stamp or a book for her mystery boyfriend. Then, when she is out of sight, Phoebe begins.

When she followed her sister in, she hadn't thought it would be this easy. She'd watched as Eve, in a really unfortunate red top and twirly green skirt, like desperate holly, left her bike neatly chained to the racks, flabbily guarded by Young Arthur, and flounced excitedly into the next quad. She looked like a normal person about to get sex but more revolting. Phoebe watched from the entrance until Eve disappeared into a doorway, then legged it across the quad. Eve was still walking up when she got there: she counted her climbing three separate lots of stairs, above the two she could see. So now Phoebe is pretty sure that it's the top floor.

There is a little board with names on at the bottom. The top one is Dr R. S. Snow. She thinks: well, I've been stupid. That can't be who Eve's been with. She'll try 'R. P. Bachelor' – much more promising.

All these staircases smell the same. Behind every door she passes will be thousands of books, rotting paper, a sucking killing dryness. She wishes she had a blowtorch. And, by the time she reaches the top, she wishes she had a cigarette. She hauls herself up by the banisters – her lungs aren't clean and pink like Eve's, and since she had to move Bilbo to Port Meadow she hardly rides him any more. No time for a fag, though: she's got to get started.

She knocks on R. P. Bachelor's door, grinning. A starved, fierce voice calls: 'Come!' Phoebe snorts. She pushes open the door. Inside, like someone from Indiana Jones, is the palest person she has ever seen: white wispy hair like Bilbo's mane; white sinking face, practically white eyes, sitting half inside a huge black fireplace.

'Fuck,' she whispers.

The person glares. Its mane shivers. 'You are?' it says.

'Nothing,' says Phoebe, retreating. She is shivery with suppressed fright and excitement. 'No one. Never mind.'

The door seems to have shut by remote control. She's tempted to go straight down again. Then she thinks of Eve's sex-expecting walk, and that steels her.

She knocks, hard and defiant, on the other door.

There is no answer.

OK. She has probably, not for the first time, made a mistake. She goes to the top of the stairwell and looks down, but there is no way, from where Eve's feet were and the number of times her steps changed direction, that it could have been a lower floor. Even Eve can't magically produce stairs. And unless she came here just to wank, there must have been someone else with her. And even if he is a doctor, this room belongs to an R.

She knocks again, and there is silence. So Phoebe opens the door.

There is a man on the other side of the room, and he is washing his dick in the basin.

He has it in his hand as he turns, and though he says, 'Jesus – what the hell—?', he keeps it there, like a hamster, where she can see it.

Jesus. She's hardly seen one before. There's just been her father's furry embarrassment and men pissing, although she's had to feel a few in her time: big blind clubs, or sticky wands. But this one—

This one has been up her sister.

'Hello,' she says.

He stares at her, as hard as he likes, then stuffs it back into his trousers and does up the fly. He wipes his hands on his jacket. He is very tall and very thin, and much, much older than she was expecting, but the way he keeps his eyes on hers, while looking like he knows this is funny, makes her smile, and he grins back, and she almost starts laughing.

'Hello,' he says.

'Hi.'

'What an interesting position.'

'Kind of.'

'Who are you?'

'Who are you?'

'I am Raymond Snow.' He waits, and she waits with him. 'Didn't you know?'

'No,' says Phoebe. 'I didn't know all that. But I know who you are.'

'Who am I then?' he asks, still grinning.

'You're the person who's fucking my sister.'

He makes her tea, and then a vodka and soda, and doesn't ask how old she is. When she mentions Eve his wolf-smile widens. 'You *are* an attentive little family,' he says.

She's still quite shocked that this is him, not a revolting chemist with a college scarf. He's old but he's funny. He asks a lot of questions, and all her answers make him grin.

'We're the same species, you and I,' he says.

He takes the piss out of her father, being grumpy. He takes the piss out of Eve, a bit.

'Do you know my mother?' she asks.

'To a certain extent,' he says. 'But there is time for that.' He draws his chair up to the fire and looks her in the eye.

Helena, meanwhile, a little late, more than usually nervous, goes to her appointment at the Gate.

'I know it's unusual,' she tells the headmaster, who is teaching an extracurricular Chinese poetry class to a group of nine-year-olds. 'But Jeffrey is an unusual boy.'

In order to speak to him confidentially she stands at his elbow. He is sitting on a desk: a vigorous seventy-five. He must know Phoebe Lux but, tempted as she is, she will not ask him. It is essential to keep cause and effect separate, at least for now.

'Please copy page 127,' he says. 'Lao Tzu.' He inclines his head, but does not lower his voice. 'Professor Potter, *undoubtedly* he is. He is certainly a favourite of mine, although I shouldn't say such a thing,' he says, still at full volume. Helena's heart lifts. Several keen-looking children glance up. 'However, as you know, we have here a great number of extremely clever but somewhat indigent boys and girls, whose paternal income, at any normal prep school, would qualify them for a scholarship, at the very least. At the very least. Unless, therefore, your circumstances have changed dramatically—'

Helena twists the leather strap of her basket around and around her fingers. Without a scholarship she will still be trapped. There will be no extra money until her next book is written, but with worry and hoping and planning she is finding it impossible to begin.

'Let us consider,' he says. 'Jeffrey is nearly ten. He knows, in addition to the usual French and Latin, a certain amount of self-taught Anglo-Saxon. He excels at chess, he writes heroic plays, in verse; he can list every battle, important casualty and technical advance of the Hundred Years War; and he can catalogue fossils. None of which, in isolation, remotely qualifies him for one of our scholarships. It takes, I'm afraid, rather more than that. And, as you know, he does so many extras that his fees rather exceed the average, which is by no means low.'

'I know,' she says unhappily. Guilt, and Jeffrey's demands, and her teaching hours mean her attempts to reduce these have always failed. 'But I—'

She could, of course, send him to a state school. Selfishness tells her that, if Jean were all that mattered, she would. But, she tells herself, he is so happy here, with everything else disintegrating around him. The least she owes him is that. Besides, he is not an easy child to defy. No: if she can't find a way to make her plan possible, she will keep him here and just try to go on, heartsinkingly, as she is.

'However, we are, as you know, enormously concerned with pastoral care here, and the development of the whole child, and we do make allowances in certain situations. Now, there have been, as you know, concerns about his welfare.'

Helena starts. 'What on earth do you mean?'

'Absolutely nothing serious,' says the headmaster. 'Did you not know?'

'No.'

'Ah – I believe his form-master spoke to your mother-in-law. Never mind. He has been a little . . . demanding at times. Rather more insurrectionary than one might hope. Is there,' he enquires delicately, 'anything perhaps *connected* with a change in financial circumstances . . .'

'I'm very sorry,' she says, as calmly as she can manage, 'that he has been, well, disobedient. It's, it's because – you see, I . . . I'm having—'

She was wrong to begin this. She should not have come. 'I'm sorry,' she says. 'I can't – there's nothing. I'm sorry to have wasted your time.'

The headmaster gives a kind, whiskery smile. 'Without wishing to pry, are you certain?'

She hesitates. The children are busy with their books. There must be a way. At her back is her cold empty study, her parents-in-laws' stuffy house, her life as it is. Before her lie this school's absurd riches, the headmaster's kindness, another life.

'As a matter of fact,' she begins.

They both know what is going on. Phoebe, on her second vodka, is laughing her head off at Raymond's impression of the President carving boar ('And for the vice-vice-deputy-senior tutor *four* inches, but rather closer to the thigh, and for the under-bursar four and a *half* inches, but towards the *back* of the thigh'), and everything he says sounds filthy, and he knows it. She has noticed, as she looked for matches, a sort of fancy narrow bed, with a paisley-shaped patch of wet on its rumpled blue cover.

She glances at the sink, and back at him. He lifts his eyebrows.

'So,' she says, and he gives her a grin. Nothing she could say would surprise him. She feels a panicky sort of flutter in her chest and finds herself thinking of Eve, but she forces through it. She opens her mouth a little bit, and gives him a hard look. 'OK then,' she says, watching for the moment he gets it. 'Now you've had my sister, what about me?'

THIRD WEEK

The little brown beetles have spread. Eve checks her sheet before she goes to bed, but she still keeps finding them on the duvet, or crushed beneath her in the night. She has started wearing leggings under her nightdress.

This morning she wakes to feel a tickling on her forearm. There is a beetle crawling over the seeping surface of her newest cut. She screams, and runs out into the hallway; her sister is just leaving the bathroom, her piss still warm on the seat.

'Get out of my way,' shouts Eve. Phoebe, to her surprise, moves.

In a paroxysm of disgust, Eve bruises her hand on the hot tap, noticing as she does so that her sister has not washed her hands, or flushed the lavatory, or bothered to hide the love-bites on her neck. Slut, thinks Eve, her throat tightening as the cut reopens and begins to leak into the swirling water.

Two hours later, as Lady Scott asks Janey Sebastopol to read, Eve reaches her limit. She puts up her hand.

'Mother – mother of Aeneas's people, pleasure of gods—' reads Janey.

'Eve, please wait,' says Lady Scott sternly. 'Put your hand down.'

'I'm sorry,' says Eve. 'I can't.'

Janey abandons her book. Everyone is watching. Eve stands.

'Sit down,' says Lady Scott. 'What on earth are you doing?'

'I'm sorry,' says Eve. 'I'm going to—' and she walks out of the room.

She goes to the lavatories and looks out of the window at the school pond: one of the many venues in which she has imagined her body being found, her friends and teachers inconsolable. Now, however, the image of her face below the surface does nothing to calm her.

Raymond does not want her. She must have known this for some days, since she's cutting again, and mad with superstition. But the last time she saw him, a couple of nights ago, he was horrible.

'Haven't you had enough for one week?' he'd said.

He'd been jumpy, too: he spent more time by the window than with her, and when he looked at her directly she could see his brain was in the way.

'What's wrong?' she asked.

'Nothing,' he said, pretending to fiddle with something on his desk. When he eventually came to her it was like he was trying to get it over with. She started crying and he moved away. After that, nothing she said made a difference.

'But what's *wrong*?' she kept asking, trying to remember what little thing she had done and could easily undo. 'Just *tell* me.' She ended up begging, and even that didn't work.

When she left he followed her to the top of the stairs and watched as she walked down.

Now she feels split in two. She runs cold water and washes her face; she will say she felt sick, which is true. Her intestines are spilling into the basin. She touches the hot tap and the cold tap, the hot tap again, but this does not balance her; she moves on to the next sink, and the next. There are twelve sinks in the room, twenty-four taps, and she touches them all. There is nothing good left. She turns on the last tap and lets it run and run until it is steaming, and then she holds her palm underneath and watches it burn.

In the second pigeon-post of the morning, Victor receives his long-awaited letter from the Lectureship committee.

The paper is almost unpleasantly thick, more like wood than wood-pulp. He reads it twice, turns it over and inspects the back, even touches his tongue to the signature, but he cannot quite absorb its meaning. He pours a glass of port, surprisingly steadily, and carries it to the window. He looks down on the idiot heads of the undergraduates, each year's crop more heedless than the last. The glass swims.

On the other side of the college, as clearly as if he held a telescope, he sees Raymond Snow open a very different letter.

They are meeting for dinner. Jean is not at all sure she wants to. Or rather, she wants nothing more, would climb mountains or kill passers-by if they tried to impede her, but she is terrified.

They have not done anything like this before. The Panty lunches have carried on as usual, and she goes to Helena's rooms as often as she can, but it isn't enough: they want more time, different contexts. Simultaneously, their options have reduced: now that the weather is growing milder, the gardens and cloisters attract students. The temptation to risk meeting somewhere else, which means somewhere more public – itself so exciting – has been growing and, as with other temptations, they have eventually yielded. A plan has been made.

She sits at the kitchen table with Phoebe with her homework, shelling broad beans into a pan. All she can think about is their dinner: how obvious they will be if anyone sees them and how urgently, despite this, she longs for it. She feels as if, for the last two or seventeen or thirty-nine years, she has been wallowing in warm and stagnant water and now, with every single breath, she scents the cold excitements of the sea.

They have, at least, a disguise. Sarah Birch, an old college friend – the only other one on her staircase from a grammar school – is coming to Oxford to hear the Poetry Professor's lecture. She has asked to see her afterwards, on the very evening Jean and Helena had managed to clear. Sarah has even insisted on booking the table far in advance, in a noisy and very popular Italian restaurant. It means sharing Helena, but this too is an exciting novelty, and it will make their flagrant act less flagrant. If they must be somewhere so very public, at least they will have the protection of being in a three.

'Dear, are we being mad?' she asks Helena, daily.

'Well, yes and no. We could avoid the risk entirely and never try it.'

'We can't *never*. If I'd said, "Yes, well, *never*," we wouldn't be here now, would we?'

'Ugh,' says Helena thoughtfully. 'Sod *never*, then.'

'Exactly. We can't hide away for ever. I couldn't stand it.'

'Then we shall take the risk. Perhaps no one will see us.'

'You know they will. It'll be stuffed with people who know us – it always is. And they'll wonder.'

'It's our only chance to meet all week. It's the best we can do; at least, until—'

At this point, Jean always changes the subject.

Victor is home early again. He keeps missing his chance to speak to Jean: she is embroiled with the girls, or uncommunicative, or absent, and he is unused to declarations. Cowardly, he has bided his time.

And now, because the Lectureship is decided, it is too late. The letter lies in his pocket like a warrant for execution; he does not know whether to tell her about it anyway, or burn it. It feels like a pocketful of ash.

Raymond Snow's mind is no better than his; he is not a better man. However, he has made it seem so, and Jean may believe him. Perhaps Victor was wrong and the Lectureship, not love, will determine the future. Perhaps, he thinks, that *is* all that matters: the surface of things, the ceremony.

Her face is beautiful. He watches her white fingers rattling the beans into the pan, and feels his heart unpeeling. In a week's time Raymond Snow will stand in Hall, the cream of the world's historians ranged on benches below him, to give the Sir Henry Spenser Memorial Lecture. He will take his place in posterity and, after that, in Jean's bed.

Moreover, according to tradition it is the Senior Dean who must introduce the Spenser Lecture, and he is the Senior Dean. There is no way round it – unless the President excuses him. He thinks, standing before his wife, of his options: stumping alone up the centre aisle, under the eyes of all their colleagues, to give his congratulations, or shutting himself alone in his rooms with his port and his misery. There is no contest.

At least, thinks Jean, home is relatively calm. Eve, who has been for a time quite sweetly relaxed, is herself once more: if anything, more so. She is prickly with her parents and crushing to Phoebe, while craving reassurance so greedily that Jean feels herself shrink away. Phoebe is back to her old exhausting delightful self too, after a funny patch of prickly distance, but somehow this doesn't reassure her. Now, on the rare occasions when she can focus on them properly, she worries about her family. She has begun to feel oddly afraid of them.

Just give me time, she prays, as Victor clumsily attempts to prepare her a grapefruit, and Eve cries about her latest practically perfect test-results, and Phoebe offers anyone who will listen her entire tape collection in exchange for feeding Bilbo; and, in another kitchen, in Jericho, Helena prepares for another day without her. Please, she begs them all silently, don't make me panic. Don't expect me to make a choice.

Helena has lied, and she is proud of it. As she hurries Jeffrey through his scrambled eggs she considers at which point, during tonight's unimaginably public dinner, to tell Jean what it will mean.

'For God's sake,' says Jeffrey crossly as she trips over his Atari on her way to change her shoes, again. 'What are you in such a flap about?'

He is not an easy boy to fool. 'I – nothing, nothing. No reason at all. You're so suspicious. Now tell me, how was . . . you know. Tennis?'

'Durr,' says Jeffrey. 'Tennis was Tuesday. Today was *real* tennis.' He looks at her with infinite disdain, like a rebellious godlet. 'Why have you become so stupid? You never used to be like this.'

In the silence that follows she thinks of a number of platitudes, even some physiological explanations, but they are all too hollow to repeat. His conker hair looks dull and scratchy; there are shadows under his enormous eyes. 'Oh, my love,' she says, sitting next to him. He folds his hands out of reach in his lap; the zip of his corduroy bomber jacket is done up right under his chin. 'Are you all right? You know I love you, don't you?'

Jeffrey, tucked away, says nothing.

She looks at him fearfully. 'Have you gone off your old ma?' she asks.

'That depends,' says Jeffrey. 'What have you done?'

Later, preparing to meet Jean, she thinks of how she will break her news. She stares boldly at herself in the hall mirror and sees, to her enormous surprise, that excitement has made her beautiful.

'I have found a way to free us,' she announces in her head.

She has, well, *forced* Jeffrey's school to give him a full scholarship, extras included, not on the basis of academic merit but because of 'psychological problems', as yet unspecified. What with this, and her recent repayment of the last of her dead husband's debts, and her new secret plan to write a different book this time, one that even non-academics will read, she thinks she and Jeffrey may be able to move out of her parents-in-laws' house at last, and into a little flat of their own. And she hopes that Jean will join them.

There are only two difficulties. First, Jeffrey does not know this; neither do her parents-in-law. What she truly dreads is that they will find out, and she will be forced to explain herself before she is ready. She fears her son's rage almost more than anything.

The second difficulty is more of a feeling, and therefore harder to argue herself out of. She is afraid that Jean will not react as she hopes she will. Helena finds her hard to predict – more so, if anything, since they . . . since circumstances . . .

since everything changed. It had seemed, standing before the headmaster, that desperate times required desperate solutions. The thought of living with Jean made her ruthless. Now, however, although she can barely breathe for excitement, she wonders if more problems have been caused than solved.

Since all this began, Jean has had the potential to destroy her. Helena hopes that, by sheer force of reason, in the light of the extraordinary thing which has grown between them, Jean can be made to see that they must be together soon, now if possible. There is no other way – Helena cannot live like this much longer. The next chance she gets, she will ask Jean to decide.

By the time Jean arrives at the restaurant, her composure, which has been threatening to dissolve for several days, is in pieces. At the last possible moment, when her hair was brushed and her teeth cleaned and the evening had taken on that nacreous glow, that taste of excitement, with which she is coming to associate all such evenings, she had found a message from Sarah Birch, her college friend, adrift on the kitchen table. Victor, on cross-examination, admitted she had phoned last night, cancelling dinner.

'But why didn't you tell me?' asked Jean, stretched to the point of tears.

'Because, my dear,' said Victor, infuriatingly mildly, 'I had hoped that . . . well, I had thought – that perhaps you and I could go out for dinner. Together. It would be . . . we need to . . . I would rather—'

'Jesus!' said Jean. 'The first time in – how many? Four years? Five? Your timing, for God's sake. Jesus. Well, no.'

So it will be just her and Helena. The restaurant occupies

several Elizabethan garrets above a stationer's on Cornmarket, at the end of hundreds of stairs. At last, delayed by a battle with Phoebe, Jean arrives and, breathless, hauls herself to the top. Then, on the brink, she hesitates.

She thinks: if a table for three in a noisy restaurant was the least dangerous, then a table for three in a quiet restaurant is more dangerous, followed by a table for two in a quiet restaurant, followed by a table for two in a noisy restaurant. This could not be worse. They will be a scented island in a sea of curious acquaintances: an illicit microscope slide. Every word will give them away; they cannot possibly touch, but how will they resist it? She can feel Helena's need, radiating out towards the doorway, and it scares her. Her own need scares her. Everything is drawing tighter. She waits for the snap.

He phones. Just like that.

When Phoebe hears his big man's voice, she is amazed. She didn't expect to hear from *him* again, at least not on the phone like a normal person. But she's pleased he's there, sounding wicked.

'You shouldn't ring,' she says. 'You're illegal.'

'That's why I did it,' he says. 'Or where's the fun?'

She thinks of him on his college phone, at his college desk, just round the corner from her father. About a minute away from this house, from her and Eve. She imagines a glass case on the end of his desk and, inside it, the thing she gave him: fluorescent blue and flickering, like electricity trapped.

'So,' she says. She hears him smiling; his teeth.

'So.'

She thinks of her virginity, flickering in the glass: she was so right to ask him to relieve her of it. She smiles.

'What do you want,' she says.

Eve listens to the slamming of the door with her eyes closed. She has argued with everyone in her family today, including her father, who has been irascibly gloomy all week. Gemma is not speaking to her, and her other friends know nothing. Even the Samaritans have been no use at all.

She has thrown out her stolen scalpel in a moment of panic, but instead has swallowed nine of the ibuprofen pills sent from America for Phoebe, who won't take aspirin. She expects nothing in particular: only a small cut, this time inside. I don't know what to do, she thinks, over and over again. I have to do something. A fat drop of blood is running around her arm like a bracelet, and the upper part of her forearm is a mess.

She touches her mother's potato-knife, the arm of the chair, the knife, the chair. She is thinking of rituals too quickly to keep up. Everything is thick with dread. I cannot hang on, she thinks, over and over again. My skin is too thin.

She needs blood to let the blackness out. Before it was very limited: she did not buy razor-blades, or keep knives in her room. It was all about a little at a time. Now, unexpectedly, she is reaching the next stage, and it's exciting. Above her, between volumes K and L of her father's encyclopedia, the Finnish knife is waiting for its moment.

Helena is glowing. Jean can see it – surely the entire restaurant can see it, but Jean's own glow makes it impossible to tell.

Everything is exciting; even mozzarella. They drink red wine and talk. I am in love, thinks Jean, as Helena's amazing eyes catch her and hold her. Beneath the table their toes touch.

'I have something to tell you,' says Helena, happily.

Raymond, who is explaining exactly what, if this restaurant went dark, he would do to Phoebe, how much and how softly and how hard, has just reached, verbally, her waist. She's a little bit drunk, and can't stop grinning. She has just realized that she is very wet.

They are celebrating something. He said so, before, on the phone. He's won something from the college, and now there's more money, or something, what does it matter, and she really doesn't care but he obviously does. He says that, because of the timing, because he heard about it just after their fuck, she has to be the one to celebrate with him. She's not sure she understands, but what matters is that he's hard under the table. So would she be if she was a man. They are on a stage, shining, surrounded by a glare of light and noise.

'And what,' she says, 'exactly,' looking at him sideways, 'would you do when you got there? Just think: your hands on my waist.'

Then she looks up and sees her mother.

'Oh, hello,' says Raymond, smoothly.

Jean looks from him to Phoebe. She feels herself frown. She feels Helena, very slowly, remove her hand from the small of her back.

She is as confused as Phoebe looks. She dares not turn to see Helena, but her back is blazing. The discussion they had just begun, and then postponed for the privacy of Helena's rooms, is gnawing at her. She wants it to continue, but here is the first man she ever slept with, and here is her barely fourteen-year-old daughter.

'Phoebe?' she says. 'Why—'

'Why—?' says Phoebe.

Jean waits to make the missing connection. She looks away from her lovely daughter, across the table to Raymond Snow.

'You again,' she says. 'What are you doing here?'

Phoebe stares. 'Do you two – do you know each other?' she asks.

'Well, yes,' begins Jean, as Phoebe looks up and registers the presence of Helena. Her wide eyes narrow.

'But how – why do you?' asks Jean.

Phoebe's eyes return to hers, and all the surprise has left her face. She is composed and hard and beautiful: she lifts her chin, and stretches out her arms luxuriously. 'Well,' she says. 'Since you ask—'

'Didn't Victor tell you?' Raymond interrupts, looking from Jean to Helena and back again. 'How very strange. He asked me to help young Phoebe here with her coursework: not really his field, you see. Ottoman, largely.'

'Oh,' says Jean.

Then Raymond stands. He holds out his hand. 'Forgive me,' he says, looking over her shoulder at Helena. 'Raymond Snow. St James's – Victor's colleague. I'm sure you know Victor.'

'Ah,' says Helena bravely.

Her voice is delicious; an almost unendurable relief. Jean longs to turn to her, to escape with her. Instead, she forces herself to face outwards, towards this man whose eyes, and grin, and very presence, make her feel investigated. She is too hot to think.

'Quite,' says Helena. 'Yes. Helena Potter.'

'Professor Potter,' says Raymond, with a radiant smile. 'Ah yes. I know your . . . face.'

There is a pause, imperceptibly weighted, as if a bell has just finished ringing.

'But why,' says Phoebe, her cheeks flushed, her eyes fixed on her mother, 'are you here? You said you were seeing that friend, you know, from school.'

'From college,' says Jean automatically – for this, at least, she is prepared. 'Sarah couldn't come at the last minute. She told us just to have dinner anyway, without her. Which is, you know, very sad, because I was so . . . I was—'

She looks at Raymond, whose bright eyes are still fixed on Helena. She longs for Helena's hand on her back again. Something about Raymond's stare is making her uncomfortable; she wants to move Helena out of the way.

'Well,' she says. 'If you're . . .'

'Actually,' he interrupts, dropping his napkin on to his plate. He reminds her of a locust. Jean, dazed, takes a step backwards, and collides softly with Helena, who moves away. 'I think we've covered the main points,' says Raymond. 'It's a school night, after all. Phoebe, if you encounter any further problems, please don't hesitate to let me know. Your father – indeed, your mother – will know how to find me. Jean,' he continues, 'you'll be taking young Phoebe home, I take it? Unless you have other plans?'

Jean turns to see Helena's reaction, but Helena is looking down. She thinks of tearing, of witch-trials and wild horses. Phoebe's angry voice tugs her back.

'Well, I think it's very strange. And you still haven't explained how you two know each other.'

'Oh,' says Raymond silkily. 'It was all a very long time ago.'

Jean stiffens. She can no longer feel Helena behind her.

'I'll finish my wine,' Raymond says. 'Off you go, Phoebe.'

There is pale green fury in Phoebe's eyes. She stares at her mother but, it seems to Jean, the waves of hatred which pour from her are aimed at Helena. Instinctively, Jean steps between them.

'Fine,' Phoebe snaps, grabbing her schoolbag. She drains her wineglass – she has been drinking, thinks Jean slowly, as if from a distance – and stands, nearly eye to eye with her mother. She ignores Helena. 'Fine.'

Raymond is looking at his plate, but Jean knows he is smiling. She is beginning to realize something, but its exact shape is unclear. We should go home, she thinks, still hoping that Helena might come with them, that she might wait with her until the others are in bed. She looks over her shoulder again, and Helena's wary smile rockets through her. 'Come on,' she says to Phoebe, her eyes still on Helena.

Then she turns back to the table.

Phoebe's eyes are fixed, hard and bright, on her mother. She lowers her head and kisses Raymond Snow, hard, on the mouth.

It is impossible. Jean tries for hours to talk to her daughter, on the way home and then in Phoebe's room, but Phoebe, after her initial bravado, is refusing to confide. She claims that she was simply 'being nice to Raymond'. Eventually Jean, exhausted, decides to believe her. She cannot entirely free her mind from Helena, from whatever it was she had begun to say when Jean had panicked and decided they should leave. They barely had a chance to say goodbye outside the restaurant. Jean wishes she were here.

'Do you promise there is really nothing I should worry about?' she asks.

There is a sound in the doorway. Eve is standing there, puffy-eyed.

'What's going on?' she asks.

'Why don't you just piss off,' says Phoebe. 'We don't want you here.'

'What's going on?' says Eve again.

Jean looks at her pink-cheeked daughter, furious and wet-faced, and the sallow one, her negative. 'Forget it,' she says, but Eve remains in the doorway.

'You want to know?' says Phoebe. 'I'll tell you. I was at—'

Eve's eyes well up. 'Oh, look, I don't want to know,' she says, sounding very tired and very sad. She is somehow lop-sided, her left hand and arm hidden by her right. Jean feels a clutch of pity. 'I just don't . . . I can't—'

'Go on then,' says Jean, rather more abruptly than she meant to. She thinks of stretching out to stroke Eve's arm, but the gap is too wide. 'See you in the morning,' she says, watching her elder daughter, ignorant and safe for just one more night, take herself to bed.

The next day begins bright and cold: a perfect Oxford morning. Gilded cupolas, decomposing angels, the delicate vertebrae of pinnacles are acid-etched on a background of fourteenth-century blue, although there is still mist in the hollows of the Meadow. After a night of resolutions and silent promises, everyone is being very normal. The Lux family, having rejected a trip to the Botanical Gardens because Phoebe is feeling tired, have just returned from a short walk in the University Parks.

'Anyone want tea?' asks Eve, holding up the red tea-tin.

'Please,' says Jean. 'Phoebe, you have some.'

Eve looks calmer than she has been for some time; her cheeks are flushed. We must go for more walks, thinks Jean vaguely. It seems to agree with us. The kitchen smells of fresh air and oranges. She looks around at her family: the way they fit together, look right together. Their naturalness. This is good, she thinks.

She says, 'I'm leaving.'

There is a fan of fallen tea-leaves on the floor. Phoebe and Eve are staring at her, identically open-mouthed. The tea-tin circles once, twice and is silent. They are all waiting for Victor, but he is writing in his notebook, and does not look up.

'I'm leaving,' says Jean, a little louder.

Then the spell breaks, and there is chaos. Eve, surprisingly, reacts first. She screams at her, 'What are you talking about? Since when? How—'

Phoebe sweeps her plate from the table and rushes towards her. She shouts: 'No you're not! You're not! You can't!'

Only Victor, slowly returning his notebook to his pocket, seems calm. Thank God, thinks Jean, who has nursed a secret hope that he has known all along, and is going to release her. Then he lifts his face and she sees that she was wrong.

Their daughters fall silent. Everyone listens to his breathing as he rises to his feet, almost a foot above them. His chair skids away from him, and everyone flinches. He is looking at Jean alone. She begins to move away, but he heads straight for her. She retreats until her back bumps against the dresser: she is trapped. Time is a silver stretch, at the end of which she waits for him.

Then he is there, huge in front of her. She reaches out a placating hand; he bats it aside and grabs it. His teeth are clenched. She thinks, for the first time in years: he loves me. Oh Victor, too late.

His fist is tight around her fingers. She opens her mouth, and shuts it again. He brings his face right down to hers, so she can see every white hair and crazed tooth and discoloration: the collapsing of his old-man's flesh. When this man she once thought she loved opens his mouth, she is bathed in his breath. She leans away.

He screams at her: 'I will break his fucking neck!'

The kitchen goes silent. Jean frowns.

'Who?' Her voice sounds remarkably calm and strong. '*Who*?'

'Raymond fucking Snow, of course!' roars Victor.

And Eve, behind him, screams, '*No!*'

No one breathes. Victor, Jean and Phoebe slowly turn their heads to where, white-faced, huge-eyed, Eve stands at the table, like a girl possessed.

'My God,' says Jean.

Victor's face turns from red to grey. He stares from Jean to Eve and back again. 'But,' he says, 'you – you didn't – Jean? Eve? What in God's name is going on?'

Jean rubs her hand over her eyes. Everything seems out of kilter, as if whoever was issuing 3-D spectacles forgot to give her hers.

'Jean?' says Victor dazedly.

'I've no idea,' she says, although the impossible truth threatens to show itself. 'I've no idea!' she says, more forcefully. 'Phe— Eve, what on earth have you been—'

'No,' says Victor, beginning to shout again. 'Let me understand. Are you saying,' he asks Jean, his huge old-man's finger in her face, 'that you have *both*—'

Eve sits heavily on her chair. Tears are pouring from her face, but her fists are clenched, and she is furious. 'Are you *serious*?' she screams. With a moment's delay, Jean realizes that Eve is shouting at her. '*Tell* me you're not serious? Have you – have you—?'

'What?'

'No,' shouts Victor to Eve. 'Have *you*?'

'*What*?' Eve screams. 'What's *wrong* with it? It's – it's *beautiful* . . . he's *wonderful*! It would all *be* wonderful if it wasn't for Mum – you . . . *bitch*!'

No one moves. They are all looking at Jean: Victor, shaking his head like an idiot; Phoebe, rosy, bright-eyed, half smiling.

'*What* did you call me?' Jean says quietly.

'A bitch! A bitch! That's what you are! You can't let me be happy – you, or *her*, you take *everything* from me—'

Jean takes a breath. She looks at her brainy needy daughter – the cuckoo in her nest. She feels surprisingly calm; it is oddly refreshing to have it all exposed. 'I have taken nothing from you,' she says levelly.

'It was my *only good thing*,' screams Eve. 'Everything is *hell* apart from him – and now you— I know you hate me, but now you've done this, I . . . I know you just don't care if I, if I, if I *die*—'

'*I* have had nothing to do with that man,' Jean says and,

266

all at once, the force of what has happened hits her. She looks at Eve's mouth, her hands, and thinks, I am going to be sick. I should sit down.

She cannot sit down. She begins to shout, and does not stop. 'Are you telling me,' she says, 'are you *telling* me that you have—'

'What?' Eve shrieks. 'What's wrong with it? Why shouldn't I?'

'Have you no idea?' shouts Jean. 'He's – he's your father's age! It's *disgusting*! How can you possibly think—'

'Don't you *dare* even *think* you know *anything* about what I think!'

'Don't tell me what to do! You're still my bloody daughter!' She glances at Phoebe, who is fiddling with her collar, face averted, and banishes from her mind the image of her kissing Raymond. She returns to Eve.

'Have you any idea what you're doing? You could get pregnant! He is *using* you!'

'He is not!' shrieks Eve.

'He is! He is a pervert! He should be locked up!' she says, working herself up to new heights of rage. 'What the hell were you thinking? Have you any idea what men like that are? What they think of girls like you? Christ, Eve! The thought—'

'Don't think then!' yells Eve.

'How can I not? Oh – it makes me sick . . . he must have thought it was Christmas. He's a pervert! If I see him again, I'll kill him. I mean it.'

She thinks: even now, in the middle of everything, I *would* kill for you – and, as she thinks this, she sees Eve's face changing. Eve knows it too. They stare at each other, eyes wet.

Then Jean catches herself. Her escape is beginning to slip away. She forces her heart closed, releasing Eve and realizing, as she wipes her eyes, that she had forgotten about Victor.

Where is he, now she needs him? He should be going after that filthy man, his colleague, but he's just sitting there, looking squashed. He is a shabby, stooping, incompetent old man. Seventeen years, walled up alive.

Guilt is scrabbling at her. She thinks: I have to do it now. They will be all right, one day, and I will not. I can help them if I go, not if I stay.

Her mouth is dry. She flexes her fingers. She doesn't dare look at Phoebe, can't bear to look at Eve, will not look at Victor. The floor is muddy, the table is covered with their jumbled possessions. There is something to tie her everywhere. She lifts her head and looks through the kitchen window, at the cold world outside. She forces herself to be strong.

'I'm going to pack,' she says.

She shuts the door behind her. Eve sits down with a bump and covers her face. Phoebe and Victor gape at each other.

'I do not understand,' says Victor. His words seem to take a long time reaching the surface, as though he has fallen into a hole. He feels immensely stupid, heavy-headed, as if everyone else has been following a different version of the text. There is no one to ask for help but Phoebe, his little one, who seems, thankfully, separate from this mess.

He turns his good ear towards her. 'Your mother – is she—'

Phoebe turns, her expression unreadable. 'So?' she says, cold as stone. 'She's going. So what?'

'But . . . but not with him?'

Phoebe sneers. 'Is that what you thought?'

'Who, then?' begs Victor.

Eve lifts her head from her arms; her face is terrible, colourless, as if she is bleeding to death.

'Helena, you fool,' she cries. '*Helena*. Can't you see? Why did you think it would be *him*? If he was going to go off with anyone, it would be *me*! Why can't any of you see that?'

Victor's brain refuses to engage. He's thinking: thank you God, not Raymond Snow. Thank God; thank God. Anything but that.

'No. You're all wrong,' says Phoebe, her voice strangely dense, self-satisfied. 'He wouldn't want either of you.'

'Hush now,' he says to her. 'Let us—'

'How do *you* know?' Eve screams at Phoebe. 'This is nothing *at all* to do with you. It's my business, mine and Mum's, and—'

'That's what you think,' Phoebe says. Her smile gives Victor the sensation of looking through water, at shivering shapes, horrible and insubstantial, which he hopes will not resolve.

'Not think,' shouts Eve. '*Know.*'

'Well, you know fuck all. In fact, for your information, he doesn't want you.'

'Oh yeah? How the hell would you know?'

'Because he told me when he fucked me. He wants *me*.'

'Cunt!'

Eve and Phoebe whirl around, but he is not looking at them. His vision is black and red, like a nightmare, except that his nightmares are a fraction of the truth.

'I will tear his balls off!' he roars. 'I will kill that fucking

fucking – I will kill him. Do you hear me? He is evil, and I will stop him – both my daughters! That arsehole! That shit of a man! Both my girls? *Both* of them? Tell me the truth. Did he – *both* of you?'

His eyes feel hot, enormous. He stares at his girls, who seem very small and far away, and frightened, but not of him. No, not of him – it is Raymond Snow they should be afraid of. The air is full of poison.

'*Did* he?' he bellows. Phoebe, wide-eyed, nods. Eve's eyes are closed, but she too, his girl, his first-born, nods her head.

'Right!'

He wants to do damage. He kicks hard at the table. Its leg screeches and gives way but the corner, supported by the others, merely droops, like the bent corner of a book. He grows angrier by the second. 'Bastard,' he roars in rage and pain and grief, driving his foot into the side of the dresser. Two old ugly plates, once his mother's, slide from their shelf and snap. 'Damn him. Damn him! *Damn him! Damn him damn him damn him.*' He kicks the biggest fragment against the dresser to shatter it again. 'All three! All three! How could he, that little bastard fucker? I will break his neck! He thinks I am nothing, that shit, that intellectual vacuum, that fraud! Standing on that stage tonight like he is a *saint*!'

With that, Victor stops. He lowers his hands. Breathing hard through his nose, he approaches his daughters, who gasp as he lowers his face to theirs. Eve looks broken. He will try her first.

'Did he,' he begins, speaking slowly to avoid alarming her, and only realizing as she flinches that he is still shouting. He lowers his voice to a hiss. 'Did he hurt you?' he asks.

Eve frantically shakes her head.

'Did—' he begins, turning to Phoebe and seeing at once

that there was no need. Who would dare hurt Phoebe? He takes a deep breath and tries to think clearly, but he *is* thinking clearly, as if curved stained glass has been held up to his eye: magnifying and brightening.

'Never mind,' he says, calmly observing that, despite the foreignness of his accent, his English continues to flow smoothly, even now. Every grain of skin and section of hair are bathed in hatred; he is wild and strong with it. It is better than love.

'I tell you now,' he says, very quietly, staring into the faces of his ruined girls, 'that this is it. This is absolutely it. This man is nothing, his life is nothing, he will be *nothing* when I have finished with him. Nothing. So, believe me. I will make him suffer. I will ruin his life as he has yours and mine. I will ruin him. I cannot wait. It begins tonight. This will be his last mistake.'

They listen as their father climbs the stairs to his study. Eve looks at her hands. The silence builds like water rising, until it fills the room. At the last possible moment, Phoebe speaks.

'What did he mean, "All three"?'

Eve turns to her. She cannot speak – her lips are made of straw, her eyes are dusty – but it is as if a great wave of loathing, pure and poisonous, has been trembling, growing fuller. Now, with a little motion, she feels it break and begin to fall.

Some time later, as Victor sits silently and Jean, sorting through her papers, goes to the bathroom to wash her face, the front door slams. It takes a moment for the sound to register. Then, very slowly, Eve moves to the kitchen window and sees her sister tearing across the garden on her bike.

She's in her jeans, with a bag in the basket, and Eve knows where she will be going. She listens to the side gate swinging shut, and smiles. Feeling wonderfully calm, she climbs the stairs to her bedroom.

From the arm of her big chair she can, with a satisfying effort, just reach the top shelf. She runs her fingers over the old terrarium, the dusty shells, the microscope and slides of human organs that her father borrowed from a biologist at his college. Then, if she stretches a little further, she can touch the tight-packed volumes of his old encyclopedia: too dated to use, impossible to throw away. It has, at least, served one purpose. She closes her eyes and breathes in the books' dusty flesh-smell. Then she slides her hand between them, and reaches for the Finnish knife.

She thinks with disdain of the last time she went after her sister. This time there will be no Raymond to stop her, and this time she knows what she wants.

She leaves her bicycle by the kissing-gate, in the mud. The sky is cold violet-blue behind her; on the other side of Port Meadow the sun is setting in a red and orange mess. There are ponies nearby, but she can barely see them: living lumps of twilight, curiously silent on the rough wet grass. She shivers as wind rattles through the pollarded willows. Even the dry parts of the meadow feel marshy tonight.

She can see no one. She does not know where to begin. She thinks of the ponies' hot tight skin, the hairs and sleek muscles; and of the softness of human forearms, the smooth unresisting flesh. So far she has only once allowed herself to try the blade, and then just on the edge of a sheet of paper. It cut like an oar through water. She is in love with sharpness. She does not feel like someone she should be near.

At first she keeps between the Rainbow Bridge and the canal, where most of the horses gather. She is slightly afraid of them in the coming darkness, but, compared to her sudden terror of this wild space at night, they seem to promise a little safety. The Meadow is more Phoebe's place than hers: the out-of-controlness, the potential for accidents. She wraps her fingers protectively around the knife.

The ponies stare at her with black jelly eyes and show their teeth. She swears miserably at them as she passes. She is crying again, and the hummocks and thistles slow her down. It's growing darker, but she can still tell that these ponies are smaller than her sister's will be, and scrappier. She won't find her here.

One thing is certain. Whatever happens when Phoebe sees her, she will make sure that she sees Phoebe first.

'I've done it,' says Jean.

Helena presses the receiver hard against her ear. Her body aches, as if she is trying to force herself through the mouthpiece. It is late; she is whispering. 'What have you done?' she asks, hopefully.

'Done it. Said it. I'm leaving.'

'You're joking.'

'I'm not.'

'Darling.'

The space between them softens. They concentrate on their idea of each other's faces.

'Oh, God,' says Jean. 'It's been hell. I can't believe I've done it. It has been hell.'

'I know, I know. It must have been. You're wonderfully brave. Where – how did you . . . who—'

'Don't. It was terrible – really terrible. I'll tell you later, when I see you.'

'When *will* I see you?' asks Helena. 'Where are you?'

'Still at home, in the, you know, bedroom. On the terrible phone. He's just next door. Oh God. I don't know what's going to happen with the girls.'

'Do they know everything?'

'I don't know. Don't think so. Oh – I see what you mean. You mean: about you?'

'Well, yes. What else?'

'Actually, there was a bit of a misunderstanding. It was – God Almighty. I'll tell you later. It wasn't bad in the way you're thinking, or at least— Should I tell them, do you think?'

'I don't see how. Or how not. They're going to hate it, the . . . the le—'

'Don't,' says Jean.

Both fall silent, thinking of their children.

'I feel sick,' says Jean.

'So do I. But in a wonderful way.'

Jean breathes a laugh, like fire down the telephone. They can both hear it. 'Me too,' she says. 'Apart from the girls, I really do. God. I can't believe it.'

'Does it – does it feel like the right thing?'

'Of course it does. Dear, dear Helena. Of course. How could it not?'

'I can't – oh, bugger.' There is a knock at the door. 'What is it?'

Jeffrey's face, hot and creased with sleep, appears in the doorway. 'What are you doing?' he says, fiercely.

'I'm on the phone.' She gives him a bright, reassuring smile, but he will not move. Jean's open mouth is at her ear. 'Sorry, sorry,' she whispers. 'Hang on.'

'*Mum*,' says Jeffrey.

'Um . . . it's – look,' she murmurs to Jean, 'can I ring you back? A bit of local trouble. I'll – I'll ring you right back. Just – don't . . . I'll be right back.'

By the time Eve finds her sister by the water, night has settled over the ponies at the eastern edge of the meadow. As if to compensate, the sky above the canal has grown more florid, like a trifle. Pink light glints off the roofs and windows of the houseboats. It looks as if the river is on fire.

Most winters, when they were children, this whole area would flood and freeze. Everyone would spend the next Saturday on the bubbly ice, looking down at the grass trapped beneath them, shaving the surface with the blunt blades of their fourth-hand skates. As Eve walks beside it to where, beyond the Rainbow Bridge, her thieving sister is racing her silver pony up and down a little stretch of path, she thinks about blunt metal and slow-flowing water, the many uses of ice. If she hadn't stolen the Finnish knife she would have to improvise – if they hadn't made her so unhappy that she'd had to steal it. But they did, and as a result she has everything she needs in the palm of her hand.

She has stopped crying. She is steely and furious like a needle colouring over a flame; as a body becoming stronger, finer, when you let some blood. The last time she felt anything like this angry with Phoebe, the night she met Raymond, she had felt bold, but that had been an illusion. It had been to do with Phoebe getting a pony, and the *idea* of shouting at her – if she'd ever got to the stables, shouting would have been enough. It won't be now.

When Phoebe turns her pony and, saddleless, helmetless, races back the way she came, Eve is standing in her path. She thinks she sees her jump. Then, as she'd known she would, Phoebe continues at the same speed towards her and Eve, strengthened by fury, her mind fixed on Phoebe's latest, unforgivable, act, stands in her path, unmoving.

It is Phoebe, for once, who loses her nerve first. She pulls hard on Bilbo's reins to slow him, then steers him straight past her sister, as if it means nothing that she is there. Bilbo slows to a canter, a trot. Eve holds tightly to the scabbard in her pocket and, with her other hand, feels through the fabric for the catch.

'Wait.'

Eve's voice is dry and cracked, but it is loud enough to make Phoebe stop. She looks down at her sister and smirks, scratching her bare head. Eve doesn't react.

'Why should I wait?' Phoebe says.

'Because I say so.'

Phoebe stills the pony. She waits, growing cold in her T-shirt, and Eve waits too, feeling herself glow as if she's standing by a fire. Then, slowly, Phoebe climbs down and comes towards her, leading Bilbo like a slave.

'What are you doing here?' she says.

'You know,' says Eve. 'You know.'

'No, I don't. Tell me.'

Eve speaks quite coolly, feeling the shapes her mouth

makes, glad it's come to this. She says: 'You have ruined everything. There is nothing left you haven't pissed on. You took Raymond, and I'll never, ever forgive you. But that's just the start of it. My entire life is you doing things to me, tramping all over me. You both do it, and I can't stand it. I cannot stand it. I cannot—' and at that, Phoebe grins.

'Come here,' says Eve.

So Phoebe walks towards her.

It's very quick. Phoebe's there in front of her, pushing at her arm, and a murderous rage overtakes Eve, requiring release. It's swift and sudden, like a back-street stabbing, except that this *is* a stabbing. There's a knife in her hand.

Then it is over. The sky is streaked with smoky purple, and they are on the rosy grass, and wet blood is falling out of Phoebe's arm as if it's nothing to do with either of them.

'Oh—' says Phoebe.

'Oh my God,' says Eve, staring at her sister's face.

'I'm going to be sick,' says Phoebe.

'No you're not,' says Eve, as if the blood is flowing of Phoebe's own accord, and then she looks down, and her mind empties.

It's nothing like anything she has seen before. It is much longer – horrible, like a cut in meat and, because of the speed, it's curved, finishing on the side of Phoebe's forearm with a . . . a sort of *flap*—

Phoebe puts her good arm on her sister's shoulder. Eve, torn between pushing her away and pulling her closer, merely hunches. The pink light makes Phoebe look like a film star. Under that, she is very pale.

Eve watches her. She tries to think of something to do.

'Are you going to faint?' she asks.

'No. Don't think so. Fuck. What were – how *could* you—'

Eve seems to be looking down from an enormous height. She can only remember how they came to this in patches; everything else is soggy with shock and amazement. A jagged sleeve of blood is spreading down Phoebe's white inner arm. Eve's stomach rolls.

'I'd better,' she begins, 'you'd – Christ. I don't know where to – oh Jesus. I'm sorry—'

'Are you?' says Phoebe.

'Shut up. Don't start now. We've got to – shit. We've got to do something about the, sssomething about the—'

'Your teeth are chattering.'

'No they're not,' says Eve. 'Shit. Fuck. We've got to—'

'Well, what *can* we do?'

'Why are your eyes closed?'

'It hurts,' whispers Phoebe.

Eve is crying, quiet silvery tears, but Phoebe doesn't feel like crying yet. This burning sensation, and the red all over her fingers and T-shirt, seem unconnected. She has one overwhelming feeling, stronger than pain: astonishment.

Eve has decided something. She will not look at Phoebe, but she takes her arm and holds the sides of it together. It hurts, but not in the way Phoebe would expect. She looks down on herself, on Eve and the huge cut, and watches Eve's lips move.

'What?'

'Scarf,' says Eve. 'On my neck.'

Phoebe unwinds the scarf. It is long green lambswool. It is not going to help.

'Now,' says Eve, more clearly, but less calmly. 'Got to wrap it around your arm. You help me.'

'Fuck,' says Phoebe. 'It hurts.'

'Shut up,' says Eve.

It's like tying a bow on a present. Eve holds Phoebe's skin together until the last minute, then takes the end of the scarf and carries on winding it around her arm. Bilbo tears at the grass around them, ignored by them both. At Phoebe's elbow, Eve tucks in the soft fringe.

The pain is worse. Phoebe feels herself drift into tears. 'I don't *want* . . . I don't *want* a stupid fucking scarf on my arm. What the *fuck* were you doing? You hurt me. You *hurt* me. Why did you do it?' she begins to shout.

Eve's teeth are still chattering; she cannot anchor her mind to this place or this time. Besides, she is terrified – of the size of the wound, of Phoebe's rage, of the distance across the meadow and, most of all, of her parents. No – most of all, of herself.

A church bell is faintly striking the half-hour. The sky above them is darkening. However bad home will be, night on the meadow will be worse.

'We'd better try and get back,' she says wiping her face with her sleeve. She picks up Phoebe's bag, and Phoebe. 'What do we do with Bilbo?'

'Leave him here.'

They walk, slowly, towards the path across the meadow. Behind them, a horse whinnies.

'Will he be all right?' Eve asks.

Phoebe turns on her, furious. '*He'll* be all right. Yeah, thanks. Fuck me, though, with half my arm cut off.'

Eve digs her fingernails into her palms, stuffs her hands

in her pockets, and discovers that she has left the Finnish knife on the grass beside the river.

Victor sits at his desk. Before him lies a sheet of thick college paper; his fountain pen rests on it, perfectly aligned with the edge. He has measured the space in between, just out of interest. He has cleared his throat, uncapped his pen, licked the nib, put the lid between his teeth to help him concentrate.

Yet the page remains blank. He screws the lid on to his little finger thoughtfully, sniffing at the comforting smell of warm dust from the threads. Then it comes to him. He will do what he did in his youth, in his heyday, before his nerve failed him and the false security of planning and note-taking hemmed him in. He does not need notes: he knows his subject perfectly. The worst has happened, and now he is unafraid.

They stand still, beside the kissing-gate. It is night on the road up into Jericho. The sky above the river is streaked with black and green.

'Are you all right?' asks Eve.

Phoebe opens her eyes. 'It really hurts,' she says. There is a light by the gate and Eve can see that the top layer of her scarf is spotted with blood.

'Do you . . . do you feel like you're bleeding a lot?' she asks, feeling a bubble of hysteria settle and swell. It is oddly difficult to breathe, as if the wide meadow behind them is a solid block, moving closer.

'I feel weird,' says Phoebe crossly.

'I've got my bike,' says Eve, still determined not to panic, to remain calm and sisterly and tolerant. 'Shall we bring yours too?'

'Leave it.'

'I'll just – hang on.' She pulls her own from the mud and wheels it over. 'Do you want to lean on it? We've got to get you home, to—' For the first time since she reached the Meadow, Eve remembers about their mother, leaving. 'Um,' she says. 'Oh shit.'

'I can't lean on it,' says Phoebe scornfully. 'And I'm cold.'

'OK.' Eve breathes in carefully, out and in. Her lungs feel full of holes. 'Well, let's just . . . let's get home as soon as we can,' she says, as an awful thought seizes her. 'Oh, God. What are we going to tell them?'

'Dunno.'

'Well, what?' says Eve, hearing her voice rising. 'I mean, I know this was – horrible, a horrible thing to happen, to do, you know, to you, but—'

'I don't care what you tell them.'

'Seriously?'

'No,' says Phoebe. 'Really. Why should I?'

'But – I mean—'

'Make it up,' says Phoebe, shivering. 'It's nothing to do with them.'

A surge of love sweeps Eve up and deposits her beyond what she thought she was feeling. She starts to cry again.

'Are you sure? God, that's lovely of you. Can we – shall we say it was an accident? Some . . . well, I don't know, glass? Can we? Oh God, thank you. That's such a relief. I—'

Her tears are hot and uncontrollable. All her terror and shame is exposed to Phoebe, like a gift. This horrible mess, she thinks, is what will save us. We can begin again.

'Forget it,' says Phoebe, dismissively

'But . . .' says Eve, and hesitates. Phoebe's face is impassive, faintly bored. She sounds exactly like she always has done. Eve's face is wet with gratitude, her hand is on her sister's warm arm but, at the sound of Phoebe's voice, she feels herself beginning to seethe with irritation. Or no, not irritation: fury.

Three-quarters of a mile away, their mother snatches up the phone.

'It's me.'

'At last. Thank God. You were – I didn't know. . . .'

It has taken much longer than Helena had expected to settle Jeffrey again. He had been too vulnerable and persistent to refuse, and the stories he chose were particularly long ones, and he had insisted on being cuddled to sleep. By the time she is able to call Jean back, she has developed a terrible fear that Jean will have changed her mind – a fear she knows is irrational. Nevertheless, it is a great relief to speak.

'What shall we do?' she asks. 'When are you coming over?' There is a pause. 'Jean?'

'I'm here,' says Jean.

'Well? Shall I come and get you? We could put your bags on our bicycles. If—'

'Helena, listen. I'm not coming to your house.'

'Sorry?'

'I'm not.'

Helena covers her eyes. Everything is sliding in the wrong direction. 'I don't understand,' she says.

'I'm not going to *you*,' says Jean. 'Oh no, is that what you thought? I didn't mean . . . I mean, that's not the idea, at all.'

Helena grips the receiver. 'Well, yes,' she says. 'That *is* what I thought.' She is trying not to cry. She thinks of the restraint of chrysalises, of worms wrapped in silk. 'I thought – I thought . . .'

'But what were you – how did you think it would *work*?' asks Jean. 'I've been sitting here waiting, but I didn't honestly think – how could you expect me to be ready for *that*?'

'For what?'

'Jesus!' Jean's voice is rising. 'Ready to – to go from a standing start to public . . . *lesbianism*! After sixteen, no, seventeen years of marriage!'

'Well, I—'

'And how did you think it would work? You and me in your single bed at your parents'-in-law? Do you think Jeffrey would be tucking us in? Or did you think that we'd find a flat straight away, you know, just breeze into an estate agent, and find somewhere perfect for you and me and Jeffrey and Phoebe? Happy families? How, tell me? *How*?'

'And Eve,' says Helena, knowing that Jean can hear her crying, and well past caring.

'Well yes, Eve too, if she wanted to, which I doubt. But that's not—'

'But we – I thought—'

'We've got *children*, Helena. We aren't *free*. I don't want a shitty little flat with you. I want a shitty little flat of my own. I've got to decide what to do. Do you understand? Do you? Helena?'

As they walk down the dark slope of Walton Well Road it begins to drizzle. At once, as if they were Sea Monkeys merely needing rehydration, the arguing begins.

'Well, why *did* you?' Phoebe keeps saying.

'Don't keep asking,' Eve tells her. She is feeling peculiarly weak: is there not enough air for the two of them? Is she faint with guilt? She doesn't feel guilty. 'I've said I'm sorry. I've *said*.'

'But – Jesus,' says Phoebe. 'You cut me. You *stabbed* me. You can't just—'

Eve thinks: one cut is nothing; you're lucky that was all. It wasn't even nearly as deep as it looked. Then, although she is trying hard to resist it, an image of the alternatives lodges in her mind: Phoebe's stomach, Phoebe's wrist.

The pavement lurches. She rests both hands against somebody's wall and lowers her head. Below her, rolling upwards with every breath, she sees a basement kitchen. It's like a version of theirs: stripped pine, primary colours, cork-board, but there's a little child riding a rocking caterpillar on the tiles. She closes her eyes.

'It's *me* that's hurt,' says Phoebe petulantly. Eve clenches her fists and her teeth and her mind. When she opens them again she sees Phoebe in Raymond's study, in his arms. She feels rage clamp down, like a drawbridge.

'Do you want to know,' she says, slowly, ferociously, 'why I did it?'

Phoebe bites her lip. In the streetlight the scarf on her arm seems to glint; more blood. For the moment Eve doesn't care.

'Do you want to know, I said.'

'Yes,' whispers Phoebe.

'Right.'

Jean is making phone calls. She tries Helena's number at home, at college, at home again, but both telephones ring and ring and there is no one, not even a parent-in-law or a grumpy porter, to reassure her. She begins to visualize all the awful things that might be happening: the vows Helena might make never to see her again; the confessions, or worse. Suicide. Could Helena commit suicide? If she, Jean, were convinced that, after all this, she could not have Helena, what would *she* do?

Her hand on the dial looks so old. She tries Helena's home number one more time. With every second that passes she is more certain that Helena will answer, and more alarmed that she does not. The phone keeps ringing.

There is no need to worry. You always worry, she tells herself, about everyone, and they are all all right. There is no need to worry, but she *is* worried, and as she takes a folded place-card from her bag she sees that her old hand is trembling. With excessive care, she dials the telephone number written on the back.

'Yes?'

'Um.' Her voice is a tiny squeak. She coughs: now she sounds even stranger. 'Hello. Is that – um . . . Professor Ramos?'

'Yes?'

'My name is Jean Lux . . . ah, Jean. I sat next to you at a dinner in All Saints'. Some weeks ago – last term, actually. Do you remember?'

'Ah, yes,' says the voice: kind, extremely foreign, very old. 'You kept me company during that dull banquet at your friend's—'

'How . . . um, how are you?'

'Very well. Very happy. And you?'

'Yes,' says Jean. 'Yes. Well. Um. That's what I wanted to speak to you about.'

*

Next door, in the study, Victor, who has been listening to the faint clatter audible every time the telephone receiver in the bedroom is picked up, or put down, lets one final growl escape him. He can hear nothing else: the walls are too thick and he is too deaf. However, he seems to sense furtive movement.

It is very nearly time for the lecture. There is nothing for him to do but to wait. He returns his fountain pen to the inside pocket of his jacket, beside his heart. Then he rests his fingertips on the envelope in front of him, addressed, in the copperplate for which he is modestly famous: *Jean Lux*. It is almost an afterthought, but he knows it will please her, and he does feel oddly liberated by its contents – even if, for a love-letter, it is about seventeen years too late.

It is impossible to argue with Phoebe. Her weapons are blank denial and illogicality, or vicious insults which leave Eve empty-mouthed. She tries to give the smallest clue to how she has been feeling, hoping to exonerate herself, or even – although she would deny it – to provoke pity. Phoebe is, however, like a wall with claws. As they turn into the lane and approach the side-gate, Eve sees again that mocking half-smile as her sister walked towards her, and tastes that hard, swift rage: self-defence, or its opposite.

Beside her, Phoebe is bleeding. Eve stretches out her fingers like a cat flexing its paws, and wills herself calm. Then she looks up at the house, and sees a light in their parents' bedroom.

This is it. If they go in now, with Phoebe wrapped in blood-soaked lambswool, they will be trapped for ever in this one-off contrary moment, when she is bad, and Phoebe good.

'Listen,' she says, in a last-minute surge of self-preservation. 'We'll – let's talk about this later. But do you want to go straight in? Are you, do you think you . . . need to show them? Either of them? Or can we just—'

Phoebe shakes her head. 'It's fine,' she says, which reminds Eve of the one good thing she can think of in her sister's favour: she may be grotesquely, insanely selfish, but she isn't vindictive. At least, not yet.

She must concentrate on getting Phoebe indoors without anyone seeing. Their mother won't have left, she tells herself doggedly. She can't have left. There's too much going on. Which means, as she's bound to want to see Phoebe, that unless they hurry they will come face to face with her. Their father is slower-moving, but less predictable. Would he necessarily notice a great gash on his daughter's arm? Eve thinks bitterly of her own, but this is different, much . . . messier. And Phoebe is wearing short sleeves.

She takes a raggedy breath. Her mouth is full of saliva; she wants to spit. She wants to lie down. 'OK,' she says. 'Let's just . . . walk. Through the garden. Like . . . I don't know. Like we've been, been off for a talk.'

'Ha ha,' says Phoebe.

'Yes, I know,' says Eve weakly, 'but try. Pretend. Please.'

She stands next to her, closer than they've stood for years, and they begin to walk across the thick wet grass. They look like sisters, like love unites them, with Phoebe's arm hidden in the shadows between their bodies. They look almost normal. Eve opens the back door, and they walk in to the dark kitchen.

*

There is no one there. Her heart is beating so loudly that the room seems to rustle. She looks down at Phoebe's arm; the scarf seems possibly even blacker than before. But she doesn't seem to need a doctor. 'How—?' she begins.

'Shh,' says Phoebe. 'Let's just – upstairs.'

It's almost too dark to make it across the room, but it feels safer with the light off. The house is strangely quiet. 'OK,' she says.

Every stair creaks, and there are fifty-one to the top floor. They pass their parents' bedroom, and everyone holds their breath – her, and Phoebe, and even, she imagines, their mother and father. No one comes out. No one accuses or unmasks her. They reach the top of the stairs.

'Come in here,' she says, and opens the door to her bedroom.

'No,' says Phoebe. 'Mine.'

'Eve frowns. Her own room is so obviously better: fairly clean, except for the beetles, and she has tissues and even a bandage. Besides, she has hardly been in Phoebe's room for years.

'What are you afraid of?' says Phoebe.

It used to be fear of attack; then it was not wanting evidence of Phoebe's growing rebellion, as if both were her fault and a danger to her. Now, however, she has seen Phoebe's dark heart, and Phoebe has seen hers. How much worse than that could a bedroom be?

'Why should I be afraid?' she says.

She is wrong.

Phoebe's room is like something glimpsed down an alley in a documentary. Nothing is its original colour: every surface is stained and burnt and gouged into, covered in obscene and childish pictures or posters of Eastern gods, speckled with burning joss-stick or sticky drips. The floor, to shin-height, is an ashtray: littered with tape-boxes, books about astrology, flat cans of lighter fluid, tantric leaflets, cigarette papers, encrusted bowls, kitchen scissors, silted glasses, crisp packets, Phoebe's clothes, Eve's clothes, a man's muddy boot, defaced copies of *Horse and Pony*, a filthy sleeping-bag, rings and feathers and photographs and drums and matchsticks and, on top of it all, like a switchblade shining in the stink, a mahogany plaque, stolen from the board at the bottom of a familiar staircase, painted, in gold letters: Dr R. S. Snow.

All the shame and protectiveness and gratitude evaporates. She turns to face her sister.

'You,' she says, almost too angry to speak, 'are an animal.'

Then they are upon each other, hissing whispered insults, leaning in from uncertain footholds like seabirds fighting on a shit-encrusted rock.

'Shut *up*,' snarls Eve as Phoebe's voice begins to rise.

'I will not shut up. Why the fuck should I?'

Eve grabs the name-plaque and holds it right in Phoebe's face. She is gripping it so tightly it shakes, but her voice is steady and venomous. 'Because—'

She looks at the sharp corners of the plaque, and Phoebe's lovely skin. Raymond's name is engraving itself on to her palm, and Phoebe has – Phoebe has—

'Because . . .' she says. It feels as if everything beneath the surface of her skin has come away and slumped towards the floor. Her muscles seem too weak to keep her upright.

'I—'

Phoebe snatches the other end. It trembles between them. 'What I want to know,' whispers Phoebe, 'is why you are being such a *bitch* about this *one thing*.'

Eve unclenches her hand and lets it fall. The soft skin

slowly surrenders the wood's shape. She stares at her sister in amazement.

'One thing?' she says. 'Are you *mad*? One thing?'

'Yes!' says Phoebe.

'But you have *everything.*'

Phoebe, still gripping the plaque, gestures furiously at her bombsite bedroom. 'This crap? I don't want *this*! Why would I want this? It's all rubbish! It's . . . I haven't got what I *need*, have I?'

'*What*? How can you *say* that?' Furiously, Eve swipes away the tears that have gathered on her eyes and nose.

'Why not?'

'That's shit!'

'*You're* talking shit.'

'No, you are! You took what *I* need.'

'I—'

'Why? Why did you have to?' A can rolls off a pile and nestles against her ankle, depositing brown beads on her shoe.

'Oh, right,' says Phoebe, sarcastic and vicious. '*I* don't need anything. You—'

'I don't believe this. You don't!'

'I do.'

'Crap you do. You didn't need him. He was the only thing *I* had.' She glances down; her other foot is resting in a pool of damp ash on a mouldy saucer. She snatches it away.

'Give me that,' says Phoebe, pulling at the plaque.

'Take it. It makes me *sick.*'

'Thanks.'

'All this stupid pretending—'

'I'm not fucking pretending!'

'You are! Don't you dare pretend *you're* not happy. Don't be so *stupid*.'

'Don't call *me* stupid. You're the stupid one. You don't get it—'

'I get it.'

'You don't.'

'So what is it?'

'Never mind.'

'No, go on. If you're so miserable, you tell me. Amaze me. You're—'

'Shut up.'

Eve wipes the ash off her shoe. She sits on a paperback, and tries to look reasonable, but she is breathless, as if she has been dragged to the top of a too-high mountain, and a fist of anger is pressing into her throat. '*Tell* me. Or fine, don't tell me. I don't ca—'

'You have no idea,' says Phoebe. 'You think it's all—' Her voice wobbles. Eve looks at her with interest.

'Just tell me.'

'It's not that simple.'

'I didn't *say* it was simple,' says Eve. 'I *said* you've got everything.'

'Well, I *haven't*,' spits Phoebe. 'There's things you've got I'll *never* have. All right?'

Eve takes a great breath. Her lungs, finally, seem to fill. She feels invigorated. She will not let this go.

'*What?*' she says. 'How can you say—'

'Forget it.'

'*No!* You can't just – what are you . . . don't just say that. What things?'

'Things.'

'Don't talk crap. I said, what things?'

'Don't even start – if you don't know, there's no point—'

Eve is awash in tears and snot; she's drowning in frustrated fury. She wipes her nose on her woollen sleeve, past caring what Phoebe thinks – well, almost. 'I don't know,' she says. 'Tell me.'

'The stuff you get! From them!'

'From who? Mum and Dad?'

'*Yes*!'

'I get – it's *you* who gets—'

'Stuff! That's all!'

'It's not all!'

'They're only interested in me to see when I'm going to *fail*. So they can feel sorry for me.'

'Oh, come—'

'How do you think that feels, being the only *dunce* in this fucking place? Don't look so disgusted,' she says, as a tear rolls out of the corner of each eye and begins to make their way over her cheekbones.

'I'm not. I'm – I . . .' Eve looks at her sister, her bandaged arm, her revolting bedroom, and something hot and appalled and confusing, like a single drop of water, gathers and falls. It is pity.

'They don't think you're going to fail,' she says, more softly. 'They don't. Why should they?'

'Because,' says Phoebe. 'I'm – I can't – I *do*.'

'No you don't.'

'I do.' Phoebe gives an enormous sniff and starts coughing, hand pressed to her chest. 'I . . . all the *time*,' she says.

'No . . .' Eve begins.

'While you're this untouchable golden fucking girl—'

'Crap!'

'Not crap! Look at yourself!'

'I'm looking! Look at you! I'm the crap one; if you hate me, think how much *I* hate me. Hate myself. Don't snort!'

'I'm not—'

'I'm *never* fucking good enough.'

'How can you think that?'

'You – you're so full of—'

'Shut up!' says Phoebe, beginning to sob. 'If you're not good enough, if you're not . . .'

'I'm not!'

'If you're not good enough, where's that leave me?'

'What do you mean? Jesus, what do you—'

'I can *never* do what you do!'

'What do you mean? You don't try!'

'Because I *can't*. I'm *bad*, that's what I do, *all* I can do—'

'Not true—'

'And now you've done that too . . .'

'I haven't – well, I—'

'Well, now what do you think I've got? What *am* I, if I'm not that?'

'But . . .'

'Yeah, well. And now it doesn't even – even Mum's stopped noticing—'

'Has she?'

'*Yes*! And at least *you* worried about me, and now even—'

'I do,' says Eve. 'I still *do* worry – God, you're hardly . . . And anyway, you didn't care if I *did* worry. You thought I was crap—'

'Says who? I never thought that.'

'Don't lie. You're lying.'

'You were—' Phoebe begins, but Eve has to stop her,

because she has begun to unwind the green scarf from her arm.

'Leave that,' she says.

Phoebe will not leave it. The scarf is patched with blood, each layer more stained than the last. She gasps as the bottom layer pulls away. A blackening slash, as long as her palm, stands out from the red-smeared skin of her arm.

At the sight of it, Eve crumbles. 'Oh, Jesus, I'm sorry,' she says. 'I didn't – I—'

'Yeah, but you did do it, didn't you?' cries Phoebe.

'I know—'

'So you meant it.'

Eve swallows. 'Well,' she says. 'I—'

'That's the point! Don't pretend you didn't.'

'I'm not—'

'It's better if you *did*.'

'Why? Jesus, that—'

'I want you to,' Phoebe mutters.

'Don't be ridiculous.'

She looks away. 'Forget it.'

'Are you serious?'

'No.'

'Tell me why.'

'Because – because,' begins Phoebe, but she is crying too hard to speak. Eve reaches out a hand, uncertainly, and to her surprise Phoebe slides underneath it and sits beside her on the mattress.

'Because?' says Eve, cautiously patting Phoebe's back.

'Because,' she sobs, 'because then . . . I know . . . you don't think . . . I'm *stupid*. And *useless*. I'd count. That's what I want.'

'What?'

'I want to count to you.'

The air in Phoebe's bedroom is stinging with TCP. She is biting down, hard, on Eve's left index finger, as Eve uses her other hand and festoons of toilet paper to mop the skin around the cut.

'Enough,' says Eve. She withdraws her finger. 'Should I do the actual cut, do you think? I'm worried that—'

'What? That I'll bleed to death?'

'Yes.'

'It sealed up the first time. It'll do it again, won't it. You're not very good at fatal wounding, are you?'

With the last of the toilet paper, Eve swabs her sister's arm until the black blood melts.

'Fuck. That hurts.' Phoebe purses her lips and breathes in. 'Enough. I can't believe what you said, about hating yourself. If I was you I'd fucking love myself. Who do you hate more now, me or you?'

'You. Me. No, Mum. No, after what you did, I think it's still you.'

'Fine.'

'I do love you too,' mumbles Eve.

'What a way to show it.'

After twenty rings, Jean knows the worst has happened. She has been packing her last possessions slowly, to allow them both a chance to calm down, and now she knows she has made a fatal misjudgement. Should she go straight there, or stay at the end of the telephone, in case? With every second of waiting, it becomes more impossible to put it down. Then, as she reaches her wits' end, someone picks up.

'Hello?' they croak.

'Who's that?' snaps Jean. The voice sounds desolate. 'Is that Norah?'

'Jean, it's me,' says Helena. 'What is it?' Jean's mind is blank but for Helena, risen from the grave. 'Jean?'

'Sorry. I'm here. I didn't expect you.'

'I see,' says Helena, her voice clipped and bitter. 'Well, my parents-in-law have kindly taken Jeffrey out for dinner. I have work to do. Now,' she says, and her voice, still furious, begins to quiver, 'if that's all . . .'

Jean feels a sharp tear inside her chest. 'Helena,' she begins, 'please—'

'I don't want to speak to you. I don't want to think about you. I don't want anything to do with you. Leave me alone.'

'But – I don't understand. What's this about?'

'Don't joke with me.'

'I'm *not* – please, just . . . really, I don't know. What?'

'I'll tell you,' says Helena, 'what this is "all about". It's about the fact that I – I can't believe you want me to tell you – you know what I did. What happened—'

'Of course I know. I was *there*. I'm not pretending . . .'

'You had everything, my whole – everything, and you let me believe that it was – well, you know . . .'

'I know. It *was*. I—'

'But I was just an excuse! That's all I was!'

'You weren't!'

'I *was*! And how do you think that feels?'

'But love, listen to me . . .'

'Don't love me. I'm not your love.'

'You are. You are . . . Come on. Talk to me. I know you're there.'

'Say it again.'

'You are my love.'

Jean lies down on the bed. At the squeak of its springs, Victor pushes himself to his feet. He picks up a bundle from the floor, buttons up his jacket, takes an ugly woollen hat, stiff with age and Jean's distaste, from the hook on the back of his study door. Quietly, he slides his letter under the bedroom door and then, before he has had time to reconsider, he walks out into the night.

'What are you saying?' asks Helena. 'Who?'

She is sounding a little happier. Jean has soothed her as much as circumstances allow, but she has waited until now to explain her plan. She is afraid of sounding silly – even with her, after everything.

'That man,' she says. 'Professor Ramos. You remember.'

'No. I know who you mean, but I don't understand—'

'He told me all about it at that banquet, the All Saints' banquet. I was between you two.'

'Oh . . . I remember. He's a lovely man.'

'He is – he certainly seems to be. The point is that . . . well, he told me about living with his scout, in her house not in his college flat. But I wasn't listening.'

Helena's voice turns to honey. 'Good. I should hope not.'

'Well, yes. But the thing is that it sank in. What he was saying. Do you know about his scout?'

'Well, amazingly I do. Quite young, isn't she? One of the

297

other scouts told me. Do you . . . oh hell. Do you think there's anything like that going round about *us*?'

'No. Oh, no,' says Jean. 'Anyway, so he's living with her, sweetly – though I don't see why it's quite such a scandal.'

'Well, you know she's younger than us. And he's ninety-two.'

'Jesus. Anyway, I think he . . . I think he may have picked up something from, um, us, at that dinner.'

'Like what?'

'Like . . . I don't know. Would you . . . would you be very worried if he'd guessed?'

'Do you think he did? My God. How could he?'

'We were holding hands. Under the table, but still.'

'I suppose we were.'

'I don't know. Maybe it's . . . sympathy? I mean, he and his scout must be sixty years apart, even if they are . . . well, different sexes. And she *was* his scout. They're not exactly your average couple . . .'

'Maybe. Maybe. But—'

'Anyway, there was this funny moment right at the end, over the crystallized fruit, when he . . . he put his hand on mine. But not in a creepy way. And said it was a . . . a pleasure to meet me.'

'Well, it is.'

'Thank you. And he gave me his, their, telephone number.'

'Really?'

'So the point is, I rang him. Just now. And he – and I – basically, I told him; not everything, but a bit. I didn't actually refer to you. I just said – look, it just seemed obvious. He's in his love-nest, so he's not in his college flat – he doesn't need it, but it's his for the year. And he wants it to be used – he lends to all his friends. He said, at the dinner. And I thought, because he'd been so kindly and twinkly with me . . .'

'I can't believe you asked him.'

'Well, I did. I had to. Even if there are other people staying, it's somewhere for two months, at least . . . You know, dear, don't you, that we can't live at yours or mine, and there's no money to rent—'

'Well, actually, there's going to be a little more—'

'Is there?'

'Yes. I—'

'Well, still, I've none at all. I don't want to be *kept*; I'd go mad. And even if you could afford to get out of Hugh and Norah's, it's not realistic to expect the children to want to set up home with us together – which reminds me, I can't believe I haven't told you, there's something awful—'

'What? Us?'

'No, no. I'll tell you when I see you. I can't face . . . that, until we've sorted this out. I want you to understand.'

'I do.'

'I hope you do. I just need time, before . . .'

'With the girls, though.'

'Well, yes, with Phoebe.'

'What about Eve?'

Jean opens her mouth, and shuts it again as she thinks of Eve's face. She glances at her case, whose ugly leatherette side is bulging with old photographs: she hadn't expected to find so many of Eve as a little girl, or to want them all. She says: 'She's sixteen. I don't know if I can make her.'

'She'll want to be with you.'

'I don't know,' says Jean, swallowing hard. 'I really don't know . . . She might want to stay with her father. She might, you know.'

'Just ask her.'

'I will. I will. Christ, there'll be so much awful stuff to sort out, with Victor too . . .' Then she rallies. 'In any case, even more so if it's *both* of them, we can't just merrily move in with you. How could we possibly? And I don't think it would be right, for me: going straight from him to you. So if I stay in José Ramos's flat, with whichever of them wants to be with me, that's an interim stage. And we can see each other freely, more freely. You understand, don't you?'

'I . . .'

'I need a new life first, and then, with that as a – you know, foundation – I can be with, we can share . . .'

'What?'

'Don't make me say it.'

'You're going to have to say it, if we do it.'

'I'm not brave enough. I'm really not. Maybe not for any of it.'

'Yes you are.'

'Yes I am,' says Jean. 'Live together. That's what I want. To live with you.'

The air is silvery with anticipation. The eminent, the grand, the very old, jostle on benches like undergraduates. Before every man – and even, despite the endowment's wording, every woman present – stands a tall cup of sweet wine and a dish of walnuts: sustenance, from the days when the Lecture could last for hours.

As Victor Lux walks slowly up the central aisle, heads turn. Both he and Raymond Snow were obvious candidates for the Lectureship; some of his colleagues, moreover, will have realized that the Introduction falls to him. Nevertheless, they seem a little surprised that he is present. Even the President, debonair as ever in a marvellously brocaded gown, lifts his eyebrows infinitesimally. Victor, however, keeps his eyes fixed on a black spot straight ahead: Raymond Snow, who has turned in his chair to address the beautiful young Prime Minister of Pakistan, who still retains an interest in her old college.

The hall grows quiet. Victor's feet resound as he climbs the three steps to High Table, around which, as at a last supper, the luminaries wait. Raymond Snow turns his sleek head, concealing his surprise. He gives Victor a smile of triumph. Blankly, Victor returns his stare. Then, although he can sense the President attempting to catch his eye, he stands at the lectern and shrugs on his gown. For five, ten, twenty seconds, Victor's gaze sweeps the room: professors whose books he grew up on, celebrities from distant universities, dons with whose children his daughters have played. He is terribly nervous, but this excites him; he has not felt nervous for years. It reminds him of how good, in his brief heyday, he used to be.

The clock strikes the hour. Then, as the last note fades, filling the hall with a deep great silence, he swallows, clears his throat, nods to the President, and begins.

'My learned friends, Prime, Prime Minister, President. You will all, I am sure, be a little surprised to see an . . . ah, a defeated candidate for the Sir Henry Spenser Memorial Lecture standing before you tonight. However, I am Senior

Dean. And only a Senior Dean ah, *unworthy* of the title would allow professional envy to stand in the way of, well, his official duties.'

His listeners nod; one or two smile. Encouraged, Victor attempts his first joke. 'I am sure that none of us are prone to such a vice as *that*.'

Cautious laughter ripples up towards the lectern. Victor stands a little straighter.

'Yes, aha, well. It was with interest, this morning, that I saw the announcement of the subject of Dr Snow's lecture: Crime and Punishment in Late Medieval Italy. Now, if you will permit me one brief observation of my own on the subject – as is, I believe, ah, traditional in these circumstances – President, if I may?'

Jim Kramer raises an eyebrow, his head to one side.

'We will all, I think, agree that, in different cities and states, or nations, crimes may be said to differ? That what may be a crime in one place may not, under a different set of legal codes, be, ah, *considered* a crime elsewhere?'

Here Victor smiles pleasantly at his audience. A sprinkling of dons, suspecting that this may be the beginning of another joke, titter drily. Behind Victor's left shoulder, where the President and Raymond Snow are sitting, someone shifts in their chair.

'For example. In *Romeo and Juliet*, Juliet, as I need not remind you, is thirteen. Ah . . . "My child is yet a stranger in the world / She hath not see the change of fourteen years." Ahem. Now, in contemporary Verona this was young, but not *too* young. And Romeo could have been considerably older – a man of her father's age, for example – without experiencing the, ah, the *opprobrium* which would face him in England, indeed in Oxford, today.'

He looks down upon the rows of curious, clever, ignorant faces. They cannot fault his grammar, or his extemporization; he has, without question, right on his side. He smiles.

'Which is, not to put too fine, ah, a point on it, ah, my point. Ahem. Here the young are protected, not only from their peers but from their elders. Sometimes elders are *not* betters. And some minors are more fortunate than others, because they are subject to protections – protections beyond English law.'

To Victor's left, a chair scrapes across the floorboards. There is a whispering; then he hears the President murmur: '. . . I assure you. Please.' Raymond Snow's bony body settles back into his chair, but Victor can feel the tension emanating from him. Not long now, you bastard, he thinks.

'One or two of you may have noticed that, when I entered the Hall, the doors behind me were firmly shut; I asked for them to be shut. Since then, no one has been admitted. This is a stipulation of the college statutes when a . . . ah, a *crime* has been committed.'

Victor pauses. His heart hangs in his chest. He thinks: have I made a terrible mistake? Is this too much? He thinks of his girls, his daughters; there is no mistake and nothing is too much for them, or for the man who sits behind him. This, he tells himself, summoning all the courage and showmanship and fury which has been festering inside him – this, tonight, is what he was born for.

He clears his throat and clasps the sides of the lectern, feeling the muscles at the base of his thumbs tighten against the polished wood. It is a good, strong feeling. 'I must ask your forgiveness,' he tells his audience, who are shifting uncomfortably on their benches, 'for the . . . well, perhaps rather *melodramatic* turn this evening is about to take. It is not in keeping with the tone of the Sir Henry Spenser Lecture. However, I am afraid that, tonight, very little is. I mentioned a crime. A crime has, ah, recently been committed, against the laws of this country and against the, ah, this college, the college itself.'

Behind Victor, Raymond Snow pushes back his chair. He clears his throat.

'Ladies and gentlemen,' he begins, 'I'm afraid that, aha, emotions may have got the better—'

'Kindly sit down, Dr Snow,' says Victor, his voice rising with determination and embarrassment. 'As the Senior Dean of this college, I, ah, I must *command* you to sit down. President, colleagues, ah, Prime Minister, I do not wish to give you the details, but in the circumstances I must. A pair of girls, sisters, one aged merely sixteen, one aged barely fourteen, have been, well, abused, or at least taken, ah, taken advantage of, within the very walls of this college, by a man forty years their senior – Raymond Snow.'

There is an outraged rustle of gowns and confused voices; grey heads lean back into the aisles for a better view of High Table. The President stands; Victor looks into his blue eyes and does not quail. He turns back to the well of the hall.

'It is my, my *duty*, my *obligation*, as Senior Dean, on discovery of a crime within the college – and, ah, I assure you that what has happened to the younger girl *is* a crime – to do two things, under the statutes and the law of England respectively. I must first convene a disciplinary tribunal, and I have done so. I must also inform the city police which, also, I have done. And I am, believe me, truly sorry that it must be tonight, before you all, that this, this, this *act* must be revealed. And I do, I do have proof.'

He points to the package he has deposited on the table; it contains Eve's dedicated volume of Latin erotic poetry, several unsent letters of love and recrimination, clearly addressed and, taken from his younger daughter's bedroom floor, a paper napkin from a pizza restaurant written on in two distinct hands, ending 'Remember this: talking to a waiter with my fingers up you', in the unmistakable writing of Raymond Snow.

'Unfortunately I do. The disciplinary committee and the police will have to see it. But there is, I can assure you, no doubt of . . . no doubt that this has taken place. These girls are . . .' He coughs and continues. 'They are my daughters. The younger is the goddaughter of the President. But, which is most important *legally*, if not otherwise, they are under my protection as the disciplinary head of this college. One more point, President, if I may?'

He turns to meet the President's eye. The President nods.

'As, as Senior Dean, I have certain powers. The Sir Henry Spenser must only go to 'a goode man', as you may know. And it is for me, as Dean, to determine – if the elected candidate's virtue is in question – whether or not he is a good man. And he is not.'

Victor takes a deep breath. 'I can, I have discovered, if I have evidence of, ah, this, strip him of the Lectureship. I can do so. And . . . and to do so is the one thing that, with pleasure, I do tonight.'

He steps back carefully from the lectern. Raymond Snow, white-faced, begins explaining to his neighbours the circumstances in which—

No one, however, will catch his eye. Victor walks past

him to the President, alone at the end of the table. 'I'm sorry, Jim,' he murmurs.

Jim Kramer nods. Gravely, slowly, he rubs his hands together, pushes them hard against his lap until his elbows lock. 'Hmm,' he says. 'Bit of a mess.'

'Yes.'

'And true, all true? Of course it is. I know you wouldn't . . . I know it must be, to come to this.'

Victor nods. His eyes are burning.

'Take my chair.'

He lowers himself into it. He rests his heavy head against the carved wood. Unauthorized teardrops have, to his amazement, begun to squeeze between his lashes. However, he is smiling. His work is done.

'Don't worry, old man,' says the President. 'I'll sort it out.'

Phoebe's arm is clean, rebound with one of her sister's bandages. They are sitting together on the end of Eve's bed.

'You've got a beetle,' says Phoebe.

Eve glares at her – then sees, on the end of her sister's pink and childish finger, a small bronze beetle walking neatly around her cuticle.

'Ugh!' says Eve. She leaps to her feet, flapping her hands. 'Shake it off! Shake it out of the window! Ugh! Get rid of it!'

Phoebe stares in mild surprise. 'It's only a beetle.'

'It might be dirty! It'll spread something – I can't bear it. Get rid of it!'

'God, calm down. You are *really* uptight, aren't you?'

Eve forces open the jammed window, grabs her sister's brutally nailbitten hand and shakes it over the parapet.

'Calm down,' says Phoebe. 'It won't eat you. Unless you're a creeper.'

Eve is searching the duvet for other beetles. 'What are you talking about?'

'It's a creeper beetle. Dad said. You know, Virginia Creeper. That's where it lives.'

'Come on.'

'I'm serious. They're everywhere. Dad's got them at college. Why? What did you think? You've got a thing about them, haven't you?'

'No.'

'You have. You've got a thing about everything. You won't even touch doorhandles.'

'Yes I will.'

'You're lying,' says Phoebe. 'Not my doorhandle – I saw you. Do you think you'll catch thickness from me?'

Eve looks at the section of duvet where Phoebe is sitting. 'No!' she says.

'You think I make things dirty, don't you? How *shit* do you think that makes me feel? I hate you, sometimes – it's not just me pissing *you* off, in case you hadn't noticed.'

'Oh.'

'Yeah, well. And this other thing – OK if you want to feel sorry for yourself about Mum all the time, but it's only her *buying* me stuff. She doesn't *think* about me. It's you she thinks about.'

'Rubbish. It's rubbish, isn't it?'

'All the time. Or you wouldn't wind her up.'

'Do you think?'

'Yes I do. Except now she doesn't think about anyone. She's leaving us, isn't she.'

They stare at each other.

'What are we going to do?' Phoebe says.

'She'll take you.'

'I know. And you.'

'Doubt it.'

'Hope so.'

She returns the receiver to its plastic cradle. Her flesh, which had begun to feel dry and shrunken, blooms again. She is fat with love.

They have reached a decision. Jean will move tonight to Professor Ramos's flat, by taxi, having explained the situation to both her daughters. The girls will follow in the next day or two, if they choose. Helena, who cannot imagine Eve and Jean coexisting in a cramped college flat for more than an hour, or herself and Phoebe getting on anywhere at all, plans to find a flat big enough for them all, as soon as Jean is ready. However, she is keeping this to herself.

She sits straight in her chair, as if about to begin an examination. On the surface of her desk lie books and papers and index cards, thousands and thousands of words, all adding up, so far, to nothing. Her subject is enormous; perhaps, she has thought lately, too enormous, and too dangerous. Too public. Now, however, she is past all that.

She rests her hands on top of the piles of paper, fingers splayed, as if to contain her endless notes, or her happiness. It is impossible. She is too excited to work, but she must work. She takes a fresh sheet of paper, and begins at the beginning:

LOVE: AN ANATOMY
Helena Potter

and then the dedication, for all the world to see:

For Jean Lux, with all my heart

'I'm scared.'

Phoebe's bottom lip begins to tremble. Eve watches, fascinated, failing to notice that her sister's arms are outstretched until Phoebe begins to growl impatiently and wave her hands. Gingerly, Eve takes her in her arms. She closes her eyes. She rests her chin on Phoebe's back and breathes in her smell. It is White Musk, smoke and joss-sticks, unwashed hair and then, when she dares to move closer, something that Phoebe has always smelt of – there, at the back of her neck, like a birthmark: milk.

'I still hate you,' mutters Phoebe into her shoulder.

Eve strokes her back. 'Shh. Sh-shh. I know,' she murmurs. 'I hate you too.'